THE SIGHT OF HEATHER

Ally Stirling

For more information contact:
authorallystirling@gmail.com
http://www.authorallystirling.com

Book design by Evolve Unlimited Pty Ltd
Cover design by Jeanine Henning

ISBN – Paperback: 978-0-6397-9895-0
ISBN – e-book: 978-0-6397-9896-7

First Edition: September 2023

Billy, Ross, Alistair & Robyn

My beginning, my end, and everything in between.
May you have walls for the wind
And a roof for the rain
Drinks beside the fire
Laughter to cheer you
Those you love near you
And all that your heart may desire.

Glossary

As a native of Scotland, I have written this book using British English as well as some of the Scots vernacular familiar to me. People not of Scots heritage may find this a little odd – or incorrect. I have listed a few words below to make this easier, and to ensure you don't think my spell check isn't working.

Wheisht: *pronounced wheisht* – *Hush! Be quiet.*
Och: *a term of acknowledgement*
Aye: *pronounced I* – *yes*
Yer, yerselves: *you, yourselves*
Feart: *pronounced feert* – *scared*
Tae: *pronounced tay* – *to*
Oot: *pronounced oot* – *out*
Git: *pronounced git* – *get*
Didnae: *pronounced didnay* – *didn't*
Reekin: *pronounced reekin* – *smelling*
Quaich: *pronounced quake* – *two handed drinking cup, traditionally used at weddings.*
Tairsgeir: *pronounced tarsee-er* – *peat cutting tool with a sharp metal blade*
Cannae: *pronounced canny* – *can't*
Weans: *pronounced wains* – *babies*
Bairns: *pronounced bairns* – *children*

For those who may want to delve deeper, I have included some interesting information and links below.

Munro

Munros are named after Sir Hugh Munro, the mountaineer who compiled the original list of Scotland's highest peaks. Munro was a founding member of the Scottish Mountaineering Club (SMC) in 1889, and he later served as the club's third president. In 1891 he was tasked with cataloguing all Scottish peaks over 3000 feet, a list that became known as "Munro's Tables." He admitted that "when first this work was commenced, I had little idea of the enormous amount of labour and research which it would entail." The original list featured 283 separate mountains and 538 tops, which are lesser summits still over 3000 feet that are judged as not being distinctly separate from the primary mountain peak. Given the rudimentary nature of the maps Munro was limited to, his number was surprisingly accurate, off by just one peak from today's tally of 282. Munro was actually revising the list at the time of his death in 1919; the SMC has updated it several times to ensure it's as accurate as possible. Despite giving his name to Scotland's tallest mountains, Munro unfortunately died before managing to climb all of them. Just three peaks escaped him: Carn Cloich-mhuilinn, Sgùrr Dearg, and Carn an Fhidleir. Carn Cloich-mhuilinn was later demoted from Munro to Munro Top.

Mother Cailleach

In Wonder Tales from Scottish Myth and Legend, Donald Alexander McKenzie hails the Cailleach as the mother of all gods and goddesses in Scotland, and Scottish folk tale collector J.G MacKay refers to her as the most tremendous figure in Gaelic myth today. Although her name can be found throughout Scotland in folklore, customs, ancient monuments and the natural landscape, the Cailleach is one of the lesser-known figures of Celtic mythology and is often overlooked. Her true origins have been lost over time. She is vastly ancient and predates even the Celtic mythology of which she has become a part. One Highland folk tale states that she existed 'from the long eternity of the world'.

Comparisons and claims to her beginnings are made in places as far-reaching as Spain and India. Some suggest that she was originally a Spanish princess named Beara, others that she is a bastardised version of the great Hindu mother goddess, Kali, brought to Britain by Indian immigrants. The Cailleach is a crone goddess, usually depicted dressed entirely in grey with a dun-coloured plaid wrapped around her shoulders. Her face is wan and blue, like that of a corpse, and her hair is long and white and speckled with frost. She has a single eye in the centre of her forehead, a trait characteristic of deities who can see beyond this world and into the next.

Older Than Time: The Myth of the Cailleach, The Great Mother – Wee White Hoose

Haar

Scotland is surely not the only place in the world where a mist from the sea comes rolling in and blankets everything. But it does have the distinction of having a word to describe that fine mist, and the word is 'haar'. To feel haar on one's face is like being on the receiving end of spray from one of those fine mist sprayers used for houseplants. Walking around in haar is like chasing a phantom. Wherever you are standing seems clear of haar, save for the fine wet spray in your face to tell you it is there. The haar seems to be over in the distance, where everything is white and indistinct. But walk to where the haar is and it disappears. Turn around and look back, and the haar seems to be where you just came from.

The Concise Dictionary Of Scottish Words And Phrases defines haar as:

"a cold sea mist which drifts in from the North Sea along the east coast."

Edinburgh Haar – What It Is And How To Embrace It – The Quill*cards Blog*

Prologue

In this eyrie of haar and heaths, where the ancient mingle with the present-day innocent – obscure, mystifying or shamelessly overt – all credit must go to mother Cailleach who stomped through the world, the sheer strength of her shillelagh's blackthorn club crushing the land into a shattered assortment of islands, Munros and glens, before reaching into her creel and tossing boulders in a frenzy of her winter temper; unwittingly creating and blessing the universe with the most magnificent land in the world: Scotland.

Unfulfilled by her creation, she sprinkled her magical jewels, their random, and imperfect display seen as standing stones, imbued with her capacity for creation and sight, gifted only to those of her choosing. Ones deemed worthy of her motherhood; guardians of spirits, healers of misery and defenders of persecution: Spaes.

In the shadow of a Munro scarred by aeons of frozen waterfalls, a glorious moon fired shards of light across a cloudless sky, through bare tree branches, and into a room where three women gripped the hands, and wiped the brow of a friend as she laboured. Their chanting pulsed within the walls, choreographing the candle flames in a shadow dance as they beseeched their spirits and guides. The weary mother-to-be cried out to the spirit of Cailleach to bring forth the child she'd wrestled for twenty-one hours, and in the moment of birth a tidal wave of relief dumped its weight. A child wailed, women whooped, and a mother cried. Fingers and toes counted, and a kiss on each eyelid confirmed her blessings. In the moments of respite and euphoria, a screech sliced through the air. Another child demanded to be born, oblivious to the exhaustion draining the life from her mother. All hands rushed to witnesses a dark crowning. Within seconds, time reminded its limit and only the mother's yells echoed in the hollow silence of panic. The unexpected child wriggled and squealed her way into the traumatised hands of the midwife. Attendants stared, mouths dropped open, and an explanation remained buried in confusion. Overwhelming thoughts ended when the child's demands triggered a rush of activity. When the two babies lay clean and swaddled, quiet and gurgling, all attention swung to their mother. Eyes staring into the unseen, cheeks retreating to their hollows, and lips unable to move as they took on the colour of an angry sea, silently begged her attendants for help. Doors slammed, the cold stone floor rang out with each hurried step, and water basins overflowed in the rush from the hearth to the bedside. Blood-soaked cloths piled, eyes drowned in sweat and tears, and a husband's voice bellowed from outside. The mother's closest friend, no longer able to watch the proceedings, gripped a hand and begged her dearest to stay strong, and breathe, knowing breath depended on her rapidly decreasing blood pressure. With the unwelcome but inevitable outcome looming, she gripped both hands and pressed her forehead against the near-unconscious mothers'. In her heart she understood, and so she hummed, and prayed, and with a voice summonsed from the depth of her soul, charged with the blessings of mother Cailleach, she sang her friend on to her next world.

Outside, her husband beat leaves beneath his feet with each stride up and down his cobbled path; clawing at his wiry beard and pulling hair on the back of his head. His mind reeled and sweat beads merged on his forehead with every rushed heartbeat. Smoke snaking from his chimney offered no familiar comfort, and red-berried holly bushes proposed no guarantee of a merry Christmas. Two brothers swung from one knotted rope tied on a branch three times their young height, as their father's heart swung from hope to despair. The younger boy revelled in an entire day's attention from his hero, as boredom nudged the older to consider tossing his sibling into the icy pond – to end the monotony and provide some entertainment.

In the house, screaming hearts clashed with the quiet chill of winter. The midwife stuffed bundles of bloodied rags into a sack. She then supported the young mothers' friends as they washed away every trace of her torment, replaced her soiled birthing shirt with a nightdress, freshly sewn and laundered in preparation of presenting her new child to her husband and sons, and placed a wreath of fresh heather on her head. In the corner, sharing a crib carved by their father, two baby girls lay content and unaware of their combined loss. Quiet sobbing resounded in a room bereft of energy and anticipation. Even the candles stilled. A timid yelp from the crib interrupted everyone's musings. The midwife clasped her hands and her in-breath echoed. "We must tell him."

A voice stammered from the woman still clutching her friend's hand. "I will."

Clyde gripped the tree trunk and his chest heaved. His nostrils flared when he gripped Morag's shoulders. "It's not possible. How did she have two weans in her tiny body?"

Morag shuddered. "We don't know."

A few remaining leaves, refusing to accept winter's demands, fluttered to his feet when he roared. "How did this happen?"

His two sons fell from the rope and rushed to his side, their sudden puzzlement sitting in the creases of their foreheads and tired eyes. "Da, what's happening?" the older asked. "Is the wean here yet?" the younger quizzed.

Clyde's stare hurt. Morag's wet eyes said everything. "Boys, your Da needs to tell you." She left him consoling his sons and returned to her friend's bedside.

Moments after the wailing reduced to sobs, the stone floor rang out again, this time with solid stomping that trembled from far below the slate. The door clung to its hinges when Clyde barged into the room. The midwife and attendants retreated like mice to the corner, heads bowed, hands clasped in as much armour as deference. He barely acknowledged them. His wife's perfectly still body distressed him from within his bones, and his sudden collapse snuffed out the candle illuminating her colourless, but peaceful expression. Not yet dismissed, the women dammed their tears and dug fingernails into already painful palms. In one sudden movement, Clyde bolted upright and swung to look at them. "Where is my daughter?" he thundered.

The midwife rushed to the crib and placed his firstborn into his trembling arms. When she returned with his twin daughter, he was already striding out of the room. She rushed after him. "Your second wean," she called.

Clyde swung around. "The one who killed my Ailsa?"

The midwife clung to the innocent babe and begged her knees to hold firm. She shook her head, but her jaw trembled. "Clyde. Please."

His eyes glazed over. He glanced down at the child in his arms. "Take it away. Prepare Ailsa for her journey."

"Clyde. No!" Morag rushed to his side.

"She killed Ailsa. I never want to see her again."

Clyde left his home with his two boys and newborn daughter while the women gathered around the crib where her twin sister lay, now alone.

"She needs to be nursed," said the midwife.

"I can do it," replied one attendant, a new mother herself.

Morag sobbed. "Then what?"

After two days of preparations, announcements, and prayers, they laid Ailsa to rest alongside her parents and brothers. Solemn as the occasion warranted, the situation regarding an unwanted child threatened to crush everyone who stood by the graveside. None brave enough to broach it or to decide on where the child should go, all were relieved when the rain arrived, and only the closest family risked attending the wake. Morag, unable to contain her sorrow, grabbed Clyde's arm as he left. "This is wrong. You cannae do this."

He ignored her. Morag pursued him. "Take some time, then think again."

He turned on her. "I've done my thinking."

Morag sighed her defeat. "And how is the wee one doing? Have you named her?

"Heather," he replied before marching off.

When the daylight gave way to the dull early evening, the midwife and attendants gathered in Morag's house. They shared bread, herbal tea, hugs, and tears. When the moon appeared at its highest, Morag went to her room and returned with a blackthorn wood box, carved and hinged. She removed two stones, each with a hole through the middle and etched with Gaelic symbols. After holding them between her palms for a few moments, she handed them to the woman next to her. The stones continued their journey from hand to hand while humming ascended to a chant, reverberating from deep in their souls to the thatch above. The walls heaved as the volume increased, before descending again into silence. Each woman opened her eyes and looked at Morag. She took a stone in one hand and a hammer in the other. Even the candle flames flinched when she smashed the stone, retrieved the pieces, and tossed them into her fireplace. She returned the other stone to the box and tied a piece of narrow muslin around it. The nursing mother's loud exhale disturbed the moment. "It's done."

"Yes," Morag replied. "I will take this to Heather."

The midwife crossed her arms. "Who will teach her?"

Morag pressed the box against her heart. "We will."

Chapter 1

A FIRST DAUGHTER, JESSIE would still learn the significance of her place in the world, and the insignificance of Tom's. Jessie had no way of understanding the way her cheeky grin pierced his heart and soul the day he locked eyes with her outside the milk yard at the edge of one of the smallest, but prettiest villages in the highlands; or how it would forever change the path of her life.

Neither the chill of an early Scottish autumn, nor its ominous tidings dulled freckles the colour of crushed autumn leaves dancing across her pale face. Tom worried his chest might burst when she dropped a full pail of milk, but it was simply their fates colliding; determined long before they were born. She shrieked when the precious milk splashed over her feet, shook her head, retrieved the empty bucket, then flopped onto the grass. Tom's smirk rose from his belly. "Well, that wasn't too clever."

Jessie tucked loose wisps into her overstuffed cap, looked up and spotted his bright blue eyes and baffled expression. She extended a slim, mottled arm matching her complexion and pushed a clenched fist into her waist. "You could stand there gawking, or you might help me up." She cocked her head, straightening the bulging headgear. "If you've any manners, that is."

Tom ignored the thumping in his chest, dropped his farming gloves, gripped her hand, then yanked her off the ground.

"Steady on," she yelped, "I'm not a heifer," before landing gracelessly on the path.

A rush of colour flushed his face. "Sorry, I'm more used to pulling sheep out the mire."

After brushing herself off, she picked up her pail and winked. "I'll remember that next time I get stuck in a mire."

Tom stared as she sauntered off, skirts swinging, down the gravel path bordered by colourful and dependable common heather. His heart hadn't yet recovered when the boy from the milk yard nudged him. "Hiya Tom, what's up? You seen a ghost?"

Tom's head tilted sideways as he gazed at the spot where Jessie released a mane of glowing red hair from the inefficient cap, before disappearing around a tight bend leading to a dense forest of sky-high pines. "No, Donald, not a ghost. I think I just saw an angel."

Donald shrugged. "Well, if you don't put your eyes back in yer head and get a move on, yer milk will curdle."

When Tom finally mustered the courage to ask Jessie's father for permission to marry his only daughter, he hoped his decision to die rather than live without her wouldn't be tested. Fortunately, Jessie felt the same, working her father Dougal to the point of distraction and into submission. Incapable of refusing her anything, the dowry was already agreed upon by the time the young man knocked on the door. Tom stood smart, clean, but sweating. Red faced, hands clutched to his sides, words stuttered over his dry lips. The request was no sooner made when his future father-in-law gripped him in a bear hug and gave them both an ear-splitting blessing. Tom's throat relaxed, and he beamed as Jessie jumped, squealing with delight.

Her mother, Heather, watched the greeting, then offered a firm hand; and a smile which failed to brighten her face. Two layers of wool skirts matching a patterned shawl hung from her square-shouldered body. "Welcome, young man." She glanced at Jessie. "It seems you have won our daughter's heart. I think capturing her spirit may be trickier."

Still clutching his damp hands, Tom looked at Jessie, then at his future mother-in-law. He pushed his shoulders back, ignoring the heat travelling up his neck. "I will take care of her for the remainder of her days – with your approval.

Heather steered him to a chair. "I sincerely hope so."

Brothers Fraser and Angus arrived knee-deep in dirt, exhausted from peat digging, and despite it not being Christmas or Hogmanay, Dougal hauled them into the cluttered family kitchen where he poured Atholl Brose into small clay mugs, before making an emotional toast and urging them to drink. After quaffing a few jugs, and the dowry formalised, Tom no longer had control of his legs. Jessie still jigged around the room, her bare feet dislodging any stubborn specks of dust as they slapped the stone floor, her unbound tresses flapping in time. Dougal sang folk songs to wake the dead, but not Fraser or Angus, whose toils and the Brose took their toll, rendering them both prostrate across two well-worn couches taking up most of the living space. Amazed by the volume Dougal was able to consume without slurring, Tom pondered if, although named after the expert hunter Dougal, he may well have descended from the Giant of Atholl himself. Before paralysis reached his brain, he watched Heather sitting quietly in a corner, working heather stalks into ropes which would ultimately end up forming baskets, or hanging in the barn with the multitude she'd already woven for Dougal to use on their croft. He admired the aptness of her name, knowing her legendary skills supplied the villagers with a variety of ropes they understood would last a lifetime. Her gnarly hands worked feverishly with a skill obviously learned from a master at a young age. Anyone in need of a decent rope knew which house to call upon. She scarcely spoke a word to Tom, and despite her warm hospitality and friendly smile, he could not get the making of her. Mesmerised by the synchronised movement of her fingers – and the Brose – he watched until she raised her head. Her beady green eyes fixed on him, and seconds before he passed out, his skin trembled with every hair on his body twitching.

Jessie perched on the armrest, placed a tired arm around her mother's shoulder, and fiddled with her soft dark waves fighting a grey onslaught. "Och Mam, is he not just perfect?"

Heather's lack of response dulled Jessie's enthusiasm. "Don't be sad. I'll only be a spit away, and before long you'll be a granny."

Tom's snoring rumbled from the couch. Jessie laughed. Heather didn't.

"Mam, please be happy for me. He's a good man, you'll see."

Heather stroked Jessie's free hand. "I am happy for you. Don't mind me, I'm tired. It's been an overwhelming day."

Scotland still conducted marriages based on a simple exchange of consent, but Dougal insisted on a formal church service, a legal contract, handfasting and all the traditions.

"You're doing it right or not at all, young lassie," he barked, after Jessie objected to having their feet covered in soot before

a ritual washing. "Soot is a sign of hearth and home, and a blackening brings good luck, so you'll both be having it," he declared. "Under God's eyes, in God's house, like the God-fearing people we are."

Heather's eyebrows shot up. She muttered under her breath, which didn't go unnoticed by Dougal. "I see yer look, but there'll be none of your creepy carry-ons either." He strutted out the door, presuming he'd laid down the law.

Heather and some of her friends, known to be medicine makers – amongst other less talked-about skills – created a dress of simple proportions with a colourful waistband over a padded corset. Instead of pinning the customary Arisaid cape above her heart with an ornate brooch, Heather insisted on looping both ends through the hole in an oval stone carved with intricate Gaelic symbols.

Dougal objected. "Ye cannae show off yer daft beliefs on yer lassie's wedding dress!" he hollered. "I told you, no funny business, and now look at ye."

Heather didn't flinch, but her stare pinned him to the wall. "I'll do whit I like, so you'll wheisht if you know whit's good fir ye."

Dougal twisted his russet beard until it entwined in his prominent, rough knuckles. "Ye'll have everybody clinging tae their rosaries, feart tae look at her!"

Heather banged a cast-iron pot on the hearth before striding towards him. "They'll take it any way they like. You're the one who wants a church wedding, so we're doing it, but she's mine too, so I'll bless her as I wish."

Dougal opened his mouth but bit his tongue. He knew when not to cross Heather, and although he neither understood nor liked her strange beliefs, he'd long since accepted they came part and parcel with her. He loped out the door, muttering, "I better speak tae the priest then."

Heather's best friend, Maggie, squeezed past him in the doorway. "Whit's up with him?" she chuckled, before sitting on a chair that groaned.

Heather grinned, wiping her forehead. "He's all in a worry about the stone on Jessie's dress, so now he's creepin' off to warn Father Coyle."

Maggie's chest lifted, her cackle instantly elevating the mood. "I'd give a bucket of ale to see it. That old priest will have the church carpeted in salt."

Heather couldn't help but laugh. "Aye, and we'll all be reekin' of sage for a week!"

Maggie fished out dried heather stalks hidden in her voluminous skirt. "Here, these are ready for the corset."

Heather took them, then reached out to touch Maggie's forehead. "Are you feeling all right?"

Maggie swatted the hand away, smoothing her wilful grey locks. "I'm perfect as perfect is," she groused.

"Well, yer ankles are bursting and yer the colour of an angry boil. I'll make something up for you."

Maggie shrugged. Heather's preternatural skill in reading her health and mood never ceased to surprise her. "All right then, but don't fuss with me."

Heather rolled her eyes before fetching the incomplete wedding dress, then emptying dried flowers from a muslin bag onto her heavy, carved table. Maggie heaved herself out of the unhappy chair to sit opposite.

"Help me with this," Heather pointed a finger, "and when you're done, get yerself to bed with those ankles up higher than yer heart. We want you fit for the celebration."

"Aye, I hear you. I'll be perfect for the day." Maggie picked up the hem of the dress and a few dried white heather flowers before winking. "You'd already have told me if I wasn't going to make it."

The flippant comment startled Heather. "I won't be telling you anything until it's necessary. So, you get that hemming done, take what I give you and get off yer feet."

Maggie also knew when not to cross Heather, but she leaned over and patted her hand. "I might not be a master, but I'm still a spae, so you needn't worry about giving me bad news."

Heather squeezed Maggie's hand before setting out the heather stalks to form the bones of Jessie's wedding day corset. "Skilled teachers taught me well. Anyway, get on with it, make sure you stuff that hem full of flowers ... she's going to need all the luck they possess."

After a moment's silence, Maggie's hands stilled. "She's besotted with him, he adores her, so you needn't concern yourself with that. I've never seen any two so smitten. If

17

you're worried about them being too happy, you're just being a dour Scot."

Heather focussed on arranging the stalks. "Perhaps."

"Well, I swear the sun couldn't split their shadows." She spotted Heather bite her bottom lip, but persisted. "Love is a funny business, no doubt, but if there's something you're not telling me, now would be a good time."

"I'm simply being a concerned mother."

Maggie shrugged. "If you say so, but you might want to convince your face."

Jessie arrived as if blown in on the wind, erupting at the sight of her dress in the making. Maggie's mouth dropped open. "My goodness, child, contain yerself before you explode and ruin the wedding!"

Jessie flew across the room, wrapping herself around Maggie's soft, bulky shoulders. "I'm so excited I may well burst," she squealed, her bright emerald eyes dancing in delight. Then she noticed her mother's solemn face. "What's scratching you, Mammie?"

Before Heather had time to answer, Maggie threw her a scowl. Heather reached out to her daughter. "Nothing ... I'm lost in this sewing is all."

Jessie hugged her mother tight before sidling in beside her. After picking up a handful of dried flowers, she frowned. "You've got more than plenty here. Are there any left in the fields?"

Maggie winked at Jessie. "More than you'll ever need, but there's no harm filling the hem right up ... and you'll smell wonderful."

Jessie let the dried petals fall through her long, slim fingers before turning to her mother. Her smile waned. "Da says you want me to wear a stone instead of a brooch?"

"That's right," Heather nodded.

Jessie looked at Maggie, who suddenly examined her feet.

"You haven't explained the stones to me, so why must I wear it?"

Heather took both Jessie's hands, holding them firm. "I told you I would explain in good time – and I will. When I do, you'll be happy you did." She returned to the corset. "For now, you can trust I have my reasons."

Jessie gazed at her mother's hands for a few moments before jumping out of her seat. She hugged both women, smiled, then left. She also understood when not to cross her mother. Maggie shook her head and rolled her eyes, but before she could speak, Heather raised a finger. "Wheisht, she'll learn in good time. She's one of us. What's for her won't go by her."

They toiled with the dressmaking without mention of the stone or the reason for Heather's subdued mood. When Heather noticed Maggie waning, she stopped what she was doing, collected everything from the table and took it to her bedroom, returning with a little brown bottle sealed with a cork, together with a hessian bag filled with herbs and powders. "Make sure you take this four times a day," she ordered, handing Maggie the vial and shoving the small bag into her apron pocket, "and put this in your bath."

Maggie accepted the medicine. "Aye, aye, I know what to do," she griped.

They ambled along together until they reached the end of the stone path. Maggie turned, hugged her dear friend, and whispered. "You must talk to her. It's time she understood."

Again, Heather raised her hand, shushing her. "Get yerself home now."

Maggie pulled her scarf tight, then ambled down the road.

"And for your everyone's sake, stay off the ale!" Heather hollered.

Chapter 2

JESSIE'S WEDDING DAY FULFILLED *her every wish. After an emotional talk with her mother as she dressed, they embraced, managing to smile despite a few tears. When Fraser and Angus walked into the room, the sight of them looking so clean and smart almost burst her heart wide open. They blushed when she pulled them into her arms. Heather imagined Dougal might collapse when he saw his daughter step through the doorway, so she gripped his hand and whispered. "Remember this moment, for you'll never see her happier than she is today."*

Dougal's resolve was no match for his tears. His voice broke. "Aye, God's done some fine work."

Heather bit her tongue but spotted Angus cross himself. "There'll be plenty of time for that when ye get tae church," she groaned

"Aye," he mumbled.

Dougal raised a finger in their direction. "This is no day for yer biting. We'll be in God's house, so remember that."

Angus nodded and Heather sighed. When the men turned their backs on her, she reached into a pocket, closing her hand around a smooth stone. She allowed her eyes to close briefly before releasing it. Jessie spotted the action and gripped her arm. "Mammie, stop it," she pleaded, "not today."

Heather grinned and took both Jessie's hands in hers. "Hush, child, your day will be perfect."

Tom's friends overstepped tradition, including treacle and feathers in his blackening, leaving his feet still filthy on the day of the wedding. His father Robert and sister Mary fell about laughing, but his mother Jean scowled, pinching her thin

lips, contorting her tight face more than usual. "That's no way to be seen in God's house. I'm mortified," she snapped.

"Och, be quiet," Mary chided, while finishing her best attempt to plait her long, frizzy hair. "Half her family shouldn't even get through the doors of a church."

Robert ceased straightening the heather sprig pinned to his tartan waistcoat. "Hush, both of you! After today, his feet are of no interest to anyone bar Jessie." He lowered his voice but squinted towards Mary. "I don't wish to hear any of that nonsense from you."

"It's not only me, but the entire village as well," Mary whined. "I heard her mother's a spae and the church will be full of them!"

Jean gasped. "Do not say such things in this house!" She crossed herself twice.

Robert waved a fist. "Never mind this house," he growled. "Don't you dare repeat that … anywhere. It's dangerous talk and can get people hanged!"

Jean gripped her chest, glowering at Mary. "You see what you've done? Stirring up trouble with your silly mouth."

Mary threw her arms in the air. Her words shot towards them. "I'm only telling you what I've been told. Don't pretend you haven't heard it."

Robert's ruddy complexion raged under his grey beard and the room threatened to implode. "Enough!" he roared. "Tom is marrying Jessie, which means we will be kin. We may not want it, but they are now family."

They stared silently, the significance of Robert's words unnerving. Mary fiddled with a hair ribbon. Jean's bony fingers gripped the rim of the armchair, and Robert let out a deep sigh before fixing his sporran. "Ye might know they will tar us with the same brush, so watch your step."

Tom called timeously and they filed out. Mary whispered to her mother. "Bring extra holy water – just in case."

"God help us," Jean hissed, before crossing herself again.

Children desperate for the scramble congregated outside the bride's house and the church, chanting: "Poor out, ye dirty brute. Ye canny spare a ha'penny."

Fraser and Angus showered the scrawny mob with coins to ensure a lucky day and tummies full of sweets. Heather had made the bride's cake to break over Jessie's head at the reception. Hopefully, it would crumble into multiple small pieces to signify a fruitful marriage with many children. Some mothers of brides tried to fail-safe their luck by including masses of caraway seeds in the mix. The tartan scarf for the handfasting ritual belonged to Dougal's father, satisfying the 'something old'. Toms' family provided the pewter Quaich that he would fill with whisky, then pass around to the delight of the guests – especially the men – and Maggie. Candles burned in every nook and cranny in the church, and as Maggie imagined, each pew displayed sprigs of juniper and heather tied together with a sizeable chunk of white sage. Waiting for Jessie's arrival, Maggie whispered to Heather. "Is this daft priest hoping to ward us off, protect himself, or set fire to us?"

Heather eyed her. "Well, he's going to be disappointed."

Even though the ancient stone church didn't have many pews, guests still separated themselves into groups. Bride's family on the left; groom's on the right. A third group waited until the last minute before entering, but it wasn't long before murmuring snaked its way through the attendees – on the groom's side. Six women entered the back row, distant enough to not unsettle the devout or rankle the priest. Shrouded in layers of dark fabric with lace veils concealing their faces, Heather and Maggie's fellow spaes sat still and silent. Maggie tried to speak, but Heather pinched her hand.

A bell rang out and everyone stood to listen to the piper rattling the timbers, scattering the mice, sounding the bride's arrival. Father Coyle led Jessie and Dougal through the congregation towards the altar where Tom stood, his watery eyes shining, his shirt collar already damp. Heather's skin bristled when the priest passed her, but a swell of tears followed shortly when a waft of white heather reached her. Jessie, adorned and radiant. Tom's parents remained face front, and when Dougal handed his daughter to Tom, Heather watched Jean raise her handkerchief, which wiped her tears but not her pained expression. After arriving at the church, they had simply nodded a polite, wordless greeting before walking to their respective pews in silence. Fraser and Angus stood on either side of Jessie, and Heather admired her tartan-clad boys. Angus, the eldest, stretched a good two inches above his brother and even though both had inherited their father's broad shoulders and stocky build it was Angus's fiery red hair matching his temper which set him apart from his dark-haired sibling of gentler disposition. Two sons different in every way; one a constant challenge, the other a delight. Love and protection for their younger and only sister their sole common trait. Or so it appeared.

Similar to most rural couples, Tom and Jessie enjoyed a typically festive, if modest wedding reception. The piper's skirls ousted any lurking evil spirits, blessed the bride and groom and guaranteed protection and good health. Paid in silver, together with a dram of whisky, he legitimised the contract. Heather kept company with her friends and exchanged pleasantries with those who pretended. To keep the peace, Dougal said nothing about the spaes' presence, but when he took her up to dance, he muttered through a stiff jaw. "This'll cause trouble. You should know better."

Heather squeezed his hand and pulled him closer. "This is my daughter's wedding day. If anyone's bothered, they must leave."

Dougal tensed. "I care less about their leaving, it's what they'll do after."

Heather sensed his worry so laid her head against his broad chest. "Don't fret so much. Let's enjoy our dance."

Fraser also took her up for a reel, but when she looked for Angus, her lips tightened at the sight of him deep in conversation with Father Coyle. She refrained from imagining what they were discussing, but their expressions implied it wasn't anything pleasant. She also gave up trying to limit Maggie's quaffing but whispered in her ear. "If yer not going to tend yer drinking, can you at least mind yer mouth?" Maggie scowled and resumed her merriment with the local butcher.

Heather moved to the table where the spaes sat. "Thank you for coming. I understand how it must feel." After chatting a bit, she leaned towards a grey-haired woman sitting next to her. "Myna, please make sure Maggie doesn't stay too long and gets home safely."

Myna's coat appeared to hang on her tall frame as if held by invisible clothes pegs. Her stoical spine remained upright, but she relaxed her pinched expression and her gaze softened. "We're all leaving soon, and Maggie's coming with us." Her wiry fingers wrapped around Heather's hand in her trademark grip. "Don't you worry."

Fraser danced most of the evening, clutching a jug of ale regularly topped up by an over-friendly, buxom woman who no one seemed to know. He also twirled Jessie around the room reel after reel until Tom rescued her from his wailing about how much he would miss his only sister. Angus spent time in discussion with Father Coyle and a local landowner, trying hard to ignore the attention of Tom's sister Mary who, after too many rounds of the Quaich, disregarded her fear of the spaes. This new landowner was unfamiliar to the area, but when Angus questioned his attendance, Father Coyle's eyes widened.

"I deemed it polite and prudent to invite our new resident to the first celebration since his arrival."

Angus ignored the priest's tone and held out a hand. "Then welcome. I'm Angus, the bride's eldest brother."

"Charles Wilson, good to meet you."

Surprised by Wilson's accent, Angus frowned. "Are you the new owner of Cruachan Manor?"

"I am."

Angus sighed. "I didn't realise they'd sold it to an English family."

Wilson's smile belied the tightness in his jaw. "I bought it based on price and potential, not nationality."

Fearing a confrontation, Father Coyle intervened. "Well now, that's irrelevant. I think it's important you get to know your new neighbour – and landowner."

Neither man responded, so the priest steered Wilson off for a drink. Angus remained sober, and after Charles Wilson left, he was content to listen to the fiddlers, watching the guests become louder and sillier the longer the evening wore on. He noticed Tom's mother leaving without saying goodbye to the newlyweds, followed shortly by his own, with whom he'd spent no time. He was still seething from the sight of the spaes sitting in the church, and furious with her for inviting them. This was not a penny wedding, so an invitation was necessary. Thankfully, Tom's sister found better company with a less fussy friend, and Father Coyle, now on his own, revelled *in attempting to sing along with the musicians. He spotted Fraser sliding down a gum pole so carried him home, lest the buxom one took her chances. Fraser attracted all the local girls, and in his present condition could end up in trouble. Angus dragged him through the door, dumped him on his bed, then sat a bucket close to his head, confident he would need it.*

Despite her reeling and the weight of a hem chock full of heather, Jessie's dress held together as expected. Her wild red hair wasn't so amenable, so before long, her mane of meticulously prepared curls tumbled about her face and shoulders, bobbing with as much enthusiasm as her feet. Every man present twirled her in a continuous reel, her energy charging the room. Tom circulated the Quaich more than a few times and consequently endured more backslapping and hugging than most grooms. After the sword dance ended, the guests sang Auld Lang Syne, then Jessie and Tom left their reception infatuated and hopeful. Jessie's dowry, Tom's wages, wedding gifts, and a small croft ceded to them by Tom's father set them up well, so their hearts were full. Keen to avoid any bad luck, Tom carried Jessie over their new threshold where, after frequent declarations of love, they consummated their marriage in a thatched cottage of their own, decorated with buckets of lilies and white heather. The Arisaid cape lay in a heap on the floor, still looped through the stone Heather had insisted upon.

Guests made merry into the wee hours until the beautifully decorated barn was bereft of most of its flowers, the floor strewn with empty jugs, food scraps and a carpet of trampled heather in all the shades of purple nature endowed to this striking part of the country. Those who'd quaffed liberally while underestimating their limits now lay amongst the mess – comatose, including Dougal. The following day, rumour of a search party dispatched because of the priest's no-show at mass – who they finally found unconscious behind the piano – amused everyone.

Maggie left the wedding reception assisted by the six spae women who had remained serene during the service. She was sure Father Coyle's obvious discomfort was in part because each time he had lifted his head, he could not help looking directly at them – and because Heather never took her gaze off him. Even when he'd avoided her eyes, sweat beads formed steadily under his collar until his vestments glistened. Maggie stifled a smirk each time he removed his glasses to wipe them with trembling hands. As the women walked down the long dirt path running along the forest boundary, Maggie laughed. "After today, that priest will be on his knees for a week."

Myna grimaced. "Aye, Heather certainly makes him squirm."

"He can feel her wrath from a mile away," said Maggie.

Myna halted. "You would do well to not talk about it. He's a nasty piece of work, and you blethering about him will only invite trouble."

Maggie rarely heeded her cautioning, and against Heather's advice, she had flattened more than a few ales at the reception. "He doesn't scare me. If he only understood how lucky he is our Heather is a kind lass, he might stop his rabble-rousing and leave us be."

"Maggie! Hold your tongue or we'll all be at his mercy. Heather has more at stake than us, so keep your wits about you."

The group went quiet. Maggie pulled her scarf tight before whipping her cape hood over her head. She didn't enjoy the reprimand but deferred to the wiser women – the ones who had taught her everything, stood by her for as long as she remembered, but more importantly, protected her when necessary. She looked at the clouds darkening in the distance.

"Aye," she grumbled, "I hear you. Best we be off home. There's rain coming and no moon tonight."

Myna ignored Maggie's changing of the subject. "Just mind what I've said and watch your feet on the path."

Maggie shuffled on the spot before leaning over to embrace her. "I'll be fine. I know my way."

After hugging them, they watched her take a route to the right of the forest towards her stone cottage on a larger part of the farm. Plodding down the narrow lane, she revisited every moment of the wedding, looking forward to dropping in on Heather the following day to dissect and revel in the highlights. After relishing the ale she'd swigged from the Quaich, a heaviness in her legs reminded her of Heather's warning. While puffing and sweating on her way to her cottage, she made a promise to herself – and her maker – to take better care of her body. Dark clouds hovered, diminishing any remaining prospect of a bright sunrise. She picked up her pace, her feet groaning all the way to her front door. When she put the key in the lock, her cat jumped from the nearby bush. "For the love of the moon and stars," she yelled. "You nearly stopped my heart!"

She stepped inside, still berating the cat, but no sooner had she closed her door when it crashed open again. Stunned and slow to react, she was powerless to prevent a brutal shove from sending her careering into her home. She cried out, staggered to her couch and slumped into the soft cushions. A deep voice rumbled through the room. "Stop snivelling and listen. Get yourself to the rectory tomorrow at five o'clock. Father Coyle wants a word."

The ale provided some courage, so rage fired into her ashen face. "You'll get yerself out of my house if you know what's good for you – and you can tell that evil menace to stay away from us!"

The man's immense bulk loomed over her. His unshaven face matched his enormous hands; rough, threatening. Sweat ran down the inside of Maggie's arms. She pushed her body into the couch, clenching both fists, ready to use them. He sneered as he bent towards her. She recoiled from the smell of his whisky breath, every lump within the couch imprinting on her back. The disdain in his voice and his icy stare pinned her. "I'm not interested in your drivel, just be there. I don't want to come looking for you."

He backed away and the door clicked shut behind him. She sat with trembling hands stuck to her chest, her thumping heart reverberating against her fingers. Hot tears burned her cheeks, but she forced herself to get up to take the drops Heather had given her. After preparing for bed, she made herself a cup of sweet tea, secured her windows and doors, then lay back on her pillows. Clutching her mug, she waited for the medicine to work. As her nerves settled, she cursed herself for drinking the ale – and for threatening the priest.

Heather left Dougal with her boys at the reception, and on arriving home the first thing she did was light a few candles, unwrap the two large pieces of bridecake broken over Jessie's head and toss them into the dustbin. Part of her wished she had laden it with seeds, but to her mind that would be cheating and she preferred to be forewarned than live in false hope. Two pieces were better than none, so she determined that same night she'd start praying for a granddaughter. Gripping the ends of the tartan scarf used in the handfasting ceremony, she pulled the knot tight. A glowing candlestick guided her to her bedroom where she retrieved a wooden chest from under her bed. She sat on the stone floor, the sudden cold biting through her clothing as she unlocked it with a brass key she kept hidden behind a bedpost. She lifted out a drawstring bag, the dry hessian rough against her skin, removed a smooth stone and clasped it between her palms together with the one she'd kept safe in her pocket all day. Her eyes closed, shutting out the dancing candlelight shadows. Her mind emptied as she breathed in the aroma of white heather still hanging in the air from making Jessie's dress. The stones warmed. Sitting cross-legged, she let her body sway before slipping into weightlessness. Time stood still as her surroundings melted into the dark, allowing her mind to travel. An indeterminate time passed before she opened her eyes, returned both stones to their bag, wrapped the tartan knot in brown paper with a sprig of the white heather from Jessie's bouquet, then packed both away. After pushing the chest back to its place under the bed, she changed into her nightclothes, climbed into bed, blew out the candle, then prayed to her guides ... before crying herself to sleep.

Chapter 3

THE SPAE WOMEN KNEW better than to engage Maggie when she was down one jug too many. They walked away mulling over the day's events until they reached the end of the road where the forest lay to the left, spreading far and wide. Tall, elegant pines stood guard at the few visible entry points where, regardless of the time of day, one entered an extraordinary world. Crooked tree roots pushed through a carpet of thick, moss-topped ground. Scots' Pine, Oak and Rowan trees held dominion, accompanied by holly and brambles snaking around twisted trunks. Low-hanging branches created an almost impenetrable fortress, giving home and protection to a multitude of flora and fauna. Few cared to venture into the woods for fear of losing their way – to wander forever until death rescued them. The possibility of being lost in the woods was enough to keep even the bravest away. Elders warned children: "If ye dare go in there, don't be surprised if ye never git oot." If a person happened to go missing, "The good Lord could never find himself in there," they declared.

Wild and unpredictable, the locals deemed it a hostile environment to avoid – unless you lived there. Unless you were a spae.

The group entered the woods silently, like cats, navigating to Myna's home deep in the forest by remarkable memory, a well-honed sense of direction and supreme knowledge of their territory. They meandered along invisible paths, across two rickety bridges and around a small pond, until a clearing amongst a dense spread of bluebells revealed a short pathway of cobblestones leading to an ivy-covered thatched cottage.

Myna and her husband Ewan had transformed the home where she nursed her own parents through their illnesses and deaths, from a dark hideaway in the woods into a pretty forest home. She'd gathered a multitude of evenly sized river rocks to place in a twelve-foot border, clearly demarcating her space. Holly and bramble mingled with the stones to form intense pink and white bushes in the spring, curtains of deep purple berries in the summer, leaving a hedge of rich green leaves dripping with bright red berries in the winter; a perennial smorgasbord for birds, bees and butterflies. Wild iris, lily of the valley, and white heather from cuttings she had spliced flanked the cobblestone path leading to the front door. Even the lightest of footsteps trampled the tiny twin flowers between the cobbles, releasing a light lilac fragrance which enveloped the house before drifting inside.

After Ewan had collected what he determined was enough bracken straw to re-thatch the weathered roof, Myna sent him off to collect heather stalks of the same amount. "We can't be getting the consumption the way my Mam and Da did," she'd contended. "The twins need parents for their entire lives."

Ewan worked hard on this double rooftop as Myna planted herbs she needed for her medicinal potions. She tended them with meticulous attention to ensure vigorous growth and bountiful harvests. When Ewan shuffled through the front door late one afternoon, exhausted, ready to flop onto the couch, Myna stopped him with one hand in the air, the other perched on a hip. "What are ye doing?"

Ewan only half sat. "It's done, yer new roof is complete."

Myna clapped her flour-covered hands. "Good, now get out."

Ewan had rolled his eyes before loping back out the front door. He understood when Myna gave an instruction so clearly, she wanted to do something which wouldn't wait for him to have a nap. Myna had taken a bunch of dried white sage sticks from the pantry, lit them from a log ember and blew smoke into every nook and cranny, reciting prayers of protection to the three kindreds: ancestors, earth spirits and gods. Ewan napped under the enormous oak tree behind the house until a swarm of midges reminded him outside wasn't a sensible place to sleep. He nudged the door open only enough to peer through. A waft of sage made him wrinkle his nose. "Is it safe to come in?"

Myna grinned. "It is now ... no one's coming in here uninvited."

The women walked along the path, then entered through a heavy wooden door, leaving behind the faint aroma of vanilla from crushed twinflowers mixed with fresh pine and heather. After stomping the dirt from their shoes, they piled logs in the stone fireplace, then lit candles. They gathered around the kitchen table, joined hands, closed their eyes and hummed. After a few minutes, the low resonance escalated to a chant. As the logs crackled and spat, the older woman recited in Gaelic. Candlelight cast formless shadows against rough walls in a wild dance. Hessian curtains concealed small windows, trapping the smell of wood, peat and candle wax, now imbued with the scent of white lilies and heather from overfilled clay vases. Time passed unchecked until the chanting found its natural, quieter rhythm, lowered into a deep hum, then ceased. Eyes opened, but silence prevailed until Myna spoke. "Winter is bringing darker days than before."

Some clasped their hands to their hearts.

"We need not speak of this; Heather will come and we will do what she asks."

In the tense atmosphere, a quiet voice inquired. "What about Jessie?"

"What about Maggie?" asked another.

A few days later, Angus made his way to the edge of the forest. It wasn't easy to dodge the shadows, and cursing the moon's energy didn't help. Even the shallow puddles conspired, throwing deformed shapes back from their glossy surfaces. Damp earth under soft boots muffled his steps. He slipped from wall to corner, tree to tree, ultimately hiding behind an enormous paperbark maple, hoping his instincts were correct so he wouldn't need to trudge much further. He wiped excess mud from his boots, cursing at the mess left on each trouser calf. Although severely tempted to smoke, common sense outweighed boredom. He thrust his fidgeting hands into his pockets when an overhead owl's hoot shook his bones. As his patience waned, he sighed, relieved to hear the familiar sound of gentle footsteps on boggy soil. The rough bark pressed through his wool coat, but he stood completely still, his gaze fixed on the murky darkness of the woods. When the noise faded, without moving his body, he turned his head around the trunk and peered into the dark. A hooded figure hugged the side of the path closest to the trees, each step instinctively finding easy ground. The person stopped to look behind before disappearing into the darkness. Angus' lungs deflated, dragging his shoulders down from their tight position. When he looked at the millions of stars surrounding the full moon, he conceded it was an especially delightful evening. A knot formed in his stomach while damp soaked into his soft boots. Anger held his throat until with a deep sigh he strode out onto the lane, turning away from where the figure slipped into the woods.

✿

The moon found a gap in the clouds and blazed overhead, crafting a luminous path to guide Heather through the forest. The accompanying stillness eased her nerves, slowing her thudding heart. She would not miss any unusual sound, and although she was sure no one had ever followed her, she scurried into an almost invisible entrance, her senses and warning bells remaining on high alert. Recent events had invited unwanted attention, so she understood the risk she took each time she made this journey. She'd noted the sideways glances and furtive whisperings during Jessie's wedding, so spent most of the day alternating between joy and irritation – and keeping Maggie in check. She threw off her hood and sucked in crisp air. Wafts of pine and moss filled her lungs, topping up her energy. When she left the main path, confident she was now in a safe place, her stiff fists relaxed and her arms swung loose by her sides. Within minutes, tree trunks wide enough to hide behind surrounded her, their dense, entwined branches weaving towards the moon.

It was easy for her to thread her way through these familiar allies without the need to watch her feet. She knew the terrain well but blessed this moon for its presence. Marrying Dougal took her away from the forest, condemning her to secret visits and a denial of her friends living there. It was a promise she made to him when agreeing to marry and live on the croft – a promise made with a warm embrace and a glint in her eye.

One she had no intention of keeping. She allowed his limited understanding of the depth of her beliefs and devotion to its practices to prevail, knowing she could never sway him towards her ways, and it would achieve nothing but harm to try. Their impasse, imprinted on her heart, still made her smile.

"Ye cannae be behaving like those crazy wives from the forest," he'd chided her, the arm around her shoulders slipping to rest on her buttock while they strolled through a heather copse.

"Dougal, mind yourself, my beliefs aren't crazy, I simply don't care for that church of yours."

His wide grin had morphed into pursed lips and his arms slumped to his sides. "Can ye just try? Maybe ye'll realise God's word is divine, it's only he who heals, and forgives."

Heather had pushed him away but eyed him carefully. "If ye want to marry me, you must accept I have traits you may not understand – just as there are things about you I'm not fond of."

Dougal reached for her hand but she'd pulled away. Her head cocked sideways, fists denting her tiny waist. He'd huffed and scowled. "Well, will ye promise not to swan around with them in public – and stay away from the forest?"

Heather simply rolled her eyes. "There's nothing wrong with the forest. You're listening to gossip and fear-mongering, but if ye insist, I'll be careful."

Dougal had shuffled, kicking imaginary stones at his feet and chewing his bottom lip. Heather had inched towards him until he could breathe her in; it worked. "Aye, all right then, if ye promise," he'd mumbled.

Heather grinned and his face responded with delight. Golden flecks danced around his hazel eyes and his shoulders lifted. He pulled her close, smothering her with kisses. When he ultimately came up for air, he held her tight. "Will ye come with me to church?"

"No."

His eyebrows met. "Did you say there are things about me you don't care for?"

Heather's laugh rattled her entire body. "No Dougal, you're perfect. Of course you are."

Fine lacy ferns skirting the pond and rock pool skimmed her legs, and her feet hardly made a sound, finding firm, spongy ground with each step. Moonlight gleamed on the surface of the water. She smiled thinking of summer approaching with cool dips to look forward to. Tawny owls screeched in competition with the usual nocturnals. This creepy cacophony might unnerve others but it was familiar music to Heather. The door creaked open after two gentle knocks. Firelight and friendly faces welcomed her inside. The candlelight shrunk the space. Tavia loaded fresh logs, and wild red flashes of bright light cast shadows around the room. Or was it Tevia? Since Heather first met the twins, she could seldom tell them apart. Shining, pin-straight dark hair, innocent blue eyes, porcelain skin and soft pink lips protected their cheery smiles. Each so tiny they suspected God may have accidentally created two people from one. No amount of help from the elder Myna, strong Aila or experienced midwife Aileen was enough to save their poor mother's life after she laboured for thirty-eight hours to deliver her identical, precious daughters. Myna undertook the mothering duties to support their father who took off to Lanark (the black country) to earn better money. He never returned, so the girls grew up accepting Myna and Ewan as their parents. Myna had miscarried each of her pregnancies so this responsibility thrilled her.

She handed Heather a mug of warm herbal infusion but a frown settled on her face. "Should you be here so soon after the wedding?"

Heather sipped the fragrant liquid before replying. "I didn't notice anyone watching me – more than usual, and Dougal thinks I'm off visiting Maggie."

Myna's eyes narrowed. "Have you seen Maggie?"

Heather placed her cup down on the low wood table in front of her and clasped her hands. "That's why I'm here. I needed to make sure she'd survived the wedding. She's poorly, so I gave her some more medicine, but I haven't seen her again."

Heather sensed the women watching her but only Myna spoke. "She may be poorly but it's from the drink so she only has herself to blame."

"She's her own worst enemy, I know. I told her so before the wedding. I gave her a potion to reduce the swelling in her ankles, but she simply can't help herself. She has one drink then nothing can stop her."

Myna glanced at the others before asking. "What did she say?"

Heather leaned back. "Nothing important, we chatted about the service, the daft priest, and how beautiful Jessie looked."

Myna clenched and unclenched her fists. "What about the priest?"

Heather sensed the air thicken. Watching the fidgeting of Myna's fingers extend to her feet, she glanced at the other women but none responded. She eyed Myna. "Why are you so troubled about Maggie? Have you seen something?"

Heather sensed the others shift before lowering their eyes. Myna breathed deep. "Yes."

Heather slumped forward resting her head in her palms. Logs collapsed in the fire sending tiny orange embers into the strained atmosphere. She watched them turn white then black before drifting back into the fireplace. Her lungs emptied as she lifted her eyes to Myna's.

"Tell me."

Chapter 4

THEIR HONEYMOON FLEW BY *in a week of relaxing, hiking through the mountains and forests, swimming in the still, chilly lochs, and copious lovemaking; indoors and out. Tom delighted in Jessie's enthusiasm to have sex anywhere, any time. Watching her smooth her skirts for the third time that day he chuckled. "We'll be having our own football team before long."*

Sunrays illuminated Jessies' hair, flashing golden shadows across Tom's face. "That's fine by me," she winked.

Tom reached up and pulled her down next to him against the wide tree trunk. He laced his thick fingers through hers, marvelling at how these fine freckled hands held both strength and tenderness equally. He drew her close enough to breathe in her scent and see his reflection in her luminous green eyes. Her energy sucked him in, engulfing his entire body, leaving him both powerless and euphoric. Each morning he gave thanks to God for blessing him with his new wife, praying to remain by her side for all eternity. His voice softened and his eyes glistened. "You are my life, I promise to give you everything you want, and I will protect you as long as I have breath in my lungs."

Jessie's heart ached beneath her ribs. She leaned in and kissed him. Tom's fingers traced each feature of her face as if for the first time as she listened to his heart beat against hers. In their own bubble, impervious to sounds or movement, they caressed each other, lost in the joy of their love. Then Jessie pulled away. "As many children as I want?"

"Yes." Tom pushed her down onto the grass, "but if it's a football team you want, then we better get on it."

Jessie's miscarriage took everyone by surprise, except Heather. "You're only married a year and you're young," she consoled, but Jessie cried for days after the blood appeared. Not yet five months pregnant, her belly had twinged as she beat dust from a loose carpet. She ignored it at first but as terrifying minutes flew by the twinges strengthened until she raced to her mother's house in a panic. Heather heard the frantic footsteps and flung open the door before Jessie reached it. She helped her into a back room slightly bigger than a broom cupboard and held her close. She'd forced Dougal to create this private women's chamber after complaining she and Jessie shouldn't have to endure the stink left by the three men of the house. Heather took great pride in her sacred place, forbidding any man to set foot in it. She kept it pristine, daily placing a fresh vase of heather on a small table next to a chair housing the chamber pot. A carved wooden chest sat in a corner, its brass lock gleaming as if proudly protecting secrets within. Jessie wailed when Heather coaxed her into the chair before gripping her trembling fingers. "There's no stopping it now, Jess."

Jessie's moans accompanied panic-stricken tears. Heather rushed to her room, returning with a bottle of drops.

"No, please, no!" Jessie keened when Heather removed the cork.

She took hold of Jessie's face, pushed the bottle against unwilling, quivering lips and watched her pupils widen into dark pools of despair. Jessie parted her lips, closed her eyes and accepted the drops. After a few moments she leaned forward. Heather whispered in her ear as her head slumped onto her shoulder.

"Breathe deep my child, let it be."

Tom spotted young Donald racing down the path towards him. Knee-deep in the fields he instinctively dropped his tools and ran to meet him. Panting, doubled over, Donald struggled to speak.

"What?" Tom shouted.

Donald pointed towards Tom's house. "J-Jessie." He dropped to the ground and Tom took off.

Jessie's melancholy rooted itself deep, worrying Tom, upsetting Dougal, and forcing Heather to act. Her heart ached for her first and only daughter. Having lost two children, she understood the feeling well, but found consolation in the three she did have – and her life spared no time for self-pity. She cried alone, washing clothes on the iron washboard outside, her angry fingers squeezing the pain out, furiously rubbing it away little by little, day by day until it became bearable. She mourned silently to the sounds of Dougal snoring, before drifting off to sleep to greet the nightmares that dark brought. Now two healthy pine trees grew in a spot where the sun embraced them from dawn till dusk before snow wrapped a protective coat over them for the winter. She never missed a day pressing a hand against the rough bark, drawing solace from the life within. Her mind's eye watched over her babies playing and dancing in the bright summer light before bedding down safely for the long, dark months of the winter that Cailleach Bheur brings. Her belief in departed souls remaining rooted to the earth through spirit and nature consoled her more than any kind words or deeds. More than anything Dougal might say. On full moon nights she met with her spaes, sent blessings to their departed, gave thanks for the gift of Dougal and her sons, and committed to the responsibility of being gifted with a first daughter. She also besought protection for herself and Jessie – protection from those who would seek to snuff them out, who feared her spiritual beliefs, deeming them supernatural and therefore uncontrollable and dangerous. Those who deemed her unchristian therefore devilish, to be routed by whatever means – now hanging was no longer a legal option – those such as Father Coyle. Jessie had not yet cultivated these deep beliefs or the distractions and responsibilities of family life, so Heather's instincts were to tread carefully lest she slide deeper into the darkness, to lose her light and energy forever. A darkness only a bereaved mother knows – an invisible cloak requiring regular attention to avoid her soul being tormented and ultimately suffocated by it. She wanted to save her before grief overwhelmed any hope of a joyful life. It was time to teach Jessie about womanhood, motherhood and being a first daughter; the way her mother had taught her.

Heather opened Jessie's front door and the sight of dead logs in the hearth and dishevelled wool blankets on the couch did not surprise her. She didn't need to throw back the shades to see the layer of dust, or feel the iron cooking plate to discern it was some time since a decent meal warmed the house. Heather nudged the bedroom door and peered into the lightless room. Jessie's form lay huddled under blankets. As the gentle sound of her breathing reached her, she pressed her fists to her chest as a sudden rush of sadness overwhelmed her; oppressive as the stifled air. She closed the door gently then got busy cleaning the house. After sweeping, dusting, washing and polishing, she prepared a hearty meal with food she'd brought. The earthly toil of housework always fuelled her energy, so when light returned to the house accompanied by scents of freshly cut flowers and baking, her heart lifted in her chest, buoyed by optimism seeping into her soul.

"You didn't wake me?" Jessie's voice cracked, only just making it across the space between them. She stood with one hand against the doorway, trusting it to be stronger than her. Heather flinched at her daughter's pale face, almost devoid of the freckles which gave it colour and life. She stopped chopping and walked towards her. "When your heart is breaking, there's no such thing as too much rest."

Jessie's shoulders slumped and Heather held her as she sobbed. She wiped her tears, led her into the garden and sat her down on a low bench. She took out a small bottle and handed it to her. "You must take these drops daily – until you feel better."

Veins rose in Jessie's pale neck, and when she lifted sad eyes her voice broke. "Those drops took my baby away."

Heather knelt and clutched her hand. "No, they did not, they took away your pain – as will these."

Jessie gripped her knees and leaned forward. "The pain mustn't go away. I want to keep it inside. I can't let it go."

Heather pulled her grieving daughter close, feeling more bone than flesh. "You will never lose the memory, but to live unburdened you must take time to heal and accept what is. If there are more children who want to come to you, you must be prepared to receive them, to give them the life they deserve. When that time comes you must be ready."

With her own unwelcome memories bursting from their secret chamber Heather fought for composure. This was a moment to be a mother, so she surrendered her emotions to the will of her mind. "In a few days you will feel stronger and your mind will be clearer."

Tom came home and stood speechless in the doorway of his clean, warm home. Jessie asleep once more allowed Heather the opportunity to talk, to help him understand although he had also lost a child, Jessie's grief was hers alone, so required time, and much patience. Tears shone in Tom's eyes and his fingers fought with each other. "Thank you for your help, I love Jessie more than you could ever fathom, I promised to give her everything she wants for the rest of my life."

Heather hoped she was wrong, and credited his sincerity, but she feared he may be incapable of fulfilling his promise. He would never comprehend the pain of a first daughter losing a child, so Heather thanked God it was a boy. She stilled his hands. "I've never questioned your love but there are some things even a husband can't fix."

Jessie slept, ate, and took time to walk in the wild fields, soaking up the sun, strengthening her lungs with fresh air. Heather cleaned and cooked. Jessie welcomed the help, marvelling at how much her mother could get done in a day, but when she spotted sweat beads and damp wisps framing her face, guilt flooded her. Heather brushed her off, insisting she get out of the house. Every morning she issued the same instruction. "Fresh air, rest and the beauty everywhere you look will feed your body and spirit, so go feast yourself."

She took to walking to the stream, sitting on the ragged rocks, dangling her feet in the cool water, watching dragonflies flash their luminous colours as they skimmed the surface before slicing through the gaps between the overhanging willow leaves. Tadpoles zigzagged around her still feet, threading their way between her toes, gently fluttering against her cool skin; a featherlight foot massage lulling her into near oblivion. Her internal darkness seemed to live by its own rules, and although there were moments when she triumphed in a sudden battle, it would take time to be the victor in this war. Patience and mindfulness were her only armoury. Not her strongest traits, but she appreciated having a chance meant she would need to embrace them. The realisation made her smile; yet again her mother was right. Engrossed in her contemplations and mesmerised by the stream, she didn't notice Tom until he was upon her. He bent and kissed her forehead. "You look serene ... and beautiful."

Jessie didn't look up. "What brings you here at this time of day?"

Tom kicked off his boots and socks, wincing when the cool water nipped his toes. "I reckoned it was a good day to steal some time – and check on you." He wrapped an arm around her shoulder and pulled her close.

Jessie inched away, still gazing at the water. "You don't talk about the baby."

Tom dropped his arm. "I have no clue how to ease your anguish so I'm worried I'll make it worse."

Jessie's feet swished through the water, agitating tadpoles and chasing the dragonflies. "You can't ignore it and hope it will go away. I feel you grieving, and even though it's your heart to fix, I want to help you."

Tom placed a hand over his heart. "You needn't worry about my pain; I wish I had the power to take away yours – but I don't know how."

Jessie lifted her feet out of the water and pulled her knees towards her chest. She locked eyes with him. "You must stop living as if it never happened, as if it's something to hide, pretending we didn't lose our son."

"It was a boy?"

A pain stabbed Jessie in her ribs. "Does that make a difference?"

Heather stood in Jessie's garden, admiring lily buds waiting patiently for summer days. Overhead squawking and fluttering alerted her to Jessie and Tom approaching. She watched them embrace. Tom kissed Jessie's forehead before waving to Heather and heading off back to work. Jessie's feet barely lifted off the ground as she walked. Heather shivered. They were not holding hands and Jessie didn't return his embrace. She noticed Tom's shoulders droop when he disappeared down the lane. She breathed deep. It was time to take Jessie to Myna.

Chapter 5

ANGUS GLANCED OVER EACH *shoulder before pushing open the heavy door and stepping inside. With his first breath, acrid, stale incense grazed his throat. He shut the door behind him and after reaching the top of the five narrow steps within the dark passage pushed open another heavier door. Heat from a roaring fire leapt at him, accompanied by the reek of overcooked meat and alcohol. "For God's sake, this heat will fry you worse than your dinner," he barked, before removing his overcoat and throwing it over a large Chesterfield.*

A slurred voice boomed back. "Ne'er cast a clout till May be out."

His reply shot across the den. "Father Coyle, I think your weighty vestments are shrouding a cold-blooded body." Without waiting for an offer, he strode to a corner table, seized a glass decanter and poured himself a stiff drink. After a large gulp he dragged the Chesterfield into the farthest corner away from the fire and slumped into it. The deep golden amber liquid reflected the colour of his father's eyes and as he watched it swirl his grip tightened on the glass.

The priest banged his empty glass on a side table next to him. "Angus, tell me what you saw."

Angus drained his glass but his white knuckles refused to release it. "A figure disappeared into the woods. I don't know who it was, and I didn't see where they left the path."

Father Coyle gripped both arms of his chair and sneered. "That's disappointing, considering it was such a bright night. Was it a man, a woman, or perhaps a double-headed coo?"

Angus' clothes hugged his skin as if trying to escape the cloying heat as the room seemed to close in on him. "It was a still night, so I was careful not to be spotted."

The priest dragged his lugubrious body out of the armchair then lumbered to the window. With one ring-encrusted finger he flicked back a drape and peered out. "Are you certain of your desire to remain unseen or are you simply reluctant to confirm the identity of this mysterious figure?"

Angus considered for a moment. "I did not want to be seen, that would defeat the purpose."

The priest released the curtain and marched back to his chair. The floorboards moaned until he sat. Spittle crept along wine-stained lips. "We know what is going on. There is evil in there, twisting and controlling the minds of the crofters around here."

Angus wished he could twist the priest's neck but sense prevailed. "You imagine too much. I hear it is merely old women making some ancient medicinal remedies from forest plants ... poultices and such." His fingers risked shattering his glass, so he placed it on the table.

Father Coyle leaned forward, his shoulders almost swallowing his neck. "Do you understand what that is? Witchcraft! Devil worship is what it is, unchristian and evil!"

If Angus didn't know better, he would have sworn the room's temperature rose and the ceiling dropped a foot. The fire in the priest's eyes appeared capable of accomplishing that. His display of temper only added to the reasons Angus considered him unstable, but it was his volatility which made him dangerous. He got up, poured the priest another glass of wine, handed it to him and waited for him to drink it – and hopefully calm down. He watched him gulp, but it made no difference. The wine tinted Father Coyle's cheeks and his lips began an involuntary twitching which soon forced his nose to join in the dance. Angus marvelled at the power of agitation when the priest growled.

"I've already dragged that awful woman Maggie in here, I warned her that if she wants to keep her home, and her son in a job, she better mind her ways. She's too fond of the ale and reeks of contempt for our God-fearing ways. She keeps dubious company and she'll pay for it."

Talk of Maggie caused Angus to chew the inside of his bottom lip and tighten his stomach muscles lest the churning reach his throat. Maggie was as close as family. She'd been around forever. His mother cared for her as her own, but Father Coyle was right; Maggie was a drinker and blethered more than most. If Maggie found herself cornered, he believed it would be his mother she would call on for protection. Protection that may well manifest in any form – and by any means. Protection that would cause more trouble. He decided he'd speak to her, but first he needed to diffuse the priest's rage. "Most people attend church regularly, and I'm sure your books will account for the tithes coming from each crofter."

Father Coyle huffed, momentarily forgetting about Maggie. "Of course they do! It's their duty, that doesn't change the fact the devil works amongst them and currently has several wives toiling to undermine us. There have been too many unfortunate incidents since the Wilsons took over Cruachan Manor, and I strongly believe Satan and his helpers are behind them."

Angus remained quiet, hoping the wine might dispirit the priest before the conversation deteriorated further. He watched him rearrange his robes, pulling and twisting the rope belt and when his glass was almost empty, Angus walked to the window and nudged it open. His lungs swelled from the rush of welcome fresh air but the priest's sneer stole the relief.

"Remember I have positioned you in Charles Wilson's employ and I expect you to make sure all goes smoothly. He has extremely deep pockets so this wretched town will do well to respect where their livelihood comes from."

Angus sucked in a huge breath, forcing his spine to stiffen. Father Coyle's opinions regarding the town and its people grated on his conscience but he would not engage. This new job with the Wilsons afforded him several opportunities, all of which he intended to pursue. Currently, dissuading the priest of severe action against local healers, whom he deemed evil, occupied his mind. He hadn't yet mentioned his mother but Angus was sure she was top of the priest's list of deviants – especially after the wedding.

The wine found its power and Father Coyle grunted. "Enough of this distasteful matter, but be warned. These people must not think I am easily fooled, I see much more than they assume. You must uncover who is practising witchcraft and I will have them removed."

Angus pursed his lips for a second, paralysing any temptation to react. He retrieved his coat, flung it over his arm and started for the door. When he passed the priest, now moulded into his chair, he nodded. "I will look into the strange events at Cruachan Manor and investigate your so-called unchristian behaviour."

Before he closed the door the priest barked. "I expect that, and I'm sure you'll find your way home easily enough. If tonight's moon gets any bigger, we won't need candles."

Angus walked down the steps, exiting the outside door into the quiet street. When he turned towards home, he questioned how well-informed Father Coyle was, and how far he would take his persecution in pursuit of total control over the town, and its funds. He professed to see more than people were aware, but in this town those who possessed the gift of seeing outclassed him; such as his mother and her friends in the forest. Angus dug his hands deep into his pockets, striding head down until he arrived at his gate. Candlelight shone through the windows prompting him to look up at the moon. He had seen who'd disappeared into the forest – and where. No doubt Father Coyle also knew. He reached into his inside pocket and found his tobacco tin. He slid down the gate post, sat between heather bushes, rolled a cigarette and sucked in the warm tobacco. Just as his weekly dip into a warm bath soothed his muscles, so the tobacco calmed his frayed nerves. Pressure from Father Coyle, the weight of Charles Wilson's expectations, the burden of family loyalty, and knowledge of his mother's practices were more than a cigarette might settle. He doubted even his mother had a remedy for that. After one last puff before burning his fingers, he stomped the remnant and his worries into the dirt. He turned to go through the gate but the sound of movement from behind stopped him. Even with her cape and hood fastened tight he recognised her. He held the gate open. "Mother, you're out late."

Heather's green eyes shone in the moonlight. "You too, Angus, let's have some tea."

***

Charles Wilson stood furiously tossing logs into the fireplace when Angus walked into his office and remarked. "You English struggling to acclimatise?" He watched new wood firing up the already white-hot pile while sunlight streamed through enormous windows, casting streaks across a thick pile tartan carpet. He gazed into this serendipitous rainbow as Charles agitated the unnecessary fire before returning to his desk. His new overstuffed leather chair – wider and taller than his wiry frame – squeaked, disturbed by his shuffling to settle into a comfortable position.

"It's interminably damp and dull," he snorted. "I suspect one has to be born here so young bones adapt to growing in the dark." Charles's voice jolted Angus from his rainbow. Although well accustomed to insults from soft Englishmen, his toes curled in his boots and his shoulders strained to hold their straight line.

"We believe that's one of the many things which make us strong."

Charles rolled a pen back and forth on his desk. "If you say so."

Angus settled into a chair by the window where he viewed broad, heavy-set liverymen brushing pure-bred horses until they gleamed like polished floors. He remembered visiting the manor when he was a child, when his mother sent him to deliver vegetables to the cook who would meet him at the kitchen door at the rear of the house; never inside. He envisaged the cook: rotund, cheerful, she always miraculously discovered a piece of fresh fruit in her pocket, or a warm scone for him to eat on his way home. A friend of his mother who, with most of the long-serving staff, Wilson had replaced with younger employees now strutting around in uniforms as starched as their smiles. They were a miserable lot, transferred from their positions down south by the new Lady of the Manor. She preferred her own people around her – English people. Charles blamed the dreary weather for his staff's misery. Angus enjoyed knowing it was also the unwelcoming behaviour of the locals, together with the unfortunate accidents and illnesses which befell them, causing the gloomy temperaments. This he kept to himself, having no desire to assist his boss in any manner for which he wasn't being paid. If Charles Wilson trusted his own reasoning Angus felt no need to either dissuade or enlighten him.

"Let those who bring about distress suffer the same wretchedness," he'd overheard Maggie profess to his mother after Wilson replaced the old cook, her dear friend. Angus took no notice of her grumbling but was now certain the challenges *being experienced by the newcomers were not all a result of the weather.*

Angus had jumped at the chance to work for Charles Wilson. Father Coyle had facilitated their meeting at Jessie's wedding which led to the position of stable manager including a higher wage than the previous owner would have offered; especially considering Angus's limited knowledge of the finer requirements of pure-bred hunting horses. The only stables he'd managed were his Da's, with their resident Clydesdales. Charles brought his own man Eric up from England to settle in his newly gained stable, but depended on him returning south to look after his prize racehorses. Charles therefore charged him with finding a well-suited local candidate. After two weeks of interviewing, he pleaded with his boss to send him back to England, find his own replacement, and when another interview failed to impress, he complained. "I can't understand a word these people say and they stare at me as if horns are growing out of my eyebrows."

"Don't be ridiculous," Charles smacked his desk, "there must be someone around here skilled in tending horses. God knows they all spend their days in some mire or other."

Eric whined. "Well, I can't find one who wants to work here and they give me the shivers, all of them."

Father Coyle heard of the dilemma, and recognising an opportunity, he immediately suggested Angus. Charles, at the end of his tether, agreed without further information – or an interview. Angus donated his first month's wage to Father Coyle's building fund; a thank you for his recommendation, as requested by the priest.

Charles settled in his chair, leaned back and glared. "Enough about this weather, it's all anyone ever talks about. Please update me on the profitability of these crofts, who works them, and why I shouldn't flatten that ugly forest to build paddocks on it – or a golf course."

Angus bristled. Imagining his mother's forest flattened to make way for anything horrified him. He tried to explain. "The crofts are within the town boundary which includes the manor. It all belonged to the previous owner who in return for a regular supply of foodstuffs, cattle fodder, wood and peat, allowed families to live on and work the land. The crofters make a minimal living, freely giving half of what they produce to the manor. They can barely support their families without having to move away or travel to the cities for better-paying work. This town has ancestry and has lived hand-in-hand with the manor for centuries."

Charles Wilson's bottom lip curled, pushing his top lip into the coarse brown hedge that was his moustache. Other than a slight narrowing of his eyes he remained quiet.

Angus moved to the front of his chair. "They take any surplus from the manor to the city markets and sell it."

Charles leaned forward and his large chair almost tipped. He balanced himself before picking up a letter opener. Its gleaming edge caught Angus's eye. Charles's lips hardly parted. "Are you saying any profit this manor makes is from the odd leftover sheep, fish or carrots sold at a market – after first serving the entire town and the manor?"

Angus's shoulders shrunk into his jacket and his cheeks tightened. Charles leaned forward, and when the letter opener settled its point into the leather inlay of the new desk, it pierced Angus's heart. Charles continued. "Cruachan Manor owns all these crofts and land yet demands no rent, accepting mere baskets of produce for payment?" He put the letter opener to one side and tucked his fists under his chin.

Angus's throat ached. "Yes, but it's been this way for hundreds of years. It's a small community, so the manor has always allowed us to live rent free."

Charles's eyebrows shot up towards his hairline but he gestured for Angus to continue. Angus squeezed his fingers together, regretting for the first time using the term 'us'.

"Well, not only produce," his voice croaked. "They also breed cattle, pigs and sheep. They catch pheasant, rabbit and hare." Sweat warmed his neck and something twitched in his gut. He breathed deeply to lift his sagging shoulders but rambled like the nearby stream on a rainy day. "Peat, salmon, wool … the crofters supply the manor, and the manor supports the crofters."

Charles folded his arms and a smirk crept out from under his moustache. He cocked his head. "Why do people live here if they struggle to make a living?"

The vice returned, squeezing the strength from Angus's voice. "We've lived here for centuries … we have no desire to live anywhere else, this is our home."

The words floated over Charles's head, missing his ears by a country mile. "Why would the previous owners be happy with such an unprofitable arrangement?"

The words escaped from Angus's mouth before he could arrest them. "Because they were Scottish."

Charles nodded, leaning back. "Indeed, which is why they ended up bankrupt."

Chapter 6

ALTHOUGH HEATHER NO LONGER *needed to clean or cook, she still popped in daily to check on her precious child, taking it upon herself to refill vases with fresh flowers even before any wilted. Jessie reprimanded her.*

"Mammie! If you keep plundering the fields, there'll be nothing left. Those can last another few days, I'm sure."

Heather continued arranging. "The fields have plenty, with more on the way. Never let a flower die in your house, do you hear me?" She pinched the top buds.

Jessie rolled her eyes then left to make tea. She no longer laughed at her mother's strange ways, and although a clean house and a well-stocked pantry heartened Heather, she missed the spirit that sparked lively banter between them. Jessie now functioned normally, but she was not living … not truly. This colourful young woman who spread joy like fairy dust, vibrant curls bobbing with each step, now faded into the background of her own life. Previously her joy added a heaven-sent sheen to a gloomy winter day. Her wide smile lit up her eyes and cheered hearts. Heather's faith in her daughter's spirit remained strong, but her veil of grief still clung like an unwelcome stain. Unless removed carefully, Jessie may forever lose her shine.

Heather hooked arms with her when they left the path to enter the forest. "We must hurry. Myna is expecting us but we only have a few hours."

Jessie fell into step, with heartache weighing her down as if too many days of grey skies sat mere inches above. Eager to reach Myna, Heather yearned to hurry but was mindful to be gentle with her. She seemed stronger, her cheeks now blushed with colour, but her spirit lay hidden.

Myna opened the door and greeted Heather before drawing Jessie in for a hug. She relaxed her head on Myna's warm shoulders, with tears burning her eyes. Myna's soft hand stroked gently and a comforting wave washed over her. Heather sighed when she saw Jessie's body relax. Myna released her but cupped her face in her warm hands. Deep sadness darkened Jessie's eyes and Myna's heart ached. "Come, the girls are here and we have scones."

Lathering warm scones with wild berry jam, the girls jabbered on about how much they'd enjoyed the wedding, the sumptuous food and how striking Jessie had looked. Two pairs of bright eyes flashed back and forth between Jessie and each other.

Heather and Myna sat listening, smiling at the twins' double-barrelled excitement.

"One at a time!" Myna stomped a foot and the girls giggled.

"Tom looked so handsome," Tevia gushed.

Jessie's eyelids drooped. Myna noticed and clapped her hands. "Enough, you two, bring the scones before they turn to stone, then get yourselves outside while the sun's still smiling."

The girls presented the scones on a delicate blue china plate, hugged Heather and Jessie then set off for the pond, their chatter trailing behind. Myna poured tea without looking up. "Jessie, how is Tom?"

Jessie's sigh pulled at her shoulders. "He's busy ploughing for a new crop."

Myna handed a cup to Jessie and looked into her eyes, now the colour of dull winter leaves. "How is Tom?" she repeated.

The question stung. "I think we're broken."

Myna and Heather spent the afternoon consoling her, extolling their knowledge about husbands, children, motherhood and everything in between. They took turns holding her, wiping her tears until she could speak without choking. The older women listened as she purged all the emotions she'd fought since the moment she miscarried. She swung between anger and grief, from chewing her fingers to curling up in the corner of the couch. Jessie sobbed until her well of sadness ran dry. Myna left her for a moment but when she returned Jessie's body shrunk and her head dropped when she spotted two small bottles in her hands. "Not more medicine."

Myna moved to sit next to her. "Jessie, you mustn't consider what we give you as medicine. We have learned from nature and our earth. We've taken the best of everything to help us when our bodies, minds and spirits are failing us. It will make you strong, build up the parts of you that are weak and suffering. The parts you need to replenish. The parts you can't see or touch. Your body won't work properly when your heart is so wounded. You are forcing your mind to bury the things your soul is begging you to face. If you spend all your energy fighting your internal battle, you will have none to sustain the life you are born to live. You carry the gift of creating life – a precious gift – but it is not guaranteed. You cannot allow the darkness inside to take root or it will become a weed, spreading until eventually it smothers your life force."

Heather watched Jessie's legs release from her tightly tucked skirts, uncurling as she listened to Myna.

"Neither you nor Tom are to blame. Your child was not ready to come to you. It was never yours to control, however, you owe it to each other to recover and grow stronger from this tragedy. To honour the child who will come."

Jessie frowned. "Why do you say 'the child'? We plan to have many children."

Myna glanced at Heather, who nodded before removing two stones from her pocket. She placed them on the low table between them. Jessie leaned forward and picked them up. Their smooth surfaces brushed against her skin as she turned them over and over in her hands, examining the markings on each. After holding them still for a minute she returned one to the table then looked up at her mother. "I wore this one on my wedding day."

Heather reached out and took the stone. She glanced at it before curling her fingers around it. "You did. It belongs to you. I received it the day you were born."

Jessie leaned forward, tucking her fists under her chin. Heather noticed her eyes narrow. "These stones are precious to us," Heather said, "and to our daughters."

Jessie tilted her head. "Our daughters?"

Heather leaned in. "We are first daughters. You and I, my mother, my grandmother. Those before her, yours to come. We have the gift of sight and healing. We are born into this generational line to help and guide other women; despite the *turmoil it will cause in our own lives."* Heather glanced at Myna. *"The gift has consequences so it is also a choice."*

Jessie leaned back and her shoulders dropped. She looked at both stones now sitting on the table. Heather waited, braced for a reaction, but none came. She leaned forward clasping her hands. "You mustn't fear this." Her eyes shone. "This is our birth blessing ... we will teach you."

Jessie remained quiet, gazing at her mother.

"These stones come from our ancestors, blessed with the power to protect and guide. They began with a first daughter, carried and gifted only to the first daughters in our bloodline. Used in defending curses from other bloodlines practising black magic and evil. When used correctly the stones can help save you from those who would see the bloodline end."

Still Jessie sat quietly, but her fists dropped to her lap and her sigh carried the weight of her uncertainties. Myna reached over and laid a hand on her thigh. "I know how broken your heart is, how you can't see it ever being whole again. Please believe it will. We'll be with you; we are your guides and support. You were born into this bloodline to break the curse and free your own descendants from the burden of persecution. You carry the honour of being the next first daughter."

Jessie planted both hands on her belly, intuitively protecting it from the conversation. "If I am born into this bloodline, the only way it can continue is if I have another baby." She looked down at her hands and her eyes filled. "A daughter."

Heather rested her hands on Jessie's. "Yes."

Jessie's knees squeezed together as she felt the room close in. "What is the curse?"

Myna shifted when Heather pressed a palm to her mouth, pushing her lips against clenched teeth. Jessie sensed the discomfort and stood. She glared at her mother and dropped her head into her hands. Unspoken threats swirled around the room. Her words squeezed around the lump in her throat. "Is that why I lost my baby?"

They both stood but Jessie backed away towards the window. Heather paled and her shoulders sank, dragged down by the overload of her heart. She sighed. "It may have been but we can never be certain."

Jessie slumped into a chair beside the window and gripped the arms. Her anger simmered. "Did you see it? Did you know it would happen? Why didn't you warn me?"

Heather rushed to kneel at Jessie's feet. She folded her arms around her trembling legs and gazed up at her pale, tear-stained face. The pain of watching her child suffer tore her the way a storm rips branches from brittle trees, so she clung to her, fearing the pain might rip them both apart. "I can't prevent a child from leaving, I can only see the child who will come to you and the ones not meant for you."

Jessie gripped her mother's hands and Heather sank back onto her haunches. "You should have warned me," she whimpered. "Why did you not explain this to me before I married Tom? You are my mother, it's your duty to protect me."

Myna, no longer able to witness her beloved Heather and Jessie being so tormented, joined them. She reached down, took their hands and held them tight between her own. "This is part of the turmoil your mother spoke of. It is also the stuff sent to drive you apart and destroy your bloodline. In time you will understand your calling to serve, for now you must believe. Trust everything your mother may or may not do is for your wellbeing until she can no longer protect you."

Jessie looked up at Myna, her bloodshot eyes struggling to focus. "No longer protect me, what do you mean?"

Heather sighed. "I am not destined to be in this world as long as you may need me."

Jessie's mouth dropped open but Myna gestured to Heather to continue. "We have little time so you must trust me, learn as much as I can teach you; before it is too late."

Jessie gulped and pulled her hand away. Heather stood and Myna returned to her seat. Heather looked directly at Jessie. "The curse aims to end our line. It tries to prevent our bloodline from giving birth to daughters. The daughters who can pass down gifts of sight and healing. The curse works against our type of women who feel the evil energy, expose and destroy deceit. Women who enlighten and uplift others in distress. Without these gifts evil ways and dark practices will strengthen, as will oppressive cults and immoral institutions. It is our duty to make sure we continue to learn and teach our ways so generations of women become wiser, stronger."

Jessie's eyes fixed on her mother. "I always considered us different but never understood why. Da, and the boys also know something. I can tell. I wondered about the stones, why Da is so against them. What does he know?"

"Your father and I love each other, and he accepts we have different ways. He worries my ways put me in danger so he would prefer if I didn't follow my path. However, he also knows he married a woman who knows her own mind."

For the first time that day Jessie smiled. Heather's heart could have warmed the room. She took Jessie's hands again. "We are strong, wise and gifted, but also despised and persecuted. Ours is not a smooth road, so you can choose not to follow me. However, if you do, I will work my best to prepare you, but there will be sacrifices along the way. You will need to be careful of your own decisions."

Jessie wandered to the window. She stood gazing at the white heather blossoms. She tried to fathom the implications of what she'd heard, and whether any of it mattered. Most of what her mother said shocked her – but much didn't. Happily married to Tom, her world turned on their shared future – at least it had until losing the baby. Tom's grief, disappointment, and her lack of affection towards him, kept him awake at night, miserable during the day. He'd never known silence with Jessie. He professed her constant wonderings rivalled the Capercaillie's heralding the dawn. Now the pervading gloom seemed to have silenced even their song, because neither he nor Jessie remarked on them. Something about him now irked her, lurking under her skin the way a rash waits until ready to poke through. Something he could do nothing about because Myna was right. This was not Tom's fault. It was hers. She carried the curse of being a first daughter. The decision to continue, and break the curse for the generations of women to come sat with her … or not. Suddenly the twins came into view, pigtails bobbing as they bounded along the path towards the cottage. Jessie watched them skipping, stopping to pick berries, shooing away thrushes and finches raiding the bushes – their voices indistinguishable, their smiles matching. They were a double delight bursting with promise, welcoming their unknown future. Jessie tore her mind away from this enchanting view and turned to her mother. "How do you know I will have more children?"

Heather flinched but her voice held firm.
"Because I have seen it."

Chapter 7

THE TABLE LEGS SHUDDERED *when Heather placed an enormous bowl of steaming porridge before Fraser. Angus watched him ram spoonful after spoonful into his mouth without spilling a drop. He marvelled at his brother's capacity to devour vast amounts of food in a ridiculously short amount of time. Heather spotted Angus's wide-eyed scowl and punched his shoulder.*

"Don't gawk at him. He needs it for the hard work he does." *She cocked her head. "No white bread sandwiches in the fancy kitchen for him."*

"Aye," Fraser snorted between gulps.

The intense feeling in Angus's heart reminded him it wasn't his brother's appetite he yearned to match, but his enviable, unfettered spirit and contentment with his lot in life. Every day Angus justified his own earthly desires. He wanted more, he wanted better, but when Fraser's laugh rattled the walls Angus's spirit shrivelled a little. When Fraser's contented snoring threatened to blow the roof off, his own wants and needs wrestled, fuelling his impatience. He gazed at the thatch most nights until weariness doused the fire and sleep conquered. Reproach in his mother's tone always seemed to hedge between tolerance and another thumping. He also considered her hedge a little unstable, so he refrained from replying. He put on his coat, but when he reached the door Heather called.

"Here, take this, those English people don't make them the way I do." She handed him two fresh scones wrapped in a muslin cloth. Angus took the parcel, thanked her and left her standing on the doorstep.

His wavering eyes hurt her heart. "Angus," she called after him, "have a nice day."

He didn't look back. "Aye."

After Heather closed the door Fraser scowled. "Whit's up wi him?"

"Nothing, don't bother yerself." She picked up his empty bowl.

Fraser wiped his mouth then leaned back. "He's been a miserable git since he started working up the manor."

Heather banged the bowl into the sink. "Fraser, wheisht, he needs some time to adjust, God knows it can't be easy working for people who need both sides of their bread buttered."

Fraser shrugged and made for the door. "Aye, I'll stick to the fields, I can trust the magpies more than those manor folks."

"Enough of that or you'll be riling him up worse than he is."

Angus's morning dragged on like a stern church sermon, so he skipped lunch and headed to the milk yard. The walk was short, but enough to allow his lungs to breathe out stale smoke from his confined office and refresh. Soon, with attention to colourful wildflowers and snapping of twigs underfoot, his fractious musings dissipated. No sooner did he turn up the pathway towards the milk yard when Donald's whistling echoed through the wide barn doors, so it didn't take long to locate him.

Absorbed in his chores, he almost fell off his footstool when he noticed Angus standing over him. "C-creepin Jesus, wh- what are you doing here?"

"I'm here to offer you a job, so listen up."

Angus explained the new position – tending the Wilson's hunting herd and reporting their requirements back to him. Donald shoved his grimy hands into his pockets, shuffling some mushy hay with his mud-caked wellies. "Isn't that your job, Angus?"

Angus shook his head. "I manage the stables and the upkeep of the herd, but I want someone who's good with horses; to make sure they're groomed properly with attention to their daily needs. They're a special breed." He jerked his thumb towards the barn door. "Not like our nags you know."

Donald's fists flew out of his pockets straight to his hips. "Our horses are not nags, they're hard-working fellas! Kept your Da's fields right for years they have."

Angus avoided riling Donald's pride. "Probably because you've looked after them so well," he grinned, "which is why I think you're the perfect man for the task."

Donald straightened his shoulders, nodding repeatedly. "Aye, you're r-right about that. You don't know how much work it takes to keep them s-strong, healthy."

Angus ignored Donald's indignant tone; he'd pushed the right button. "It's better money than milking all day will get you," he added. One more push, then interest shone from Donald's eyes, but he looked down, scuffing the hay again. A frown creased his freckled forehead. "I'll need to be up at the m-mansion then ... with all those d-daft people?"

"Donald! Do you want the job or not?"

Donald's lips fluttered. "Well, they say W-Wilson's a dreich. Worse than a Baltic w-winter."

"Dreich or not, it's a better job than you have."

Donald's head nodded; his cheeks puffed but he could not form a word.

Angus pulled his arm. "Fine. Come with me."

He marched Donald to the manor ignoring his constant stuttering. Relieved to have convinced him, he found Donald's comparison of Wilson to the wet, miserable squalls of constant rain preceding the bitter cold of winter amusing. Wilson was indeed a dreich. However, Donald would see little of Wilson, and his inherent care for animals would more than compensate for his own offbeat character. He sometimes speculated if Donald's mother was correct in saying she dropped him on his head at birth – which removed common sense but doubled up on compassion and sincerity. Angus trusted he could count on him. He led him around the stable yard, amused by the young farm boy's inability to hide how impressed he was by the luxury afforded the hunting steeds. Unable to slow his pace or fidgeting hands, Donald's face lit up each time he ran a hand over yet another highly polished brass nameplate.

When he did speak, his admiration provoked his stutter. "D-dear God, they're just b-beautiful."

Angus patted him on the back, relief trickling through his veins. "They are, now get to work, I'll see you later." Angus strutted back to his office at the corner of the yard, crunching the gravel with each focused step. He kicked his door closed before slumping into the chair behind the bulky desk he still hadn't fathomed a use for until now. He removed a journal from the top drawer and opened it. When he'd started his new job, the pages had glared with an empty invitation, but now he silently thanked his parents for insisting he learn to read and write. He would use this journal to take notes of everything Donald required to ensure the stables and horses flourished. Donald would do his work for him – or at least the hardest part. His jaw relaxed, and for the first moment since his own appointment, he sensed his road levelling. Young Mildred from the kitchen cut short his moment of satisfaction when she knocked.

Not waiting for a reply, she nudged the door open. "Tea and scones, Angus?"

Jolted from his musings, Angus looked up, puzzled.

"Angus?" she repeated.

His mother's scones suddenly weighed down his left pocket, so he took a moment to ponder his reply. "Yes, thank you, that will be lovely."

When Mildred closed the door, Angus removed his mother's scones from his pocket, and without looking, dropped them into his dustbin. He dipped his pen into its inkwell then started making lists. When sufficiently pleased with his accomplishments, he drained his teacup, stuffed the last chunk of scone into his mouth and went to check on his new employee.

Donald's cheeks shone brighter than the rosewood table in the manor dining room, his wellies only just protecting his knees from the manure clinging to them. His crooked teeth jutted from a cavernous grin when he spotted Angus approaching. Angus suppressed his desire to laugh. "All right, Donald?"

"Great Angus, j-just great." He stuffed his mucky hands into his trousers, tilting back and forward on his heels. "Magnificent animals they are, never seen the likes of them, must have p-proper blue blood in their veins."

For the second time that day Angus patted his back. "Good to hear, I knew you were the right man for the post. Now go home. You've done your work for today – and what a fine job you're doing."

Delight from Angus's praise flashed across Donald's face. He pushed his hair back then rubbed his filthy hands on his overalls. Another button pushed, reasoned Angus.

Angus loved twilight more than any other time – not crisp and clear as morning, when the world glares with an unforgiving sharpness, nor dark and harsh as night, when the unknown looms – innocent or terrifying depending on what is most prominent in your mind. He regarded twilight as his safe zone. Shadows disappear, the air falls still, and clouds seem to relax into a fine overhead layer of grey silk. Weather permitting, even the sun softens around the edges, toning down its vivid yellow into an array of burnt oranges and muted reds. It was at this time of early evening when couples loved to go 'a roamin in the gloamin,' Angus made his way to Maggie's. His journaling complete, Donald happy, his anxieties quietened, he deemed it a good time to confront her. She seemed unsurprised to find him on her doorstep, but glanced up and down the narrow lane before inviting him in.

"It's some time since you've been here." She walked to her kitchen. "Can I make tea or is this a quick visit?"

Without removing his coat Angus perched on the edge of a chair. "Maggie, things are getting serious, you can't go mouthing off about Father Coyle."

Maggie turned, shaking her fists. "Who are you to come in here telling me what to do, young man?"

Angus sprang from the chair. "You don't understand the trouble you're causing! You do not know the power he wields; he will not abide insults or be undermined ... at least not by you."

Maggie returned from her kitchen nook to square up to him. Her words flew between them. "So, are you his lackey now? Are you doing his bidding? What kind of promise are you on? What would have you turn on your own folk? Is it the fancy new position? The money?"

Angus's nostrils flared after the barrage. "Things are changing around here whether we agree with it or not. We don't own the land we live on, so between the church and the Wilsons, we will all end up homeless unless we knuckle down and mind our ways."

Maggie threw her head back almost losing her balance. "What 'ways' do they want us to mind? What is it about our ways they find so disagreeable?"

Angus looked to the roof, groaning. "Maggie, you know what ways, and they won't stand for it. They'll root you out and God only knows what they'll do with you."

Maggie slumped into an armchair and slung her arms over the sides. "They can't punish us, they have no right. Even if they contrived enough evidence against us, hangings ended a long time ago. If anyone ought to be hanged, it's Father Coyle, he's the evil one."

"Maggie, the church is powerful and the Wilsons are only interested in their investment. Father Coyle wants to keep everything in check so they'll keep pouring money into his church, and prop up the town coffers. He won't allow deviants to disrupt his plans or scare off the Wilsons. He has the means to make things difficult for you."

Maggie gripped the arms of the chair but leaned forward. "You listen to me. He sent his other lackey to browbeat me but that didn't work. I visited Father Coyle."

Angus caught his breath. Maggie watched his eyes widen. "What did you say, Maggie?"

"I told him, and I'm telling you. We've been here forever and we'll remain here – and we'll live how we please."

Angus ran stiff fingers through his hair. "He knows you women are up to peculiar things in the forest. Since the wedding I'm sure he knows Mammie's involved, and he's determined to put a stop to it."

Maggie slumped back but held Angus's gaze. "Well, now he has you doing his dirty work, so you can either help him or make sure he doesn't do any harm."

Angus sat, the ensuing silence masking the voices screaming in both their heads. Maggie spoke first. "He assumed his bullying would scare me so I would be afraid for my own life enough to convince the others to stop practising and join his congregation. Deviants he called us, as you just did."

Angus clenched his fists and his shoulders inched towards his ears. "Dear God, Maggie, what else did you say?"

She stood, smoothing down her skirts. Angus watched her shake loose strands of hair off her face. Her chin lifted when she spoke. "I informed him he's the one who needs to be careful. The women around here know how to look after themselves ... and each other, so he ought to mind that next time he wants to send his brute around."

Angus melted into the chair and threw his head back, squeezing his eyes shut. His jaw locked tight, holding his words under guard.

Maggie lifted her chin. "You better not let your mother know about any of this, she has enough to deal with. She's at her wits' end with Jessie so will not take kindly to you pushing that rotten priest's barrow."

Angus drew a deep breath, got up and loped to the door. Before leaving he turned. Maggie stood with arms still crossed against her puffed-out chest.

"I'm not pushing his barrow, Mags, but Mam will have more to worry about if she's caught in the forest."

Chapter 8

JESSIE PLANTED EVERY HERB *necessary to concoct medicinal tinctures for treating women and children's ailments. She woke before dawn, creeping past snoring Tom while the sun's rays kindled, dissolving stubborn night clouds. Streaks of light warmed her precious plants. She loved watching them wake from their own slumber, greeting the day with a lift of their young leaves ready to embrace a new day of growth. Until learning from Myna and her mother, she understood little of how each developed its own unique character, how important its structure was to its efficacy in a remedy. Myna kept meticulous records of how many dried leaves she should crush, add to grated roots and liquid sap, before boiling, sieving and cooling. Then which herbs or plants served as masters before complementing them with a diluted form of another; without disturbing the overall constitution of the tincture. She revelled in the hum of bees buzzing from flower to flower, enticed by the abundance of her summer garden, confident such a feeding frenzy on nectar would produce a magnificent honeycomb capable of feeding, healing, and nurturing. Even the toxic spindle berry grew in her hedgerows, sandwiched between hawthorn and rowan bushes during the winter months, their bright shades of red colouring a snowy white garden. Only a knowledgeable eye might tell them apart, and unless an outbreak of lice required it, or the threat of poisoning didn't chill your blood, one stayed clear of the spindle berries.*

Each morning, the moment Tom left for the fields, she cleaned her house and prepared a wholesome meal for his return, before racing off to the forest. Most days found Heather already waiting with a mug of tea warm as her embrace. As usual, Myna's journals lay open on the table surrounded by a selection of brown bottles, corks and bowls brimming with dried substances. Jessie laughed one morning when the table groaned from the sheer volume covering its surface.

"How were you able to get all this?"

Heather chuckled. "Myna's up hard at work before the devil knows she's awake."

Jessie scanned the multitude of bowls, dissimilar only to a superbly trained eye, shaking her head. "I doubt even the devil knows how all this works."

Myna scowled. "He doesn't know this forest the way I do."

Jessie applied herself with intense dedication to the elder spae's teachings, raising concerns with both Heather and Myna. They admired her acceptance of her birth blessing but prayed she would apply the same diligence to her marriage as she now did to their teaching. Jessie however, would not be pressed on the matter. "What goes on under my roof is nothing to concern you."

Her curt dismissal of their probing left no room for discussion but Heather and Myna spoke alone. During each full moon when Jessie stayed home with Tom, they gathered around a fire with their fellow spaes – praying, chanting, calling on their ancestors for guidance; Heather meditating with her stones. Each time she sensed her ancestors drawing her closer she prayed harder for her granddaughter to come. Every day she pressed her palms against the twin pines in her garden, calling upon her lost children to bring forth the one who would bring life to Jessie. The child who would teach Jessie about motherhood the way no amount of time spent with her or Myna ever might. Jessie deserved to experience both the joy and heartache of mothering but she had locked those thoughts in the deepest recess of her mind. She never wanted to endure the pain another loss might bring, so held fast to her mother's vision of a daughter waiting for her. Although a deep ache, she would not allow that desire to distract her from what she now understood to be her true purpose – to learn and teach.

She heard that a new school had recently opened in the village. Built with Cruachan Manor funding, it stood opposite the church. Both entrance doors facing each other ensured a direct path from one to the other, with no unnecessary diversion. Coincidence or not, Father Coyle's office window looked out over this well-planned pathway. Thrilled by the opportunity to have their children educated in a formal school, without the need to travel to a larger town, residents were overjoyed by this benevolence, so flocked to enrol. However, parents of girls left the enrolment office dejected or angry – or both. The prerequisites for entry were simple: male and a congregant. Most fathers neglected to school their daughters so took no notice, but those with only young girls resented the exclusion. Some husbands forced their wives into pregnancy, hoping to bear sons, simply to avoid feeling ostracised by their community, and the chance to educate a child without cost. The religious requirement hardly bothered the menfolk. Several families even switched religious beliefs to secure a place, now sporting rosaries strung around their necks as if they'd won an award. One afternoon while shopping, Jessie's eyes burned and her tongue stuck to the roof of her mouth as she listened to a nearby conversation.

"Did you lose your marbles and find some beads?" barked the butcher to Mrs Burns who stood waiting for her square sausage. Affronted, she shimmied herself straight like a peacock rattling its train. "Och be quiet, Jock. You'd do well to pay a visit and listen to God's sacred truths."

Sniggers crept out from behind colourful headscarves tilted sideways.

"I'm perfectly fine with the local kirk, thank you very much." Jock folded his thick arms on the counter. "I don't need to pay for my prayers down our local, it's served us all well for long enough."

Mrs Burns snatched her package then turned on her heel. "Well, it's far better than the heathen nonsense going on around here." She whipped her head over her shoulder. "Father Coyle will put a stop to that, so you might want to rethink who you pray with."

A collective gasp froze the atmosphere while the headscarves all turned to face Mrs Burns who gripped her package so tightly her fingers threatened to pierce the sausage.

Jock smirked before removing a meaty pencil from behind his ear. "Well then, Mrs B. If that be so, and God's truth is to send you all on a witch-hunt, maybe I need to rethink who I sell my sausage to."

The headscarves giggled as she stomped out the door.

Unfortunately, the desire to bear more sons gave rise to an increase in Myna's visitors, which saddened her and Heather. Jessie found herself overcome by a strange new emotion creeping up her spine, twisting itself around her throat until she could no longer ignore it. Never a simpering wallflower, her conscience would not allow her to overlook this new status quo or the ensuing divisions within the community. Her watershed arrived one afternoon after she'd spent the morning boiling, steaming, drying and crushing what would become a remedy of sorts. Myna scrutinised her journals with meticulous attention while Jessie scribbled notes which she would later transcribe into her own master journal. Jessie's dedication stirred Myna's maternal blood. "You don't need to rewrite it all, lassie," she laughed. "You can have these when I die. God knows you shouldn't need them before he comes calling."

Jessie persisted with her scribbling. Heather grinned then took another sip of her tea. "Sharp as a tack … told you."

Jessie looked up, her heartfelt smile drifting across to her mother. "Thanks, Mammie."

Heather heard the knock at the door but it flew open before she reached it. A woman dressed in heavy green plaid skirts stood panting, eyes almost wider than her mouth, trying to swallow gulps of air. Heather and Myna gasped and Jessie instinctively ran to their visitor. No one spoke when Jessie led the young woman to the couch and settled her into it. Myna appeared at Jessie's side with a glass of sugar water. The woman struggled to speak through purple lips but Myna shushed her. "Be still, drink this, and for God's sake, breathe. If you die on my couch, you'll have a lot to answer for."

Jessie gasped. Heather sat next to the woman, steadying the glass as she sipped. The woman's breathing eased, her fingers clutching the glass regained colour, so Heather let go. All three women watched, aware of the unspoken instruction to hush and let this woman regain her composure. Other than the gentle sound of sipping, you may have heard the grass growing outside. When she finally drained the water, the woman stared into the glass, frowning as if surprised at how the liquid had mysteriously disappeared.

Jessie spoke first. "Are you all right? Have you run all the way here? How did you find us? Why are you here?"

Myna gripped Jessie's arm. "Jessie, one question at a time, the poor woman looks troubled enough without you badgering her."

The woman shifted then placed the glass on the table without making eye contact.

"What is your name?" Jessie tried again.

The woman prized her gaze away from the empty glass. Eyes the colour of brackish water looked out from red-rimmed lids. Her voice barely nudged her lips. "Laura, I'm Laura. I work at the manor with Angus and Mildred. I live at the end of the village, near the tavern."

"Well now Laura, I'm going to make you some tea. You seem frozen through but the sun's out, so if you have a story for us, I think you should warm up before you tell it. Jessie, put the pot on."

Jessie's fists flew to her hips but Heather's laugh softened the strained atmosphere. Laura relaxed, and although her breathing had eased, her eyes darted round the room like frightened moths. Heather shifted closer and held one of her arms but Laura winced, pulling back. She opened her mouth to speak but Heather lifted a hand.

"Have some tea, or we have broth if you prefer. Then you can tell us what's troubling you. You must think we can help, and if we can, we surely will. No rush, you're safe with us."

Myna joined Jessie in the kitchen. She poured a cup of cold water into the almost boiling pot and Jessie scowled. Myna's eyes narrowed. "Stop your huffing and puffing. We'll find out soon enough but let's give her a few minutes to steady herself."

With the tea set on a tray ready to serve, Heather joined the two in the kitchen. She put an arm around each of them and leaned in, lowering her voice. "There's something serious going on with this young woman. We must be careful."

Jessie straightened. "Well, for a start she's frozen stiff so let's get her warmed up."

Heather looked from Jessie to Myna as she contemplated. "No, she's not cold, the temperature is not the cause of her poor colour."

Myna's frown caught Jessie off-guard. Her curls bounced when her head darted between the two elder women. She inched towards her mother. "What?"

Heather held Jessie's hands. "She hasn't eaten recently and her trembling tells me something else is going on."

Jessie's hands reached for her chest then her fists slid up to press against her throat. "Oh no! Has something terrible happened to her?"

Myna took a deep breath. "Let's find out."

Jessie bit her lip, picked up the tray and led the others back to where Laura sat gazing into space. Before sitting Heather bent to Myna's ear. "We still don't know how she found us," she whispered.

Laura wept, Myna and Heather listened, Jessie fumed. Four complicated childbirths plus three miscarriages had culminated in Laura's severe anaemia. Neither of her middle boys lived six months but her husband insisted she keep trying. Their eldest was a daughter, therefore a burden, and their youngest a boy who he claimed wasn't right in the head.

"He's desperate for another son but I fear it's killing me. He claims it's my duty, screams I'm still able. The boys died so young and he blames me!" Laura's body appeared to shrink within her threadbare coat and green plaid skirt. "They were both early, but I tried my best. I didn't have good milk; they were winter weans, coughing from the day they were born." With each breath her throat tightened until she struggled to speak without choking. Myna bent and held her shoulders, loosening her grip when trembling bones pressed against her fingers.

"Slowly Laura, please, calm yourself. We understand, we hear you."

When Laura's head dropped into her wiry hands, Jessie noticed fingernails chewed to the quick, scabbed from persistent gnawing. Her own nails dug into her thighs as she watched her tremble. She nudged an angry hip past Myna and knelt before Laura. A whiff of wood smoke, damp, and stale perspiration filled the space between them. Such despair stung Jessie's heart. Laura lifted her head, and now Jessie sat close enough to look directly into her soulless eyes. Surrounded by darkness, they stirred Jessie's already uncomfortable stomach. She recognised her own grief echoing between them, her overwhelming despondency brimming within. Her toes curled in her stockings, her overfilled lungs squeezing against her ribs. Opinions, beliefs and judgements thrashed in her brain. It seemed Laura's deterioration was not her fault. Jessie leaned back on her heels, folded her arms across her tight chest and silently swore to do something about it.

Heather's eyelids slipped shut and her mind filled with the sound of howling wind and shattering wood. Laura's sob jolted her, and upon opening her eyes, she found her fists clenched in her lap. After glancing at Myna's confused expression, she turned to Laura.

"What do you need from us?"

Chapter 9

JESSIE CONSISTENTLY RETURNED HOME from her work with the spaes in time to set the fire and have Tom's supper ready for when he loped in the door, filthy and exhausted. This day her routine remained clockwork – Tom's didn't. He'd been poorly all morning, so around lunchtime he packed up and headed home. Heavy legs plus aching bones fuelled his desire to crawl into bed and he relished the delight of Jessie tending to him for the entire afternoon. His mind conjured illusions of this being the day they might shatter the invisible granite wall between them. His heart spoke with each beat, reminding him of the love they shared, the vows they'd declared to each other. Each step through the field and down the long path towards home delivered more reasoning for their heartache – a solution to their detachment, the motivation to recover, start over. Plod, plod, plod, think, reason, result. He deduced another baby would solve the problem, reignite their joy of living, dispel the trauma of the first loss and fan the embers of their love into the fire it once was. When he reached his front door, his legs quivered. A cold sweat crept up from his feet, rapidly engulfing his body. Even as he struggled to open the door, he held his theories tight, repeating them each time they tried to slip away. Having dug deep into his core, he'd unearthed the answer and needed only to present it. He'd now grasped the remedy and the resolve. Their intense love would prevail, a child would bring an end to the mourning, fulfilling their dreams. They would do this; he would make sure of it. He could almost see the phoenix rising. His heart swelled before a raging heat smothered his head, sucking oxygen from his brain. He fell against the front door which gave way into a cold, empty room. The fireplace sat prepared, dry logs piled, ready to light. Pots on the stove – full, cold. Chilly air greeted him, devoid of the familiar whiff of Jessie's scent. His throat

squeezed shut, the inferno in his head burned, his eyes closed and the weight of his burning body dragged him to the ground. In the dim light, a dull thud echoed through the empty room when his head hit the floor.

***

When Jessie turned the corner, she spotted smoke trails rising from her chimney. Her breath seized, but she broke into a run. Fear bubbled in the pit of her stomach, and startled by the sudden disturbance, swallows screeched overhead. Voices reached her before she crossed her doorway and her heart sank. It only took a few seconds to absorb the unexpected scene, her every sense feeding on an oversupply of adrenalin: the blazing fire, the overpowering stench of camphor and broth. Eyes glared at her the way predators size up their next meal. Sharp daggers fired straight to her stomach and a crushing sense of dread paralysed her. Tom's mother jumped from her seat and gripped Jessie's shoulders. "Where have you been? Why were you not here? What were you doing?"

Jessie's heart throbbed in her ears. The predators moved towards her, disordered words beat against her head, the room closed in. One deep voice stretched above the din, conquering the others with one word. "Stop!" Robert roared.

Tom's father pushed Jean and Mary aside then towered over her. His shadow chilled her to the bone. Petrified, she scanned the room and cried. "Is it Tom?" The drumming of her heart dulled their baying as she nudged open her bedroom door. Her fingers clung to the cold wood, her eyes struggling to adjust to the weak light. Candles burned on each side of their bed, still, as though painted into the scene by an unseen master. Blankets tucked under Tom's chin hid any sign of life beneath. Her knees buckled as she staggered to his bedside. His eye sockets had sunk into his face, now the colour of wet coal ash, only his dark hair confirming him as her husband. She knelt and reached for his hand.

"He's alive." Dr MacFarlane's rich voice reverberated in her ears. The doctor reached over, removed a folded wet cloth, then laid a flat palm against Tom's damp forehead before looking down at Jessie. His expression held a mix of worry and resignation, neither of which inspired comfort. Jessie gently *removed Tom's clammy hand from under the blanket and laid her head on his chest. His rapid heartbeat drummed in her ear while her own thudded. For a few minutes all other sounds disappeared as Jessie's and Tom's hearts found each other, synchronising and entering their own vacuum. Suddenly, raised voices lurched from the other room, shattering the silence. Jessie stood up and took a deep breath. "What happened?"*

Dr MacFarlane's exhale took too long. "He has terrible fevers. It may be consumption but I fear he may have suffered an apoplexy."

Jessie's jaw dropped. "Consumption, apoplexy? How can that be?"

The doctor forced a cough, twisting his neck against his collar. Jessie grabbed him.

"Doctor! what has happened to Tom? Tell me."

He pulled away. "I don't know exactly what happened first, when it happened, or how long he was here ... I mean by himself." Jessie noticed the doctor twisting the cloth from Tom's forehead, reluctant to look at her. "Tom was unwell so left work early," he continued. "One of the diggers was bringing you some honey, and to check if Tom would be well enough to work tomorrow." He glanced at Tom once more. "Tom was on the floor when he got here, so he rushed to Jean, who sent for me."

Jessie turned to Tom and squeezed his blankets with her free hand. The doctor checked his own hands as if they belonged to disobedient children.

"Tom's high fever – over some time – may have caused the apoplexy." He put the cloth to one side, his shoulders straightened, his eyes narrowed. "Jessie, you were not here. Perhaps if someone had controlled his fever, if someone had summoned me sooner ... well, perhaps he may not ... I simply do not know the sequence of events, so the treatment is difficult."

Jessie heard her own gasp. The blankets slid from her grip and her knees wobbled once more. "Tom is a young, healthy man. He left here this morning well, strong. How is this possible?"

The doctor thumbed a temple. "That is something we are all asking. It is indeed unexpected, and odd."

The room swirled and the candle flames sprung to life, burning her eyes. Scrambled worries thrashed in her mind. When she sucked a breath, something stale and pungent caught in her throat. Her head whipped towards the door. Framed in the dim light, a silhouette stood bulky, rigid. No movement, other than beads swinging from thick hands. The sound, the smell – the priest.

"Indeed, it is extremely confusing." His voice echoed the doctor's uncertainty – but heavier with accusation. "We need to investigate thoroughly."

Jessie left Tom's bedside and staggered towards Father Coyle. She barely recognised her own voice through the stranglehold on her throat. "Why are you here?"

Father Coyle grunted, shoved her aside and marched to Tom's bedside. "His family, God-fearing Christians, called for me to pray for their son's healing." Jessie clutched her chest as his gaze swept over her. "Evidently something abnormal has befallen Tom, and in your absence, theirs was an excellent decision. Anyone can see God's presence is most needed."

Before Jessie could muster a reply, yelling from the other room stole her attention. She left the priest with Tom, returning to the living room where her mother squared up to Jean. She rushed to her side. "Mammie!"

Heather pulled her tearful daughter close. "Shush, Jessie, I'm here. Hold your tongue, say nought, don't rise to their goading." She steered Jessie back to the bedchamber where Doctor MacFarlane sprang from his chair.

"Mrs Strachan." He stepped back.

Heather nodded then turned to the priest. "Father Coyle, we appreciate your attendance but we are well able, with Dr MacFarlane's help, to care for Tom and treat him as necessary."

The weight of his swinging rosary agitated the priest's cloak. "Tom's condition is a mystery; I believe he may need God's last rites before this night is done."

Jessie's gasp startled Dr MacFarlane, who rushed to cool Tom's forehead once more. "Father, I don't think there's fear of young Tom passing tonight," he spluttered.

Loud thuds echoed in the room, and all heads turned to see Dougal stride in, eyes and nostrils flaring. "Father Coyle, Dr

MacFarlane, may I have a word?" His voice boomed, fluttering the candles.

When the men left, Jessie whimpered. "Mammie, will Tom leave me tonight?"

Heather gripped Jessie's shoulders and looked into her wide eyes, dark orbs quivering in a pool of tears. "No, he will not pass tonight. I promise you."

"How do you know?"

"Trust me, his shroud has not yet reached his knees."

Jessie focused all her attention on Tom's recovery while the changing colours of the leaves and the fluttering goodbyes of the swallows remained unnoticed. Summer's vibrant colours faded, stiff breezes and winter finches nudged out the warm winds and the season's swarms of midges. During the first few weeks, Dr MacFarlane called daily to administer medicine – and report Tom's condition back to his family and Father Coyle. His constant dismissal of Jessie and her own medicinal suggestions ultimately resulted in a clash which Heather jumped to referee. After enduring Dr MacFarlane again waxing lyrical about how well Tom was responding to his medicine – and how grateful Jessie ought to be for his control over Tom's ailment – Jessie's veins pulsed in her forearms, straining against her tight grip on a creaking broom handle. The lid on her anger lost its grip, the broom flew across the room, crashed against the front door and brought Heather rushing inside. Dr MacFarlane stood in the firing line, ashen faced.

"You don't even know what ails Tom!" Jessie's wild eyes raged. "It's my medicine healing him, he'd be dead by now if I'd listened to you."

Heather yanked Jessie to the bedroom, walloping her down into the chair by Tom's bedside. After closing the door, she led the shaken doctor outside as if he were an elderly patient. "I'm sorry Doctor, Jessie is under terrible strain so she's not herself. She gets little sleep so tends to haver, take no notice."

Dr MacFarlane peered over her shoulder; his concern that Jessie may come tearing out the house after him clear by his expression. He straightened his tweed jacket but held his bag in front of him. Fallen leaves around his boots endured his annoyance, and a frown sunk into his eyebrows while he stomped. "There better not be any strange medicines being administered to Tom," he grumbled under his twitching moustache. "His parents expect me to control everything given to him. They're not pleased about this, not pleased at all." The loud crunching under Dr MacFarlane's feet warned Heather to tread lightly.

"Of course, Doctor, as I said, she tends to haver when she's out of sorts."

Dr MacFarlane puffed out his chest, nodding. "Take heed, Father Coyle will not abide any deviance from proper treatment. He will be swift to punish anything not done in God's name."

Heather's jaw ached and she forced her fingers not to curl. "Of course, Doctor, we're all doing our best for Tom."

She watched him stride away, wrapped her arms around herself and looked up at grey clouds sinking towards her. She walked towards the house glancing right and left, admiring the plants lining the path, then ran a palm across white heather blossoms which stubbornly held on to the last of the season's sunshine. When she spotted young holly berries already peeking out from under thick shiny leaves she winced at the prospect of a harsh winter. She crossed the path to inspect Jessie's hedgerow. Next to the house stood the rowan tree, branches laden with berries, its rich red autumn leaves reaching out to test the air. An uneasy tremor in her stomach stopped her. Nestled between holly bushes, dark red spindle berry buds gleamed their sinister glow. She rested her forehead on the purplish grey bark of the tree, squeezing her eyes shut, praying for strength to survive the dark days ahead.

Chapter 10

FATHER COYLE USHERED TOM'S *family into his office where they spent the larger part of an afternoon debating the cause of Tom's sudden illness, arguing about who they deemed responsible, and deliberating on a course of action. Jean's ankle bones knocked together, synchronised with stiff fingers drumming on her knees – until Robert's elbow almost cracked her ribs. He clapped his hands. "Stop fidgeting."*

Mary stood at the window pondering over asking Mrs Bain if she'd received any new wool from Glasgow. Robert turned to her. "Pay attention, Mary, Father Coyle is speaking."

Mary slumped into a chair and fiddled with her scarf. "I don't understand what you are talking about. I do not know why Tom is ill, and I have worthier things to do than sit here listening to this."

Robert's huff almost rekindled the fire while Jean grumbled under her breath. Father Coyle's fists bounced on his arm rests a few times before he stood and reached for a leather-bound book on the table. He waved it around, almost slapping Jean with the red ribbon markers when they flew past her face, its gold-edged pages flashing through the air. The floorboards squealed while all three strived to avoid missiles of perspiration leaping from the priest's head as it whipped from one to the other. He delivered a rousing sermon on the evil living amongst them and the need to purge the town, with emotion enough to stir William Wallace. Jean's head bobbed like an apple in the dooking bucket, Robert's eyes widened with each statement while Mary focused on avoiding the errant sweat – silently praying they would leave before it rained. The walls seemed to shake, and even though the sun no longer shone, the priest blew enough hot air into the room for his guests to swelter. Tom's illness was indeed sudden, unexpected, still undiagnosed. His family's loyalty and desire for his speedy recovery stirred resentment: partly caused by their suspicions of what Jessie may have been up to when Tom lay dying on his floor, plus their knowledge of the couple's discontent since the miscarriage. Rumours floated from house to house, kept afloat by Sunday sermons where Father Coyle indiscriminately doled out lashings of fire and brimstone, resulting in innocent parishioners casting sideways glances at each other. Children ran into their homes pale and wide-eyed after Father Coyle asked if their conkers came from the schoolyard or the forest.

Jean whimpered and Robert grunted when the priest hollered, "I will drive these evildoers out of this town!"

Mary slid further into her chair as the priest ranted. "That forest is hiding pagan practices and evil deeds. It needs to be cleared and put to good use." He stomped up and down punching invisible enemies. "I'm sure Lord Wilson will want to turn the land into something to better prosper the entire town." He reached the window then swung around with clenched fists, glaring at Robert. "God took away her child – for its own safety no doubt – and now poor Tom is paying the price. I will make sure someone answers for this."

At the mention of Tom, Robert stood. "If there's even the slightest chance anyone hurt Tom, I want to know." He turned to Jean, still wringing her hands. "Jean, do you have anything to say?"

Jean's gasp matched her horrified expression. "Robert, this is all too terrible, I don't know what to think any more. I told you marrying that girl would be a disaster. We allowed it, and now look." She dropped her head into her hands.

Robert fumed. "Well, that's not helping now, is it?"

"Dad, stop it!" Mary's sneer flew across the room. "We're all upset. I warned you on the day but you dismissed me." Her heels clacked on the stone floor when she strode back to the window. "They were desperately in love and he was determined to marry her."

"Until she lost the baby and it all turned to ashes," Robert barked. "If Charles Wilson took over the farm, he would expect them to work for him – if they wanted to remain living there – and we all know she hates the Wilsons. She's been at loggerheads with Angus since he started working for them and swore Tom against having any dealings with them."

Father Coyle's mouth twisted. "Exactly! I was told she and her kind would love to drive them out."

Jean's snivelling escalated to sobs. Mary rushed to her side. "I think you've said enough, look how you've upset mother."

Robert snatched his coat then swung his scarf around his neck. "They have ways we simply don't understand, God knows they're capable of anything – if the rumours are true."

"They certainly seem to be." The priest interjected. "There's no place here for pagan beliefs or evil ways, we must rid our town of them."

Tom's family shuffled out of Father Coyle's office in silence; more bewildered than when they entered. Mary tightened her scarf, murmuring to her father. "Do you think she poisoned him?"

Robert clasped his hands and glanced up at Father Coyle's window. "I'm not sure, but my son is lying like a possessed cripple, so if she does have any part in it, she'll be sorry she ever met him."

"Oh, dear God help us," Jean whimpered.

"I'm not sure how much God can help us now!" Robert barked.

Jean turned on him, her eyes flashing. "Well then, I'll speak to someone who might."

Robert's eyebrows crunched. "Who?"

"Laura McLean. She cannae hold her water."

Across the street, Heather and Maggie found themselves alone, the townsfolk forewarned of their presence. They also found themselves alone in the few shops they frequented. Even young Alec now left their milk bottles at the farm gate instead of delivering them on his way home. Maggie glared at the window of the wool shop with the 'closed' sign. She spotted Mrs Bain's rotund belly peeking out from behind the curtain.

"They're gathering against us. Father Coyle has them all in a state."

Heather pulled on her elbow. "Let's go before they have something to bleat about."

Heather grasped Maggie's elbow tightly to avoid her from marching across the street and terrifying Mrs. Bain. Cold air suddenly chilling her lungs made her realise she needed Maggie to drag her home. Maggie blethered all the way without a sideways glance at Heather, who by the time they got to her gate, looked the colour of damp concrete.

Maggie turned mid-sentence and held Heather's shoulders. "For the love of Airmid, what's wrong with you?" She yelled up the path: "Dougal, Angus, Fraser ... anyone!"

Dougal and Fraser rushed out, and in one swift movement Dougal swept Heather into his arms then fled into the house. Fraser stood hands on hips; head bowed so low he looked shrunk. Maggie's eyes flashed between the closed door and Fraser. She sucked in a deep breath then slapped Fraser to attention. "What's come over her so suddenly?"

Fraser's arms flopped to his sides. "She says it's the dying disease, says there's no cure."

Maggie rushed towards the door but Dougal emerged before she got there. He held her at arm's length. "Tomorrow, Maggie, she needs to rest, she'll explain tomorrow."

Maggie stood frozen on the cold doorstep still beseeching Airmid, the Gaelic Goddess of health. Fraser's hand on her back startled her, and when she turned, her own sadness reflected in his drooping eyes. He squeezed her shoulder before returning inside. She tried to dislodge the lump in her throat but it was stronger than her resolve. Heather's worries had piled higher than she should need to cope with: Jessie's miscarriage, Father Coyle's unwanted attention, his involvement with Angus – enough to exhaust her life force. Heather's health had deteriorated rapidly, but she found her ways to keep it well managed, and mostly hidden. Similar to trees, one minute the leaves are brown, then suddenly when you're not paying attention they disappear. Maggie left, but cried all the way home.

On the opposite side of the village, Jessie sat by Tom's bedside. His rhythmic breathing reminded her of faraway thunder, lulling her into a daydream where they walked hand-in-hand through thistle fields, across gurgling streams surrounded by multicoloured heather spreading farther than their sight permitted. His eyes fluttered beneath pale lids and she questioned if his dreams gave him peace, or whether his mind tormented him with the memory of lying helpless, struggling for breath as she gave her time and attention to a desperate young mother. She ran her fingers across his smooth forehead, down his cheek, the stubble prickling her fingers on their way to his soft neck. When the fevers subsided and Tom's clarity returned, relief bubbled through Jessie's veins, breathing life into her tight chest. Determination to dedicate herself to making him well again overpowered her previous yearnings to learn everything to do with nature's medicines, her inherited ability for healing, and the power of the stones. Guilt proved to be a tough taskmaster, waking her each morning, driving her throughout the day, making sure she didn't sleep until she paid her dues. Sleep no longer came easily, most nights her mind tossed around wants and needs. Tom appeared to be on the mend, and with the passing weeks he regained both strength and appetite. Soon he was up and about desperate to get back to work, and despite Jessie's misgivings and pleading for him to rest a little longer, he insisted he'd spent enough time in bed. He no longer wanted to be a burden to her, so one morning he declared it was time. Jessie watched him dressing. Her brain silenced his excited babbling while her eyes moved with his fingers as he buttoned his shirt and tied his shoelaces. Spiders crawled up her spine and her stomach twinged each time a finger missed its button. When disobedient shoelaces repeatedly slipped away from his thumb, her chest twitched.

Tom interrupted her thinking when he laughed. "Jess, I'm asking you what's for tea?"

Jessie snapped to attention. "Something warm."

Tom wolfed down salted oats with stewed apples before walking out their front door. Jessie followed him to the gate, careful not to make a sound. The gate post grazed the inside of her grip as he sauntered down the road. She noticed his gait, slightly lopsided, and her stomach twinged again. Cleaning the house from top to bottom and washing all Tom's clothing depleted most of the morning but took minimal energy. She flung open every window, sweeping until her arms ached. Images of Myna's house flashed in her mind but she beat them as she did her dusty carpets, finding another chore to drain her energy. Hanging up wet bed sheets, wafts of fresh herbs stung *her nostrils but to prevent them demanding her attention she held her breath. By lunchtime all her housework was complete – and no amount of wilful determination eased the nausea plaguing her.*

She made tea and sat outside, resting her head against the rough stone of the back wall. She looked out to where dark clouds promised rain, realising she'd missed most of the leaves falling from her favourite tree. Even the nests stood empty, waiting for a harsh wind to send them flying off into the winter grass, their jobs done for the season. Her eyes followed a flock of swallows heading south and she marvelled at their inherent sense of formation, direction and routine. Engrossed in the serenity and simplicity of her surroundings, she didn't hear her mother at the back door. Heather stood watching her daughter, who at first glance seemed peaceful, with no sign of the inner torments draining her colour. Jessie's instincts nudged her, and she turned to see her mother leaning against the doorframe. Again, something disturbed her stomach, and the spiders revisited her spine.

"You're sick."

"I am."

"Tom will never be well."

"No."

"I'm pregnant."

"I know."

Chapter 11

THE WAGE ANGUS NOW earned pleased him, but his family rarely inquired about his new job, and even though he wanted to give his mother more 'keep' money, his father refused. When Angus offered, Dougal hadn't looked up from his soup, but his words stung. "We don't need more, Angus, certainly not Wilson money, so you keep it, turn it into something useful or save it for a rainy day."

Angus tried to control the heat in his chest but failed to contain it from spreading across his cheeks. Fraser laughed. "Awe, Dad, you've riled him now. He wants to throw English money at you."

Although frail, Heather's yell flew from the kitchen. "Wheisht!"

Angus thundered. "Money's money, isn't it?"

Heather strode to the table, standing between the boys, wiping her hands on her apron. "Angus, thank you. All he's saying is it's your money. You give us enough, and it's always good to save some."

Fraser huffed. "Aye, for when they fire you. They love to fire us folk, keeps us desperate, they think."

Angus looked down at his white-knuckled grip on his mug. For all Fraser's niggling and his mother's pacifying, it was his father's reaction which sent his muscles into a clench. He sipped his tea, eyes downcast, ignoring his mother. Fraser's chewing sanded every nerve until he was sure his bones would crumble, so he marched to his room, slamming the door behind him.

Morning came after a restless sleep accompanied by the anxiety of a meeting he was required to attend, but began with a distressed Laura. She flew into Angus's office, her green plaid skirts hitched up between tight fists. Angus gawked from behind his desk when she bared her teeth.

"He's a bloody monster, that one."

Angus shrugged. "Can you not speak to cook?"

She turned from the door and pushed her fists into her hips. "He's one of Wilson's men. Who am I to say anything? I'll lose me job and go hungry."

Angus got up and walked to her. "I'm sorry Laura, it's difficult for us I know, but it's a decent living."

Laura nudged the door open just enough to see if her escape was possible. Before leaving, she turned to Angus. "Dinnae you worry about us, we'll sort it out."

Wilson's men were an unwelcome bunch: loud-mouthed, rough, unaccustomed to the regular use of soap. The house and dairy maids lived in terror, complaining regularly to Angus about the leering, lecherous advances, but Laura's problems weren't his therefore no reason he should get involved. He credited himself for hiring Donald, and even though he rarely set eyes on Charles Wilson, he was confident he found his work acceptable, even if Wilson never said it. Trudging along the damp road to the priest's office, he pushed her words aside. His mood hung heavier than the morning fog while he aimlessly flicked through an old Bible waiting for Father Coyle to arrive. The clock chimed a reminder of his own punctuality compared to the priest's bad manners. When the door opened, it was not Father Coyle. A young boy carrying a tray with tea, and a plate laden with shortbread, gasped and his eyes darted around the room. Angus frowned at the youngster with the shaky hands. "You were expecting Father Coyle?" The boy nodded and a greasy lock of red hair tumbled onto his forehead as he set the tray down. Angus eyed his grubby fingernails when the cups rattled. He leaned forward, steadying the tray. "I'm a visitor not an intruder. Is there something wrong?"

The boy kept his head down. "No sir, I'm only delivering the tea."

"Thank you. I'll have some while I wait."

The boy turned and Angus listened to his quick feet racing down the steps. He was still mulling over this strange behaviour when the door flew open and Father Coyle huffed and puffed his way to his chair.

"Those stairs will be the death of me," he grumbled.

"Have some tea," Angus offered.

Father Coyle wiped his sweaty cheeks with a well-used handkerchief. "Yes, I will. Where did it come from?"

"Your servant boy brought it."

The priest leaned forward and took the cup from Angus. "Don't be silly, I don't have a servant boy."

Angus rolled his eyes. "Father, a young boy brought it."

The priest sank back into his chair, grumbling between slurps. "Laura must be off again. Damn unreliable, these local women, damn unreliable. Must have been her daft son, he's a tricky character, needs watching."

Angus pushed his feet into the carpet. "Laura works up at the manor. How can she work for you too?"

The priest rattled his cup into the saucer. "She keeps my carpets and curtains in a respectable condition, but clearly not today. I arranged for her son to attend school, so she owes me."

Angus rolled his eyes. "It is excellent tea, so perhaps enjoy it then tell me why I'm here."

The priest gulped, then banged the cup and saucer on the table. Angus flinched, relieved to see it didn't break.

"This ugly business with the women in the woods is getting out of control and we are no further forward. You seem to be especially comfortable in your new office so have you perhaps forgotten my instructions?"

Angus noticed the priest's cheeks flush; his fat fingers squashing his rope belt. He'd hoped the priest would be far too busy with his new school, upgrades to the church, and preaching to his new devotees to worry about the forest women. He dug his fingernails into his palms when the priest wiped spittle from his mouth before wagging a damp finger at him. "I've heard too many stories of more and more women visiting these witches, using potions against their husbands and employers. They do not attend my mass and only a few ask for confession."

Preferring not to rattle the priest's beads, Angus remained quiet, keeping a neutral expression. The priest punched the arm of his chair.

"Angus, it is time to stop this, time to bring these women out of their lair and charge them."

"Charge them with what?"

Father Coyle leaned forward. Angus watched his eyes contract. "They are practising witchcraft! They are concocting poisons to turn women against the church and their menfolk." Angus melted into his chair when the priest's glare turned into a snarl. "I warned you Angus. I ordered you to get your mother and her people to stop. You have had enough time so you better say who is responsible and what you intend doing about it."

Angus's hands were almost numbed from his constant squeezing, while silence hung heavy; a black cloud about to burst. Blood rushed to his cheeks at the reference to his mother. He cleared his throat.

"Father Coyle, I don't know of any harm to anyone. If some choose not to attend your church surely that is their right? I don't see how women are being turned against their menfolk. That makes no sense, and your obsession with my mother is uncalled for."

Father Coyle heaved out of his armchair and marched to the window. The relief from the distance between them was short-lived. When he swung around, Angus prayed the colour of the priest's face pre-empted a stroke. It did not. "They are practising witchcraft!" he repeated. "Casting spells on men to render them impotent. One minute a woman is with child, the next she is not. Men have mysteriously disappeared and almost no young girls attend mass."

Angus jumped to his feet. "Father Coyle! This is an ancient town full of stories and hearsay. You cannot take any truth from it. Most of Wilson's men are drunkards, bullies, relentlessly bothering our young girls, so if they are indeed missing and not lying in a brothel somewhere, I can't imagine anyone will miss them."

The priest's roar flew at him. "Miss them? They are employees of Charles Wilson! They have families back in England waiting for their wages. He is not happy about this; he expects something to be done. Not least of all, flattening that forest."

Only the need for breath ceased his rant, and Angus thanked God the windows were closed lest the street hear the furore. The priest regained his breath then loped across to face him. "Your mother is at the root of this. I have been told she descends from witches and has more power than all of them."

A lump in Angus's throat prevented him from answering.

The priest leered. "That shocks you, or are you shocked I know it?"

Angus's brain scrambled to understand the priest's tirade, so he remained speechless. Father Coyle raised his fists. "Now there's this wretched situation with Tom."

Angus gulped. "You cannot be implying my mother was involved with the disappearance of those missing men, or Tom? For God's sake, she's a poorly old woman."

The priest shook his head, his lips curled. "She may be old but she can still teach and pass on her pagan ways."

Bells louder than any Sunday morning rang in Angus's head. "Are you saying you think my mother and Jessie caused Tom's illness? He is family!"

The priest thumped the arm of the chair. "How else can we explain it? We know your mother is a witch – and Jessie is her daughter. They have made their dislike of both the Wilsons and the school well known. Especially since Charles Wilson intends buying the farm they live on. You are family so may not see it, but it is what they do. This is the evil they practise and I will stop it." He whacked the chair again and Angus's mouth dropped open. They locked eyes while the room seemed to disappear into the priest's dark glare. "Either you end this or I will have someone arrested. I will flatten that forest, any dwelling in it, occupied or not, and burn it to the ground."

Angus's words sounded as though sand filled his mouth. "You can't be serious, surely you don't intend—" His words dangled between them until the priest pounced.

"I am deadly serious. If you want to keep your job, and your family safe, you must do what I asked you." His lips formed one fat line, beads of perspiration edging them.

"I am doing a fine job; Charles Wilson is happy with me." Angus cringed at his own whine.

Father Coyle's sneer could have stripped the paint from the walls. "If Charles Wilson decides he's run out of patience with this godforsaken town and the problems it brings, he will pack up and go back to England, leaving you and all your peasant people jobless. Now get out, get it done."

Angus left the office in a daze, and the minute the fresh air reached his lungs he almost choked. He ran his hands through his hair while he stood staring at the pavement. Movement in his periphery jolted him from his shock, and he turned to see the young tea boy staring at him. Angus opened his mouth to speak, but neither his brain nor his mouth obliged. The young boy dropped his eyes, turned and ran around the corner.

Hours later, Angus sat at his desk, his head and heart wrangling. No sooner had he finished his tea, about to transfer Donald's requirements into his journal, when he heard a light knock on the door. He assumed it would be Mildred returning to fetch his dirty crockery, so without looking up he bellowed: "Come in."

"My, my, that's quite a tone to take."

Angus's jaw dropped when he looked up to see his mother standing in his doorway. She'd never visited him at work. In fact, no family ever visited him – not when Jessie miscarried or when Tom fell ill. He was always the last to be told anything; or at least he viewed it that way. Now she stood in his office doorway and it struck him how brightly her eyes shone, in notable contrast to her pale face. He rushed to grab a chair from the corner. "Mam, this is a surprise. Come in, sit down, is something wrong?"

Heather sat and loosened her scarf before speaking. "I wanted to talk – just the two of us."

Angus slumped into his chair. This wasn't a visit to see his employment. The tightening in his muscles signalled the conversation would not be pleasant.

Heather wasted no time. "I know you've been visiting Maggie and I know you're in some agreement with Father Coyle."

Angus's mouth dropped open. "I asked Maggie to keep it between us. Dear God, is there no end to that woman's tattling? As for Father Coyle, he needed someone to help the Wilsons because no one around here can see any benefit from their presence." He waved his arm the way a painter sweeps his brush across a new canvas. "Can you not see it's a well-paying job? Far better than lugging a kishie loaded with peat?" Heather's hands rolled into fists, prompting Angus to lower his voice. "Mam, it's not all bad. One hand washes the other so everyone benefits. What's amiss with that?"

Heather remained quiet, allowing Angus time for his mind to run around like a headless chicken, unable to decide what he ought to reveal or discern what his mother already knew. A tightness in his chest nudged him to open a window – the expression on his mother's face told him she understood why.

"Father Coyle is not, and will never be your friend," she warned. "His interests are his own, so he will use you, the Wilsons, and his position, to line his pockets and increase his influence and power."

Angus bristled. "I know you dislike him and all he stands for, but he got me this job."

Heather raised her hands. "Don't you see? That's what he does. He builds a church that divides people, a school that separates children. He controls with money and fear, causing bitterness and jealousy amongst our people. Families turning against each other because their boys are being favoured over their girls."

Heather's passion surprised and irritated Angus. "What is wrong with a new school? The old one isn't turning out professors, is it?"

Heather's eyes narrowed as she leaned forward. "It was good enough for you, your brother and Jessie. It doesn't ram religion down the bairns' throats either."

Angus leaned back. "That's what this is about, isn't it? Religion, you're all in a huff because the church is behind it."

"Angus, there are a lot of us in a huff – because it's a brainwashing school, it excludes lassies, it's turning folk against each other."

"Mam, you can't talk about brainwashing when you're out in those woods dancing around fires, howling at the moon, turning half the village women. Even Da is against it."

Outside, the early afternoon brought clouds spewing fine rain, adding an unwanted chill to Angus's office and Heather's tone. Her eyes darkened. "You know nothing of what we do so your disdain pains me. You know Father Coyle is riling Tom's family against Jessie, harassing Maggie to turn me in as if it's still the auld days. His threats don't scare me, Angus. My shroud won't wait much longer, but you have time, and you owe it to your family to look after them, especially your sister. Yet you sit here drinking tea, ordering Donald around as if you're the lord of the manor. If you let these outsiders destroy our ways, you'll be no better than them. Just don't expect them to help if ever you're in need."

Angus snapped the pencil he'd held prisoner since Heather sat down. The mention of Jessie and Maggie flipped his stomach like a waging coin, but his mother's awareness poured cold water on his simmering arrogance. He shifted in his chair then threw the pencil fatalities into his dustbin.

"Jessie's not been right since she lost the bairn, now this trouble with Tom ..." his voice faded in the room's heaviness.

Heather's chest lifted as if pushing against an onerous weight. "She's been to her darkest corners, Angus, she's trying to find her own way."

Angus fumed. "Mam, I know you've been taking her to the forest. You must know it would cause trouble. She should've been at home when Tom fell ill. You're bringing this trouble to us all, you and the others with your pagan practices. Even Da can see she's turned, so what comes to her is her own doing – and yours."

Heather lifted her scarf and wrapped it around her neck. She locked eyes with him but her expression sent no signals. Angus ignored the screaming in his head as she buttoned her woollen coat. He smothered his rage, straightened his shoulders, and clasped his hands on the desk. Heather folded her scarf into her collar as a tight smile tugged at the corner of her mouth – enough to wake the hairs on Angus's neck. Without making a sound, she stood and slowly moved towards the desk. Angus called on his entire resolve when her stare pinned him to his seat, but the air in his lungs refused to leave.

Heather's voice floated down gently like the breath of an angel, but landed with the strength of an army. "You have choices to make with only your heart and conscience to guide you. Jessie will need you to take her side, so when the time comes, I hope you choose wisely. Nothing I say will make any difference now. You've heard enough from me."

The walls seemed to close in when she turned towards the door. His anger flew after her. "For God's sake, Mam, you must stop her! What you're doing is dangerous and might get somebody killed."

Heather turned. "I won't be stopping Jessie from becoming who she's meant to be. I suggest you don't either. Her journey was determined long before her. You say somebody may die, but you do not know who."

Angus squeezed his eyes so tight his eyelids hurt. "Mam, you can't force me to choose, so for all our sake please stop this before it gets worse."

A gust of wind almost rattled the door off its hinges, and when he opened his eyes, she was gone. Torrential rain pelting onto the roof deafened his thinking. He longed for silence, but the drumming and howling swirled around the room, throwing him off balance, unable to focus. No amount of stabbing weak-tipped pencils into his leather-bound journal eased his need to grind his teeth. He sank his head into his fists and his elbows landed on the desk with a thud.

Chapter 12

JESSIE'S PREGNANCY TESTED HER ability to bounce between her emotional strain and the physical demands she'd taken on. Tom was back at work, his cheeks found their colour, but he was far from recovered, still struggling with most of his basic abilities. Jessie noticed his unsteadiness – how uneven ground tested his balance. His left eye drooping long before bedtime, and his battle with buttons and laces persisted. She heard him stumble, trying to manoeuvre around the chanty, knowing at the very least he'd leave a puddle of pee for her to clean. Broken pieces of cups and plates that didn't make the tin wash tub without hitting the edge caused her heart to ache as she watched remnants of their wedding gifts rattle to the bottom of the bin. She'd become accustomed to the extra cleaning, discarding her good crockery, but it was Tom's mental deficits which disturbed her sleep. He repeated himself, forcing her to repeat herself in response. He often walked out the door only to return minutes later, looking for the lunch Jessie had packed into his canvas satchel, or the cap already on his head. His gaze would fix upon a spot only he could see, and when Jessie nudged him to attention, his dark vacant stare left her cold. His restless sleep tangled the blankets, his mutterings made no sense. He called out for the son he had lost, wailing until Jessie forced him awake to calm him. Some days he got excited about her pregnancy. However, until her bump became impossible to miss, he often forgot she was pregnant, asking when they would try to have another baby. One evening, her energy already drained by the day's toils, she concluded reminding him was a futile exercise, so she took his unsteady hands and placed them on her belly.

"Soon, Tom, soon." She smiled, but his expression remained unchanged. Despite her pregnancy, Tom's family continued to blame her for his illness, picking holes in everything she did in her care of him. On one visit, they noticed Tom's hand bandaged, berating her for not paying better attention. He had poured tea straight from the pot onto his hand. Jessie had heard the scream, rushed from cleaning the bedroom and found Tom staring at his scalded skin. There was no cup on the table, the pot lay on the floor, tea soaked into the stone; sadness into Jessie's heart.

Dr MacFarlane now visited only to deliver medicine, check on Tom's progress and retrieve the empty bottles from previous deliveries. He skirted around Tom's ailments, his eyes preferring to flit about the room than face Jessie's glare. Her nostrils flared and his moustache twitched when he spoke. "These are complicated matters, but I believe if you give him the correct medicines he'll mend in good time," he muttered.

Jessie knew better – so did Heather. They tried all their known remedies, including the ones recently developed in Myna's rudimentary kitchen. When Tom slept, Jessie spent hours poring over Myna's journals, or roaming the woods looking for plants, hidden flora and roots unknown to her. She scrambled up slippery rocks, under dense hedgerows, yanking stems and roots with one hand, while balancing precariously on moss-coated boulders or fallen tree trunks. She often arrived at her mother with a haul stashed under her pregnant bulge; for Myna to identify, dry, boil, grate or crush into what would become a powder or tincture. Then wait anxiously for a result. Some worked, most didn't, so Jessie's frustration grew.

Concerned about her friend's failing health, Myna convinced Heather to substitute her rope-making for an easier task. She placed a pile of bright, multicoloured threads she'd acquired from Mrs Bain's latest delivery into Heather's pale, stringy fingers. "Please turn these into hair braids. The girls will love them."

Heather twirled the rainbow of threads around her fingers, grinning. "Don't you work your charm on me now."

Myna ignored her. "Heather, we can never have enough luck so make sure they're colourful. Not flimsy – and give them a good blessing."

Jessie's impatience soon got the better of her, so despite warnings, once again the minute Tom left for work, she rushed to Heather and they walked to Myna's. She appeared focused on her endeavours to heal Tom, and although Heather and

Myna admired her determination, they worried her desire for knowledge and skills were her true driving force. Knowing they had limited time, spending every possible moment together, regardless of the pursuit, became their unspoken intent. It was a conversation they avoided. Heather resigned herself to being unable to temper Jessie's wilfulness, so prayed for her protection, and enough time to pass on her wisdom. She would not hold Jessie back, but her intensity exhausted her. Early one morning, scrambling through the woods, she yanked Jessie's arm. "You're going to have to slow your pace if I'm to survive another day."

Jessie let Heather catch her breath. "Sorry Mammie, I forget you are not so strong."

Heather sucked in the fresh air, then took Jessie's hands. "Close your eyes."

Jessie stood still with her mother's hands curled around hers. The forest sounds-which she'd failed to notice in recent weeks as she rushed in and out on her clandestine ventures-enveloped her, gently reaching into the deepest parts of her brain. Her heart seemed to lose its beat, each breath drifting silently. Her mother's grip warmed until the damp seeping into her feet no longer registered. The vision came gradually until nothing else existed. Her mind's eye watched her mother's glowing face, wide shining eyes gliding towards her, followed by a child. An image formed, as sharp as the reflection from a crystal-clear pond – her younger self holding her mother's hand. All physical sense disappeared as Jessie's vision fixed on the child moving towards her until it filled her entire view. For a moment, or eternity, the child's luminous expression held her gaze, then smiled. Jessie's heart ached and her breath froze in her throat. When she opened her eyes, her mother's face beamed. Heather released Jessie's hands, revealing a stone sitting in her palm. Jessie's mouth dropped. "Mammie, why did you do that?"

"I want you to slow down, centre yourself. You're becoming fractured, you will harm yourself if you're not mindful. The fire in your soul will destroy you if you cannot contain it."

Jessie ignored the warning. "Was that me?"

"Perhaps."

"Why did she come to me?"

Heather wrapped her arms around herself. "You are pregnant and you're not looking after yourself. Please manage your time and efforts so your child can arrive healthy. She feeds on your energy. Stop scrambling to find something to heal Tom. We both know we can't fix him. His damage is too much – even for us."

Jessie's eyes filled. "I know."

"You know I won't be here to help you."

Jessie's tears tumbled unhindered onto her scarf. Heather leaned forward and stroked her cheek. "Toms' family and Father Coyle will make life hell for you if you're not careful. Myna will do her best, but even she won't be able to stop them. She has her girls to protect."

Jessie's legs stiffened. "I can't keep everyone happy; they can't force me to stop doing what I choose." She gripped her mother's hands. "I love Tom with all my heart, but I'm losing him, day by day."

Heather noticed Jessie's foot funnelling into the damp ground. "You've chosen your path Jess, but I must remind you it comes with dangers. I know your priorities but you still need to welcome your child and make sure she's safe."

Jessie stroked Heather's hands then rested her head on her shoulder. "I will remember all you've taught me; I will protect my child with my life – no matter what. The way you have protected me."

They stood holding each other until the forest sounds reminded them of their purpose. Heather released Jessie. "We should go now. Myna will worry."

Jessie squeezed Heather's hands. "You're convinced I'm having a girl."

Heather grinned. "I am."

Jessie's pregnancy advanced without concern or hampering her efforts to deal with Tom's ever-changing behaviours – or her study and practice with Heather, Myna and the spaes. However, her increasing proficiency resulted in an increase in the number of visitors to the forest cottage. By varying the route and covering their tracks, the women reliant on help worked hard at protecting its location, keeping their activity secret. *Within a few months Jessie had commandeered anyone with a spare minute plus the fearlessness to assist. The couch endured more traffic than the kettle could keep up with and her heart swelled each time a despairing woman left more hopeful than when she arrived. Some circumstances proved more serious than others but a kind ear and an understanding of women's health formed the starting point for all who knocked on the door looking to resolve something in their life. A cup of sweet tea and a hug eased much anxiety and although she crossed some invisible lines, she did whatever she deemed necessary. Myna marvelled at Jessie's ability to recognise the cause of distress swiftly and accurately, but often reprimanded her methods. Jessie took little notice.*

"She'll never carry without pain, suffering, more stillbirths," she remarked, hands on hips when Heather and Myna exchanged glances after watching a tearful young woman leave.

"Be careful Jessie, there's a fine line between healing and playing God," Myna warned.

Jessie's eyes flashed. "Well, God should be kinder."

Heather clutched her chest. "Jessie! Mind your mouth, we all live under the same God, none of us are above that will."

The thud of the front door slamming signalled Jessie's exit, but her bluster hung over them. Myna held Heather's trembling hand. "It's not your job any more, her intentions are pure. Let her be." Heather's eyes filled and her heart pushed against weak ribs. Myna wiped an escaped tear from her friend's drawn face. "We both know there's no negotiating with destiny – and it's time you were off home."

Heather took a deep breath and cast her eyes skywards. "The moon will be especially full tonight so we must gather."

Myna nodded. "Then you must rest now."

On that clear Beltane night when the air stilled even the breathing of the leaves, and the movement within the pond – morphed into the exact shape of the giant orb sitting high – the moon did indeed fill the sky. All the spaes turned out to pray beneath this super-moon, to give thanks and absorb its energy. A larger than normal fire glowed and the moon's powerful light snatched the smoke billows, scattering them throughout the trees into the atmosphere. Gentle humming followed murmured invocations before each woman joined hands in a large circle surrounding the flames, combining fellowship and energy.

Heather stood between Jessie and Myna, eyes closed, heart full. Bodies swayed with the rise and fall of chanting and beating hearts. One by one, each woman threw something into the fire – a piece of fabric, a flower, a sprinkle of dried herbs, a letter. Each item burned while the women watched the ashes flicker and rise before disappearing into the dark. Both Myna and Jessie tossed handfuls of dried mixtures before Heather stepped forward to toss a bunch of white heather into the flames. Within seconds, sweetness infused the air. Wails, moans and gentle sobs filled the space until the women's chanting rose to a crescendo. When the fire dwindled to orange and white cinders, the chanting ceased. The women broke their bonds then huddled together on a grassy patch next to an enormous rowan tree, to share their experiences, visions. Each woman held Heather, kissed her hands, then gently touched Jessie's belly before saying goodbye. Heather, Myna and Jessie sat in silence, watching the fire disintegrate into a heap of grey and white embers. The nocturnal forest creatures crept from their hiding spots while stars sent silver streaks of light through the leaves. Heather's drooped shoulders and drawn face stirred Jessie from her stillness, and her heart ached.

"Mammie, you're exhausted. I'm taking you home." She turned and dumped damp earth on the warm ash. Myna eased Heather into her coat, tucking her scarf inside the collar, before clasping her. Moonlight caught both Heather's brilliant eyes, and a heavy tear as it slid down Myna's chin.

Heather wiped it then placed her palm on her cheek. "We know our journey, my friend. I counted my blessings long ago. I lack none." Myna's crushing embrace gave Heather the opportunity to whisper. "Jessie's force is nothing we've known; I fear I will see her sooner than I want."

Myna released her but held her elbows. "I will do what I can."

Heather tilted her head, so the moon caught her smile. "You've done more than enough."

Jessie turned and noticed their shining eyes. She thrust her hands into her pockets. "This is indeed a super-moon. You two are overflowing with emotion."

Heather kissed Myna on each cheek before turning to Jessie. "We are. Let's go."

Heather insisted they stop at the pond before leaving the forest. Fuelled by the energy of the evening Jessie didn't argue. Heather sat on her favourite rock where she watched the stars glint between the tree's reflections on the pond's glassy surface. Jessie sat, hooked arms, and with her head nestled on Heather's shoulder, listened to her mother's soft breathing. The forest's moonlight sonata lulled their minds and calmed their spirits. Heather pulled Jessie close, basking in the warmth of her daughter's body against hers. Soon the air cooled. Jessie stood.

"Mammie let's go. I must get you home before the chill gets into your bones."

They walked silently, arm in arm until they reached Heather's gate. With a promise to visit the following day, they hugged and said their goodbyes. Dougal opened the front door then joined them at the gate. He hugged Jessie, before leading Heather inside, his arm draped around her as gently as the shawl protecting her shoulders.

Jessie turned towards home then walked straight into Angus. She clutched her scarf. "Dear God, Angus, why are you creeping around at all hours?"

He cocked his head. "I don't need to ask the same of you, do I?"

She bristled. "Leave me alone, I do no harm to you."

"Tom is asleep on his own again ... and you're out roaming while pregnant. Is it any wonder they suspect you?"

Jessie stepped forward, her belly creating a natural barrier between them. "I don't care what they think or what they do. I'm not afraid of any trouble they bring my way."

Even in the moonlight she spotted Angus's jaw clench. "I'm warning you, Jessie, they'll find something you won't be able to fight."

She whipped her hood up and shook her head. "Angus, they don't frighten me. Goodnight."

The crunching of the ground being pummelled beneath her boots matched her thumping heart and heavy breathing as she stomped home. She squeezed her eyes and took a long breath before creeping into her house and sliding into bed. Tom's snores rumbled in the silence and she marvelled at how he slept through it. She found it impossible. Her mind would not settle. Her body found no comfortable position, so when the geese called the world to attention, her sandy eyes struggled to open. The routine of getting Tom off to work flew by in an exhausted haze, so she determined to get the cleaning and washing done before taking a nap.

Her waters broke with a searing, unexpected pain after she hung the last bedsheet on the washing line. Panic rushed from her feet to her heart. Her knees gave way and she collapsed on all fours. Tears burned with the realisation her child was on its way; fast, early, without help. Her eyes darted around the garden then out to the fields, desperately looking for someone, knowing no one was nearby. Each overwhelming contraction turned into a scream which flew into the air, dying in the clouds. Screams which started in her belly and tore up through her throat, terrifying the birds and chasing every living thing into hiding. When she tried to stand her muscles stiffened. After reaching between wet skirts, she soon understood her child would not wait much longer. Between increasing contractions, she crawled across the garden to the rowan tree, heaved herself up against its trunk with nettle-stung hands and drew her scraped knees towards her chest. Soon each breath proved a monumental struggle. Between cursing the universe, her guides, and Tom for leaving her stranded to give birth on her own, she drew on all Heather and Myna had taught her. When pain and breathlessness overtook all other sensations, she focused inwards, begging her child to come – and end the torture. She summoned every ounce of strength, forced her heels into the stubborn earth, and begged all the angels, spirits and spaes for help. She suddenly remembered her mother's words:

"It is when you are sure you have nothing left, the universe gives you what you need."

Hot tears stung her eyes but suddenly she envisioned her mother's face, inches from her own, bright and comforting. She reached out but pain held her just out of reach. With one last push she screamed for her mother and her child crowned. A little more agony, two more pushes, then after bearing down with every ounce of strength she possessed, Jessie reached down and lifted her screeching child to her chest. She ripped open her blouse with trembling hands. Her body shivered with *a power of its own, so she snuggled her baby against her breasts, breathing through teeth-rattling sobs. Newborn fingers clutched her skin, and when a tiny mouth searched before latching onto her nipple, Jessie's body reacted with a rush of hormones flooding her from head to toe. No amount of effort ceased her sobbing, so she rested against the tree, cradled her child and allowed her body to control itself. After a few moments she lifted her blouse, marvelling at ten little fingers and toes, a perfect pink body, plump arms and legs. A full head of dark hair explained the constant heartburn and although exhausted she managed a grin.*

"Welcome baby girl, your grandmother was right, again."

Jessie sobbed when she cut the umbilical cord with a paring knife still in her apron pocket from peeling pie apples earlier. She thanked whomever was responsible for providing her with this necessary and timeous instrument. She tied the cord with a fine braided hair tie, smiling at the irony of how before giving it to her, her mother had chastised Maggie for making one so thin it wouldn't hold a toddler's ponytail.

"Keep it for your child, but it won't last."

Jessie remained under the tree cradling her newborn, allowing her body to complete the birthing process, and so she might regain some sense of normalcy. She gazed at the sky wondering if she would ever recover. In this surreal moment she ignored the rough tree bark digging into her back and the relentless stinging of her grazed knees. The birds revisited the trees, and as she marvelled at the gentle rise and fall of the child breathing against her chest, she gazed across her garden. A new sprouting of one of her favourite flowers caught her eye and her heart swelled. She looked at her daughter then peeled back her blouse once more. Her voice quivered. "Hello, Lily."

When she found enough strength to stand, she carried Lily inside, one unsteady step at a time. She bathed, inspected and revelled in each minute detail, before wrapping her perfect child in clean swaddling gifted to her by Myna. Lily found her appetite and Jessie was both overwhelmed and delighted to oblige. It crossed her mind Tom ought to have been at home to witness their miracle, but this precious time alone with her baby filled her with a joy she'd never known. Left to rely on herself to give birth alone, she now wished to remain in their cocoon forever. Content to be clean and fed, Lily slept while Jessie's body relaxed, finding its natural rhythm. She was about to doze when she heard footsteps on the path. Too exhausted to move she called out. "Tom, come here, quickly."

Within seconds, Fraser stood in the bedroom doorway. She beamed. "Fraser, look, I birthed a baby girl. Come, you're the first to see her ... she's perfect." Her words danced with delight and wonder. "Now you'll have to be her godfather."

Breathless, wide-eyed, Fraser tiptoed to the bedside. Lily didn't stir when Jessie peeled back the swaddling. "Isn't she the most beautiful thing you've ever seen?" she whispered.

Fraser knelt, gazing at his new niece. Tears spilled onto his cheeks, but he smiled, running a finger across Lily's tiny chin. "Ah, Jessie, she is," his hand shook as he wiped his tears.

Jessie reached up and stroked his face. "Och, look at you, she's got you soft already."

Fraser took Jessie's hand and squeezed it. "Mammie's passed."

Chapter 13

HEATHER PASSED PEACEFULLY, NESTLED in Dougal's brawny arms. He listened to her last breath brush his chest, clasping her hand when it went limp. He wept into her hair, breathing in the scent of her as her spirit left her body. In the crushing silence he laid her head tenderly on the pillow before opening each window in the house. He left them open for a few minutes then tearfully wished her spirit safe travels before closing them, as well as every curtain.

Birds welcomed the sunrise with their song, and fine shards of sunlight broke through the darkness, scattering the shadows for another day. Prepared as best for this moment, his hands still trembled when he covered the only mirror, removed the striking weight from the clock, before returning to lie beside his beloved Heather once more. He no longer needed to be strong for his dear wife, so soon his chest heaved, allowing long-suppressed tears to flow. His heart ached when he woke his boys to inform them of their mother's passing. Although aware of Heather's failing health, the finality of death unleashed inconsolable anguish and sorrow on her men. Angus and Fraser sat on either side of their mother, each holding a hand. Sobs echoed around the room. Dougal fetched two coins from a wooden dresser he'd carved for Heather early in their marriage, and after closing each eye he placed them delicately on her eyelids. He laid a hand on Fraser's shoulder. "Please tell Jessie, bring her here."

His hollow voice stirred Angus. "I'll fetch Maggie, you sit with Mammie."

Maggie understood the moment she opened her door and saw Angus's ashen face. "Oh, dear God, has she gone?" Tears filled her eyes as she fell against the door frame.

Angus nodded. "Aye, can you come?"

Maggie fetched her coat and closed the door behind her. She squeezed his arm. "Is Jessie there?"

"No, Fraser will bring her."

The moment they reached the gate they heard the wailing. Angus stopped and caught Maggie's elbow. "I can't go back in there, not yet."

Maggie turned and gripped his shoulders. "You take five minutes, no more, you need to be strong for each other." She let go but clutched her chest. "Especially Jessie."

Maggie rushed straight to Heather's room, peeled Jessie off the bed and held her as sobs wracked them both. Then Maggie pushed her back, looked at her belly and wailed, "Jessie, what's happened? What's happened to your baby?"

Before Jessie had time to explain, Fraser tugged at Maggie's sleeve. She swung around. Lily lay cradled in the crook of his arm. Maggie gasped then slumped onto the side of the deathbed. She wrapped her arms around herself and rocked. "Oh my, what has God done on this morning?"

It took a few hours to compose themselves, to take stock of what this day had brought – the trauma of Heather's passing coupled with the joy of Lily's birth. Emotions seesawed; tears flowed. Maggie and Myna, assisted by a house filled with women, soon got to work on the tasks at hand. They ordered the men out to the barn where they spent the afternoon cutting and sanding eight spokes to support Heather's funeral board. Even though coffins were now routinely used in Scotland, Heather demanded she be put into the earth with only her 'dead clothes' and winding sheet. Jessie, Maggie and Myna washed Heather's lifeless body before dressing her in the shroud she'd made herself. Five heather sprigs embroidered on the front; one for each child, living and passed, tugged at their hearts. Dougal placed the funeral board on the seats of six chairs. Maggie spread the winding sheet as she would a tablecloth and as they all stood with heads bowed in silence, he lifted Heather from her deathbed then laid her gently on the board. Myna brought two plates, placing them carefully on Heather's chest – one filled with salt, the other with fresh earth from the garden. No one doubted the immortality of Heather's soul, or that she would indeed return to the earth, but they still honoured the custom.

The bell-ringer walked through the village for two days, house to house to the kirkyard. Farmers put their livestock into their barns, all means of business closed, dark curtains concealing any sign of life behind every window. The women baked oatcakes, bread and scones, soups and stews simmered on the hearth.

"Heather will be proud of this," Maggie sniffed, cutting an enormous clootie dumpling into slices.

Myna stroked her arm. "Of course she will, that smells so good it may well raise the dead."

Tevia, Tavia, Donald, together with three other young people chosen for their love of Heather (and their ability to stay awake) were tasked with watching over her body through the nights, before being relieved from dawn till dusk by dark-clad mourners filing through the house to touch her forehead and bless her journey. Such was this careful attention, not even the devil would get near Heather. Even though the youngsters took great pride in carrying out this important task, the slightest noise curdled their blood and rattled their bones. They did pray for Heather's soul, but more for the night to pass before the shadows from the oil lamps demented their young minds. These 'dead' days dragged like a weary winter but were necessary to respect Heather's wishes and custom.

Tom's health took a turn for the worse after he was told of her passing and he now appeared to be in a state of constant bewilderment. He would refer to Lily as Heather, often becoming confused by her 'sudden' appearance in his home. On the day of the funeral Jessie left Tom asleep, wrapped Lily in a bundle of blankets and set off to join her family. She asked his sister Mary to sit with him, to avoid subjecting him to what was sure to be a long, unhappy day. Mary agreed – a relief to them both. Jessie had little desire to manage Tom the day she was to bury her mother, and Mary was more than happy to steer clear of any misconstrued involvement with Heather's forest friends her attendance might imply. During her slow walk to the house Jessie's mind flipped between distress caused by Tom's health, and amusement by Mary's behaviour. When Lily's wriggling progressed to whimpering, she stopped beside a large juniper bush. The moment she eased her grip Lily settled, so she sat on the stone wall allowing her body to relax. "Sorry, baby, I'm new to this, I was sure I'd have your granny to help me."

She ran her free hand over the green and silvery leaves, observing the blue berries. Her mother's voice sounded in her mind.

"Don't be picking them Jessie, they're still babies and the birds are waiting to be fed."

"How do you know they're babies?" Jessie recalled her own curiosity.

"They're blue as a summer sky until they grow up, then they become black like a dark, moonless night."

Jessie had pointed to the short, stubby bush next to it. "So why are those yellow?"

Remembering her mother's laugh filled Jessie's heart.

"Because that's a boy bush; not so pretty."

She appreciated it was possibly her first lesson in the way mother nature works, followed by the knowledge that if she noticed juniper sprigs pinned to a coat or displayed on a window ledge, the owner fretted over the presence of witches. She wiped her wet cheeks and at the risk of disturbing Lily's deep slumber, decided this was not a time to dither or torture her soul further. The walk took her past the stone cottages she'd known since birth and with each step she remembered the countless times her mother walked with her. Their small enclave comprised ten identical homes evenly spaced with various outbuildings beyond. A low wall surrounding the entire area from the banks of the river to the end of the forest gave it a self-contained community feel. She remembered the day her mother took her to the farthest edge of the property to pick wild daffodils.

"What's out there?" Jessie had pointed to the craggy mountains in the distance.

"That's God's country, and he shares it with Mother nature."

Heather's eyes had scanned the countryside that never failed to stir her blood. Jessie's inquisitive mind had worked hard. "Do they have children?"

She would never forget the way the sun lit up her mother's eyes so even the grass melted away.

"Of course! We are all Mother Nature's children."

It was after she passed the fourth cottage that something tweaked her attention. She stopped, looked around and listened, but all appeared normal. She tucked Lily's blanket under her chin but when she looked up again, she caught her breath. Her eyes darted up and down the street, following the line of windows. Flowers from the Beltane and May Day celebrations no longer brightened the homes but there was not a juniper sprig in sight. White heather hung in enormous bunches inside the windows of every cottage in the street, each door brandishing a circular wreath of purple heather entwined with lily of the valley. The street remained quiet, no faces peered from the windows, but Jessie's heart almost burst with overwhelming gratitude.

She reached her mother's gate willing her jangled nerves and anxious stomach to settle, then she viewed the house she cherished. Originally built to house people and their livestock, the low height of the dry packed stone cottage belied the lofty space inside, so a straightforward renovation resulted in separate living, eating and sleeping areas. Heather pioneered this conversion when she married Dougal then moved into what was still a thatched, one-room dwelling, with a wooden fence partition down the middle separating humans from their livestock. Jessie had heard the story many times over the years but it still amused and impressed her.

After a long night shovelling runny cow dung out the front door when one of their herd of three had fallen ill, Heather had thwacked the broom on the stone floor for the umpteenth time and screeched:

"This is an abomination; we are not animals! Unless you sort this out, Dougal, I swear I will take my gibbles and go back to my Mam, I'm not living in a byre."

Dougal's flaughter had hit the floor and Heather's hands flew to her ears. A pig squealed and Dougal's breath almost blew out the oil lamps. "I hear you Heather, God knows the whole croft hears you, but I cannae tonight."

Heather wiped her dirty hands on an already grubby apron, scowled and strode towards him. "Well, tomorrow will do." Her eyes flashed. "And if you've broken that flaughter, you better know how to fix it, it's the best tool we have."

Dougal had picked up his discarded spade, inspected it for damage, and with an exaggerated bow to Heather and a thank you to the God of tools, they cleaned up the mess in silence before falling into bed exhausted. Heather looked forward to her new living area and Dougal prayed for strength. It wasn't long before she convinced the other crofters to follow suit; making sure they employed Dougal to do the building. His cheeks still bulged with hot porridge when he was told he would convert all the cottages. He'd dropped his spoon.

"So, I'm a builder now, am I?"

Heather sidled up to him, wrapped her arms around his broad shoulders and nuzzled his neck. Her breath warmed his ears. "You'll do whatever needs done to feed the three of us."

Dougal's bowl had hit the floor when he swung around. "Three?" His eyes bulged.

"Aye," her laugh brightened the room, "so you better get on it for you've also a crib to build."

Warmed by the memory Jessie inhaled a deep breath, squeezed Lily once again and pushed open the gate. She avoided the rows of white heather lining the footpath to her mother's front door lest her heart burst, but the aroma swept into her nostrils, filling her lungs the moment she walked in the door. Maggie rushed to meet her, carrying Lily inside.

"Thank you, Maggie, how are they?" She removed her headscarf and straightened her skirt as if she were a nurse appearing for duty. Maggie frowned, cocked her head towards the bedroom and lowered her eyes. "Dire Jess, dire."

Jessie took a deep breath then walked past her mother's body into the room. She remembered the last time she'd seen her father and brothers look so smart had been on her wedding day, and it tested her resolve not to collapse onto her mother's bed, hold her father and cry until she ran out of tears. Dougal sat hunched at the edge of the wooden box bed he'd shared with Heather for fewer years than he'd expected. Angus and Fraser stood still, silent like young soldiers waiting for their commands. The room they'd forever known to be their mother's sacred place, crammed with pewter vases of heather in every colour, now smothered them with the cloak of darkness only grief possesses. She placed a light hand on Dougal's shoulder. Stifled sobs hiding within his thick tweed jacket trembled against her skin. A fleeting glance at the boys' ashen faces confirmed her suspicion ... no one was managing *the shock of Heather's passing and this would be a day that would scar each of their hearts.*

"I'm sorry Da, we'll need to be leaving soon." She stroked his thick hands. "Are you all right? Can you manage?"

Dougal turned, lifted his shoulders and sucked in a breath. Jessie squeezed her lips together when heavy tears spilled from his dark-shadowed eyes onto his crumpled face. His choked reply was almost unrecognisable. "Aye."

She got up, pushed Angus and Fraser out, pulled the door closed and after swallowing the lump in her throat, fired at Angus. "You can't hang around him staring into space."

Angus flinched from the slap of her words. "It's all right for you, but we live here and he doesn't say a word. He sits on the bed all day."

Fraser grunted. "Hardly eats a thing."

Angus threw Fraser a scowl. "And all he does is complain about food, even though the kitchen is heaving."

Fraser wrapped his arms around himself. "It's not the same as Mammie's."

"You see?" Angus clutched his hair.

Jessie slapped both their arms. "Don't tell me about being all right. Only three days ago I was on my own in my garden giving birth, and now Mammie's gone without ever seeing my child." She ran her fingers through hair now looking as if she'd been pulling at it all morning. Her eyebrows almost met in the middle as her lips curled inwards. "This is the day we put Mammie in the ground, so you two need to get yourselves together ... for Da."

Fraser's gasp calmed her rant, softening her tone. "Fraser, how are you going to drive the cart if you can hardly breathe?"

Angus shot a frown at Jessie then turned to his brother. He stretched an arm around Fraser's quivering shoulders. "You'll be fine, and you'll do fine by Mam."

"I'll make us some tea," Jessie groaned, "we'll all feel better for it."

Maggie sat in Heather's favourite armchair by the window, Lily asleep in her arms. Jessie tiptoed across to them. "She'll have me up all night if you keep spoiling her."

Maggie signalled for Jessie to bend down then whispered. "You leave us alone. Didn't do you any harm now, did it?"

Jessie swung on her heels and headed back to making tea. Heather's death overshadowed any post birth attention her body needed, so now standing waiting for the water to boil, her muscles complained, her legs buckled, her breasts ached. She ran weary hands up and down her aching thighs, contemplating the day ahead. A glimpse of Angus still comforting Fraser tweaked her stubborn conscience, and she chewed her bottom lip. Her own heart ached with desire to have her mother back for any amount of time God would gift her, and she knew Fraser's gentle character would struggle under the weight of having to hold his own. Her mind shifted to Angus, and as quick as day turns to night her jaw clenched. Sparring with her older brother was commonplace, especially after Tom's collapse. In her opinion her mother's wrangling with Angus, and the constant worry, had drained her energy. Memories of her mother's pained expression came to mind and her fists clenched. Bubbling water disrupted her contemplations, so she filled the teapot. She waited for it to brew, twisting a washcloth, pondering how much Angus's interference in her mother's lifestyle and her own subsequent situation had contributed to their mother's ill health. She squeezed the cloth then tossed it into the sink.

Maggie joined her, hands on hips. "I see your maternal hormones haven't softened your mood."

Jessie raised her head to the roof lest a tear escape. "Oh, Maggie, my head and my heart are beating each other and I can't seem to calm either." Her body shivered as she lifted her palms to her face. Maggie pulled her into her arms.

"They'll sort themselves out without too much interference from you. These are the hard days, but after we've laid her to rest and sent her spirit home, she'll settle in your heart and help you find your way."

Jessie wiped her swollen eyes and crossed her hands over her heart. Maggie placed her hand over Jessie's. "Yes, right there."

Heather had not wanted them to walk to the kirkyard.

"It's too far. If it rains, you'll all get soaked and end up with me."

Exasperated by her peculiar ways, Dougal had pleaded. "Heather, it's the way it's done."

She wouldn't budge:

"Not for me it isn't, and I'll not be in a coffin. I don't want my winding sheet ruined. It took me weeks to embroider it."

So, with eight spokes carved with love and dedication supporting the funeral board, the men carried Heather out of her home and placed her on a low, four-wheeled trap, driven by Fraser, pulled by their two well-groomed, black-plumed Clydesdales. Perfectly braided ropes secured her shroud around her neck, waist and ankles. Jessie entwined her mother's home-made ropes with white heather stalks and lilies before pinning all colours of heather to the board beneath her body. Dougal insisted Jessie sit with Fraser. She tried to argue but despite his despair he glowered. "You've given birth and lost your Mammie. Don't be daft. You're a mother now, your wee lass needs you well."

Everyone else followed on foot with the bell-ringer sounding their steps. Each family from the crofters' cottages completed the gathering, but when the horses turned into the village Jessie caught her breath and grabbed Fraser's arm. Outside each house, shop, business, women with their daughters stood with bowed heads, clutching bunches of white heather. Her heart burst at the sight of her mother's favourite flowers and an entire village showing love ... or at least respect.

Father Coyle stood at this window watching the cortege go by. His nostrils flared, his fingers curled and his teeth chewed his fat lips.

Chapter 14

AFTER A FITFUL NIGHT'S sleep Myna woke early, the
weight of her grieving heart pinning her to her bed. She heaved
herself up, fetched her shawl, tied a headscarf under her chin,
then checked on her girls. She found them in a half-asleep daze,
tucked into each other like one large spoon waiting for a
bigger pot. "Girls, I'm going to the village but I won't be long."
 The twins looked up through sleepy eyes and nodded. After
swapping her slippers for boots, Myna hurried sure-footed
through the forest until she reached the pond. Stepping close to
the edge, she gazed into the crystal-clear water, still, flat
without even the attention of a dragonfly to wrinkle its
surface. She picked up a small pebble, pink as a baby's cheek,
and tossed it in, rippling the water, but within seconds the
pebble disappeared into the abyss. She envisaged Heather
sitting on the large rock on the opposite side. After a silent
prayer she glanced right towards the furrowed path leading to
the village then turned left. The forest closed in, wrapping her
in a blanket of green and brown. Unforgiving bramble bushes
snagged her skirts and her eyes inspected every inch in front
before she allowed her feet to follow. The gentle rustle of
overhead branches disappeared, sucking the light with them
until she needed to navigate by instinct as ancient hunters did.
Only she and Heather knew this obscure path left for them by
those gone before – those who also needed an escape route. Her
feet did her bidding, and before long, light filtered in from
above and the trees thinned enough to allow her to stand clear
of overhead branches. She took a minute to catch her breath
and absorb the distant squawk of blackbirds being chased by
buzzard bullies, squirrels scratching up rough bark, hedgehogs
crunching through dead leaves. A few steps further a clearing
emerged, scarcely big enough for half a dozen girls to play
Ring-a-Rosie. Myna stepped into this ethereal verdant patch;

grass, soft and plump as if it had never known the pressure of human feet. She stared at the skies and inhaled its purity. When her heartbeat no longer sounded in her ears, she stepped towards the centre of the clearing and rested her hand on the low stone wall of an ancient well. Her hand slid along the rough, mossy surface like an eel around kelp, the damp, satiated leaves tickling her inquiring fingers. When she leaned over the narrow edge, darkness drew her eyes into a void deeper than an echo might travel. Relief settled in her bones. Although she had supposed she may well find her way back to this well, she sometimes worried if after so many years it may have become lost in the forest's growth ... or her memory. A shiver unsettled her confidence. It was her sense of foreboding and Heather's warnings which had prompted her to make sure, but the well was only halfway to where they would need to travel, so she took a moment to pray it may never be necessary, then left.

Retracing her steps proved easier than expected so she paused, breathing in the air, damp, heavy, infused with a mixture of woodland essence. Picking wood sage gave her the opportunity to replenish her stock – and provided an excuse for being out. She was still bent over when a noise startled her. Straight ahead a young boy stood dishevelled and snivelling. Her heart skipped a beat and her wood sage landed at her feet when she bolted upright.

"Dear God, laddie, who are you? What on earth are you doing here?"

The young boy stared out of purple-rimmed eyes from a face smeared with as much muck as snot. Rooted to the spot, he trembled from his toes to his hair. They stood gazing at each other until his condition overshadowed Myna's fright from being discovered this close to the well. She eased towards him. "What has happened to you?"

He took a step back and pushed his hands into his pockets. "I'm lost."

Myna eyed him. "You certainly are," she looked him up and down then rested her fists on her hips, "and how did you get into that state?"

He looked down at his muddy boots, ripped trousers, torn jumper. "I was chasing a hare and just kept following it ... now I'm lost."

Myna cocked her head. "You look like the hare attacked you. Is that blood?"

His hands shot to his face. "It's just scratches from the bracken," he blurted, and wiped furiously.

Myna scanned the area then back at the boy. "I haven't seen many hares around here so you've probably lost that too. I think you should get home now."

The boy's eyes widened; his curls wobbled. "Yes, yes, I just want to get home. Can you show me?"

Myna gave him directions back to the main road – as far away from her cottage as possible. He stood expressionless as his body still shuddered. She doubted he was fit to remember. "You're in a right mess. Do you want me to take you home?" she offered, reluctantly.

He looked at his feet. "No, no, I'll find my way now."

Myna stepped back. "What's your name?"

"Callan."

Myna deliberated for a minute. "And who's your Mam?"

"Laura McLean."

Myna's breath caught in her throat. "Oh my, I know your Mam. You better get home and sort yourself out. When your Da sees the state of your clothes, you'll be in the mire."

Callan nodded. "Aye, I'll be away then."

Unsure of his ability to find his way, she watched the boy scurry off then disappear into the thickets. She looked around still dumbfounded by the boy's appearance, then picked up her wood sage and headed home.

❧

Jessie hummed softly, lulling Lily to sleep as she walked through the forest to Myna's house. Unlike the fresh air out on the road, within the forest it still hung heavy, waiting for a cool breeze to sweep it away. Birds and insects lumbered from one spot to another, slowed by the lingering summer's weight, the overpowering aroma of blooms and pollen cloaking every living thing. Jessie slowed her pace to absorb each sound and smell and when she reached the cottage, she stood for a moment enjoying the vibrant colours of Myna's summer garden. Her love of this place, the women within, had intensified since her mother's death, so now it didn't take long for her to get her house in order, find a routine and return to her obligations in the forest. She harboured a longing to move in with these exceptional, supportive women, to make the cottage her permanent home. She conceded it was impossible and relied on her sense of belonging to something important for solace. The weeks following Heather's funeral were bleak for all. Lily became the sun shining through their tears. Her sweet nature surprised no one, everyone trusted Heather's spirit was at work. Jessie was sure it was her mother trying to comfort her.

"It's her way of making up for leaving you so soon." Maggie said.

Jessie grinned. "It may well be, and long may it continue."

Myna, Maggie and the twins couldn't get enough of Lily, fighting each other for the chance to play with her. Jessie loved to see her surrounded by such love and was sincerely grateful for the help. Her days tested her stamina and Tom's health denied her any practical help with chores or baby minding. However, she persevered, determined to do her best for her father, Tom and Lily, with every shred of strength she possessed. She dreamed each night, waking with her mind full, but Lily's early morning demands prevented her from recalling the details. It was only during her daily walks through the forest to Myna's she took the opportunity to sift through the remnants trying to unearth anything meaningful or significant. She was sure her mother would not only visit her dreams, but she would also guide her, now she was the current first daughter. Tom would not be a long-term father so Lily's future depended on her. Making the right decisions would ensure both her safety and her ability to continue their line. She would bear no more children so she would immerse herself in motherhood, learning and healing. She'd contemplated meditating with the stones but Myna advised her against it.

"It's too soon, Jessie." Her words crept from deep inside, careful not to be overheard. "Your Mam's only just rested but you are not. You can't prompt the stones to give you what you are looking for. They will guide you and provide what you need, but only when you need it."

Jessie didn't doubt Myna. However, she also trusted her gut and worried Myna may be withholding. She wiped her hair from her forehead. "Mam trusted you with her life, her beliefs, her history."

Myna folded her arms. Her voice remained gentle; each word wrapped in sincerity. "Your impatience works for you in many things but our ways need time, attention and understanding or you risk distorting the true meaning of your blessings. Your work here is vital but you must always know there are those who believe it's dangerous and will try to destroy it."

Jessie felt her spine tingle and her fingers curled around her apron ties. The suggestion of anything destroying the gifts passed down from her mother, and those before her, riled her more than Tom's mother's Sunday morning interrogations. She forced her teeth to part. "I will allow no one to destroy what we have here, it is our legacy, my child's destiny."

Myna uncurled Jessie's fingers from the trapped ties. Her voice softened. "My child, we love you and will protect you, but I want you to be kind to yourself, the way you help the women here." She put her arm around Jessie's stiff shoulders. "Look around you, there is nothing but love and compassion amongst us and right now that's all you need for what you were born to do." Lily screeched from the corner and Myna laughed. "And it looks like Lily needs to eat."

Jessie folded her arms and stood pondering her way forward. Across the room Maggie watched her before exchanging a glance with Myna. She called out. "Jess, Lily needs a feed, she's not happy waiting."

Jessie put her musings aside, called Tevia to take her place at the herb table, and settled into the chair normally occupied by her mother. Feeding Lily always eased her heartache, stilling her fractious mind. She marvelled at her body's ability to feed and nourish another human being, reasoning this was one of God's ways of creating a fiercely protective bond between mother and child. She observed the room. Maggie's fingers worked carefully, with gentle attention to a poultice she was applying to an elderly woman's elbow. Myna sat huddled in the corner counselling a tearful Laura, pressing a cold compress to her left eye. The twins muttered, heads bobbing and knocking each other, similar to lovebirds on a branch. Tevia crushed herbs and Tavia braided threads with deft hands and a cadence born of practise and devotion. Three women huddled on the couch waiting for Myna, Maggie or

Jessie to attend to them. They arrived looking solemn, shawls wrapped tight, held between fingers which either trembled, grasped or fidgeted. Jessie watched them, confident that if they were strangers when they entered, they would be friends when they left. She returned their gaze, followed by smiles, and as Lily suckled, the entire room took on its own unique rhythm and mood. A whiff from the garden floated through the open windows and her eyes closed. She surrendered to her body and her senses, content in the knowledge her mother remained amongst them. Gorged and sleepy, Lily sounded her contentment with a burp, disrupting everyone's occupations and sending a ripple of laughter around the room.

"Well, you can always count on a bairn to lighten the mood," giggled Maggie as she tightened the bandage around a treated elbow.

Tevia giggled, and with a wink from Jessie, she sprung across to take Lily off into the corner where a clean nappy awaited. Jessie joined Myna and bent down. Laura's head hung low and Myna reacted to Jessie's grim expression with a shrug. Jessie knelt, took Laura's hands and caressed them, careful to avoid her bruised fingers now missing nails. Laura's neck struggled to support her head, and Jessie flinched at the scabbed-over bald patches on her crown. She gently lifted Laura's chin until level with hers. Despite Myna's best efforts Laura's left eye remained black, swollen shut.

Heat in Jessie's chest fired her. "This must stop! How much more of this can you take?" she blurted.

Laura's tears trickled down her face, and although her lips moved, no words formed. Jessie's rage burned in her throat. She glared at Myna. "It's enough! We need to stop this before he kills her."

Myna caught Jessie's elbow and flashed a warning. "Calm, Jessie. We'll fix her up then let her rest here a bit before making any trouble."

Jessie pulled away. "Trouble? Look at her. How many times must he be lifted only to get out the next morning? If Mr Drummond can't see what's going on, and get him locked up for good, what's the use in having an overseer?" Jessie's cheeks raged as her eyes fired daggers. Myna yanked her sleeve and motioned her outside. Jessie stomped out. Every eye in the room followed her from under furrowed brows. Myna swung her around.

"Jessie, I'm warning you now. Laura's in no state to listen to what she already knows. Her poor boy is demented with it, and her worry is not for herself. If that boy takes it upon himself, well, God knows what'll happen."

Jessie ripped a stem off a climbing sweet pea and her nostrils flared. "Myna, how can you stand it?"

Myna seized her shoulders. "Hush now, we'll mend her."

"I'll speak to him," Jessie raged.

"You must not!" Myna's grip tightened until Jessie winced. "None of us knows what goes on behind closed doors. I've never seen her in this state before, so my bones tell me we may not know the complete story. She looks as if she's been in some fight for sure. I'll have a word with Mr Drummond. He may have heard something, but he's only the overseer of the crofts … and takes more than his share of free drams to look the other way."

Jessie dropped the shredded sweet pea, pulled away and crossed her arms. "Myna, it's not right. Every day another one arrives with fingers worked to the bone, some without shoes, others with bairns not much older than themselves."

Myna shook her head. "You're right, Jess. That's why we're here, but we can only help so much. We need to be cautious or we'll find ourselves in bigger trouble than them. There's already rumbling, and the path to this house is wearing thin. The powers won't find it too hard to get what they need to destroy us. From the ones who can't hold their water, or from the ones they can pay."

Jessie grumbled. "I hear you, Myna, but it drives me crazy."

Myna wrapped an arm around Jessie's stiff shoulder. "I know, but can you not see how far we've come, thanks to your mother?" She squeezed her tight, and Jessie's tension eased. "And now, you."

Jessie's mind shifted to Father Coyle. Myna didn't need to name him; she was certain he would be happier if she didn't exist. His influence over Angus jangled her nerves like a woodpecker in a frenzy, but he was her brother and hell would freeze over before she would allow him any part in whatever devious plan the priest was cooking. Angus was obviously avoiding her since the funeral, and her father did little to appease the foreboding circling her heart when thinking of him. Myna implored her to reflect and act wisely, but her spirit wrestled. She didn't need the stones to suggest Father Coyle was her arch-enemy, but it was now up to her to make sure Angus didn't follow suit. Unless it was already too late.

Chapter 15

LILY GREW INTO A perfect, healthy infant. After only a few weeks she slept through the night, allowing Jessie to rest, regain her strength and mourn the loss of her beloved mother. A contented child, she chortled her way through each day, arms and legs stretching and reaching out like eager young beanstalks twisting around trees. Innate sense of timing or not, she always gave Jessie something to smile about each time her heart ached.

Dougal's heartache permeated his entire house, and neither Fraser nor Angus could dispel his sadness. Only Lily held that power, so it became Jessie's daily mission to visit him. She claimed it was Lily's need to see her grandpa, but she used the opportunity to do the housework, lay the fire and prepare a meal. In the weeks after losing Heather, Dougal didn't notice the work she did, but when his forty days of mourning passed and his physical grieving eased, he grasped the extent of her efforts, appreciating how difficult it must be. One morning when she arrived, he surprised her with a hug. Not wanting to wake Lily he lowered his head to Jessie's ear. "I'm so sorry Jess."

Jessie handed Lily to him. "For what, Da?"

Dougal cocked his head. "You don't fool me. I wouldn't have lived through this without you propping me up. God knows you've enough to do but you've looked after me too."

Jessie stroked his unshaven face and looked down at Lily in his arms. "Not so long ago you were holding me, and Mammie looked after us both. We need you and I'm here for however long you need me."

Dougal's eyes filled. "I miss her every day."

Jessie smiled. "I know Da, me too. So, let me make some soup, those useless brothers of mine will have you starved."

Dougal defended his sons. "Aye, they're hopeless I know, but they're taking this hard too."

"They might be, but they were hopeless before – from all ma's spoiling."

Dougal huffed. "Aye, yer right, I'll have a word with them tonight."

"Good, tell them it's time they cleaned their own chanties. I've enough wiping up to do after Tom."

The remark about Tom stalled their banter, and they turned from each other. Jessie started on a pot of soup while Dougal fetched wood from the outside bunker. It was enough to cope with their grief without mulling Tom's condition. That would come in its own time, so both Dougal and Jessie chose avoidance by silent, mutual agreement. Jessie finished the chores, did a stir of the soup and a last sweep of the floor before wrestling Lily from his arms. His forlorn expression tugged at her heart so she hugged him. "Da, we'll be back tomorrow."

Lily's gurgle disrupted the moment, so she turned away before the conversation became maudlin.

"Tomorrow then," Dougal called after her.

"Remember to shave," she called, without looking back. Her grief remained parcelled, timed within her busy routine, and she wouldn't risk allowing her floodgates to be opened. Not until she was strong enough not to drown.

⟨❀⟩

Her hair bristled when the rapid-fire knocking on the door reminded her it was Sunday morning, which meant a visit from her mother-in-law. "Dear Mammie, give me strength," she muttered.

"Halloo!" shrieked Jean.

Jessie flung her dishcloth onto the hearth then straightened her hair and apron before loping to the door. Jean's hand floated in mid-air when the door flew open. "Good morning, Jean, you can stop knocking, I'm here." Jessie stepped aside resisting the temptation to grab the tightly pinned bun sitting at the nape of Jean's neck when it swept past her, rolling her eyes instead. "Do come in."

Jean marched straight to the bedroom where Tom lay fast asleep. Jessie followed, watching from the doorway. Jean conducted her weekly routine of touching Tom's forehead with the back of her hand, straightening his blankets, inspecting every item on the bedside table, from over and under her wire-framed spectacles. After whipping the curtains open and kneeling at his bedside, she placed her Bible on his chest and recited whichever prayers she deemed necessary. She called upon every saint to get to work on Tom's behalf – and fix whatever ailed him – starting with St Camillus, the general all-rounder of illness and healing, ending with a heartfelt plea to the almighty Archangel Raphael. If Tom looked particularly off-colour and perhaps requiring a miracle, she implored St Anthony to work harder. Jessie invoked the calming spirit of her mother to prevent her from screaming while Tom remained still and oblivious to the surrounding battle. The prayers complete, Jean invited herself for tea. Jessie squirmed when she settled herself in the chair which in Jessie's mind would forever belong to her mother. She quizzed Jessie on how often Dr MacFarlane visited, whether he'd prescribed anything additional, and if Jessie remained diligent in her administration of Tom's medicines. Jessie answered only what Jean needed to hear – true or otherwise. When satisfied, Jean considered Lily and her lips parted enough to hint at a smile. "Now, where is my grandchild?" Her eyes flitted around the way a sparrow looks for worms, and Jessie envisioned Jean's neat little head flipping off her neck, into the fireplace quicker than St Anthony might save her, but she forced a smile.

"I'm sorry. I fed and put her down only a minute ago."

Jean feigned disappointment. "Oh dear, that's a pity, perhaps next time."

Jessie almost stirred through the bottom of her teacup. "Of course, next time."

Jean's lack of interest in Lily no longer annoyed her. Her behaviour clearly suggested until Tom became healthy and able, Lily would remain an extension of Jessie ... and Heather. Jessie's initial disappointment soon swung to relief. If Tom were to die, an overbearing grandmother using Lily to fill her own void would be far more intolerable than the grief his passing would bring. She expected if Tom was no longer with her, she would never see his family again.

Their absence from Heather's funeral did not go unnoticed. Robert appeared at the last minute, without a word to Jessie. He walked with the procession, head down, hands pushed so far into his pockets, his shoulders hunched further with each step. Mary babysat and Jean paid her condolences with the delivery of a batch of scones, which Jessie fed to the pigs that evening. She conceded Tom's family was uncomfortable with Heather's ways and her reputation. However, their inability to step up for the family Tom married into only fed her resentment, so part of her relished their discomfort. Her mother's ways were now her ways, so she cared less about their disfavour. She fully intended to raise Lily as a first daughter, but she understood if Tom were healthy his family would make it problematic. Jean's eyes scanning the room as she sipped her tea reminded her of Father Coyle so her grip on her teacup tightened. If Jean picked up anything to suggest she was guilty of alternative healing or pagan worship, she would run to the priest faster than a stiff wind could carry her, and Jessie would suffer another of his impromptu visits. She reminded herself to confront Angus about his relationship with the priest.

Jean reached out her cup. "I'll be going now."

Jessie took the cup to the kitchen but Jean followed her. When she reached the sink Jessie's spine tingled.

"What's this?" Jean held a small brown bottle up to Jessie's face. Her feet clenched but a moment's silence allowed her to hold still the hand wanting to rip the bottle from Jean's bony fingers. She focused on her breath but Jean's eyes fixed on her.

"No need to panic, Jean." She surprised herself with the steadiness of her voice, but her brain hunted for the right words. "It's some medicine to help with my milk. You know, after the trauma of the birth and losing my Mam."

Jean fiddled with the bottle while Jessie prayed for the sweat tickling her neck to stay hidden. Jean shrugged, put the bottle down, then turned to reach for her shawl. Jessie held her breath. Jean opened the door then turned, her narrowed, beady eyes scarcely visible.

"I don't remember getting medicine like this when my bairns were born."

Jessie understood it was a question, not a statement. She coaxed the words out, smoothing off the sharp edges before speaking. "Did your mother die the day Tom was born?"

When the door closed, Jessie exhaled and leaned against the wall before hastily tucking the bottle into her apron pocket. Tom snored, so she walked to the bedroom and stood over him, breathing deeply to steady her heartbeat. It still amazed her that the man she fell in love with, and planned to spend her life with, looked so serene in sleep yet in wakefulness he seemed to have not fully returned from where his dreams took him. Each time he woke, a little more of 'her' Tom stayed behind and it broke her heart. She traced a finger over his forehead, tenderly easing his hair back. She wanted to remember every detail, for one day she would need to describe him to Lily.

A squeal jolted her, so she smoothed Tom's blanket before going to Lily's crib. No sooner did she lift her when more knocking boomed through the house. Clutching her child and muttering under her breath about lightning striking Father Coyle, she opened the door to find Angus on her doorstep – holding a basket.

He shrugged his shoulders. "Don't look so pleased to see me."

Jessie grimaced. "I'm sorry, I was expecting someone else. Someone not so friendly, and certainly not bearing gifts."

He followed her into the house and shoved the basket of wild berries from the manor gardens into her free hand before tickling Lily's chin. Jessie thanked him and sat the basket on the hearth. He settled into her mother's chair and again Jessie's teeth nipped the inside of her lip. She resolved to move the chair the minute he left.

He frowned. "What's wrong?"

Jessie sat on Tom's home-made rocking chair with Lily nestled in her arms. "Nothing, but I'm surprised to see you. I want to think you're here to see how we're doing, and spend some time with your niece, but your fidgeting suggests not."

Angus wiped his forehead and leaned forward. "I am concerned about you, and of course I want to see Lily."

"Your face tells a different story, so spit it out."

"You know I disapproved of what Mam got up to with Maggie and those spaes."

Jessie tried to ignore the sudden fluttering in her stomach.

"She's gone, Jess, and Tom's not right, so you should stay away from them. Stay home, look after yourself – and Lily."

Lily whined so Jessie loosened her grip. "Is this you, Angus, or is it your friend Father Coyle speaking?"

He snarled. "He's not my friend Jess."

Jessie pulled Lily's blanket tight and the rockers of the chair crunched against the stone floor. She leaned towards him. "If he's not your friend, you're spending more time with him than you should."

Angus grabbed his hair. "He got me my job, Jess! He gets Wilson to spend money and I keep him updated, nothing more."

Jessie sprang from the rocker and settled Lily back into her crib. She returned to stand over him. "Update him on what? Did you update him on Mam? Or me?" Her face burned.

Angus jumped up and stood toe-to-toe. Jessie searched his face as the heat between them intensified. She watched his eyes tighten when he spoke. "If you think I would hurt Mam, you've lost your wits. You know how we've lived because of her beliefs. You might want it but Fraser and I had no control, we're fed up with it.

Jessie stepped back. Her mouth dropped open. "Choose? Are you mad? I didn't get to choose either." She pushed her fists into her chest but her tone softened. "It's who she was, who she was born to be, so if people disapprove that's up to them. She never did a harmful thing in her life."

Angus reached for his hair. "People hate it. Don't you get it, Jess? This is Church of Scotland country now, which is bad enough, and the history of this place provokes suspicion."

Red curls framed Jessie's flushed face in a ring of fire. "The history here is sacred." Her jaw stiffened. "They burned or slaughtered our grandmothers here, and those before them. Or simply drove them out of their own lands to survive with nothing!"

"That matters no more, most of these villagers only care about feeding their own. Now with Coyle's church and school here, they'll side where it suits them best."

Jessie's nostrils flared. "You mean they'll run with the hounds and hide with the hares? Not all of them, Angus, not all of them."

He sat. *"The sensible ones, yes, don't think all these followers of yours have gone unnoticed."* His head jerked towards her. *"Stop pacing. Sit down!"*

Jessie's chest lifted so much she almost lost her balance. "Don't you come in here thinking you know more than you do. My 'followers' are simply poor women with real troubles, and all we do is help them in the way we know how."

"You're doing more than that from what I hear, and there's more than a few men riled around here."

"Men! Aye, it would be them filling your head with shite. The same lot who drinks their wages before they've even earned them. Only happy when they're brawling, plundering their wives, singing merry songs about sad times."

"Jessie, stop!" Angus jumped and seized her shoulders. "It's not your place to mend anybody's woes but your own. You have a bairn to look after and Tom isn't right. Leave those spaes to it but you mind your own."

Tears burned but Jessie's simmering rage gathered strength. "I won't have you standing in my house telling me what to mind. Tom has long gone with the spirits and I'll be mourning him too soon. I'll take good care of Lily and anyone else who needs it."

He took a step forward. "Tom is a problem, Jess, there're rumours."

"For heaven's sake, Angus, stop with the rumours, I'm not interested. Something happened to Tom, and he's not been right since ... I've tried everything."

Angus glared. "People think it's you, they think you've cursed him."

The power of his words sucked the air from the room leaving them both speechless. After a few seconds she reached out but he stepped away.

"You can't believe that! My whole heart belongs to Tom. My entire life on this earth is to be spent with him. Why would you even think I would hurt him?" No amount of self-control stemmed her tears. They tumbled down her cheeks and a flash of regret swept across Angus's face. Her opinion seesawed, did he know better or did he believe the rumours?

Angus slumped into the chair and his head dropped into his hands. "Jess, you need to hear me. Mam isn't here to protect you, Da hardly has the strength to carry his grief, and those spaes are not your family. Maggie can't protect you."

She cut him off. *"You're wrong, Angus. They are my family. Why bring Maggie into this? Mam trusted her with her life and so do I."*

He threw his head back and sniggered. "Maggie is an old widow who loves a dram and can't hold her water. She might love you and sure she loved Mam, but if you're expecting more from her than she can offer, you'll be sorely disappointed."

Jessie breathed deep trying to ease the dragon stirring within. Her love for Angus, sure as the sunrise, struggled with her desire to throttle him at this moment. The contest bruised her heart. She uncurled her fingers and pushed her wild hair back. Suddenly, her mother's words rattled around in her mind like bright river stones in a strong current. She heard the whisper break through the clatter.

"Our journey is not without turmoil and heartache."

She composed herself and straightened. Angus's expression unnerved her. He leaned back in the chair. She took a step closer and her words floated towards him, clear and clipped. "What do I need protection from?"

Angus stood, his cheeks reddening. "If some had their way that house in the woods would've burned to the ground long ago. You must be careful, Jess, if you're not this will not end well."

Despite his threat she met his glare. "You make your choices, Angus. In my house I'll make mine."

He marched to the door, flinging it open before turning back. "Your house? If Tom dies, they'll throw you out before he's cold."

The door slammed shut and Jessie stood with her eyes burning holes into the back of it. In the silence she held herself tight, willing her breath to silence the commotion in her head. Before long only her heartbeat sounded in her ears as her arms unfolded and dropped by her sides. Her eyes slipped shut and she relaxed, inhaling the scent of white heather wafting through the windows. She reached into her apron, clasped her trembling fingers around the brown bottle and sighed.

"I know Mam. I know."

Chapter 16

MAGGIE'S DELIGHT WHEN SHE saw Jessie on her doorstep ended when she noticed dark shadows under her eyes. After a hasty glance back along the path, she took Lily, guiding Jessie to sit before rushing to place a teapot on the hearth. Jessie removed her shawl and flung it over the arm before slumping into a chair. The comforting aroma of fresh oatcakes and wildflowers saturated her lungs, so it didn't surprise her to see jugs of fresh white heather on the fire mantle. She hadn't visited Maggie for some time and now struggled to ignore the twitching in her heart signalling her mother's absence. Her hand stroked the rough wool blanket draped over the chair. Memories visited, reminding her how deeply ingrained her mother's spirit was into the fabric of this home. She pondered the multitude of hushed conversations between her mother and her treasured Auntie Mags, and how many faeries they had dispatched her to find so they could have 'big people's' talks. She let her eyes slip shut for a moment, letting sweet recollections caress her troubled mind, the way early morning sunlight sweeps across sleeping fields – gradually waking and calling them to their purpose. Maggie busied herself preparing cups while cooing to Lily, even though she remained fast asleep. Jessie watched until her patience ran out.

"Maggie, she's asleep and you're avoiding me. Leave the kettle, it'll boil itself, come talk to me."

Maggie sat opposite her, with Lily still close against her chest. "You're troubled Jess. I can see your steam rising, settle for a minute. Have some tea before your thoughts boil the sense out of your brain."

Jessie fumed. "You're right Mags, I'm in a stew but tea won't fix it."

She stared straight ahead while Maggie patted Lily, rocking back and forth. Her gentle rhythm soon improved the fractious mood. Jessie's muscles relaxed, her fingers uncurled, and her body surrendered to the comfort offered by the warm embrace of the room. Maggie placed Lily in a basket of soft wool blankets before attending to the boiling water. She returned with a steaming cup. "Slowly Jess, there's no rush."

After three sips Jessie's complexion regained its autumn glimmer and her eyes brightened. Maggie would not press her so she finished her tea before leaning forward. "Angus and I almost came to blows yesterday, and it's left me feeling anxious and angry."

Maggie nodded. "I can imagine he's torn. He wants to do right by you, but he's in a thorny spot."

Jessie punched the air. "He's scheming with Father Coyle against us!"

Maggie seized Jessie's hands. "Calm, Jess, don't make it worse than it is. You don't know everything."

The room closed in and Jessie's chest tightened. "He knows more than he's telling, warning and threatening me at the same time. That priest wants Myna's house destroyed. He wants rid of us, and if Angus takes any part in it, I swear I will—"

"Wheisht, Jess! Not one more word or you'll have your Mammie turning in her grave. He would love nothing better than to turn you against each other, and frighten us to death, but this is no time for it." Maggie released Jessie's hands but clutched her own. "I've already enjoyed a run-in with Father Coyle. He wanted me to tell him where Myna's house is, who your mother worked with, and taught."

Jessie clutched at her skirt. "What does he want to do if he finds it?"

Maggie shrugged. "The Wilsons are fretting about strange things going on up at the manor. Father Coyle is blaming the spaes. A few of those vile men he employs have disappeared, but if you ask me, they were probably too thin for our weather and not quick enough for our type. They'll have bolted back to England. Good riddance, we all say."

Jessie's brows almost met in the middle. "Did anything strange happen to them?"

Maggie ignored the question. "Regardless, it's precisely the excuse that priest needs. He wants Wilson to flatten the forest, and everything in it. He's sure if he drives us out everyone will rush back to his church. Wilson is only interested in money and believes the land is worth more without the crofters. Between the two of them, they will control the lands, the crofts and the entire village."

Jessie seethed. "He has no right, he can't. Our forest has been here for thousands of years, our families built the crofts, they're ours."

Maggie stood. "He hasn't a clue where Myna's house is, and it's too dangerous a place for his fat feet. He wouldn't chance getting lost, too fond of himself for that. None of his visitors would dare tell him, for they know what's good for them." She glanced over to Lily's basket before lowering her voice to a murmur. "With Angus at the manor we can find out what they're planning. You and Lily can be safe ... if you stay on the right side of him."

Jessie's fingers pushed against each other before curling back into fists. "Angus wants me to turn my back on the spaes, to accept that others' troubles are not mine. He warned me of danger if I don't stay home, but didn't say what danger."

Maggie pulled at her sleeves. "I'd be wasting my breath to advise you to do his will, but if he's warning you, he must have wind of something. Tom isn't well, so perhaps it's better you stay home for a bit. I'll speak with Myna then visit you when I find out more."

Jessie looked to the heavens and cupped her face in her hands. Despair overcame her, and she spoke from an unknown place in her mind, a place she'd never considered visiting. "What if they drive us out, Mags? What if they burn the forest? If all we're doing is for nothing?"

Maggie knelt and held Jessie's knees, the warmth of her hands passing through her skirts into her skin. She looked into Maggie's round eyes – dark amber flecks floating in pools the colour of hot tea, surrounded by folds of paper-thin skin. Resisting the desire to rest her head on her shoulder, she searched her face for guidance.

"They will never drive us out, Jess. A house is only stone and thatch. We are blessed with this precious place in the most

magical of forests, but it's our actions and your gifts that give it energy. You can do that anywhere."

Jessie detected a resilience in Maggie's expression and leaned back. "You know of another place?" she quizzed.

Maggie's eyes shifted. "If we need, but for now we won't talk about it. I want you to go home. Look after Tom. God only knows how old his shroud is, and it breaks my heart to see you both suffering. These ought to be your happy days."

Jessie shrugged. "Mammie told me my journey wouldn't be easy."

Maggie pulled her out of the chair and held her tight. Jessie now let her head rest on Maggie's soft shoulder.

"For the good your mother did, and you do now, it's a high price to pay … most wouldn't. The world will always comprise givers and takers. I know which is easier, but I also know whom God prefers."

Maggie's embrace squeezed Jessie's heart, and tears trickled down her cheeks. She wiped her face. "I miss her so much, Mags."

Maggie smoothed her curls back. "Listen to your heart, Jess, she's in there."

Maggie lifted Lily as Jessie wrapped her shawl around her shoulders. Maggie handed Lily to her then picked up her own shawl and followed her outside.

Jessie turned. "Where are you going?"

Maggie grinned, and her eyes narrowed. "I'm off to see a friend. I'll find out what's going on with those vile men at the manor."

Jessie gripped her elbow. "Maggie, don't cause or get yourself in any trouble."

Maggie sniggered, tightening her shawl. "Don't worry yourself over me. Now you be off home."

Jessie watched Maggie stride off, a halo of ash-grey hair above stiff shoulders, her feet crunching the unfortunate twigs in her path. She took a moment to listen to Lily gurgle before picking a dandelion from Maggie's overgrown hedge and twirling it between her fingers. She watched its seeds float into the warm air then turned Lily's face towards them. "Look Lily, they're taking all our love and hope up to your granny."

She strolled along the quiet road humming, rocking Lily who snuggled peacefully. Angus interfered with her attention at every other step but she forced him back into the part of her mind holding all the troubles her sleep fought. She stopped at the fork between the forest lane and the road to her house. A short row of cottages sat beneath a sky so blue she found it hard to believe rain hid behind the distant, glorious, heather-clad mountains, gathering angry clouds sure to sweep over them by sundown. The sound of women singing floated back and forth, carried by its best messenger. She followed it until the breeze delivered her to the front door of Laura's house.

Laura's eyes exposed her unease the moment she opened the door. She was more used to visiting Jessie at Myna's, so looked up and down the road before pulling Jessie inside. "Jessie, what a surprise! What brings you here?" She swept invisible dust off her green plaid skirts and smoothed her hair back too many times.

Jessie pondered leaving but walked past her to the nearest chair. "I'm perfectly fine. It's muggy today so I wanted to walk. I heard the singing and guessed this may be your house. May I trouble you for some water, maybe listen for a bit?"

Laura scurried to the sink. "Of course. I'll get you a drink and you can give me your wee one. The girls are busy felting but they'll be delighted to see her."

When she returned with the water, Jessie placed Lily in her arms. Laura ran a finger over Lily's cheek before kissing her forehead. Jessie spotted her eyes fill, so she patted her arm before relaxing into the chair. The music swirled around the room; leaves of sound caught in their own eddy. "Oh Jessie, I heard she was the spit of your Mammie, and so she is. This must bring you so much joy. Her voice carried delight and sorrow in equal measure, which Jessie found puzzling. A tear escaped, so she leaned over and took her hand.

"I understand Laura. It is hard, but I am also overjoyed. It breaks my heart my Mam isn't here, but she taught me well and she'll always be with me – in Lily."

Laura placed a hand on her heart. "You must miss her."

Jessie glanced to the corner where a basket overflowed with ropes of varying colours and twines. "I see you're also a fan of my Mammie's ropes?"

Laura followed Jessie's gaze. "Yes, she was certainly the most skilled."

"Well, that's quite a collection. I hope you get good use of them all – although there's a big one there in need of a wash."

Laura fidgeted and Jessie picked up on her sudden discomfort. "I don't mean to be rude."

Laura rushed to remove the mud-caked rope, then tossed it outside. "No, you're not. I think Callan used it to bring in the pigs."

"Well, it's certainly strong enough to manage a few pigs," said Jessie, before bouncing out of her armchair. "We can't be in mourning forever, and I'm not leaving here till I see your girls. Their singing is near to bursting my heart."

Laura turned and led Jessie out to the back garden, Jessie's remarks about the rope, and fury at Callan not heeding her instructions to clean it, weakening her knees. Seated around a large wooden table, long overdue a sanding, its ale barrel supports screaming for reprieve, three middle-aged women sat on one side, three young girls on the other, an older woman at the end, leading the verses, controlling the beat and ruling the effort as they engaged in the ancient tradition of singing Gaelic songs while beating cloth against a table. Singing which provided structure and personal connection to an entirely monotonous, arduous task. Tin buckets overflowing with soapy water, plus reams of raw fabric in the colours making up Scotland's vast assortment of plaids, surrounded the table. What the broad shouldered, grey-haired elders provided in technique and timing, the younger rosy-cheeked girls matched with strength and enthusiasm. Engrossed in their labours and chorus, none looked up, so Jessie and Laura leaned against the door, absorbing the lilting melodies and rhythmic movements characterising 'waulking' tartan. Jessie watched the elder at the head signal the command and the fabric swiftly shifted one to the left, in time for the next verse without missing a beat. She marvelled at their continuous efforts to drive out the soapy water to felt and shrink the fabric. She watched respectfully as their hands squeezed, pushing back and forward, even the strongest of fingers working almost to the bone. This cherished cultural feature brought pride and much needed income to supplement the inconsistent farming wage, and Jessie's heart soared. Laura's permanent uniform of green plaid spoke to her love of the process. She looked at Jessie, then down at Lily. "I think she enjoys it. She's dozed off again."

Jessie grinned. "It's in her blood."

After enjoying the mesmerising movement and song, Laura tweaked Jessie's elbow and gestured for her to follow. Once seated inside, Laura's shoulders dropped and she kept her eyes fixed on Lily. She twirled the fringes of Lily's blanket, tapping her feet on the floor – not in tune with the singing outside. Worried the blanket may not survive, Jessie probed.

"Laura, I know you're uncomfortable. I watched your jaw drop when you opened your door, so something is worrying you, will ye not tell me?"

Laura looked up. "Jess, God knows I love you, and your Mam, but there's talk all over the village and up at the manor. Willy will go mad if he knows you're here." She chewed her bottom lip, and Jessie reached out to steady her hand.

"Talk?" Jessie quizzed, before gently removing Lily and settling her in the crook of her arm. Laura didn't notice.

"Talk of the spaes and the forest, devil worship on the full moons, wickedness to Wilson's workers." Laura bounced out of her chair and paced back and forth. "It's not good Jess. They want to burn the forest. They want all the spaes thrown out and sent off to a madhouse."

Jessie gasped. "Laura, calm down. That's all nonsense and you know it."

Laura clutched her chest. Jessie watched, not daring to say a word that may agitate Laura's mind, which appeared to be spinning. Lily squeaked so Jessie rocked her, hoping to appease her until Laura explained her worries. Lily's cries nudged Laura back to earth.

"I'm sorry Jess, it makes me so anxious, and those men at the manor are foul-mouthed rabble rousers. They whistle and grab at ye every chance they get."

Jessie interrupted her rambling. "I know they're terrible but that's not what's got you riled, is it?"

Laura held her breath for a moment, and despite the weight of the world weighing her down, she pushed her shoulders back and clutched her hands. Her voice quivered. "They say your mother was a witch, and she made those Englishmen disappear. She causes our women, well, to act up against their men. *They're saying if they see any of us with you, they'll throw us out of our homes and off the land."*

Jessie's astonished expression threw her. "Frankly, we care less about Wilsons' men. We've all been through terror with them." She rubbed her belly and shook her head. "If Willy knew—"

Jessie interrupted. "Did they harm you?"

Laura's shiver travelled up and down her entire body. "Nothing you need to worry about. Understand, we women are grateful for what you and your mother have done for us." Her hands moved to snatch an errant thread, which would soon unravel her entire skirt at the rate she pulled. She dropped her head. "They just don't understand. They only want an excuse for Wilson to take over the forest, so Father Coyle can get us all in his church – with our wages."

As Jessie rocked back and forth to calm Lily's hungry girning, familiar heat flared in her chest. The increased tempo and pitch of the singing signalled a ream was nearing completion, but the crescendo only heightened Jessie's anger. She stood, wrapped Lily's blanket tight then grasped Laura's hand. "Please don't worry, I'll sort this. You know where I am if you need me, any time, day or night." She watched the skin around Laura's mouth crease, holding tight words she didn't want to utter.

"Jess, they're saying you're poisoning Tom – so you won't need to look after him, to have the house to yourself, to do your … your evil work."

Jessie dropped Laura's hand and clutched the door handle, steadying herself. Lily's cry drowned out the drums in her head and the banging in her chest. "I would never hurt Tom."

Laura nodded. "We know, Jess, we know."

Chapter 17

ANGUS WATCHED STONE CHIPS *fly off the end of his boots on his way to Charles Wilson's office. The speed of the projectiles mirrored the mood he'd been in since the usually cheery livery boy popped his head into Angus's office with shifty eyes and gritted teeth.*

"Angus, you're wanted up at the big hoose. Lord Wilson wants to see you."

Angus preferred to forget the two days it took for the skin on the inside of his cheeks to mend after his previous visit; such was the unpleasant discourse and resultant ill feeling. Far easier to hide in his own office or the stable yard in the hope his employer and Father Coyle might forget he existed. He detoured past the stables, tack room and peat bunker, convincing himself a check-in was necessary, but the rising sweat under his coat warned him stalling might well add annoyance to whatever was on Wilson's mind. Donald jumped to attention when he noticed him fiddling with the bolt on an empty stable door. He wiped his hands on his leather apron and eyed him curiously. Angus spotted him and kicked the door.

"Why is this bolt loose?" Donald's sharp in-breath and raised eyebrows checked Angus's attitude. "Sorry Donald, I didn't mean to bark." He offered a hand.

Donald shook it but stepped back like a naughty schoolboy. "S-something wrong Angus?"

Angus rolled his eyes and rubbed his forehead. "No, I'm on my way to see the boss, so I'm just stopping by to check all is in order."

Donald scratched his head and shoved his dirty hands into his pockets. "T-tiptop Angus, if they weren't h-horses, they'd be happy as pigs in shite."

His wide grin, crooked teeth and dirty cheeks lifted Angus's feet out of the mud, and for the first time in a while he belly-laughed. "Good to know, Donald. I'll leave you to it then."

"Aye," Donald nodded, but Angus heard a grumble.

"Are you all right?" he asked. Donald glanced over both shoulders. Angus's eyes narrowed. "Out with it."

Donald stuttered and stammered and his eyes roamed the area. Angus grew impatient. "Donald, you can't hold your water, so I'll be here when you burst."

Donald shuffled forward and Angus smelled the tobacco cloaking him inside and out. "There's t-trouble brewing and I don't like it, Angus, I d-don't like it." He rolled back and forward on his dung-encrusted boots, arms folded tight. Angus scratched his legs through his trouser pockets. Donald carried on. "Two of the smithies from England have gone missing and one of the kitchen maids told anyone who'd listen that it's on account of witches."

Angus put up a hand. "I've heard that already. It's drivel and you should know better."

Donald's head nodded back and forward in time with his feet, his stutter catching each nervous word. "She s-said they're everywhere," he blurted.

Angus raged. "Donald, don't be daft! Cook told me Mildred was useless and hated working for the Wilsons."

Donald wiped greasy curls off his face, still rolling on his heels. "Aye, maybe, but she said yer Mam came here and the others say Mildred was so f-f-feart she bolted."

Angus's thighs stung, so he whipped his hands out of his pockets and grabbed Donald's shoulders. "For God's sake, do you hear yourself? You knew my Mam as well as anybody, and now you're listening to English hogwash?"

Donald's greasy curls wobbled. "Naw, no me, it's everybody else. I'm only t-telling ye."

Both men stepped back. Angus sensed the sudden unease. "Yer all right, Donald." He patted his shoulder. "Just you keep yer head down and don't be bothering with any of it." Angus turned and left Donald nodding to himself. When he was almost out of sight, Donald called after him.

"I'll check the bolt but there's no horse in that stable."

Angus strode to the manor house, wishing he hadn't procrastinated. Conflicting emotions brawled within like *bullies on the playground as soon as he approached the broad stone steps leading to enormous wood carved doors framed with ornate pots overflowing with elegant roses and playful geraniums. Two fat English bulldogs lay basking in the morning sun. Familiar with the manor staff, they simply grunted when Angus knocked on the door. The butler opened and Angus watched his chest sink beneath his tailored jacket and crisp white shirt. He cast his eyes up and down.*

"Yes?" His lips barely parted.

Angus glared then nudged past him into the hallway. "I'm here to see Lord Wilson. He's expecting me." He avoided the multitude of eyes staring down at him from gold-framed oil paintings lining the walls – and all the way up the scarlet carpeted stairwell. Jewels, dripped off the end of a master's paintbrush, twinkled from the throats of thin-lipped women. Nothing riled him more than wondering about the cost of the lavish attire these individuals sported. He also questioned the use of wallpaper and wood panelling considering so little of it was visible, with wealthy ancestors dominating so much of the surface. He scowled, contemplating how many of their local treasured trees it took to fashion the highly polished floors and bannisters.

Charles Wilson opened his door. "Angus, come in."

The click of his footsteps disappeared into thick carpet, drawing Angus's eyes to swirls of green and gold, sucking him into a downward spiral. Wilson's angry voice caught him off-guard. "Angus, stop staring at the floor. Sit."

Charles shuffled some paperwork on his desk before removing his glasses. "This is not a work conversation, Angus. It is personal; therefore, it may be difficult, but I expect complete honesty from you."

Angus noticed the skin around Charles's eyes tighten and questioned what his understanding of honesty needed to be.

"Yes, sir, but what personal conversation do we need to have?"

Charles placed his glasses on the desk. "I'll get right to it. Some unusual incidents within the manor have come to my attention. I am not one to indulge rumour or gossip. I have staff to manage staff, but the situation appears to have escalated, so it seems I now have no choice but to investigate."

Although Angus surmised what might come, his body was unprepared, and sweat seeped into his undershirt. He was sure the frown formed on Wilson's forehead mirrored his own.

"You may have heard that two of my blacksmiths have not reported to work in some time. They both left their belongings behind and, to my knowledge, neither was unhappy with their work. So, it's a disturbing mystery." Charles tilted his head, but Angus preferred to let his tongue remain stuck to the top of his mouth. Charles continued. "Soon after their departure, one of the kitchen maids also left her position without explanation." Angus nodded while his tongue remained glued. Charles leaned forward and the olive-green leather inlay squashed beneath his elbows, similar to the carpet beneath Angus's feet. Wilson's moustache quivered. "Angus, do you know anything about this?"

"No, sir," he answered, too hurriedly.

"Allow me to enlighten you. It seems this area is renowned for its pagan beliefs and tribal cultures, as well as claims of people living amongst you who still practise witchcraft and evil."

Angus's feet twisted and his fingertips melted into the fabric of the chair. Still his tongue refused to budge, anchoring his words lest they fall over themselves. Charles Wilson leaned back and eyed him. "I see you don't wish to be drawn on the matter. However, all three left without collecting their due wages, and to date, the blacksmiths' families have not heard from them. Most unusual, don't you think?" He lifted a manilla envelope from the side of his desk, flapping it towards Angus. "This is a report from my head of staff and there is mention of your mother. She had an infamous reputation – and following, as does your sister."

Angus's teeth clenched behind firm lips. His mother's words repeated over and over in his head, layering the glue his tongue needed.

"The least said is the easiest mended."

However, Charles Wilson's temper rapidly unglued. "Angus, if you insist on sitting here like a dumb valet, I will bring in whichever authority necessary to investigate." His nostrils flared and his moustache fluttered like hay stalks in a breeze. "I do not believe in your hocus pocus or ancestral nonsense, but if it is true your family is meddling in the manor affairs, I will have them charged and punished."

Angus's glue came unstuck. "Sir, I do not know what you are talking about or why you think my family would be involved in anyone's disappearance." He struggled to stay composed. "Some did not understand my mother's beliefs, but she never harmed a living soul. Her practices came from her ancestral upbringing and customs."

Charles Wilson slapped the envelope on his desk. Angus heard his mother's advice once more.

"If you keep it to yourself, it can't be used to hurt you."

Charles's eyebrows shot up. "So, you admit to practices and customs still being performed."

Angus opened his mouth and his words tumbled out before he could check them. "My sister and the spaes have their own ways but I'm not aware of any harm they cause. Their practices are not evil and if their devotions appear pagan, it's because they don't believe in your church."

Angus watched Charles Wilson's sneer creep across his face, but it was too late to bite his own tongue off.

"Spaes, devotions, antichrist?"

"Sir, it may seem strange, but they're just different folk is all."

Charles jumped out of his chair. "I have no time for different around here. I have a manor and farms to manage. You should know I have invested in machinery, built a new school and currently employ more locals than I need, so if I am to be thwarted by peasants who have no idea what is good for them, I will make my decisions based on profitability alone."

Angus's tongue reverted to its noncommittal position which only agitated Wilson further. "Angus!" he bellowed. "I am not opposed to burning down the entire forest and turning those crofts into working cottages, so if you can put a stop to this behaviour, I suggest you do. My people are uncomfortable, which makes me uncomfortable, and I will not stand for it. Do you understand me?"

Angus stood. "Mr Wilson, the forest has been part of this community for so long, I think it would cause more trouble if you destroyed it. The crofts have been ours for generations. There will certainly be hostility and perhaps resistance if you were to change that."

Anger suffocated both men, the fire raging in Wilson's eyes competing with the one crackling in the enormous fireplace. Angus stood firm. He maintained eye contact, and despite wishing to rip off his tie and gasp for air, he forced his arms to remain at his sides.

Charles broke the silence. "Hostility, resistance? Do I hear you correctly? Is that a threat, or am I mistaken?"

"No, sir, no threat. I am simply trying to explain the feelings amongst the people who have lived on and worked this land for generations. They are good people, survivors of hardships from weather, pestilence and our own government. They simply want to live a good life ... they don't want much. I'm sure you have heard what has happened up North where landlords have tried to clear the crofts."

Charles Wilson's face stiffened. "Angus, let me tell you about up North. The crofts are long cleared, with most of your tribe already resettled on the coast somewhere, or on a ship bound for Canada. Any hostility or resistance has not made one bit of difference. So let me be clear. Resolve this matter soon or I will rethink my plans for the forest and the crofts."

Angus ignored the voices screaming in his ears and swallowed his pride. "Yes, sir, I understand. I will do what I can."

Charles's shoulders jiggled themselves back to their comfortable position. "I expect you back here with answers. Do not forget who you work for." With a flick of stiff fingers, he dismissed him.

Before Angus closed the door he turned. "Sir, to be clear, we are not a tribe."

He paused in the hall to catch his breath, resisting the temptation to pick up the vase of flowers on the entrance table and hurl it at one of the leering ancestors. Suddenly the front door flew open. Father Coyle, still reeking of incense from his morning mass, stood panting in the entrance. Angus decided the vase would be better served launched at his head.

The priest bared his teeth and marched towards him. "Do you realise the trouble your people are causing around here?"

Angus stepped back, avoiding both the smell and angry spittle. "You are making too much of this father, I don't know what you think I can do."

Father Coyle shook a fist at him. "One way or another I will put a stop to this. I will drive Satan and his followers out of this town, and if that includes you, so be it. Charles Wilson has run out of patience, so you'd better get your people in order."

Angus inched towards him fighting back the urge to gag. "Or what, Father, or what?"

Father Coyle sniggered. "Don't take me for a fool, Angus. Your mother passed but your sister is worse than she ever was, so I suggest you rein her in."

Angus glanced towards the vase but checked himself. His blood raced to his brain. "If you do anything to harm my sister, you will have more than me to answer to."

The priest stepped back, his wide grin splitting his fat cheeks. "She is a mother now; she needs to look out for her family.

Angus almost choked but stood his ground. "You need to take better care too, Father. You're not looking so well these days."

Angus turned and marched through the door, slamming it before the butler reached it. Walking down the steps challenged the wobble in his knees, but determined to seem composed should Wilson be spying from his window, his spine stiffened.

His heartbeat throbbed in his ears as he fished in his pockets for his tobacco. No sooner did he turn the corner when the young boy who'd served him tea in Father Coyle's office walked straight into him. They looked surprised to see each other, but Angus spoke first.

"What are you doing here?"

The boy stammered, suddenly unsure if he was heading left or right. "I came to collect something from my Mam."

Angus spotted his hands fidgeting in his pockets. "Who is your mother?"

"Laura," he said, before rushing off and disappearing around the corner.

Angus leaned against a tree, watching the clouds darken, while questioning his temper and where his resistance to Wilson and Coyle came from. His shoulders sank, the call of the magpies dancing with his heartbeat and filling his head with noise. After a few puffs the clamour quelled but regret sat like a pile of rocks on the floor of his stomach. He'd successfully aggravated both Wilson and the priest, put his job at risk, and may well have driven them more towards destroying the forest than saving it. He'd hoped to mollify Wilson, not oppose him – or appear defensive. The clouds reached bursting point, then soft raindrops disrupted his deliberations. He stomped his cigarette into the gravel and jerked his collar up before trudging towards his office. A carousel of his fight with Wilson still circled in his mind and before long it sounded familiar. He'd heard his defiant utterances before: from Jessie. The gravel endured his weighty stride as he regretted his own foolishness. His office promised comfort, a soothing blanket for his anxious body – until he closed the door and saw Jessie sitting in his chair.

Chapter 18

MAGGIE'S WHIRLWIND ENTRANCE prompted Myna to remove both scarf and hat from her tight grip and brew a special mix to settle her friend's flushed face and fidgeting hands. With each sip of herbal tea, Maggie's body relaxed, so by the time she'd finished she almost dissolved into the armchair, forgetting the purpose of her visit. Myna took the empty cup.

"Unexpected as your visit is, I'm delighted to see you, Mags. Now you're calm, we can chat."

Maggie flattened her skirt. "I'm fine. No need to worry."

Myna's mouth twisted into a lopsided grin. "Well, when you arrived, the sparks in your eyes might've set the house on fire. So, is it only my magic tea you want, or is something troubling you?"

Maggie rubbed her hands together and was about to speak when the twins barged in carrying baskets overflowing with white heather, lavender stalks and purple loosestrife. Their bright eyes and wide grins lit up the room. Delighted to see Maggie, they dropped their colourful loot and wrestled each other for the first hug.

Myna scolded. "One at a time or you'll do her an injury."

Maggie giggled and held the girls so tight they yelped. "I'll do you two an injury first."

When the chuckling ceased, Myna told the girls to take the flowers to the pantry, hang them upside down, then get on with preparing soup vegetables. Maggie kissed each warm cheek before sending them on their way. They took the atmosphere with them. Myna crossed her arms and let her breasts rest on them.

"We're not getting any younger, so if you have something to say, get it out." She didn't need to consult her guides to know Maggie's gloom was not on account of the weather, and her *reluctance to speak was as strange as a warm winter wind. "Come on, Mags," she prodded.*

The girls peeled and chopped, sending traces of heather and lavender drifting into the room. Maggie updated Myna on Jessie's spat with her brother, and her own with Father Coyle. Impending doom settled heavily on Myna's shoulders but she railed against it.

"We've always known how unwelcome we are, but you must remember we also have friends we can count on. This isn't the first time they have hounded us, and I'm sure it won't be the last, but Jessie has done well to change the minds of some with wills of stone."

Maggie groaned and her chins wobbled. "I'm not sure. It's all good and well when we're helping, but if trouble comes to their front door will they run out the back?"

Myna reached across and took her hand. "Mags don't worry. I'm ready for anything that comes to my door. They'll have to find this house before they can burn it down, and I'll know if they're on their way."

Maggie stiffened. "Do you know more than I do?"

"Don't ask questions you don't need answers to." Myna's eyes narrowed. "You can sleep easy Mags. I'll be just fine and will keep my girls safe no matter what ... and not everyone has a back door."

The two friends sat in silence. Myna's mind drew her focus inwards to ominous notions, but she cast them aside as she would dirty dishwater, and sucked in the soothing floral aromas while gazing out the window behind Maggie. Her ability to calm her mind and bring Heather's face into view provided more comfort than a Bible full of empty words. She did not allow the darkness that filled her heart when Heather passed to settle or make itself at home. It was contrary to her beliefs, and Heather's wishes; neither of which she would flout. Heather would always be her lifelong friend and ally, even in death. She called out to Tevia. "Bring a hot stone and some willow bark."

Maggie bolted upright. "What are you doing?"

Myna reached for her hand. "I want you to lie back and relax. Your worries are sitting in your ankles and under your eyes. Trust me, I know you better than you do."

Tevia fetched the hot stone and medicine. Maggie's weak objection failed, so she lifted her tired legs onto the couch then settled her head back. Myna placed the stone on her belly, and within seconds, heat seeped from its linen cover through Maggie's layered clothes, warming her skin. Soon her entire body basked in the comfort. Her joints thanked the heat by loosening their grip, allowing her blood to flow unhindered. Myna dropped three clear drops onto Maggie's tongue then smiled at her friend. "Go visit Heather."

Maggie's shoulders dropped. "That would be lovely."

Her lids closed gently. Myna stroked her arm until her breathing eased to a gentle snore, before pulling a blanket up to her chin and leaving her to rest. She found the twins under a tree, chirping; busy chicks surrounded by a rainbow of vegetables, protected by the drooping arms of willow branches dragged down by the burden of voluminous leaves. Fine light laced its way through, casting streaks of brightness on their already radiant faces. The sight never failed to swell her heart, but she was too preoccupied to wallow in it.

"Girls, we must prepare a fire, get soup on the go, and you'll need to make lots of bread today. We'll have company for the full moon tonight. It's the first without Auntie Heather so we will pay special tribute to her."

Tevia jumped up, potato peels scattering around her bare feet. "Can we come, please?" Tavia also scrambled to her feet, ignoring her bucket of peeled carrots spilling onto the grass.

"Please Mam, please!" She joined her sister in a battle of who could whine loudest.

Myna folded her arms but even in her rigid stance she struggled to contain a grin. "Do you promise to sit quietly, not speak a word of what you see or hear?"

"Yes, yes, yes!" the girls shrieked, their pigtails bouncing.

Myna's defence succumbed to the tidal wave of energy and pleading. "All right then, but we have a lot to get done today. Please also make up a cot for Auntie Mags, I want her to stay with us tonight."

"We will, thank you, thank you!"

Myna's face worked hard to remain officious. "Chop some white heather and lavender to stuff a pillow for her, and if you have time, change the straw."

She left the girls to their chores, wondering if her instructions fell on deaf ears brimming with each other's excitement. Almost of age, and having witnessed much healing and some tearful counselling without question, Myna understood the day would arrive when they would become part of her inner circle. It had been some time since the girls were surprised by any of the work the spaes did, and she thanked her spirits daily for the blessing of her beautiful daughters. She trusted that if a woman's greatest gift is to be a mother, it is also to mother any child who requires it, regardless of the origin of their umbilical cord. Her girls attended the local school without ever complaining about the bullying and nasty remarks made by children more used to listening to their parents' gossip than putting their minds to independent thinking; which spoke to their resilience and individualism. She wanted them to at least be able to read and write equal to any boy. If they became adept with numbers, it would be a bonus. Myna's nature would not indulge her own accomplishments in their upbringing, believing in a universal decree avowing children do not belong, but are God's gifts sent to teach lessons jaded hearts need to relearn. They weren't hers to begin with so their presence in her life attested to the universe's trust in her, which was reward enough.

Busying herself diluting tinctures and preparing candles for the night's gathering allowed her mind to roam amongst the memories of her baby girls – and Heather. She would wear Heather's death like a heavy coat for the rest of her days but she reasoned with the burden of grief, in equal measure came the joy of remembrance. She would carry the weight quietly, trusting the uplifting memories to more than balance the pain. Maggie stirred, but Myna made tea before settling down beside her. Maggie's squinting eyes and untidy hair prompted Myna to insist she drink before speaking.

She rubbed her eyes after swallowing half the cup. "Oh, my goodness."

Myna laughed. "That was a dead man's sleep you just had."

Maggie held the cup between her palms and rolled her shoulders back as though massaging an invisible tree. A cheeky grin snuck across Myna's face. "Did you dream?"

Maggie sighed. "You know damn well I didn't. You sent me to my next life, and even there I was sound asleep." She reached over, lifted an oatcake and asked between bites. "What have you been doing?"

Myna grinned. "These oatcakes didn't make themselves."

Maggie agreed with Myna's decision to spend the night. First, because she did not want to walk home late without Heather or Jessie to accompany her, and second, because she fully intended to enjoy a dram to celebrate Heather's life – or two.

"Or as many as you can manage," Myna teased.

The evening arrived with a mild mood and cloudless sky. An imperious moon inched its way upwards, brightening with each minute. When darkness relieved the twilight of its duty, each star journeyed to its appointed position and radiated in unison with this moon, seemingly in honour of its perfect sphere and glorious illumination. Upturned faces gazed in wonder at its blazing, stars flashing and twinkling, offering glimpses through the darkest of ceilings into another universe. A fire sizzled, spat and sparkled its best effort in response to this spectacle of natural wonder.

The women joined hands, swaying and chanting in a cadenced ritual of movement and mantra. The forest stood guard, towering, trusty sentries containing both the noise and glow of the secret ceremony. When the moon reached its highest point, the pitch and fever of the incantations bridged the distance and merged in an explosion of light and sound. Tevia and Tavia split themselves between Myna and Maggie. They'd heard many of the chants before, so were soon caught up and engulfed by the emotion and rhythm. The elders held the young in a vice of protection, breaking their union only when the last chant soared into the air. Both girls dropped to the ground, stunned by the storm of fervour. The others followed, gradually settling onto the grass in cross-legged positions – if their joints allowed. Myna and Maggie lowered themselves with awkward shifting and manoeuvring until they too sat comfortably. Maggie drew Tavia to her soft chest, smothered one small hand with one of her own and stroked her flowing hair with the other. Tavia gazed into the fire, cooried into Maggie's folds and relaxed. Soon, low humming accompanied the dwindling flames. Myna turned to Tevia and brushed a hand across her cheek. "Are you all right?" she whispered.

Tevia clutched her mother and looked up, cheeks glistening with unchecked tears. "Yes, Mam, but I don't have the words."

Myna pulled her closer, guiding her head onto her shoulder. "I know, my child, I understand. The words will come when you need them. Be still now, let your heart be full."

Tevia twisted to meet Myna's eyes. "I felt her Mam, I felt her right in front of me."

"Who?" Myna watched Tevia's lips quiver.

"Auntie Heather."

Myna hugged her, rocking her as she'd done when she was a baby, but Tevia drew back once more, frowning.

Myna assured her. "It's nothing to fret about, it's her spirit letting you know she's with us."

Tevia tightened her grip on Myna's hands. "Yes, I believe that, but I don't understand why Auntie Jessie was with her."

Myna stroked Tevia's troubled face and took a long breath. "Don't fret, Tevia."

Chapter 19

JESSIE SAT IN ANGUS'S chair, nudging half-dead logs with a poker, watching shimmers of grey sprinkle into the air. A mound of thick ash concealed any trace of simmering heat that might warm the room, suggesting Angus had been gone long enough to let it dwindle, or someone forgot to refuel and stoke it in his absence. The rough back of the chair prodded her spine, making her wonder if Angus's position was as lofty as he alleged, and whether she should give him a soft cushion and a heavy blanket. Her mother would have, and probably a mat for the cold floor too, if she'd known he sat in what seemed more like an abandoned bothy than a comfortable workspace. Noting the absence of greenery which might add a hint of the magnificent grounds surrounding his stone-walled chamber, she questioned her brother's affinity to the manor. She was about to open the only drawer in his basic desk when Angus strode into the room and closed the door behind him. His mouth dropped. She broke the awkward silence. "Not happy to see me?"

"Surprised, don't you have better things to do?" He stepped towards her and she noticed his eyes flit around the room before darting to the grubby window.

"I do, but you rarely visit, and I want to speak to you."

Without replying, he pressed his fists into his pockets.

"You can relax, Angus. I'm sure no one saw me. Unless your spies are hiding in the trees."

Angus flopped into the rickety chair opposite Jessie and rolled his eyes. "Jess, I don't have time for your fussing, so tell me why you're here."

Jessie's face warmed, and her fingernails pushed into her palms. "There's talk in the village of your boss, and your friend Father Coyle, on a witch-hunt ... and I'm top of their list. Do you have anything to do with it?"

Angus leaned back. "The talk, or the witch-hunt?"

Jessie lifted both fists and placed them on the desk. "This might be your office, but you don't need to be smart with me. I'm sick of hearing stories of my wickedness, and you seem to be in all of them."

Angus launched out of the chair. "I'm also sick of hearing the stories, Jess, but it's you who's the subject, and it's threatening my job."

Jessie's eyes fixed on him. "So, do something about it. If I get a knock at the door one night, you know Tom won't be any help. I know nothing of those missing men, and there is nothing evil going on in the forest. You should know better than to let anyone say different. Mam would turn in her grave if she thought you were siding with them."

"Them?" His eyes bulged. "They employ me, half the village, and make sure we have land to farm. Wilson has just dragged me across his carpet because he thinks I know more than I'm telling. I might lose my job if I don't go back with an explanation."

Jessie reeled from the force of his hot breath across the desk. Sweat on his brow from the fire in his cheeks clung to his skin. "What do you want me to do, Jessie?"

She unfolded from the chair, testing the strength of the desk under her fists before meeting his eyes. "We may be different, we may right some wrongs, but we are not evil – and you know it. Mam wasn't, and you know that too." She swung an arm around the room. "This isn't your home. We are your kin, not them. If you have to choose, you've lost touch with who you are." Her throat ached and her heart thumped. Anger swooped around their heads as they faced off, warriors ready to pounce.

"Jess, you don't understand!" His hands reached up, grasping the air around his head. "It's not about us and them. We don't control who lives here any longer, so it is only them. We either learn to live together or we won't have a home at all. I have no choice unless I'm willing to be thrown out – and neither do you."

His words stunned, so she struggled to speak. She reached up to hold her neck. "Angus, please kill these stories. It's hard enough with Mam gone, Lily to care for – and Tom."

Angus shook his clenched fists. "You must stop whatever is going on in the woods, Jess. The spaes, interfering in other people's lives."

"Why do I have to stop helping people because that lot don't understand?" Tears burned her eyes. "Why must I change my beliefs because they don't approve?"

Angus slumped back into the chair, the wood creaking under his angry weight. "Because they have the power, Jess. If you don't, we will all suffer. They will destroy the forest, throw us all out, and clear the land. That's what you're risking because of some ancient customs better put to rest."

Jessie squeezed her hands. With each twist, she wished her mother would walk through the door and sort it all out; with a clip across Angus's head and a remedy for everything. The heaviness in the room smothered her, her throat ached. Ideas flashed through her mind and desperation tugged her heart. "Why don't you bring them to the woods? Show them it's not evil – try to turn them around?"

Angus clutched his hair. "Have you lost your mind, Jess? You want them to go into that forest, approve of what you do with the spaes? After what they've heard?" He blew out a deep breath. "If you think Father Coyle will agree to that, you need to look at yourself." He stood up and rammed his fists into his pockets. "Go home, Jess. Look after Lily and Tom the way you're supposed to. Keep yourself busy, let things settle so Wilson forgets about it all. Maybe then we can get back to living in peace."

"Father Coyle is evil," Jessie spat. "He won't let anything settle unless it suits him; and we don't suit him."

"Let it go, Jess, please."

She made for the door, the sound of her heavy footsteps reverberating in her ears. Angus's eyes followed, boring into the back of her head as she stood before the closed door. She turned and sent her words across the room on the wings of a silent prayer. "If you have to choose, what will you do?"

Angus dropped his head onto his fists. "Go home, Jess."

She pulled her shawl tight. "Clean this office. It needs a good dusting; it's bristling with unpleasant energy." She left without closing the door. As she stomped home, she fumed. He hadn't even inquired about Lily.

Maggie almost jumped out of her chair when Jessie walked into her house without making a sound. "Oh, Dear Lord, my heart nearly stopped."

Jessie stroked her arm. "You look tired. Thank you for looking after Lily. Go home and get some rest."

Maggie eyed her, tucking escaped wisps back into her hair clips. "Did you make right with Angus?"

Jessie shrugged. "As much as anyone, with him."

Maggie patted her arm. "Gently now, he's also lost his Ma."

Jessie made herself tea, but still her feet tapped and her fingers pulled at stray threads on the couch. As soon as Lily woke, she bundled her up and headed out the door. She needed air – and some company.

When Laura opened her door and ushered Jessie in, Lily's chortles cheered everyone. Laura's daughter Iris sat on the couch, and each time her knees bounced, Lily chuckled louder. Jessie beamed. "You have a way with her."

Iris blushed and lowered her eyes. Laura gestured for Jessie to sit, then turned to Iris. "Take Lily to the garden, make her a daisy crown – before they're all gone."

Iris bundled Lily into her arms and rushed out. Jessie watched her. "Is Iris all right?"

Laura hurried to the hearth and checked on the tea. "Nearly ready, Jess, just needs to stew a minute."

Jessie followed her. "Laura, is something wrong with Iris?" she persisted.

Laura swung around. "Och, she's a bit out of sorts. Her monthly interferes with her mood. Take no notice."

Jessie accepted Iris's monthly may interfere with her mood, but questioned why it would interfere with Laura's disposition. She moved to Iris's space and waited as Laura busied herself with the tea. Lavender scent eased her mind, calmed her choppy nerves, and for a moment she melted into the warmth, letting the room soothe her. Laura sat and sipped her tea.

"You're quiet," Jessie quizzed. "Has something happened since my last visit?"

Laura gazed into her teacup. "No Jess, but with our Callan in the new school, I need to be careful." She placed the cup on a block of carved wood serving as a makeshift table. "He's warned me to stay away from trouble."

Jessie's spine stiffened. "Do you want your boy in that school? Am I trouble?"

Laura stood and her skirt almost knocked over her cup. "No Jess, I don't, but it's what Willy wants."

Jessie stood. "I understand, and God knows you have your hands full with him. I don't want to cause you any harm, so I'll fetch Lily and leave."

Laura heaved out of her chair, stepped across the divide and held Jessie's shoulders. "I'm grateful to you, but we need to watch ourselves. These stories have got the village in a panic." She avoided eye contact, and Jessie sensed a tremble in her grip. Laura brought Lily inside and Jessie wrapped her up, but something still nudged her instincts.

"Is Iris not going to school?"

Laura's groan escaped before she could catch it, but still she avoided looking at Jessie. "Not this week, she's been poorly."

"Poorly? Can I help?"

Laura shook her head and turned to the door. "No, no, she'll be fine. Myna gave her something."

Jessie said goodbye, but after she left her senses screamed something was off, and her brain toiled with reasons for Laura's temperament. She almost walked straight into Iris before noticing she was blocking her pathway.

"Oh Iris, I didn't see you. My mind was up in the clouds. Thank you for looking after Lily; you're an angel." Smiling into a blank stare, her flesh prickled. She reached out, and when she held Iris's hand, light flashed through her mind, catching her breath. Lily yelped when she held too tight. Jessie lowered her voice. "Iris, what's wrong?"

Iris stared, and whatever troubled her landed on her bottom lip, rendering her speechless. Lily cried, and Jessie pulled Iris off the pathway, behind a tree. She watched a storm build in her eyes, so she lay Lily down on a soft patch of grass, which immediately calmed her whinging. Iris stood with her back pressed against the tree, but Jessie's nerves tingled in the wave of energy between them. "You must tell me, Iris. You know I can feel it; it's dark. What's happened to you?"

Iris clutched her skirt, and her eyes darted over each of Jessie's shoulders. "Oh Jessie, I'm in terrible trouble." Her neck strained under the stiffness of her jaw. "My Da will kill me – I swear he will."

Jessie suddenly remembered Laura sitting on Myna's couch twisting her green tartan skirt; bruises and angry scratches yelping from parts of exposed skin. Her mind reeled. She stepped back, searching Iris's face, now pale and frozen, eyes like marbles cemented into stone. Jessie forced her words to be slow and kind, lest Iris fear her anger. "Has your father hurt you – the way he hurts your ma?"

Iris's forehead crunched into tight folds. Her lips trembled. "No Jessie, no, no," she whimpered, "not my Da."

Jessie took another step back. "Iris, I don't understand. Someone has hurt you. I can see it. If it's not your Da, then who? Who has hurt you?" She deliberated for a few moments then lowered her voice, praying she was wrong. "Was it those workmen from the manor?"

Iris bit her bottom lip and reached for her face. Jessie watched her flounder, grappling to string together her words, so she took hold of her shoulders. "Iris, look at me."

Iris squeezed her eyes shut and pushed her chin into her chest, but Jessie would not let her bury herself, or the truth. She peeled Iris's fingers from her face. "Speak, Iris. Tell me now. I can fix it."

Iris looked up and a waterfall of tears rushed down her colourless face. "Ma's fixed it. I must go to stay with my aunt on the coast … just for a bit."

Jessie's breath jammed in her throat. Oblivious to the rough bark snatching at her clothes, Iris slid down the tree and slumped onto the dirt. Jessie joined her and they both sat gripping their knees, the enormity of the situation screaming in their ears. Reality whipped and thrashed like sheets drying on a windy day. When Jessie was sure her head might explode, Lily whimpered. She lifted her off the grass then clutched her to her breast, breathing in the comforting scent of innocence. She didn't look up. "Does your Da know?"

Iris took a few seconds. "No."

Jessie rocked until her breathing matched Lily's. She called on the sounds of the birds and the rustling of the leaves to expel the darkness in her mind and wash the dread from her heart. When she looked up and cast her eyes from the top of Iris's head down to her feet, each instinct twitched. She looked at Iris's tear-stained face. "If your Mam fixed it, what can I do?"

Iris cleared her throat, but her words rattled. "I don't want to go."

Jessie reached out with her free arm and Iris flopped against her. Lily stilled, as though she sensed the need for comfort. Jessie's mind grappled with how she might possibly help, and despite a deep understanding of what she should undoubtedly do, her heart ached against the sobs rumbling in Iris's chest. She lifted Iris's damp chin and looked into eyes overflowing with despair. She pulled her to her feet. "Come to me later."

Iris's mouth dropped open but Jessie squeezed her. "Don't tell anyone. Now go."

Jessie watched Iris disappear. She clutched Lily tighter, turned, and left.

Father Coyle sat in his cart drumming his fat fingers against his belly. His acerbic mood lessened, and a chuckle rumbled in the back of his throat. He looked at the sky and nodded, watching Jessie disappear down the road. "Thank you," he sniggered, before lashing the back of the horse then moving on from the corner where he'd stopped to pee against a tree.

Lily whined and squirmed despite Jessie's promises of an imminent feed. No amount of stroking or back patting soothed her hungry tummy, so with a heart bursting with pain and a mind full of trouble, Jessie rushed home. The wind added to her frustration, whipping the branches into a frenzy, merging their loud rustling and snapping with the increasing volume of Lily's cries. She focused on her quick feet, each step precise, avoiding loose stones or windswept twigs determined to slow her down. Although tempted to snap at her child, and curse the wind, she accepted it was her own fault she was late, and even if he wasn't being agreeable at this moment, only God controls the weather. She chewed her lips, breathing through her nostrils, remembering her mother's words.

"Don't waste energy on battles you can't win."

By the time she turned onto the rough path leading to her house, Lily had almost wriggled out of her clothes, Jessie's hair wore a bonnet of leaves, and between the wind howling and Lily screaming, she couldn't hear herself think. No sooner had she closed her gate when Alec, Tom's colleague from the fields, appeared in her doorway and ran towards her. His mousy brown hair had long forgotten which way to grow, and with help from the wind, he appeared more like a gorgon than a farmhand. If the colour of his face revealed anything, it was a combination of fear and anxiety, coupled with two eyes ready to leap out and run away. Jessie's stomach lurched. "Alec, what's happened?"

Alec's words resembled Iris's garbled mess, so she slapped his shoulder. He stopped breathing for a second, then blurted.

"Tom's not well, Jess. I brought him home, and now they're all here, it's worse than the uproar down the tavern after last rounds." He grabbed his hair as if to stop his head from shaking, but when Jessie pushed past him, he held her arm and bent towards her ear. Jess, I have to tell you. He was roamin' around the dig, rambling to himself." He wiped his forehead, but with only one hand gripping his hair, his head shook again. Jessie tried to calm him.

"Alec, Tom's not well. He sometimes forgets where he is. I need to go in."

Alec tightened his grip on her elbow. "No, Jess, I'm sorry to tell you, but it's not just that."

"What?"

Alec caught his breath. "He was naked Jess, not a stitch in sight. Took me forever to find his clothes. Scattered all over the place, and he was getting whipped by the wind."

Jessie's knees wobbled and only Lily's yelping kept her mind from freezing. Alec rambled on but the words flew around her head like hungry birds. She forced her legs to move. "Alec, let me go. I need to be with Tom."

Alec bent towards her ear once more. "Jess, come find me. There're things I must tell ye." His bulging eyes darted towards the door, but he cocked his head towards the window. "His lot's trouble, Jess. They're up to no good. You be strong now."

He released her elbow, and she watched shadows cross his eyes. "Thank you. You're a kind man."

He shrugged. "Your Mammie was good to me my whole life. She fixed every boil I ever had, even when it was in my head."

Jess looked down at Lily's sleeping face, her hunger and energy now sapped by her crying. She breathed deep and walked to the door, keeping Lily still. Raised voices assaulted her ears the moment she entered. She looked past them into the gloom of the bedroom then lifted her free arm. "Shush! Right now." Her raspy whisper caught their attention. The commotion ceased, and all eyes swung towards Lily. Jessie walked to the middle of the room, ignoring the simmering energy. She looked towards the bedroom, but kept her hand in the air, hoping the command would work. Her words floated from her mouth, leaving her rage waiting in her throat. "I will tend to my husband, and my child needs to be fed. You can sit here quietly, or you can leave." The silence lifted her and guided her into the bedroom. She closed the door behind her.

Her senses reeled when she reached Tom's bedside. His breathing tainted the air, an ominous odour suffocating both energy and light. She briefly shut her eyes before invoking her mother and her guides to join her; to provide a ring of protection from the darkness, and fill them both with the strength they would need to see this night through She dragged the rocker close to the bedside, coaxed Lily to her breast, then lay her hand tenderly on Tom's. After watching his expressionless face for a few moments, she leaned back, listening to Lily's sucking. She begged her spirits to hold off the Grim Reaper even though the constant knocking of the wood beetle throbbed in her head.

Chapter 20

WITH JESSIE AND LILY by his side, Tom's death came in the same unremarkable way snow falls in darkness. Jessie held his hand, whispering in his ear while Lily slept. She reminded him of their love and promises, then thanked him for the gift of their precious daughter. After his last breath brushed her cheek, she opened the windows, blessed his soul and gave him permission to leave. She waited until dawn, fed and changed Lily, then moved to the front room where Robert, Jean and Mary slept. She took a moment to look at each face, knowing it would be the last time she would see them at peace. Her stomach churned, but she tiptoed around the room, lighting candles, covering her only mirror with a black cloth, and removing the chime ball from the clock, before kneeling to build the fire before the family stirred. She remained on her knees when Jean's shriek ripped through her, followed by Robert and Mary's wailing. She heard the rush of feet to Tom's bedside and didn't need to look to understand the grief had begun. The trouble would come later.

The trouble did arrive: Father Coyle and Doctor MacFarlane. Accusations and threats flew at Jessie, but she surrounded herself in white light and silent prayers. Invisible spears rattled her core in an unrelenting attack, so it took her best efforts to avoid the onslaught and remain calm. She tolerated Tom's group of tormentors, restraining her desire to throw a burning log at each of them. When the noise escalated, Lily objected and soon her screaming outperformed the mourners. Jessie seized the opportunity. She swung a shawl over her shoulders, wrapped Lily tight, and marched to the door. She begged the door handle to steady her before clearing her throat. "You may sit with your son and grieve. I need to inform my family, and Lily needs peace."

Jean's mouth dropped open, and before Father Coyle got the opportunity to voice his opinion, Jessie slammed the door behind her. She rushed to her father's house, heart racing, leaving deep boot impressions in the damp path. Her fingers snagged on the metal latch, so she kicked open the gate, staggered up the path and banged on the door. Her lungs deflated only when she heard the shuffling of slippers on stone from inside. Fraser flung open the door, squinting into the daylight. Without warning, Jessie's legs gave way, and Fraser's outline faded like a retreating ghost. As she dropped to her knees, he caught Lily. She heard him roar his father's name before she crumbled into a heap.

When her eyes opened, her cheeks were still damp, but the warmth and aroma of hot bread and burning logs soothed her for a moment. Dougal, Angus and Fraser knelt so close their warm breath competed with the surrounding air. Her fingers curled into her father's thick hands and her voice trembled. "Tom's gone."

"It's all right, lass. Just breathe. You're safe with us."

Reality slapped her. "Lily, where's Lily?"

"Hush now. She's fast asleep ... and none the wiser."

Angus retreated to the hearth, but soon the familiar sound of a boiling kettle and mugs clinking in the sink nudged her. Unwilling bones punished her with shooting pains, forcing her to lean back in the chair and be still. She looked into her father's sunken eyes and begged forgiveness from the spectre of guilt standing foremost in her mind. Her poor father grieved so for his wife. He struggled to make it through his own days, and now she sat numb, in need of his care and attention. His powerful hands reached for hers and she watched a flicker of understanding light his eyes. He raised his eyebrows. "I'm fine, Jess. This is your burden, so here is where you should be."

Hot sweet tea rushed down her throat, flattening anxious bubbles fighting for space in her stomach. She prayed she might melt into the couch, to hide until her world flipped and made things right, but reasoning subdued her wishes. Thankfully, her father and Fraser insisted on returning home with her, to help with the arrangements and manage her in-laws. Angus hesitated when Dougal asked him to join them, so Jessie took his arm. "Go to work, Angus. There's nothing you can do now; you can't lose your job on account of me."

He pulled away, and she suddenly regretted her choice of words.

"I simply don't want you to worry about me."

Angus stomped out. Fraser scratched his head. "What's got him?"

Dougal fired a glance at Jessie. "Something we're not to be involved with."

The atmosphere in Jessie's house remained cold; bleak energy greeting them the minute they walked through the door. Dougal stepped in front, and Jessie watched him straighten, his shoulders filling his coat as if blown up from the inside. "Father Coyle, it's good of you to visit." He turned towards Tom's family, huddled so tight on the small couch its legs disappeared under their mass. Jessie's instinct was to grab each one by their hair then toss them into the street, but common sense prevailed. Father Coyle moved towards Dougal; Jessie inched closer to her father. Even the rough tweed of his jacket struggled to contain his angry heat, and her own skin warmed. Before Dougal uttered one word, Jean's curses flew at him, followed by Robert's growling. He jumped out of his seat, launching himself at Dougal. "This is her fault, and by God, she'll pay."

Jean dug her fingers into Mary's arm. "She poisoned him!" she seethed. "She's evil and should burn in hell!"

"Enough!" Dougal barked. "This is a terrible time, so you all need to calm yerselves. For the love of God, my daughter has lost her husband, and her wean is without a father."

Jessie watched Robert's cheeks blow up, gradually turning purple. "God? Don't you dare use that word! You're nothing but a bunch of pagans." His eyes narrowed and his tongue fought with the spittle in his mouth. "Murdering heathens, the lot of you!"

Dougal stepped within an inch of him. "That's fighting talk, Robert, and I won't stand here listening to pure shite. You should wheisht now and show some respect for what my lassie is going through."

Robert opened his mouth, but Father Coyle stepped between them. Jessie's neck tightened and her fingers dug into her palms. The priest gripped both men by their shoulders.

"Tom is lying cold in the other room, so we should be praying over him. There'll be time enough to learn the truth of his passing ... and deal with the culprit, after his soul is at rest." He glared at Jessie. "Poor Tom didn't even get the *blessings of the last rites to unburden himself, to ease his soul." His eyes locked with hers.*

Dougal pulled away, but it was Jessie who retaliated. Her words unleashed themselves and darted past her father, aimed at the priest's smug expression. "Tom had nothing to unburden, so his soul is as content as his newborn babe. He went to his maker in peace, blessed with the love of his wife and child."

Jean leapt out of her chair and unleashed her own temper. "We should have been with him. You denied us our rights. You were never here when Tom was at his worst, he'd still be alive if he'd left you. I swear to God when I find out how you killed him, I will hang you myself!"

The room froze, and all eyes shot towards Jean. Her face matched Robert's, both testing the limits of their blood pressure. Jean's red-rimmed eyes and puffy cheeks exposed deep grief, but her clenched, white-knuckled fists and pursed lips registered her dark fury. When the enormity of her claim settled, voices rose until a windstorm of words swirled in a swiftly forming tornado of anger and intimidation. Dougal swung around to face the priest.

"I won't stand here and have anyone accuse my daughter of anything." His menacing expression stilled them. "If you have sense, you'll mind your tongues and your threats. You'll calm this fever and not make things worse than they are. There's a funeral to prepare, so if you have any love for your boy in there, you'll pull yourselves together and give him the send-off he deserves." He turned to Jessie, almost knocking her off her feet. "Jess, go be with your man, do what needs done."

The funeral proceeded in a haze of reverent ritual, but unlike the graceful rites, soulful dirge, and entirely spiritual essence of Heather's ceremony, Tom's was a full requiem mass; held in Father Coyle's church. Jessie clutched a stone in each pocket of her jacket and let her mind travel while listening to the priest swing between sad laments and pious admonitions. Only the infrequent mention of Tom's name interfered with her internal sermon – and discussion with her mother. Neither the heat simmering behind her eyes, nor the constant ache of her bruised heart, would crack the invisible armour she wore that day. She swallowed her father's advice and now worked hard to impersonate the humble daughter-in-law, and devout Christian they expected.

"This is not a day for tempers or opinions, Jess. No good will come if you poke their nest; so, do as they do, and be done with it."

His deep sigh reminded her of how difficult his life had been, juggling his own beliefs with her mother's. The sadness and worry darkening his eyes cooled her defiance, but no one could sway her regarding Maggie's attendance. She'd raged when Angus suggested otherwise.

"She will be! I need her. For me, and to manage Lily. I won't be turned."

Maggie entered the church first, slinking into the back corner, armed with a small jar of honey; should Lily wake and attract attention. It was her right to sit up front next to Jessie, but she enjoyed guilty relief – happy to be as far from Father Coyle as possible. She fixed her eyes on Lily's content expression, willing her to remain asleep, but her body flinched each time Father Coyle's voice thundered towards her; thick with insinuation and veiled threats against any who may step outside the flock. She often looked up to see Jessie, head bowed, sitting rock still between her father and Fraser.

Dougal nudged Jessie from her contemplation. "It's done, Jess."

Jessie caught Angus's tear-filled eyes when the coffin passed her. He held the back left corner, the effort turning his fingers white. Even through his illness, Tom remained a formidable size, which comforted her. A fusion of wailing and an out-of-tune hymn looped around sad-faced statues, pulsing against bright stained-glass windows, before fading into the polished timber rafters. The mourners left in a state of near hysteria, a haze of incense cloaking either fear or virtuous intent. After the last person left and silence prevailed, Maggie smiled at Lily, fast asleep. "Thank you, my angel."

Jessie waited for Maggie outside the church grounds while the men proceeded to the cemetery. Maggie ambled towards her and grinned. "She slept the entire time, and I kept her ears well covered."

Jess stroked Lily's bonnet. "Thank you, Mags. Come home with me, we can spend a quiet afternoon." Maggie's lips stiffened, but she ignored it. "They can all say what they wish. We are not going anywhere near the wake. Tom will be in the ground before long, and I have no kindness for them."

Maggie's shoulders dropped. "If that's what you want, God knows I don't want to be in their den either ... but there will be talk, and it won't take long to reach us."

Jessie hooked her arm and sighed. "Aye, so let's have some tea, she won't sleep all day."

Maggie hugged Lily tight. "She will if she's with me."

Tom was no sooner in the ground, the men dispersed to his parent's house for the wake, when Father Coyle took Robert's elbow and led him around the back wall of the cemetery. Robert took out his tobacco tin and got to work stuffing his old clay pipe. Grief masked his face, impeding his usually nimble fingers, so before long more tobacco surrounded his feet than made it into the blackened bowl. Father Coyle tapped his thumbs above his clasped hands, allowing Robert time to compose himself. Two raucous children running between gravestones, trampling flowers along the way, gave him the opportunity to release some tension. "Get out of there, you torags! I'll give your disrespectful backsides a beating if I catch you in here again."

His bellow sent the birds screeching, scattering leaves as they shot from the branches. Both children froze for a few seconds before sprinting out the gate and down the road. The commotion jolted Robert from his gloom. He sucked hard on his pipe, leaning against the mouldy stone wall. Father Coyle bent towards him. "This is a nasty business, Robert, and now your son has paid the price. It's high time we get rid of this heathen element." Eagerness shone from his bright, beady eyes, quivering on his fat lips; all propriety and reverence for the recent solemn occasion flown with the scattered birds. Robert blew smoke into the air then watched it as if expecting it to return. The priest's robes vibrated his impatience. "Robert, do you hear me? You cannot let this go; Tom deserves justice. We must be resolute!"

Robert blew out another puff. "I know, father, I know. Of course, we want justice for Tom."

The priest stomped a circle into the grass before facing him again. "We need to investigate how Tom died, and what else has been going on. We will question those he worked with, and we'll find out where she has been disappearing to. I'll also go round our parishioners and question them."

He retraced his circle, not giving the grass a chance to spring back, but when he turned, Robert raised a hand. The priest stopped blabbering. Robert's eyes narrowed. "You don't need to, Father."

The priest stepped back and opened his mouth, but Robert shook his head.

"We know how Tom died. He was poisoned."

Father Coyle spluttered, "Exactly, but we must prove she did it."

Robert raised his hand again, and now the priest's frown crunched his entire forehead.

"We can prove it." He banged his pipe against the wall, watching the burnt remnants of his tobacco flutter to the ground. "Jean has the poison. She found it in their kitchen."

Chapter 21

MAGGIE'S BABY MINDING OFFER came as welcome relief whenever Jessie needed to get out of the house or take an overdue nap. Maggie insisted she take time for herself, but restricted her to walks in the fields, tending her herbs or picking wildflowers on the copse. Her fierce expression and pointed finger appeared at any mention of going to the market though.

"You'll go nowhere near without me in tow, young lady. You'll not give anyone a chance to spit in your eye unless I'm there to belt them. Do you hear me?"

Maggie's cautions amused Jessie, but she knew not to cross her. "I hear you Mags ... again."

Maggie puffed out her chest, her resolute nod wobbling her chin. She relished her time with Lily, taking her care of duty seriously. She also kept an ear close to the ground to keep Jessie aware of the accusations and threats circling her. Tom's family would not allow their son's death to go unpunished, and stories of Jessie's imminent demise fired up the troublemakers – and kept her supporters inside. Jessie disregarded the noise as gossip and rabble-rousing, but Maggie worried. She put nothing past Father Coyle. Neither did Angus, so the day after Tom's burial, he went to warn Jessie.

Amidst the usual screeching during changing time, she barely heard him knocking. She left Lily happily wriggling around naked in her basket, slung a clean cloth nappy over her shoulder and opened the door. Her mood lifted seeing Angus on her doorstep, but it was short-lived. His jaw, stiff as his arms, matched his fists stuck fast in his pockets. She gestured for him to come inside. Hearing Lily gurgle, he relaxed and walked to her basket. As Jessie watched him play with Lily's fingers, she recalled how as children and close siblings they used to lean over the bank of the river to play with the tadpoles, feeling the featherlight sensation of new life darting in and out *of each finger. Fleeting touches brushing against their skin, the excitement it brought. Simple pleasures ... in simpler times.*

Angus turned to look at her. "She is so beautiful." His smile brightened his eyes, and Jessie believed her heart might burst. "She is."

She watched his joy wane, so she took his arm. "Sit, there's something on your mind."

"We're worried about you, and Da thinks you should live with him."

"This is my home, Angus, Lily's home. If there's to be trouble, I'm not taking it to Da."

Angus flopped into a chair. "Jess, don't be stubborn. Do you know what's being said about you?"

His expression hurt her. "I do."

"So? You should worry. Tom's family won't think twice about throwing you out of here, and that might be the least they do."

Jessie folded her arms and hugged herself. She glanced around the room, breathing in the aroma of burnt wood, sage and dry thatch. It seemed smaller, darker, but even without Tom, she still regarded it as their home. Angus's pained expression stole the colour from his eyes and pricked her conscience. "I'm sorry to bring this upon our family. The last thing I want is trouble at your door ... so I'm staying here."

Angus stood, but his shoulders sagged as if his energy were still in the chair.

Jess tried to lighten his mood. "Angus, you always say I'm a force to be reckoned with, so tell Da not to worry about me."

"Don't be silly, Jess. There're things even you can't fix."

She stood on her doorstep, watching him lope through the gate. As he disappeared around the corner, she peered up and down the desolate street in response to shivers running up her spine.

The banging came in the dead of night. Tom's father stood arms folded, grim faced, next to two police officers Jessie had never seen. In a village with relatively little crime, other than the odd drunken brawl usually sorted out by the brawler's wives, or the occasional pinching of sweets or fruit from the market, dealt with by an angry mother with a tight grip on a slipper, there was no need for a resident police force. Adults policed each other, and fear of being sent to a 'home for bad people' kept most children away from anything deserving more than a beating and bed without dinner.

"Get in here so I can tan your arse," was a common refrain soon followed by, "No, Ma, it wasn't me!" And the slamming of a front door.

So, when Jessie stood at her doorway dressed only in bedclothes, it was the sight of the police officers that surprised and confused her most. Before she managed to adjust to the darkness, the more officious-looking officer instructed her to dress and come to the church hall. The mention of church jolted her awake and ignited her fury.

"I will not! Who are you to wake me in the middle of the night when my baby is fast asleep?" Her voice rang into the emptiness of the night. Robert flinched. One officer shuffled from one foot to the other, eyes downcast, while the other rambled written instructions, and reasons she should not refuse. She did not hear one word of it. Her blood boiled, her temper raged, and as he droned on, her roar abruptly frightened the nocturnal population back to bed. "I am not moving from this house! My baby is asleep. I will not wake her, or go anywhere near your church hall at this time of night."

Ignoring her, the officer completed his formal delivery, then both police officers turned to Robert. Before he could speak, Jessie put up a hand. "If you want to discuss anything with me, come to my father's house tomorrow afternoon. Now get yerselves away from here."

She turned and slammed the door almost off its hinges. Weak knees barely made it to the chair, where she rested her head on tight fists, listening for any sound outside – praying none would come. Muffled voices rose then fell before thuds of boots on her path signalled their retreat. Only then did she feel her lungs push against her ribs, desperate for air. A deep breath relieved her stress but triggered a rush of nausea. Leaning over her sink, she drank a glass of water then paced the floor, checking on Lily more often than was necessary, until her eyes scratched. When the adrenalin finally stopped pulsing, she dropped, exhausted, onto her bed. Before sleep took her, she envisaged her mother's face, but it did not bring peace. She determined it was time to consult her stones, but first, rest.

When she woke to Lily's screams, red, swollen eyes and tear-stained face, guilt shot through her. She'd slept as if dead, but Lily hadn't and she was unhappy about it. A feed, nappy change and cuddle soon mellowed her, and she settled back in her basket so Jessie could wash, dress, and make herself tea. Her hands trembled when she replayed the night-time visit, regretting bellowing at the police officer before hearing precisely what he had to say. Inviting them back to her Da's house made her want to punch her own head. After telling Angus she didn't want to bring trouble to her Da's door, she had now done exactly that. She didn't think Robert needed police officers to remove her from the house, even if he expected her to refuse. His show of force hadn't worked, so what next, and how would she fight him? After two cups of tea, she still battled fatigue. Maggie arrived with her usual happy greeting and bone-crushing hug, but stepped back, shoved her hands onto her hips and peered at Jessie's pale face. "Have you not slept? Did Lily have a restless night?"

Maggie's oblivion of her night's trauma shocked Jessie. "Yes," she lied, "I'm exhausted, but I would love a walk, some fresh air and a bit of quiet."

Maggie hesitated, then nodded. "Off you go, sit by a tree. Rest your mind and give your body a break."

"Thank you, Mags, I'll be back before her feed." She yanked her shawl off the couch, wrapped it over her head and bolted.

Her heart thumped in time with her boots, and it took deft manoeuvring and a tight grip on her skirts to avoid sliding over mossy rocks in her rush to Myna's. There was little time before Lily's next feed.

Myna's shocked expression when she found Jessie on her doorstep didn't surprise her. Jessie leaned against the door frame, punching her chest, gulping air until Myna pulled her inside and led her to a chair. Myna knelt before Jessie's heaving body.

"Dear God, Jess, what on earth? Why are you here? You know it's not safe."

Jessie gulped a breath, filling her cheeks with colour, her eyes with fire. "Of course I know it's not safe, Myna, but if I'm to go to jail, I need to know why."

Myna's lack of surprise on hearing of Robert's visit with the police officers made Jessie think she had spent too much of her time buried in grief and motherhood, and her blank stare only fed her impatience. "Myna, look at me, tell me what is going on." Her lips throbbed and her fingers tested the strength of the chair fabric.

Myna looked over her shoulder then put a finger to her mouth. "Shush, Jessie, the girls are still asleep. Calm down, take a breath. Come outside."

Jessie sucked in the warm air from Myna's leftover evening fire, but even the inviting smell of herbs and baking, which usually provided comfort, was powerless to break through her cloak of fury. "I don't have time for calm, or a walk in the woods. Maggie doesn't know I'm here and Lily will need a feed soon."

Myna took her elbow, dragging her outside, down the path. Hands strong enough to roll a skein of wool into a perfect sphere, or turn dough into twenty identical rolls without a glance, trembled and fidgeted uncontrollably. The morning sun slept late, but as she waited for Myna to compose herself, Jessie's heart warned her the surrounding chill wasn't on account of the weather. "I know nothing about the smithies and neither did my Mam."

Myna held up her hands in prayer. "Yes, Jess, we don't think you do, but you've drawn so many people to visit us it's caused a huge amount of talking. You can't protect everyone, and you've already attracted too much attention.

Jessie reached for the air. "Myna, if it's not the smithies, why are they after me at all? What are you not telling me?"

Myna stepped closer and her eyes filled. "Tom, Jess, they believe you poisoned Tom. Someone gave them a bottle from your house ... they're convinced it's poison."

Jessie's knees buckled as Jean's face blazed in her mind. "I didn't poison Tom. I couldn't possibly have done that. No matter how difficult the situation became, I never stopped loving him. They surely don't think I would, and they can't believe I know anything about the smithies." Her mind reeled. "Did you know Iris was pregnant?"

Myna stiffened. "Yes, and that's why you're in trouble with Laura."

Jessie stepped back. "Why?"

Myna clasped her hands. "I treated her injuries and gave her medicine ... to settle her. Laura planned for her to go to her sister on the pretence of learning how to weave. She would return with an orphan child who Laura would raise as her own. She arranged it … then you gave Iris the potion."

Each waited for the other to speak, but neither found the words until the door opened and Tevia appeared. Myna swung around, glaring at the young girl.

"Tevia, go inside."

Before the door closed, Jessie watched Tevia's eyes flash towards her, then look away. Her heart missed a beat. "Myna, are the girls angry with me?"

Myna's frown provided the answer. "You shouldn't have done it, Jess. We warned you to be careful. We told you over and over to be patient, not to push our ways on others. Now everything is at risk. I'm trying to protect you on account of your mother and Lily, but we're all in danger now. We'll be lucky if we survive this. Only Laura and I know about Iris, so the police aren't coming after you for that."

Jessie's tears came fast and heavy. "I didn't mean to harm anyone, Myna. I only want to improve life for all of us women. It's my calling, my history, my obligation."

"Jess, your gifts and your destiny don't put you above the safety of others. The gifts you possess are for the good of us all, but you must manage them carefully. Your mother warned you. This will not work out well. Not for you, for us, or for Laura and her family. I understand better than you think, so please go home now. Come back tomorrow morning before sunrise. I need to show you something."

Jessie's anger gave way to bewilderment. "How can I? I need Maggie to take care of Lily. What does she know?"

Myna glanced around as if there were eyes in the trees. "Bring them with you. Just do as I say, but for the love of your child please mind your temper … and keep your mouth shut."

Jessie nodded then turned to leave, but turned back, pain hurting her throat. "Am I truly in such danger?"

Myna raised her hands in prayer again. "Father Coyle will try whatever he can to burn you on his own home-made stake."

Like a homing bird, Jessie's natural instincts guided her back through the forest, but she cried the entire way. Muddled thoughts churned her anxious stomach. When she reached her front door, she wiped her face and straightened, but the instant

Maggie looked at her, the room stilled. Jessie leaned against her soft chest and sobbed.

Maggie remained quiet until Jessie calmed, then lifted her chin. "I knew you needed more than a walk. Tell me."

Chapter 22

FATHER COYLE TAPPED A *gleaming brass letter opener against his tight, white knuckles. His slitted eyes followed wisps of smoke snaking their way up from his early morning fire around the multitude of statues lining the carved mantelpiece. Only when a knuckle objected did he break his mindfulness, toss the opener aside, lurch out of his armchair and go to the window. Smoke billowed, agitated by his flapping robes, layering an ashen facade on his underlying fury. Peering up and down the empty street did nothing to appease his mood, but when a few young boys appeared on the path to the school, he marched out of his office down the stone steps, slamming the door behind him. He strode across the road and stood with clenched fists, watching the boys file past – some offering a courteous nod, but most keeping their eyes downcast, following their shoes. He snarled at the bowed heads. "Get a move on. You'll learn nothing by dragging your feet. God has no time for laziness."*

When a group of three young boys walked by, he whipped out an arm and seized the young redhead by his collar. Laura's son, Callan, almost lost his footing, and when he turned to the priest, his eyes bulged from his petrified face and every freckle faded beneath his skin. Father Coyle bent towards his ear.

"You go straight home after classes and tell your mother to come see me." The young boy nodded, but the priest barked. "Did you hear me? Today!"

"Aye, father."

The priest poked a finger into the boy's bony chest. "It's 'yes, Father', not Aye. Make sure you tell her."

"Yes, Father." Callan stammered, turned and ran.

The priest marched to the old cowshed behind the church housing equal amounts of building stone, chopped wood and broken tools. Having not homed any cows for some years, Father Coyle's ageing horse and cart occupied the bulk of its space. Left behind by a farmer who'd gone off to make a better living kelp farming on the islands, it provided the most basic form of transport for the priest, a constant source of his irritation. On his arrival to minister to his new parish, he could not conceal his horror when presented with it. He had stomped into the dusty space, disturbing the cobwebs lining the crumbling walls and boarded-up windows.

"If you expect me to bestow sacraments from that claptrap, I suggest you get to work and transform it into a carriage worthy of my station!"

Two Gaelic speaking farmers had exchanged looks, adding exasperation to his humiliation. Picking up a hammer which may well have come from the Battle of Culloden, the priest threw it at the confused farmers, snorting when it fell apart upon hitting the ground, rousing a family of mice from their sleep. The farmers had watched in silence as he turned on his heel and marched out leaving a mini tornado of dust and hay behind his flapping robes. Although the cart underwent some minor refurbishments, Father Coyle's bulk tested the already weakened wheels to their limits. When they squealed their distress, even his lofty robes could not mask the shame on his face, so he avoided using it – citing unfavourable weather – which he deemed a permanent problem in Scotland.

Now his immediate desire to visit Wilson left him no choice but to stem his self-importance and feign the humility his position presumed. Framed in the barn's arched doorway beams, he bellowed for attention. Within minutes, his cart prepared, he headed off to the manor, venting his mortification and discomfort by whipping the elderly horse at each bounce over rocks or splash through puddles. Donald helped him disembark, watching the flustered priest dust himself down, remove fallen leaves from his shoulders, then rearrange his voluminous overcoat. When composed, the priest snarled. "Check the wheels on my cart. I want them spotless ... and get that nag cleaned up before I leave."

Fearing Father Coyle's face may explode, Donald avoided engaging, simply nodding. He took the horse's reins and turned away. "If he lives," he muttered, stroking the horse's heaving belly.

From behind his desk, Charles Wilson's irritation twitched in his eyes and crackled in his voice as the priest settled himself into a large chair, before snapping at Wilson's doorman to bring him tea.

"Coyle, I am busy and this is not a good day. I wish you would give me notice when you plan to visit."

The priest patted the armrests and huffed. "You are the only person this side of London with a telephone, and with the tardy disposition of everybody around here it might be weeks before I reach you."

Charles pushed aside his journals, rolled his eyes and leaned back. "Nevertheless, you are here. What do you want?"

Studded leather squeaked beneath the priest when he leaned forward to rest his fists on his knees. "I feel I need to update you on the matter of the missing blacksmiths ... and the unfortunate practices of these pagan women."

Wilson folded his arms. "I see."

Father Coyle clasped his hands together, but even their weight didn't prevent his knees bouncing happily as soon as Wilson stopped and paid him attention. Like a child about to present a gift, his eyes widened and a grin spread across his face. "I always trusted my suspicions and now we have proof. That old witch's daughter is exactly like her mother, and caused the death of her poor husband."

Wilson's frown spread as swiftly as Father Coyle's grin. "Good God! She murdered her husband?"

"She most certainly did." The priest thumped the arm rest, unsettling the only few hidden dust mites. "He was a poorly man, a burden to her, so she poisoned him, in order to grab the home for herself and practise her evil without him stopping her."

Wilson's jaw twitched and his moustache followed. "If you have proof, have the authorities arrested her yet ... and what does she have to do with my men disappearing?"

Father Coyle shifted in his chair. "Police visited her house just last night, but her baby was asleep, so she refused to be taken."

"Refused? Is it common practice around here to refuse to be arrested?" Wilson's sneer wiped the smirk off the priest's face, unsettling the spittle balancing on the corners of his lips.

"No, it is not. However, these officers are not familiar with this part of Scotland, so were unsure of what to do considering the baby. I now have information linking her to your missing *workmen, so any minute we will remove her from her home and deal with her." He puffed out his chest and clasped his hands on his lap.*

Wilson eyed the priest. "Unless, of course, the infant objects?"

This swift slap to the priest's endeavours heated his face but chilled the room. He pulled himself out of his armchair, lifted his shoulders and glared. "The infant will be removed, taken to a children's home, brought up in God's good faith. That pagan will spend the rest of her life in a women's prison far away from here. It will be a lesson to anyone around these parts: evil will not be tolerated."

Wilson rose and walked to the large window overlooking the gravel yard. He gazed out towards the forest, tapping his gold family ring on the polished window ledge. The sun blinked through a smattering of determined cloud bubbles struggling to lighten the day. Father Coyle wrung his hands and chewed his bottom lip. When Wilson turned to face him, neither man spoke, and the air hung expectantly, waiting to be breathed in or blown out. Wilson traced the toe of his shoe around a gold leaf pattern on the carpet, his gaze fixed on the polished toe cap. He straightened before sauntering back to his seat. His snide expression gave way to a tight-lipped stiffness.

"Father Coyle, whatever becomes of that woman is of no interest to me. Arrest her, don't arrest her. Unless, of course, you have solid proof she is to blame for the disappearance of my workmen, in which case I will have her arrested myself. I am paying wages to both families until I have reason not to, so the sooner you resolve this, the better."

"Imminently, I guarantee you," the priest spluttered.

Wilson put up his hand. "I want to know what has happened to my men, and frankly I believe it would be worthwhile for me to go ahead with my plans to flatten the forest once and for all. If they have nowhere to hide, perhaps they will move on. Alternatively, I will move them on."

The priest twisted his sweaty hands. "I understand, of course. However, perhaps you ought to hold off on destroying the forest as it has great sentimental value to the families here. Many of whom have children in our school."

Wilson sneered. "They can look for another school, or return to whichever trees they sat under before I agreed to fund your plans. This school of yours looks like it's creating more problems than it's worth. Your assertion of an educated community serving me better than an uneducated rabble remains an expensive gamble, for here I am, constantly throwing money your way. Yet despite that, they behave like rabble."

The priest sucked in, almost choking. He tried to speak, but Wilson thundered. "Get these people in order or I will burn down that forest and your school!"

Before the priest replied, a kitchen maid knocked and entered carrying Wilson's morning tea.

"I'm sorry sir, I didn't realise you had company. Shall I bring another cup?"

To Father Coyle's horror, Wilson shook his head. "No, that will not be necessary. Please find Angus and tell him to report to me immediately."

The maid scurried off and Father Coyle pushed his fists into his robe's pockets. "Angus, what is your intention with him?"

Wilson ignored the priest and busied himself with pouring his tea.

Donald's whistling had disrupted Angus's daily log of tackle, shoes and feed stores requiring attention, but the minute a horse's stringy mane filled his window when he led it past, Angus jumped out of his chair, rushing outside. Donald had nodded his usual greeting, but Angus stepped out and blocked his way, so he cocked his head towards the horse and a frown crinkled his freckled forehead. "Hiya Angus, look who's visiting."

"I see. Do you know why?" Angus hoped his words belied the tightness in his throat, but Donald's eyes narrowed. "No, but he never brings good news. You worried about something?"

Angus shook his head without conviction, taking the reins from Donald, and walking the horse to the stables. Donald followed in silence, but after he'd removed the hefty tack and given the horse a drink, he handed Angus a bunch of carrots. "Well, if yer hanging around, feed the poor nag. After that journey he might just keel over."

Angus chuckled, always amused by Donald's lack of regard for the priest's status. Watching the rhythmic precision and natural affection of Donald's brushing, he considered how simple life was before he'd become a Wilson employee; before he'd yearned for better things, a more dignified future – before he'd met Father Coyle.

His mother's words rang in his ears:

"Be careful when you reach for grander things. You may lose your soul along the way. Even the moon has its dark side."

The horse, unaware of the increasing tension around him, chomped happily on his carrots while Angus and Donald avoided eye contact. Donald brushed and Angus fed until the sound of feet crunching the gravel interrupted them. Wilson's out of breath tea lady appeared, wisps of dark curls escaping from her cotton cap. After catching her breath, she wiped her brow and tried to stuff them back under the unwilling elastic. Angus dropped the carrots. "What's up?"

"Lord Wilson wants to see you, now. The fat priest is with him, and they both look dour."

Angus picked up the discarded carrots, handing them to Donald before casually dusting himself off. Though sweat pooled under his collar, and his feet insisted on rooting him to the soft earth, he took a deep breath. "I'll see you later, Donald."

Donald scowled. Angus's feeble attempt at nonchalance hadn't worked. Donald stepped in front of him. A few missing teeth – and eyes often struggling to work in unison – often prevented him from being taken seriously, but now his earnest expression and stiff jaw compensated. He glanced at the tea lady still fighting with her unmanageable curls, then bent towards Angus's ear. "I'm on your side, whatever you need."

Blood rushed to Angus's heart, warmed by Donald's concern. It had been a long time since he'd experienced such sincerity. Both men nodded, but Angus turned away before Donald might see his face redden.

Angus arrived within minutes, but stood back, far enough from both men so neither might notice the sweat seeping into his collar. He clutched his damp hands behind his back, struggling to hold his composure. His heart and head perched on a seesaw, the ground stirring under his feet. He spotted Father Coyle's bulk first. Preferring to avoid the man he considered the snake in the garden, he watched Wilson arranging papers on his desk. For a few moments, clangs reverberating from the grandfather clock standing guard in the corner occupied the atmosphere. It crossed Angus's mind how awful it must be to be reminded of the passing of each hour of one's life by a sound so gloomy. Perhaps it contributed to Wilson's contemptuous nature. The time it took for eleven chimes gave Angus a chance to remind himself; although an employee of lesser means, he and his kin held themselves to far more noble standards. He didn't need to look at the fat priest to know he was surely sweating under robes that served no purpose other than to promote his position; one favoured by few around these parts. Sweating – surely a result of apprehension or self-satisfaction – depending on the strength of his influence over Wilson to grant him his devious way. Angus recognised he may well prolong the priest's discomfort depending on his own response to Wilson, but satisfying as it might be, he'd prefer to not spend one extra second in his company. Wilson obviously held the power to make them both sweat, so if this was to be an hour of reckoning, his immediate wish was for the chiming to cease.

Chapter 23

JESSIE AND MAGGIE SPENT the afternoon with Dougal on the pretence of a visit with Lily. Although his eyes lit up, dark shadows sat under hooded eyes, and his unshaven beard only partially hid greying skin. When he shuffled to the kitchen on unsteady legs, hunched shoulders exposing a mess of curls clinging to the back of his neck, Jessie's heart ached. How much he must miss his monthly haircuts from his wife. His bulk no longer filled the room, his vigour no longer gave it life. Their love stood as an example to any considering marriage. Her parents had lived their lives as one complete unit. Without his other half, his spirit now lacked the desire to live, even if he pretended otherwise. The afternoon dragged on, testing Maggie's anxiety to the point she swore the clock had lost its second hand. They took turns keeping watch at the window, making tea, preparing a stew for Dougal, entertaining Lily. When Dougal dozed off with his granddaughter already asleep in his arms, Jessie walked to the bedroom and rested on the corner of the cot bed. Few traces of her beloved mother remained. No happy flowers to brighten the dark wooden chest of drawers – now demoted to housing only Dougal's belongings – desperate for a polish. Her mother's clove trinket box sat on the windowsill undisturbed, and her fingers trembled when she lifted it. She removed the lid, careful not to disturb the cinnamon sticks adorning its surface, then removed her mother's wedding band: a pewter Luckenbooth ring similar to the one she still wore on her finger. Entwined hearts set in a narrow band, topped with a crown, given to each of them with the promise of a glorious life, love and eternal unity. The sun cast a gloomy light through unwashed windows, and if the unmade bed and dirty clothes piled on a chair could speak, they would complain this was sadly now her father's space. However, she only needed to clasp the ring, close her eyes, and her mother's spirit surrounded her. She drew her mind inwards, and soon the gentle touch of her mother's hand stroking her

hair soothed her anxious nerves, followed by the faint aroma of white heather easing her breathing, lulling her into a state of peace where only she and her mother existed. Her heart slowed in time with her mother's stroking, and her shoulders relaxed. She melted into her gentle embrace and watched her mother's face glow, green eyes twinkling, swathing them in a bright, exquisite light. At that moment of serene presence, Jessie wished her mother would take her into the spirit life and hold her in her arms for eternity. Unaware of unchecked tears soaking her cheeks, when she opened her eyes and saw Maggie sitting in the corner, she couldn't help but smile. Maggie reached over and handed her a handkerchief. She took the ring from Jessie's palm and held it.

"She never took this off from the day your Da gave it to her."

Jessie wiped her eyes. "I think we've been here long enough. They'd have come by now."

Maggie nodded, placed the ring back in the clove box, and left the room.

Dougal delighted in the visit – and the stew – snorting when Jessie chided him. "Get those boys to wash the windows, and next time I'm cutting your hair."

She hugged him tight, Maggie promised to visit again, and they left thankful he remained none the wiser to what might have happened. They remained silent on the walk home, other than replying to Lily's babbling, but unspoken worry lingered between them. The authorities had not appeared at Dougal's house, so they may indeed decide to drag Jessie off in the middle of the night. Maggie insisted on sleeping over, offering help with Lily, and a right hook for any police officers who may decide to visit again. "They'll need to get past me first," she assured. After kissing Lily goodnight, she grabbed the broom and stomped off to bed. Jessie insisted Maggie sleep in her bed – she didn't object. "These bones are getting on a bit, and these ankles are not as slim as Myna's," she grumbled. "So, if I'm to be traipsing through the forest tomorrow, I better get them rested."

Jessie spent a fitful night on the couch, desperate for sleep, listening to Lily's contented snuffling and Maggie's rumbling snores. The occasional nocturnal call of owls and frogs distracted her from her inner worries, but each creak and crackle of the thatch above reminded her that her home and safety were now fragile. She considered her stones, but thought better of using them with Maggie in the house. She doubted even if they should appear whether her fractious mind would still sufficiently to feel the energy and understand the visions. Waiting until after her visit to Myna seemed a better idea. Her mother warned her never to consult the stones with an angry or impulsive heart, so this time she elected to heed her advice.

Lily set the day off before the worms rushed into hiding, the light only just filtering sleepily through the branches of the trees, when Jessie bundled her up before helping Maggie into her coat. When they stepped outside, Maggie tucked her scarf into her coat.

"I see neither of us prayed to Cailleach for decent weather."

Jessie looked at the ominous grey not too far above. "I hope the weather is our only trouble today."

The journey proved tricky. Manoeuvring through mud-sodden ground with a wriggling child strapped to her belly, and steadying Maggie up and over tree roots, tested Jessie's strength, balance and temperament. The weather proved contrary, so Jessie soon understood that even with the shelter of thick trees, rain would soak right through if they didn't speed up. Maggie, however, refused to be pushed.

"If I didn't trust you, I'd swear you were trying to kill me," she declared, after grabbing Jessie's arm to slow her down for the third time. "If it's a choice between breaking my neck or getting wet, I'll take my chances with the rain."

Jessie pressed Lily tighter to her chest, but slowed her pace, hoping Myna's reason for the visit would be worth it. The front door flew open before they reached it and Myna huddled them all into the warmth of her kitchen. Cups sat ready, her fire glowing so brightly, Jessie reasoned Myna had also got up before dawn. The twins remained asleep while the women warmed themselves with hot tea and potato scones. They chatted about Lily's gentle personality, and Maggie's grumbling about her damp feet, until Jessie finished feeding Lily and laid her in a basket. Then Jessie turned to Myna.

"Why are we here?"

Myna checked on her girls, and once satisfied they slept soundly, she led Maggie to the chair in the corner and joined

Jessie on the couch. She took her hand. "I have something to show you and somewhere I must take you."

Before she could continue, Maggie thumped the arm of her chair. "Somewhere to go?" she whined. "I've half killed myself coming here at the crack of dawn."

Myna jumped up and stood before her. "Wheisht, you'll wake the girls. There's something I need to explain. God knows I wish I didn't. I never imagined I'd see this day."

Jessie watched her shoulders drop. "Maggie, be quiet. Let Myna speak."

Myna sat with her hands clasped on her lap, speaking as though to herself, and Jessie's heart thumped as she listened.

"I believe we are all in danger now. Heather and I spoke of it happening, never believing it would. We've managed to survive and practise without attracting attention or fear, but now I think Wilson and Father Coyle will track us down then do whatever they think will give them complete control of the village."

Jessie and Maggie sat motionless.

"So," Myna straightened. "If we need to leave in a rush, you need to know how and where."

Myna left Jessie and Maggie donning their coats and went to the twins' bedroom. Puffy eyes and messy hair peeked out from under the folds of a red woollen blanket. When she was sure who the eyes belonged to, she gestured with a finger to her lips and an outstretched hand. Tevia uncurled herself from her sister and followed her mother to the kitchen. Even half awake, Maggie and Jessie standing in their coats startled her, and she wrapped her arms around her shoulders. Myna took her to one side, and after receiving instructions for Lily's care with scant explanation, Tevia settled in the chair beside Lily's basket.

Jessie moved to check on her, but Myna took her arm. "She'll be perfect. We need to go."

Myna led them around the back, through a gap in the fence, along a short, narrow dirt path in the opposite direction to the way Jessie usually approached the house. After a few metres the path led to rough ground until they reached denser woodland. Sun rays tried hard to fight their way through, but when the branches thickened it proved an almost impossible task, and soon the women found themselves in minimal light, *trudging through damp undergrowth and around mouldy tree trunks. The air appeared to crystallise with each breath, and other than the odd mating call of the Pine Martens, the forest remained ominously quiet. Myna led the way while Jessie watched her feet navigate with an ease borne of familiarity. Maggie's laboured breathing throbbed behind, and she hoped the journey would not be too strenuous lest they end up carrying her home. It didn't take long before they reached a clearing, and when Myna stopped, then turned to face them, both Jessie and Maggie looked around in silent wonder. An expanse of lush grass reaching their calves, but only spacious enough for a family picnic, surrounded the low stone wall of a well. Maggie and Jessie gasped, and for a few moments all three stood staring at the rough, moss-embroidered stonework, each deep in their own imaginings.*

Jessie walked towards the well. "How do you know about this place?"

Myna joined her. "Your mom revealed it to me. Her mother showed it to her."

Jessie lifted her hands to her cheeks, and Maggie grumbled. "Is there no end to the mysteries and misgivings around here?"

Myna took Jessie's hand, pulling her away. "We don't have time for stories right now. Follow me."

Maggie grunted. "Would explaining where you're taking us be a story?"

Myna ignored the remark, walked around the well towards more thick trees, then turned and gestured for them to follow. Sometime later, when Jessie deemed this another arduous hike through the forestry, Myna stopped in front of a tall, sheer wall of shrubbery.

"Are we lost now?" Maggie whinged.

"For heaven's above, Maggie, stop moaning! We're not lost, but I need your help."

Myna stepped forward and started pulling at stringy branches of thick entwined bracken, bog myrtle and creeping cowberry. Jessie and Maggie stood transfixed by Myna's assault on the foliage until she turned, glaring. "Don't just stand there, get pulling."

Although Jessie suspected Myna of losing both her way and mind, she launched herself at the bushes, joining her in pulling back ropy stems, stalks and branches, ignoring thorns desperate to thwart their efforts. Maggie grunted before joining them. A few moments later Myna broke through and touched metal. One more fierce pull and a clump of mangled creeper broke away, revealing a short, wrought-iron gate fitted into a narrow gap in a stone wall. All three women stepped back, catching their breath, staring at the gate. Without a word Myna reached into her pocket and removed a large, rusty key. The lock screeched its objection so Jessie stepped forward to help force it. Fragments of stone broke away from either side, defeated by the sudden pressure, then soon the sound of squeaking metal broke the silence. Myna climbed over the mangle of broken shrubbery and kicked her way through to stand on the other side.

Jessie turned and offered a hand to Maggie who wore her reticence like a mask. "Come on, Maggie, I'll help you."

Wild heather, cotton grass and nettle bushes fought for space and dominance over peaty mounds and enormous rocks. Once again Jessie suspected they may be lost, and looking at Maggie's tight mouth confirmed she was not alone in her thinking.

Myna ignored their reluctance. "Follow me," she ordered, "but watch your feet."

Jessie and Maggie followed, avoiding hidden stones, and kicking at nettles until they rounded a low hillock, only to come face to face with a larger mound. Maggie, out of patience, sat on a low rock and rubbed her knees. "Myna, if we're lost, please don't make it worse. We can trace our steps and get back before we end up dying out here. Not a soul will ever find us, and your lassies will be rearing a bairn on their own."

Myna joined Maggie on the rock, leaving Jessie to search for signs that may lead them home safely. Myna relaxed and dusted herself off. "We're here. Rest a bit and I'll show you."

Jessie returned to join them on the rock. Closing her eyes and listening to birds welcoming the day, the scent of fragrant heather slipped into her lungs, soothing her anxious mind. Nothing in their surroundings signalled them being anywhere in particular, regardless of the attractive view.

Maggie did not hide her grimace. "Myna, this better be worth it for I might not make it back."

Myna stood, renewed vigour lifting her posture. "Come."

Not waiting for a response, she marched towards what Jessie guessed may be a cairn. She removed a few small rocks, then without being asked or knowing why, Jessie took off her coat and got to work. Myna glanced over her shoulder, nodded and grinned. Maggie remained on the rock, arms crossed, her face still contorted. Combined efforts rewarded them, so soon they stood looking into a dark, gaping hole in the hill. Jessie's heart thumped, effort and anticipation jockeying for credit. The darkness yielded no clues, but Myna's face glowed with satisfaction.

Maggie's voice floated into the back of their heads. "Whatever's in there better be dead."

For the first time since Jessie left home that morning her anxiety eased. Maggie's humour and Myna's smile lifted her spirits, but was this only part of the journey Myna planned? Suddenly Lily's face flashed through her mind. "Myna, it's time you explained. Do you expect Tevia to mind Lily all day?"

Myna held Jessie's hand. "I needed to make sure I found this place once more before telling you why. Your mom and I were young girls when we first arrived here, but we always kept it concealed to protect ourselves in case of a need."

Jessie shivered. "Is there a need?"

Myna nodded towards the gaping wound in the hill. "This is what she meant."

Jessie's voice broke. "Are we supposed to hide out in a cave? With your girls and Lily?"

Myna took her hand. "No Jess, it's not a cave, it's a tunnel, a route to safety. So far from here they'd never think to look for you. This tunnel has survived hundreds of years and saved the lives of too many souls to count."

Myna glanced at Maggie. "Did Heather ever speak of this to you?"

Maggie shrugged. "Not so I remember, but she always said if ever they came, they'd have a hard time finding us."

Jessie's mind reeled, and Maggie dug her fingers into her cheeks once more. Myna squeezed Jessie's hand.

"I know it's hard to understand, but after your grandmother passed, your mother and I were the only ones left, and we kept it our secret. There's no one who knows it's still here except my sister Morag. She's the one who will take care of us."

Maggie sucked in a great gulp of air. "Myna, are you saying we'll be fleeing sometime soon?"

Myna fixed her gaze on the tunnel. "I pray not, but the noise gets louder by the day. I promised Heather I would do whatever was needed to protect Jessie and Lily."

Jessie's mouth dropped open. "Myna, no."

"Jess, I promised. Even if it means protecting you from yourself."

Confident and relieved an escape route still existed, Myna said it was time to go home, leaving Jessie concerned, Maggie bewildered. During the walk she explained the tunnel's origins, dating back to the Jacobite's uprisings, its use during the Battle of Sheriffmuir, and subsequent frequent escape route and hiding place for anyone suspected of witchcraft. Jessie's mind reeled with the implications of fleeing. Resentment of the reasons warmed her blood. Myna stopped for breath and Jessie's distracted feet missed their spot. She reached out and caught Myna's shoulders, almost pulling them both down. Myna shrieked, swung around, and gripped Jessie's shoulders. "Jess, be careful!"

Jessie's tear-stained face surprised her, so she pulled her into a tight embrace. Maggie stepped close and stroked Jessie's trembling back, and although quiet since leaving the entrance to the tunnel, she bent towards Jessie's ear. "Don't fret, Jess. It will sort itself out, and we'll be with you no matter what."

Jessie straightened, swiping her tears. She watched the clouds turning grey and narrowed her eyes, daring them to gather. Her chest lifted. She glanced at Myna, then Maggie, who both took a step back.

"They will not drive me out, punish me, or condemn my child. They will rue the day before I let them destroy me."

Maggie groaned, and Myna gripped Jessie's arm. "Jess, your mother warned you. I warned you. Some battles are easy to win, but others are best left alone. I will do my best to protect you and Lily, but if you don't heed the warnings, it is you who will rue the day."

She stomped off, followed by Maggie mumbling under her breath. Jessie watched them until they were almost out of sight, then cast defiant eyes at the clouds, sweeping her indignation to the corner of her mind before rushing to catch up. She focused on her surroundings, noting the size, colour and shape of tree trunks, and any special features she may need to recall, stopping occasionally to look up to where the treetops reached up to the sun, instructing her memory to hold the detail safe should she become dependent on it. When they finally reached Myna's house, concentration and holding rein on her temper had left her exhausted, but she immediately relaxed when she looked into the basket to see Lily fast asleep.

Tevia appeared from the kitchen and grinned. "It's been a busy morning playing in the garden so she's just fallen asleep."

Maggie slumped into a chair. "Well, I'm about to join her. As soon as you've fed and watered me, thank you."

Myna chuckled. "Maggie, put those feet up. Tevia, please make some tea."

After feeding Lily and having something to eat, Jessie hankered to leave. Tension occupied the space like a child in the middle of a parents' argument – moving from one part of the room to another depending on whose mood ruled. Jessie clutched her teacup, avoiding eye contact with Myna. Maggie slurped, continuously shifting in her seat. Jessie coaxed her appetite, but with each mouthful her sandwich fought with her throat. Tevia disappeared outside and Jessie's heart sank. As each woman silenced their agitations, Lily sat close to her mother, babbling and pulling at Jessie's skirt, unaware of how she'd become the sole artificial focus in the room. When sufficiently rested, Maggie declared it time to go, but never one for mincing her words, she whipped her scarf around her neck, swinging a pointed finger between Jessie and Myna.

"You two may not agree on the best way to handle this, but you'd better mend your fence before trouble tramples it. This is no time to be fretting over who's right or wrong."

Jessie wrapped Lily and pulled on her coat, avoiding Myna, who would not allow Jess to leave without an agreement, or at least a truce. Jessie turned towards the door, but Myna called after her.

"Jess, we're all in this together. Please don't do anything rash."

Maggie nodded. "Come, Jess, let's get going."

Jessie left, her senses telling her Myna remained on her doorstep watching her. When she turned to close the gate, Tevia rushed down the path and flung her arms around her.

Jessie looked into her wide eyes, but before she could speak, Tevia gripped her shoulders.

"Please be careful, Auntie Jess. I love you."

Chapter 24

WILSON APPEARED TO BE *in no rush to assuage Father Coyle's curiosity or Angus's mental strain. He stirred his tea as if reluctant to disturb the liquid, and only after a tentative sip and depositing the gold-rimmed cup into its delicate saucer, did he push his spectacles up the bridge of his long narrow nose to look up – first at Father Coyle, then Angus. He showed no hint of rhyme or reason for the unexpected meeting, but Angus's tightening skin reminded him to assume nothing, trust neither. Father Coyle fidgeted.*

"Charles, please enlighten us." A creak of leather beneath his portly backside prompted Wilson to grip the front of his desk and address Angus. "I am growing weary of hearing tales and accusations regarding your family and their habits. I am none the wiser regarding the whereabouts of my missing men, and Father Coyle has made some alarming claims regarding your sister."

Angus fired a glance at Father Coyle whose sneer contorted his pug-like face. He turned to Wilson. "We have discussed this before. I don't understand your grievances or how you think I can help."

Wilson sighed. "Are you aware of an attempt to have your sister arrested just the other evening?"

Angus held his temper. "No." His expression concealed his shock.

Wilson's eyebrows shot up, and he nodded to Father Coyle. "Perhaps you wish to enlighten him?"

The priest lurched out of his chair, thumping his way to Wilson's desk, one hand clenched into a mottled, puffy fist while he waved the other in Angus's direction.

"You can say nothing and keep what you know to yourself, but it will not do you one bit of good. If you value your employment and your home, you would do well to understand it is our intention to put an end to this pagan behaviour. Your

sister, with your mother before her, is at the centre of every demonic incident amongst our people, and it is high time she answered for it. You have a fortunate position, with prospects and a secure future, which will come to a swift end if you choose to support her evil ways."

Angus's anger promptly dissipated and his chest no longer pounded beneath his shirt buttons. He saw Father Coyle's face change colour, beads of sweat congregating on his upper lip, blood rushing to the surface of his greasy cheeks. A glance at Wilson confirmed his suspicion: neither man had enough evidence to act upon, so now looked to him for it. He could offer whatever it was they needed to crucify his sister. Perhaps he might string them along with denials, or yield to their threats. Or simply warn them of the fire and damnation they risk should they harm one hair on her body. His shoulders relaxed, as did his heartbeat. A whiff of pine from the pile of evenly chopped logs stacked up on each side of the fireplace stirred memories of walks in the forest with his mother – and a desire to repeat those with his niece. Wilson nonchalantly drummed his fingers on his desk, but his chest heaved with restrained breath.

Angus turned to Father Coyle. "Our people? Whom exactly would they be?"

Only the distance between them saved Angus from the flight of the priest's spittle and the force of his breath. "Our people!" he roared. "The God-fearing and pious congregants who practise their faith daily." His bulging eyes couldn't decide between glaring at Wilson or Angus, but Angus retaliated.

"You mean those who show their faith by handing over their hard-earned wages to you every Sunday, leaving them with barely enough to eat?"

"Enough!" Wilson thumped his desk. Both Angus and Father Coyle froze. Wilson's once calm exterior shuddered under his stiff tweed and his moustache twitched. He scowled at the priest. "Do what you need to do. If this woman is indeed guilty of both her husband's death and the disappearance of my men, she ought to be locked up and punished."

Angus's breath caught in his throat. Stunned by the realisation of what they judged Jessie guilty of, his anger flared and burned the back of his eyes. "Are you mad?"

"Be quiet! I have lost all patience with this, and if burning that goddamn forest to the ground flushes out these pagans you speak of, I am more than happy to get on with it." He got up from his desk and stepped towards Angus. "A word of warning. You may do a fine job here, but if you turn out to be more trouble than you are worth, I will fire you before the week's end. I suggest you decide what your livelihood is worth."

The priest snorted. "Hear, hear."

Angus struggled to contain words desperate to be screamed. His throat ached and a sudden crackle of a log snapping in the fireplace jolted his nerves. "You can't be serious. You don't truly believe my sister is a criminal?"

Wilson sauntered to the window then turned. "It appears so. If you were unaware, you can now be rid of her and her ilk. It would certainly go some way to ensuring your permanent employment." He glanced at his watch then waved a hand. "I have a busy afternoon so please leave and get on with it." Angus turned to leave, but the priest stood his ground. Wilson's lips disappeared under his moustache before he hissed. "Both of you."

Angus rushed from the office and headed towards the front door with the priest scurrying behind him. The priest grabbed his arm when he flung open the double doors. "We have warned you. Your sister has gone too far and she will pay the price. If you have any sense, you'll save yourself."

Angus swung around, almost knocking him off his feet. The heat in his face and rage in his eyes could have set fire to the priest's robes. He bent towards his smug face. "If you lay one finger on my sister or her child, even God won't be able to save you."

The priest stepped back, his eyes almost disappearing into folds of fat. "You be mindful of threatening me. I won't think twice about sending you down with her."

Angus drew in a breath and his whole body lifted. "Just try."

The priest stood on the step shuffling in his robes and patting himself down as Angus marched down the steps. Charles Wilson stood at his office window watching the altercation while smoothing his moustache with a stiff index finger. After the men went their separate ways, he grabbed his hat and coat from his mahogany coat-stand then made his way through the kitchen, out the back door.

In the barn, the priest's horse munched hay from a large rusty pail, while Donald loaded bales onto an already sizeable pile. Humming to himself, he glanced at the bunch of carrots pilfered from the kitchen store. He leaned his pitchfork against the rough stone wall, offering the horse the biggest one. His body shuddered when Father Coyle marched into the barn and bellowed: "Get him hitched. I need to get going. Now!"

Donald rushed to fetch the harness lying over the fence, gleaming from its recent polish. After securing the collar and reins, he backed the horse up, attached the shafts and whispered in his ear. "Go easy, big boy. If he whips you, just you bolt down the hill then toss the old bastard into the river." He intended to give the priest a leg-up, but fat hands snatched the reins from him.

"Out of my way!"

Donald stepped back, watching the priest huff and puff his way up the narrow boards into his seat. "Aye, off you go then," he mumbled.

After the cart disappeared out the gate, Donald picked up the leftover carrots then headed to the kitchen. Returning them rather than leaving them to rot seemed the sensible thing to do. He might have tucked them into his overalls to take home, but he feared his mother would either jump out of her grave or slap him in his sleep; which she did each time he dreamed of Tevia. Although out of bounds for labourers, cutting through the garden then sneaking around the back of the manor provided a shortcut to the kitchen. After a quick look around to make sure it was safe, he snuck across the lawn, stopping twice to admire determined daisies pushing through the immaculately manicured grass. He pondered doing the gardener a favour by pulling them out, but simply winked at the bright yellow clusters before moving on. Never had he walked on a lawn that seemed to caress his gnarly boots; it was the closest thing to velvet he'd ever feel. It seemed criminal to step on it, and because he'd never seen another soul walking on the grass, he questioned why they killed all the daisies in the first place. When it was still an open field, he'd spent many summer days making daisy chains for his sisters, and holding delicate buttercups under their chins simply to see them glow. He was sure his ancestors turned in her grave the day they cleared it to make way for the manor. With fists full of carrots, his mind tossing around memories, he almost didn't see Charles Wilson turning the corner facing the yard and the kitchen door opposite. Instinct halted him, so he stood pressed against the ivy-covered wall, clutching carrots to his chest.

On the rare occasion he'd seen the lord of the manor it was at the stables, inspecting his prize possessions – they'd not exchanged one word. His employer always appeared pleased, mumbling nonsense to each horse. Cook said it was the only time he ever smiled. Donald took it as a sign he was doing a good job, and his boss was simply short on manners. He understood it to be an English trait for which he should pity him. But now his skin crawled, so he peered around the wall to find the source of his discomfort.

Wilson stood with his back to him, talking to two burly men in hunter hats and long wool coats. The distance between their bowed heads suggested an important and confidential conversation. His mother always told him to turn his nose in the opposite direction of a stranger's business, but after already watching Angus stride off thumping his thighs, then Father Coyle's bad-tempered mood, he sensed trouble brewing. He'd also heard of those two thugs causing havoc in the tavern, so if they were planning something, this might be the time to find out.

To avoid walking across the yard, he ran back across the lawn to approach from the other direction. Soon he stood pressed against another ivy-clad wall, close enough to make out hushed bits of conversation. When the talking ceased, his chest heaved and he slid to the ground. His head fell back against the unforgiving wall and he looked at the sky. Words flew around his brain as he tried to arrange them into something other than what he'd heard. He dropped his head into his hands, squeezing his hair with fingers refusing to remain still. He took a few moments to slow his breathing, looking towards the border of the woodland, willing his trembling to cease. The breeze swayed the tops of the trees in their unique rhythm. A multifarious selection of lush greens and solid browns turned in and out with each rush of air. A sway of mottled branches amid a flurry of glossy leaves enjoyed nature's Ceilidh, oblivious to the tumult below. When the thumping within his chest diminished, he jumped up and took off across the lawn, leaving behind a trail of trampled, emerald green velvet, and a scattered pile of carrots.

Father Coyle whipped the poor horse all the way back to the barn before climbing off the cart and throwing the reins at a young boy chopping wood. After stomping across the road to his office, he slammed the ground floor door behind him then huffed his way up the steps to his office. His fat arms fought with his sleeves until they finally released him, and he tossed the coat over the arm of his couch. He headed straight for the window table where he decanted a glass of red wine that overflowed down his sweaty hand and onto his robe. He swiped it off with the back of his hand, draining the glass in one gulp before collapsing into his chair. When he kicked off his boots, one near-missed landing in the fireplace. He spotted his fire dead from the previous evening, still overflowing with ash. He hauled himself out of his chair, cursing under his breath, then thumped to the door on stocking-clad feet. Leaning into the stairwell, he bellowed:

"Mrs Ramsey, are you there?"

Within seconds Mrs Ramsay appeared, wiping wet hands on her apron. "Yes, Father, do you need me? I'm busy with your food."

"No one has cleaned or prepared my fire. Where is that Callan boy?"

Mrs Ramsay's hands reached for each other. "I think he's out back with the chickens. I'll send him up."

"Tell him to bring fresh wood!"

Callan arrived laden with logs. He avoided eye contact, silently praying to be left alone. God didn't hear him, and the priest's words flew into his face. "Callan, did you tell your mother I want to see her?"

"Yes, Father, she will come after she finishes her shift." He turned and knelt before the fire, hurriedly piling on more logs

than necessary, while wishing his back would shield him from further onslaught.

The priest marched to the window. "Ah, here she is."

Callan made for the door, but the priest shouted. "You can stay right here until I dismiss you." He loped to the door and opened it for Laura, who soon appeared. Spotting Callan, her face turned the colour of the dead fire. Stuffy air clung to her throat. "Callan, why are you here?"

"Someone forgot to lay my fire," the priest barked, "so he's doing it now. God knows I'll have a chill by the time it's ready."

Laura forced her hands to be still, nodding towards Callan. "Well, seems you're done now, so get on home."

Callan launched himself towards the exit and Laura noticed his lips trembling.

"Aye."

"Not so fast. Sit right down, you two. We have some important matters to discuss."

Chapter 25

ANGUS FLEW TO JESSIE'S house without feeling his feet, or the spatters from puddles he sloshed through. His jacket snagged on bushes; startled frogs leapt out of his way. When he reached her gate, he leaned on the posts, his chest heaving. He took a few minutes to recover, relieving his wobbly knees and jangled nerves. His breathing steadied but his eyes burned, and when a tear splashed onto his tight grip, his heart took control of his mind, which was not helpful.

He reached up, wiped damp cheeks and tried to right himself. The anxiety of confronting Jessie tingled in his belly as he stood gazing at her front garden, suddenly realising the care and attention she paid it. Having never seen the deftly carved bird feeders hanging from each tree, he wondered if they were Tom's handiwork or his father's. Neither ever took credit for them. Plants and shrubs inhabited their allotted space without wandering. Carefully pruned and painstakingly tended, unlike his mother's garden, now seriously neglected since her passing. He made a mental note to rectify that, but an ominous shiver, accompanied by the shriek of an overhead hawk reminded him of his visit, warning him he may not get the chance. Jessie routinely demolished him in a challenge, and if he allowed his heart to lead him, she would mash him into fairy dust before he might coax her into his way of thinking. His teeth nipped his bottom lip, but he resolved to remain strong. She might listen to his advice if he managed her will without agitating her pride. He inhaled, opened the gate, and forced his apprehensive spirit to the front door. His only one incentive to sway her into seeing sense was Lily – or so he hoped.

Jessie opened the door and immediately squinted at him. "Angus, why are you here?" She looked down the empty road. "You should be at work."

Angus brushed past her. "I need to speak to you. Please sit, and promise you'll hear me out before blowing the roof off."

Jessie sat on the edge of a chair and smirked. "If you think I might, then we're not off to a good start. I've already told you I'm not going back to Da."

Angus glared and Jessie's skin prickled. She trusted she understood her brother better than he, but now his dark energy dulled the light in the room. His eyes blinked too often and the tremor in his voice rumbled through her blood. She leaned back and watched him flex his fingers. "Out with it, Angus."

He scanned the room then sat. "Where's Lily?"

"She's in her cot playing with toys. Speak."

His fingers curled around the chair arms. "I can't believe what I've just heard from Wilson and Coyle. If what they say is true, you are in real danger of being arrested."

Jessie tossed her hair back. "I've heard that before, and they've tried it already." She swept her arms around the room. "Yet look, I'm still here. They're all threats and noise, Angus. I've done nothing, so they can't do a thing to me."

Angus leapt from his chair. "No, Jess, they are looking to blame you for Tom's death – and the missing smithies."

Jessie's arms dropped to her sides. "Why would they blame me?"

Angus reached for his hair, dragging his hands down to clutch his neck. "Coyle has been after you forever, and Mam before you. You haven't been careful the way she was, and it's common knowledge you despise his church, school and religion."

Jessie shook clenched fists. "His church is his own personal bank. He's a monster to those young boys, and his religion is control, not faith."

Angus puffed his cheeks. "Jess, I'm not here to argue with you. I loathe his ways, but I don't agree with yours either. You've given him ammunition with your … well … helping the women around here, and the strange things you get up to in those woods. God knows I don't understand it, but I don't think it's evil, and I know you would never harm a soul. He doesn't believe it, and he's convinced Wilson you're to blame for every mishap since he took over the manor – and why the women congregants and tithes are dwindling. Wilson doesn't know any better. He will not rest until he finds out where his smithies are."

Jessie stepped back, catching her breath. She glanced towards Lily's cot, willing the walls to stop closing in. Angus studied her face and lowered his voice.

"Jess, do you know anything about the smithies?" Dark images whipped around her brain. She watched his eyes widen as the walls crept forward. "Jess, please tell me you're not involved in their disappearance." He dropped into the chair. "Please tell me you didn't hurt Tom."

Jessie lowered herself into her chair, pressing both hands against her trembling belly. Tears welled behind her eyes. Her throat tightened as anxious words frightened to be heard, crept over her lips. "I didn't hurt Tom. I only eased his pain." Her voice faded, her explanation withering before forming.

Angus's mouth dropped open. The frozen space between them barely registered his words. "Dear God, Jess."

Jessie dropped her chin onto her fists. As the enormity of the situation pounded them, they sat staring at each other until Lily cried. Jessie jumped up and Angus put his head in his hands. She used the distraction to get her notions in order. The timing of Myna's trip to the tunnel, Laura's comments about the smithies, Iris, and Angus's visit clanged like church bells, and the wind whistling through the window wailed an ominous siren. Angus used the distraction to recall his mother's visit to his office, and her words:

"Jessie will need you to take her side, and when the time comes, I hope you choose wisely."

When Jessie returned clutching Lily, Angus stood, reaching out to take his niece's outstretched hand. When she grabbed his fingers, his heart leapt.

"I will find out what they're planning, Jess. I don't want to know how far you've gone, but to protect Lily, and stop whatever it is they have in mind for you, we need to fix this. You may need to leave here, and take Da with you, so prepare for it."

Jessie's eyes brimmed once more and Angus's shoulders dropped. "I hope it's worth it, Jess. Whatever drives you to do what you do."

Jessie rocked Lily on her hip, stroking her head. "You will never understand. I don't expect you to. Please promise me, no matter what happens, you will keep Lily safe."

Angus stepped back and put his hands on his hips. "I will, but promise me you won't do anything stupid."

Jessie smiled. For the first time since Angus arrived, warmth hugged her, and the walls stepped back. "I only do what I was born to do."

Angus strode to the door. "That's not what I want to hear. Keep this door locked and wait for me to return. Be ready to come home with me."

Jessie watched him rush out the gate before she locked the door. She stroked Lily's smiling face and played with her plump fingers. "Enough playing, it's time for your nap, and time I spoke with your granny."

Angus rushed home with a mind full of torment. A fleeting question of his job security would have made him laugh if it weren't already obvious; like watching a squall rush toward you, pretending it may pass you by. Wilson's tone exposed more than his words, and although he phrased them as a solution, his need for a patsy lay hidden under his stiff collar. Angus recognised this easily, knowing the importance of a poker face when confronted – unlike Coyle, whose blatant bullying tactics only made his jaw ache. Angus understood Wilson's power and Coyle's vindictiveness, fearing both may decide to disregard the other and execute their own plan. He picked up his pace and begged heaven for time.

Dougal raised his hands when Angus burst through the door. "Why is no one at work today? Have I missed a holiday?"

"No, Da, what are you on about?" Angus peered into each room before standing at the fireplace, hands on his hips.

Dougal shrugged his shoulders. "Well, you've just missed Donald, who I understood works for you. Are you both skiving today?"

Angus rushed to the window. "Why was he here? What did he want?"

Dougal shook his head. "He cannae string two words together, so I don't know what he was jabbering about."

Angus's conscience tweaked at the sight of Dougal's grey pallor under his dull beard. "Sorry Da, it's a funny day. Where's Fraser?"

Dougal threw up his arms again. "For God's sake, he's at work, I would hope. Where you and Donald ought to be."

Angus knelt before him and held his knees. "Da, can you get the food done early today? Jess is coming, and she may stay the night."

Dougal's eyes brightened, his shoulders lifted, anticipation hitching up his braces. "Och, that's grand. I'll get started right now."

Angus headed for the door but Dougal called after him: "You off back to work now before you get fired?"

Angus waved. "Aye, I'll see you later."

Angus stood at the gate deliberating where to go first. He bounced his fists on the gate post before deciding he must speak to Fraser and Maggie. Although Donald's visit baffled him, he found no sinister reason for it. Donald did have a soft spot for Dougal, although Wilson may well have gone on the rampage and fired them both. Or Donald may be skiving, but he doubted that.

Before leaving, he gazed into his mother's garden, which only reminded him again of his part in its obvious neglect. Angus's familiarity with the route to the peat fields meant he could have walked with his eyes closed. Today however, he had not dressed for the occasion, so every few minutes his feet informed him his shoes were unlikely to survive. He cursed Jessie and her spae friends, even sending a rebuke to his mother, which he promptly retracted when he remembered her scolding about speaking ill of the dead:

"Everyone becomes an angel when they die, so it's best to forget their earthly sins and pray for only good things for them."

This was her mantra each time he or Fraser cursed the old man who'd whipped them with a whittled branch when he caught them stealing his gooseberries. He still refused to believe the old man became an angel. Just as he would die before believing any God would transform Father Coyle into one. Scrambled worries and memories fragmented his mind as he laboured through the bog. He found Fraser at the far end of the vast dig area, and if not for his too familiar whistling he may never have spotted him. By the time he reached the enormous black hole surrounded by layers of dense, wet peat – packed tight by aeons of constant pressure – his trousers appeared two-tone; black from the knees down. Sweat marks stained his collar, his damp dark curls hung limp. He caught his breath and almost laughed. Only Fraser's bright green eyes – and a flash of white when he parted his lips – confirmed a human lay beneath the layer of black caking him from head to toe. He did not miss his days in the peat bogs and lacked any desire to return. Fraser, however, stood relaxed, leaning on his tairsgeir, undaunted by his bleak surroundings.

His radiant, crescent moon grin cut through his black encrusted face. "Angus, what the hell? Has the Sassenach eventually fired you?"

"Not yet, but there's always tomorrow."

"Och no, but I warned you." His grin disappeared. "Is something wrong with Da, Jess, Lily?"

"No, they're all fine, for now. There's a wee problem with Jess. Can you please get home early so we can talk to her, and decide what to do?"

Fraser shrugged. "Aye, sure, is it because of the medicine she's been giving all the women? It was sure to bring trouble."

Angus stepped back. "What do you know about it?"

Fraser leaned forward, balancing precariously on the wooden post of his tairsgeir, avoiding the sharp, forged iron blades on either side of the unique tool used to carve peat as easily as butter. He wouldn't be the first to slice through a foot if not careful.

"Well, if you don't know, you're on your own. Or they've buried you too deep in the soft carpets up at the manor," he eyed Angus's trousers, "and now you're going to need new breeks."

Angus cringed, looked at the sky and cleared his throat. "Fraser, can ye just get home early?"

Fraser lifted his tairsgeir in salute. "Aye."

By the time Angus trudged back through the bogs to Maggie's house his body ached with each step and his knees threatened to buckle.

Maggie opened her door and grabbed his shoulders. "Dear God Angus, get yerself in here. You look about to expire."

Angus mumbled his thanks, sinking into her soft armchair while she rushed to put the kettle on.

"Thank God I lit the fire earlier today. The tea will be ready in a flash."

He sat examining his hands and the peat dirt from slipping in the bog lodged under his fingernails. Another reason he didn't miss the digging, but the impact of losing his job was forever on his mind.

"I wanted to get my baking done before going round to Jessie. I don't want her being on her own."

Most of Maggie's jabbering from the kitchen rolled past his ears, but when he heard Jessie's name, it caught his attention. "Jess won't be there. I'm taking her home with me."

Maggie returned from the kitchen and stood before him. She handed him a buttered scone thick enough to feed a family. Angus broke it in half before devouring it, almost choking. He raised a hand. "Sorry Mags, my stomach thinks my throat's been cut. Please excuse my hands."

Maggie nodded and slumped into the chair opposite. "Your mother would have something to say about that, but I'd prefer to know why you're here and what's got you in this state? Where's the trouble?" She tossed a tea towel into his lap. He swallowed, twisting the towel in his hands. After recounting his meeting at the manor, and his visit to Jessie, Maggie's chest heaved and her lips disappeared into a thin line. She thumped the arms of her chair.

"Angus, we have warned her more times than need be, so this isn't surprising, but you can't underestimate Coyle's determination to get rid of her ... to be rid of us all."

Angus dropped the tea towel. "I don't understand her connection to Wilson's men, and why he thinks he can pin it on her."

Maggie side-eyed him. "Did she say anything about those men?"

"No, and I told her I don't want to know, but Mags, there was something in her eyes. She didn't look right. Do you know if she harmed Tom?"

Maggie avoided the question and made off to the kitchen, ruminating his words before returning with a mug of hot tea. Angus held the cup with both hands, gazing into it as if making a wish. After a gulp he relaxed into the chair, scanning the room, remembering his last visit with Maggie. Since his mother's passing, she was now her stand-in. A vase chock full of white heather filling the window space wafted its familiar perfume towards him, pricking his heart. He regretted his prior unkindness towards her. He squeezed the cup between his hands. "Mags, I don't know how to fix this."

Maggie leaned forward over folded arms. "I'm not sure you can, but for now we need to keep her and Lily safe."

He nodded. "That's why I'm taking her with me. Fraser, Da and I won't let anyone pass the door."

She shook her head. "No, Angus, she won't be safe with you. Some of us worried it might come to this, especially with Coyle strutting about frightening the life out of anyone who speaks her name."

He took another gulp, but it failed to ease his deep frown and pinched eyebrows. "What then, Mags?"

"I'll take her where she will be safe."

"Not the damn forest."

Maggie punched the air. "Don't you start. You'll listen to me and be happy about it. She'll come with me and you will go home to look after your Da. If he gets wind of this, I swear it'll send him to your mother before she knows he's dead. We'll keep her safe until you can sort it out." She loped to the vase of heather and fiddled with the stalks. "However long that may be."

The cup rattled when he put it on the table. Worry and fear paled his skin. "She's a law unto herself, isn't she?"

Maggie turned. "Come, we should go. The sooner I get her out of her house the better."

As he lifted his weary body from the chair, Maggie tied her boots and buttoned her coat. "Who would want to harm Jess?" he moaned. "Who would help Father Coyle?"

Maggie lifted her chin and almost spat. "Jean Fraser and Laura McLean. They have more faces than you will ever have time to meet. They're devils dressed in green tartan."

Chapter 26

LILY'S PINK FACE GLOWED *after her bath, feed and change. Faint sunshine creeping through the bedroom window created a soft radiance hanging over the cot where she slept. Jessie caressed her daughter's head, with an occasional twirl of a lock of fine hair; midnight black, similar to her grandmother's. Even the birds sat quietly in the trees, in unintentional but timely respect for the need for peace and quiet. Jessie loved this time of day; when the busyness of chore-filled mornings withdrew, making way for gentler afternoons filled with what she liked to term 'life's pleasures': baking, sewing, gardening, her beloved study of herbs and tinctures, playtime with her precious daughter, before preparation of dinner and the mysteries evenings brought. Before her mother left her. Before Tom's passing, Iris and the smithies – before this. Lily's restful breathing mirrored hers, but the serenity only amplified the sound of her heart beating, fear ringing in her ears. Fear had never occupied space in her consciousness. She allowed it no room, nor the requirement to feel it. Her mother served as her guard and guide – her father and brothers her protectors. Fear came as an unwanted gift, packaged with responsibility and endowed with the risk of loss. It came with Lily, but without her mother or Tom, its weight required every ounce of strength to prevent her heart from imploding. She gazed at Lily's fluttering eyelashes, her eyes sweeping down her snuggled body, cocooned and calm, wondering how something so delicate held the power to command such overwhelming emotion.*

After kissing her forehead, she drew the curtain across the window, reached under her bed and retrieved the wooden box her mother had given her. She closed her eyes, holding it against her chest. Rubbing her fingers across the rough wood her heartbeat throbbed against her ribs, as if reaching out to it. On the few occasions where she'd considered using her stones to find reasons for her mother and Tom's untimely deaths, she'd refrained. What difference would it make? Both now gone, with her powerless to prevent either of those losses.

Still clutching the box, she moved to the couch, leaned back and rested it in her lap. After a few moments, she hesitantly removed the lid. Two stones shone from their nest of emerald velvet. She placed one in each hand and closed her fingers around them, letting her eyes slip shut. In the dark silence, her senses probed the room like curious children in a traveller's wagon. The itchy thatch crackled. Swollen window frames groaned, only just holding their own against wind pummelling the stone-packed walls, but proving their determination to stand strong enough to guard her. The door rattled its familiar tune in response to intermittent gusts which swept down the chimney, puffing pale grey clouds of soot into the still room, filling Jessie's nostrils. Soon her lungs swelled with a mixture of wood smoke, fresh pine and yesterday's soup, all vying for attention; none able to overpower the ever-present, comforting essence of the scent of white heather.

She cast her mind to the depths of the forest, drawing stillness into her consciousness, until her body succumbed to the support of the couch. Her heart and soul draped her in a mantle as gentle and warm as her mother's embrace. White light danced across her eyelids, followed by blues the colour of shifting skies, drawing her from the physical world into the depths of her being – where her spirit lay. The stones warmed before releasing timeless energy. Soon, light pulled her into a space illuminated by the brightest of forest greens, surrounded by interwoven tree branches. The visions came in lightning flashes, a kaleidoscope of colours impossible to separate. Tree branches meshed into solid dark walls, shifting closer. Even in her transcendental state, her heart pulsed against her ribs as though trying to flee. A force pulled from behind, and whirling light drew her deeper into a vortex of opposing energies. She held her space, begging her guides for protection and calm. Gradually, the orbiting colours stalled, the surrounding space transforming into a wall of dazzling white light holding back the darkness. It calmed her throbbing heart, and when her spirit settled, her mother's face appeared, glowing, soothing the aether, her green eyes piercing the brilliant white. Having restrained the dark energy, Heather led Jessie into a centre space, where she stood on a carpet of vivid green moss. More visions came in a flurry of random figures, impressions and concepts, a delirium of images in varying degrees of agitation, elation and spiritual fervour. In a frenzy of light and colour, representations and metaphors, clarity remained hidden. Her body swayed while the stones pulsed against her fists. As fleeting as the colours had appeared, so they dissipated. Heather's face faded as though sinking under water, and in Jessie's last vision, her mother's hands reached out, and her eyes faded into an unfamiliar and distressing expression … sadness.

Despite her best efforts to stay in her vision state, Jessie opened her eyes. When she uncurled her fingers, the stones appeared lifeless, sitting heavy and cold, exhausted of their energy. Her heart resumed its natural rhythm but her senses sharpened. She looked around the room, inspecting every corner as though something sinister lay hidden. She glanced towards Lily's crib, but the child slept peacefully, oblivious to her mothers' state. An icy shiver prompted her to close her eyes, to think of what her experience with the stones had revealed. Her mother's firm opinion of the valuable guidance they offered seemed to be in stark contrast to her own visions. Dark, faceless silhouettes leering from a background of murky grey, frightened her. Seeing her mother's face look so forlorn, together with the overpowering colours of red, orange and black, consumed her with stomach-tightening dread. Tears rolled down her cheeks, landing on her clenched fists. The way her mother had reached out to her stirred something deep inside, and now every fibre of her being knitted together in a tapestry of clear communication. She would join her mother soon, but first she would need to walk through fire.

After returning the stones to their box, she heaved herself off the couch, went into the bedroom and removed a brown tanned leather bag from a wooden chest Tom had made for her shortly after their wedding. She unfolded a knitted scarf, wrapping it securely around the box. Reaching down into the chest she removed her wedding handfaster and sash, which still held the dried sprig of white heather pinned to it by her mother on her wedding day. She rested a hand on the closed lid of the chest for a moment. Memories of Tom ached in her throat, but she hoisted her skirts then climbed onto the chest to reach her precious notebooks; stashed out of sight on top of her wardrobe. Clutching the books under one arm, she sat on the edge of her bed. As she flicked through each book, she hoped one day Lily would be proficient enough to decipher her handwriting. Although familiar to her, it looked as if she'd let loose an army of spiders on each page. She held the books against her chest, allowing the smoky aroma of birch-tarred leather and grassy rope to settle in her lungs. A vision of her mother twining rope strands, looping them through pierced holes to form a binder for her copious notes, stirred her heart, so she carefully encased the books in her wedding corset, still reinforced by the dried heather stalks carefully gathered by Maggie. With little space remaining, Jessie gathered Lily's warmest clothing and shawls, stuffed them into the top, stretched the flap over and fastened the buckles. Satisfied she'd left nothing of importance behind, she pulled on her coat, slung the bag over her shoulder then lifted Lily into her arms. Keeping her swaddled in the warm blankets, Jessie kissed the top of her head. Lily gurgled in response, so Jessie bent and nuzzled her ear.

"We're going on a journey. We may not go together, but I will always be with you." With one last sweeping glance around her home, she stepped outside.

"Jessie." Father Coyle's eyes pinned her to the ground and her blood froze.

The same two police officers who had tried unsuccessfully to arrest her stood stiff-spined, hands behind their backs, glaring defiantly. Father Coyle's chest heaved too rapidly, and he wore the strain of the walk on his sweaty face. But self-satisfaction overrode his discomfort, leaching from him like the stench of tooth decay. Most surprising was his housekeeper, Mrs Ramsay, who stood a little back from the men. Her eyes stuck to the space between her boots, avoiding Jessie's gaze, trying unsuccessfully to still her trembling hands. Jessie stood quietly, but a flinch from Lily forced her to loosen her grip. Father Coyle stepped forward, but before speaking, one police officer took his elbow, moving him aside. The soulless drone of the man's voice drummed in Jessie's ears, dragging her heart into her stomach.

"I warrant you to be taken to the school hall for questioning. You will be remanded into custody until a prosecutor is available to present formal charges."

Jessie opened her mouth, but the priest's head popped forward. His chins shuddered under the weight of his venom. "He is on his way from Glasgow."

Jessie hugged Lily closer and another yelp startled Mrs Ramsay, who looked at Jessie with eyes only just holding fast in their sockets. Father Coyle grabbed her elbow and pushed her forward. "Take the child to Jean."

Jessie dug her nails into Lily's blanket and turned away, but Mrs Ramsay crossed her arms over her chest, pleading: "Jess, let me take her."

Jessie's roar stirred the birds. "No! You are not giving my child to Jean. You will need to tear her from me screaming before I'll let you!"

Mrs Ramsay stroked Jessie's arm. "Then I'll keep her with me. I promise we'll look after her better than our own. She'll be in kind hands."

Father Coyle and the two police officers exchanged glances. No one moved; none prepared to be the heartless bastard known forever as the man who ripped a helpless child from her screaming mother.

Mrs Ramsay stepped closer to Jess. "It's settled then. I'll take her home with me."

Jessie watched the woman's eyes fill, her lips quiver, and as though guided by an invisible force, she placed Lily into her outstretched arms. Mrs Ramsay nodded then narrowed her eyes. "You'll be home soon. Don't fret."

Tears poured down Jessie's face, but she breathed deep before slipping the bag off her shoulder. She placed it over Mrs Ramsay's shoulder before lowering her head onto the strap. She turned her mouth towards Mrs Ramsay's ear: "Take care of this bag as carefully as Lily."

Mrs Ramsay slipped her free hand between them and squeezed Jessie's thigh.

Impatience prodded Father Coyle. "Enough. We must go."

The two police officers stepped forward to take Jessie's arms, but she lifted her shoulders, thrust out her chin then glared from one to the other. "There's no need. I know the way."

Jessie walked to the school hall carried on a wave of emotion, detached from all sights, sounds and movements. Distorted voices and blurred images remained outside her consciousness as her mind rationalised what was happening to her, and more importantly, why. The familiarity of the route allowed her to be swept along powerlessly. Every warning ever given to her repeated in her head – each louder than the other. Lost in the journey, she almost missed the school, but a police officer pulled her back, escorted her inside, then left her to sit alone in a small storeroom. When the door closed, she took a breath and inspected her surroundings. Wall-to-wall damp formed intricate patterns as if millions of snowflakes clung to the walls – interspersed with buds of black, spongy blobs creeping out of the stonework. Spores permeated the air with a pungent reek, and in a fleeting moment of awareness, Jessie considered she may die of consumption before they hanged her.

✿

Outside, on the opposite side of the street, Callan stood paralysed by what he was witnessing. When the police officers led Jessie into the school grounds, he prayed that if the ground would not swallow him, may it at least make him invisible. The moment the large school doors closed, he took off, bolting down the street as though hell's fire licked at his heels. He raced through the village, down past the border of the forest, heart thumping, his feet skimming the ground. When he reached the corner, he swung around, almost knocking Maggie off her feet.

She grabbed a fence post and shrieked. "Dear God, boy, are ye trying to kill me?" Callan doubled over and pinched his waist. Maggie slapped his shoulder. "Have you seen a ghost? Are ye ill? For God's sake sit down, take a breath." Callan looked up and tears sprung from his eyes.

She stepped closer and lifted her hands to her head. "What, Callan?"

Callan's face crunched into a red, blotchy mess. "I must find Angus," he cried, "it's all my fault!"

Maggie grabbed his shoulders. "Laddie, I swear I'll rattle your bones right out of you if you don't explain yourself."

Callan dropped to his knees wailing. "They've arrested Jessie, and they've taken her baby."

ALLY STIRLING

Chapter 27

ANGUS'S FEET DRAGGED ALONG *the dirt road like stubborn donkeys minus the braying. The walk home from Maggie's seemed interminable, and such was his anger he wanted to return the magpies' call with his own screams. However, he let his frustration balloon in his chest lest he be arrested for lunacy. After the nightmare of his day, he dreaded facing his father's disappointment, certain he'd spent the entire afternoon preparing a hearty stew and pot of lentil soup – perhaps even a clootie dumpling – and some custard for the bairn. With few pleasures left since losing Heather, Dougal loved to cook for, and spend time with his family – especially Jessie.*

Fraser belly-laughed each time the smell of stew wafting down the path greeted him. "It's a good thing those rabbits breed the way they do."

"Your Mam will haunt me if I don't keep you fed," Dougal would say, stirring a pot big enough to sustain the street. Angus pictured him sweeping until his arms ached, to avoid a tongue-lashing from Jessie, who checked every room when she visited. He'd likely whistled the birds from the trees with his delight, and bathed – so she wouldn't call him a minger unfit to hold his granddaughter – and placed a fresh vase of white heather on the windowsill to welcome her as she walked in the door. Angus justified Jessie's cancelled visit as preferable to her being arrested in front of their father – and the distress that would cause. However, he had no plausible explanation for her no-show, with no guarantee of another dinner visit soon. He stomped his ruined shoes into the gravel, ground his teeth and wished he'd never planned it. When he arrived at the gate and spotted a lone magpie perched on the fence, he narrowed his eyes and lifted a stone.

"One for trouble, two for joy."

His mother's words reminded him of her peculiar ways; possibly the root of their present trouble. The hooded magpie eyed him without flinching as he scanned the trees for its grey-mantled mate, without success. He rolled the stone around in his hand for a few seconds before taking aim. Suddenly the front door opened and Fraser called him. The startled magpie spread its glossy wings and flew off in a flash of iridescent blue, green and deep purple. Angus followed his flight and grumbled under his breath. "Off ye go ... and take yer trouble with ye."

When he walked up the path Fraser spotted the stone in his hand. "Fighting with the locals now are ye?"

Angus tossed the stone into the bushes. "Jess isn't coming."

"Och, no! We'll be eating his stew for a month."

Angus followed Fraser to the hearth where Dougal stirred attentively. "Won't be long now."

The delight in his voice punched Angus in his gut. Fraser elbowed him.

"Da, Jessie can't make it tonight. She's truly sorry, but—"

Dougal swung around, the spoon flying from his hand and sending stew splatters straight to Angus's shoes. "Why, what's the matter? Is she not well?"

Angus glanced at Fraser's expressionless face; his arms folded across a clean shirt. He would be no help.

"No, Da, Jess is fine, but it's been a terrible night and a horrible day for her. Lily's cutting more teeth so hasn't slept a wink." In his periphery he caught Fraser's head jutting forward, so flashed him a frown. Fraser's eyebrows lifted and Angus prayed his father wouldn't sense his heavy heart.

Dougal bent to pick up the spoon, his happiness vanished and his shoulders drooped. "Och well, that's bairns. There's always something when they're wee. I'll pop over tomorrow with food."

Again, Fraser's head tilted, but Angus's resolve retreated in the face of his father's dejection. "Aye, I'm sure that'll be fine."

Fraser elbowed Angus. "Let's eat then. Glad she's not here to see your shoes messing Da's spotless floor."

Angus hung up his jacket then ran his fingers through his hair. He took a few moments to close his eyes and breathe in the familiar smells, willing them to settle his twitching stomach and calm his fractious mind – as they'd done his entire life. Soon the table overflowed with hearty food, and Angus watched Fraser and his father shovel mouthful after mouthful, praying his meal would not join the mess on his shoes. His brain worked harder than his knife and fork but a solution refused to come to the table. Fraser rambled on about the dig, but between mouthfuls Angus sensed his eyes boring into the side of his head, so he chewed and prayed, swallowed and prayed. When Dougal pushed his empty plate into the centre of the table and leaned back in his chair, Angus deemed it a good time to broach the subject churning in his stomach. He avoided Fraser's gaze but hooked his ankles together as though they may anchor him. He tried to speak but stopped to clear his throat.

"Are you choking, Angus?" Fraser smirked.

Angus raged but held his temper. "No Fraser, but carry on being smart and I might choke you."

Dougal lifted a tired arm. "Are you two not weary of riling each other by now? Give it a rest, please."

Fraser bowed to Angus. "You were about to say?"

"Nothing important, Da, I was wondering if you still have family on the coast?"

"Why? Are you thinking of moving?" Fraser grumbled.

Angus thumped the table. "Can ye just wheisht? I'm asking Da."

Dougal rolled his eyes. "Will you two ever grow up? Aye, I have my brother and a cousin. Been kelping down there forever. Haven't seen them for years."

Angus nodded. "Maybe now Ma's not here, ye might want to visit them, or go stay awhile. See out the winter by the sea."

Fraser inched forward, so Angus unhooked his ankles and kicked him before continuing. "I might skip a few days' work to take you."

Dougal gawked like a red deer waiting for the first move, and Fraser's gasp startled Angus, who kicked him once more. Dougal's expression morphed from surprise to puzzlement. After a glance towards the windowsill, it settled into how he'd looked since his wife passed: sad. Angus's throat pulsed as he reached over and patted his father's arm. "It was just an idea. I reckoned it might be nice. I worry about you being on your own so much." He paused for a moment. "Jess might want to take Lily."

Dougal's head popped up. "Do you think she would?"

Angus turned, his stiff jaw and angry eyes catching his brother's attention. "What do you think, Fraser?"

Fraser gulped down the last of his ale, set his tankard down then cast Angus a resigned look. "Aye, I'm with Angus, Da. Sounds like a grand idea."

Angus drained his tankard. "Good, then let's get it sorted. The sooner the better ... before the dreich starts."

Fraser gazed, too many unasked questions creasing his face and hanging off his bottom lip. "Aye, before the dreich," he mumbled.

Dougal remained quiet, his melancholy smothering Angus like lava looking for earth to scorch. He'd never lied to his father, and through no fault of his, the only solution he'd fathomed involved deceiving the person he loved most. If he hadn't already lost his job, it surely wouldn't be long in coming. The sudden realisation burned his eyes. He vowed once he sorted out Coyle and Wilson, he'd rake Jessie over the coals for the trouble she'd caused. He'd make sure she wound her neck in and behaved. Perhaps he would move in with her and Lily to make sure she didn't get up to any more of her nonsense. With a child to look after, and no man in the house, it was time she got in line. Again, the temptation to scold his mother chipped at his conscience but he ignored it. He'd also find a way to make right with his father, so he might sleep easier – and his mother would stop tormenting his dreams. He waved the empty tankards.

"Fraser, let's clean up so Da can get to bed. He's overdone himself today."

Fraser gawked as if he'd popped down from the moon. Angus grabbed his arm. "Come on, don't stand there like a spade. Let's get it done." The plates were no sooner in the sink when sounds from outside sent blood rushing to his feet. He gripped Fraser's arm. "Stay here, I'll go."

Fraser dropped a spoon into the sink. "Not without me, you won't."

Before they reached the front door it flew open and an overheated Maggie stood on the front step, Callan lagging behind. Her head swivelled in a quick scan of the room before heading towards Dougal. He heaved himself out of his chair but she put a hand up.

"No Dougal, don't you get up. I'm minding Callan tonight so thought I'd pop in to see you and the boys." She flashed wide eyes between Angus and Fraser. "I know it's a bit late but Callan's been desperate to see your tairsgeier. Fraser, can you show it to him?"

Fraser's bewilderment froze his expression and his lips almost disappeared into his dark beard while Angus nudged him towards the door. "Aye, of course, no bother at all ... Fraser?"

Fraser struggled to answer as the room stilled. Dougal broke the silence. "Well, don't stand about, take the laddie. I'll boil a kettle." He winked at Maggie, oblivious to her flushed cheeks and trembling hands. "Or would you prefer a wee dram, Mags?"

She forced a smile, wiping her forehead. "That will be lovely, but it's awful warm in here, so you pour it while I catch my breath outside for a minute."

Angus stepped towards her. "Good idea. Da, you get sorted and I'll make sure Mags doesn't collapse in Ma's bushes."

The second Dougal turned his back they rushed out the door, careful to close it behind them. Maggie grabbed Angus's shoulders. "They've taken her, Angus. They've arrested her, and they've taken Lily." She keened like a mourning wife, shaking him. "You need to do something. You must get her out!" Her anguish punched both Angus and Fraser, rendering them both breathless for a second.

Angus held her face and pleaded. "Mags, calm yerself and tell me what happened. Where is she?"

Maggie sucked into the depth of her belly. She looked at Callan, whose face resembled a statue of highland marble; varying yellow and green hues streaking through damp skin.

"Callan, he was there. He watched them take her into the school." Callan stared at his feet until she elbowed him. "Callan, tell them. Tell them what you saw, what you heard and when it happened."

Callan's lips moved, but no words formed. Fraser, speechless and still mystified from the moment they arrived, grabbed both his arms and shook him like a dirty rag doll. "Laddie, do I need to beat it out of you? Open your mouth, tell us what happened."

Through sobs and stammers Callan described everything he'd witnessed at Jessie's house, including when the police led Jessie into the school. He bawled describing the way they'd taken Lily from her. Everyone's shock registered – Callan's sniffling increased. Maggie held her head in her hands, Angus tore at his hair and Fraser beat his thighs with clenched fists. When Dougal called out the window, Angus huddled them.

"Fraser, tell Da I'm walking Mags home because she's overheating, then I'm going to call in on Jessie to make sure she's managing." He held Maggie's clenched fists. "Take Callan to Mrs Ramsay's and tell her Coyle sent you to fetch Lily. You're her godmother and will look after her. Callan can vouch Coyle sent him to you."

Angus and Fraser watched Maggie scurry out the gate with a firm grip on Callan's jumper. Angus caught his breath when she swiped the revisiting magpie off the fence post.

"Away with you and your trouble," she hissed.

He waited until they were out of sight before he turned to Fraser. "Keep Da calm, but get him ready to leave at first light." Fraser shook his head and his mouth dropped open. Angus leaned into him. "Don't ask me how. There's too much to explain. Trust me and get him sorted."

Fraser stepped back, and for the first time in Angus's life he watched fear transform his face. He grabbed his dark curls and held his head. Even though his throat hurt, his voice thundered. "No one in this family is going to jail. They will not take any child of ours, and no one will hang our kin."

Fraser stammered. "Where are you going?"

"To bring Jess home."

Chapter 28

DR MACFARLANE THANKED HIS *wife Irene for dinner and accepted her offer of tea, when thunderous knocking on his door threatened to burst its hinges and his heart. Irene put a hand against the wall and grumbled. "Dear Lord, who is that at dinner time? Is someone in labour?"*

The doctor leapt out of his armchair. "Well, if they are, they're not due."

He barely opened the door and Angus burst into the room. "Doctor, I need to speak to you urgently." He glanced at Irene then back at the doctor's crumpled face. "In private, outside."

Irene rushed towards the men. "Is your Da ill?"

Angus turned. "No, it's Jess." He watched her expression change, the panic in her eyes fade and her jaw tighten.

"Well, I'll get back to the dishes."

He ignored her scorn and gestured to the doctor. "Outside, please?"

Dr MacFarlane followed Angus to the front yard, where they stood amongst meticulously tended petunias and primroses, their petals already folded over, tucked in for the night. Only the sound of Angus's heavy breathing broke the stillness of the late twilight. The doctor shoved his hands into his pockets. "What's wrong?"

Angus lurched at him. "You know what's wrong! You know very well. Did you have anything to do with Jessie's arrest?"

The doctor stepped back. Angus watched his eyes widen. "No, I did not. I am aware of certain investigations, but I did not know it was imminent."

"Imminent?" Angus's eyes bulged. "So, you knew it would happen, and after all the years you've known our family, you didn't warn us?"

The doctor's spine stiffened. "Angus, your sister may be responsible for Tom's death … not to mention other, well, incidents."

Angus grabbed the doctor's jersey, his fingers curling so tight around the fine Hebridean wool his knuckles pushed through the knit against hard collarbones.

"The only way anyone might blame Jess for Tom's death is if you confirmed it." He stepped to within an inch of the doctor's nose and shook him almost off his feet. "Did you tell anyone Jess poisoned Tom?"

Dr MacFarlane's realisation that Angus may know he was the one who suggested the bottle Jean removed from Jessie's house was poison sent fear rushing from his ankles up into his throat.

"Your sister and her spae friends are guilty of many things," he whined. "They administer medicines with no proof of efficacy, and they twist people's minds with their hocus pocus and pagan rituals. Who knows what she puts in those potions, or what damage they do?"

Angus flung the doctor against a wooden fence that only just held firm. He stomped into the sleeping petunias and towered over the trembling man, pinning him against the narrow wood slats. "You told my family Tom's illness was probably the result of an apoplexy, after a consumption fever. Jessie was nowhere near him when he collapsed."

The doctor rambled incoherently about Jessie's lack of care, and mismanagement of Tom's health, while trying to escape the restraint of the damaged fence and Angus's bulk. Angus's swell of fury drowned his voice. He yanked the doctor by the hair, pulling him straight, holding him with one hand tight around his neck. Again, their noses almost touched. His words rumbled from the back of his throat. "You are coming with me, and you will do whatever it takes to release my sister."

The doctor's eyes bulged, and although trying to wipe spittle from his mouth, Angus only loosened his grip enough for him to speak. "I don't want any part of this. Father Coyle will, Wilson will—" Words failed him and he squeezed his eyes closed.

Angus let go of his throat. "So, this is their doing?"

The doctor held his head with one hand, soothing his throat with the other, but Angus grabbed his chin. "Look at me. If you truly believe my sister and her spaes have the power to kill people, you'll be far better off siding with me … if you know what's healthy for you, and your kin. Get your coat." He *waited outside, but spotted Irene watching him from a window. He cursed then turned his back on her, trying to slow his pounding heart and gather his scattered wits. In a fleeting moment of clarity, he noted there was not a sprig of heather in the MacFarlane's garden.*

Angus dragged the unwilling doctor to the school while Maggie dragged an even less willing Callan to Mrs Ramsay's house. With no tolerance for his snivelling or malingering she barked:

"Lift your feet before I knock you into next week," yanking his jumper at each slow step. "If my old legs can move quicker than yours, you're not worth the space you take up."

Mrs Ramsay lived on the far end of the village, but Maggie's energy, driven by her fierce protection of Jessie, carried her along the dirt road from Dougal's house and along the periphery of the woodland without missing a beat or stumbling over loose stones.

When they reached the closest edge of the forest Callan pulled back. "I don't want to go there. I'm scared."

Maggie stopped and turned to him. "Scared of what?"

Callan looked toward the forest and his head shrunk into his shoulders. "I'm not going near the woods at night. My Mam will kill me, or the faes will drown me."

Maggie's laugh echoed through the narrow tree-lined path. She bent over and glowered into Callan's large, wet eyes. "Laddie, if you don't lift your feet and get a move on, you'll have no need to fear the faes, for I'll wring your neck. I think you've caused too much trouble for the faes to want you. Now, wheisht and move."

She gave him no time to resist. She pushed him forward and they carried on past the forest – one of Callan's hands stuck to the side of his face. Upon reaching Mrs Ramsay's, Maggie's chest heaved, so she stood at the gate inhaling deep into her lungs until her panting ceased. Callan stood gazing at his feet, fidgeting with his buttons. Mrs Ramsay's husband Gordon opened the door, promptly folding his burly arms over his chest. He looked over his nose and frowned.

"With all this trouble I'm not surprised to get a visit, but I didn't think it would be you, Mags." A whiff of chicken broth assaulted Maggie.

"Hello, Gordon, I'm sorry I'm disturbing you, but if you don't mind, I need to speak with Elsie."

Gordon eyed her from head to toe then looked at Callan. "What's he up to?"

Her fists immediately clenched inside her pockets. "Father Coyle sent him to ask me to fetch wee Lily. You might know I'm her godmother."

Gordon grunted, turned his head and called into the space behind him: "Elsie, you've got visitors."

Elsie appeared and Maggie spotted one of Lily's blankets in her hand. Her throat tightened. "Hello, Elsie."

Elsie glanced at Callan drilling his feet into the path, and Maggie cleared her throat.

"I'm here to fetch Lily. I'm sure Jessie's extremely grateful to you, but I'm her godmother so I'll be happy to take her home with me."

Elsie twisted the blanket between her fingers. Maggie's heart pounded. She gestured to Callan. "Father Coyle sent Callan to tell me to—"

"Maggie, stop." Elsie raised a hand. "You need not explain to me. I know who Lily is."

Maggie chewed the inside of her cheeks. She resisted her immediate desire to barge into the house and rip Lily from wherever she lay. She met Mrs Ramsay's narrowed eyes. The woman waved Lily's blanket towards Gordon. "Go check the kettle. You're not needed here."

Gordon shrugged and loped back into the house. Maggie opened her mouth but Mrs Ramsay spoke first. "This is terrible trouble, Mags, God knows how it'll all end. The poor child is in the middle of it – through no fault of her own – and she'll probably end up paying for it." Maggie's chest puffed and her nostrils flared. Elsie sighed. "You don't need to get into me about it, Mags. I have six of my own, and if anyone tried to take even one of them, I'd chop their legs off."

Maggie's jaw dropped. "You'll give her to me?"

Elsie glanced at Callan then leaned towards Maggie. "Aye, but you'd better not take her home. That daft priest plans on having her taken to the orphanage in Glasgow ... first thing tomorrow morning. So, if she's not here, yours will be the first house he races to."

Maggie's knees buckled, so she leaned on the door frame. Mrs Ramsay turned and disappeared into the house. Within a few moments she reappeared holding Lily – Jessie's bag hanging over a shoulder. Maggie took Lily and held her tight.

Mrs Ramsay patted her gently. "She has her granny's eyes … they look right into your soul."

Maggie extended a hand. "Thank you, Elsie. You'll be in my prayers forever."

Mrs Ramsay raised her eyebrows then transferred the bag to Maggie. "It's not me who needs your prayers."

Maggie nodded. "What will you tell Father Coyle?"

Mrs Ramsay eyed Callan. "I'll blame him. He looks as if he's overdue a hiding."

After arriving on the doorstep, and having destroyed every blade of grass under his feet, Callan's head suddenly shot up. His colour hadn't returned and his red-rimmed eyes stared at Mrs Ramsay. She bent until her eyes levelled with his. "You better get yourself home before your Mam looks for you."

She leaned over to Maggie. "That boy's not right. He always seems to be where trouble is."

Maggie frowned. "Aye, I'm glad he's not mine. Thank you, Elsie. Jessie will be forever grateful."

Mrs Ramsay turned, still holding her door. "Heather was a wonderful woman. I hope Jessie remembers what she taught her."

Maggie and Callan walked back down the path, but when they reached the corner, she took hold of Callan's jersey once more. "Keep your mouth shut," she growled, "if I hear you've uttered one word to Father Coyle, you'll wish the faes took you."

Callan turned and within seconds disappeared down the road.

Maggie stopped at her house just long enough to rest her legs, swig a dram, and fill a bag with a few of her things. Mrs Ramsay's warning rang in her ears, and even though the burden of carrying Lily plus two bags didn't sit lightly, she wouldn't take a chance with her safety. She beseeched Heather. "I don't know how I came to have this burden, but for the love of our ancestors, help me carry it, for I'm not sure my legs are fit."

With scant light filtering through the dense branches of the forest, Maggie made her way warily, mindful of her steps. She hummed softly, hoping Lily didn't pick up on her anxiety. She stopped for a rest at the pond for Lily to stretch her chubby legs and play with the soft grass. Maggie reminisced. She couldn't count the number of times she'd shared this space with Heather, or the stories framing their lives. The last of the days' midges still hovered, but the dragonflies and ladybirds had long gone to rest. The pond sent no glistening welcome, and a shudder rumbled up her spine as she looked at the still darkness of the water. After a brief rest, she gathered Lily, their bags, then trundled on, hopeful the light would last enough to guide her safely. Lily gurgled, jabbering nonsense and amusing Maggie – distracting her from her troubles – and her painful body. The light faded as dancing shadows gave way to dull stillness, and Maggie begged her legs to stay strong. When the faint smell of familiar wood smoke reached her, the relief that she'd almost made it to Myna's house spurred her on. By the time she arrived, she barely managed enough strength to knock. When the door opened, she dropped Lily into Myna's arms before slumping onto the doorstep.

Myna caught Lily and yelled: "Girls, come quickly!"

Tevia and Tavia rushed to the door. One took the bags, the other helped Maggie into the house. No one spoke until she settled on the couch and caught her breath. Myna turned to the girls. "Tevia, take Lily to the bedroom. Tavia, bring some water."

The girls burst into action, and soon Maggie was gulping down a mug of water as Myna sat wringing her hands – until she was about to burst. "Maggie, you're terrifying me. What's happened?"

Maggie drained the mug then held it between her palms. She shot a look at Tavia, so Myna instructed the young girl to join her sister. Tavia left without a word. Maggie put the mug on the table then leaned forward. "They've taken Jessie. I've just fetched Lily from Elsie Ramsay, and Angus is on the warpath. Myna, it's our worst nightmare."

Myna sank back and the chair creaked its objection. She reached for her hair and met the eyes of her weary friend. "We need to have faith in Angus. We'll keep Lily safe here until Jessie is free. He won't let them hurt her."

Maggie's eyes filled, then overflowed with the day's turmoil. She dropped her face into her hands and sobbed. Myna reached over and held her. "It'll be fine, Mags. We'll be all right."

Maggie rocked. "No, Myna, Heather saw this. She knew."

Myna sighed. "Then we know what to do."

Maggie and Myna held each other and the room went quiet. In this moment of uncertainty, an observation floated into the foremost of Maggie's mind, but overwhelmed by the present crisis, and despite the smell of smoke, it left before she acknowledged it.

Myna's fire wasn't lit yet.

Chapter 29

AFTER JESSIE'S ARREST, *Father Coyle wasted no time in rushing to the manor. He flew into the cowshed and bellowed: "Get my horse hitched!"*

A young boy chopping wood dropped his axe then snatched his shirt from the dirt. Without bothering to shake it clean or button it up correctly, he hitched the horse and cart – the priest continually yelling for him to hurry. When done, he supported the priest's bulk as he heaved himself into the cart. He watched the wheels bounce over stones and through puddles, the priest's whip working furiously. No sooner had he resumed his chopping when Donald arrived, doubled over and gasping for breath. He asked the boy if he'd seen Angus, and immediately noticed his uneasiness. "What's up with you? Have you seen Angus or not?"

"No, but that priest was here all in a panic about something, then raced out of here cursing him."

Donald's head pounded. Controlling his stutter was worse than catching a pocketful of escaped marbles. "C-cursing Angus? W-where is he off to?"

The young boy pointed in the direction of the road. "To the manor, you've just missed him."

Donald swore into the air, then took off back down the road. His mind flipped a coin: find Angus or find out what Coyle is up to with Wilson? Turmoil throbbed against the back of his eyes, his chest burning as he sprinted back across the fields he'd just come from. Coyle's smug face when he'd left the manor earlier infuriated him, then the conversation he'd overheard in the yard had prompted him to follow the priest, even though he had no idea what he'd do when he caught up with him. His senses fired and his gut warned him things were not right, but he convinced himself whatever it was, Angus would fix it.

Coyle rode into the stable yard at the manor, shouting. When Donald didn't come rushing, he muttered, lowered himself onto the gravel then headed to Wilson's office. The dour doorman answered his impatient knocking, casting his eyes up and down.

"Is Lord Wilson expecting you?"

The priest pushed his way in and banged on Wilson's office door, striding in without waiting for a reply. Wilson jumped from his chair. "Why have you barged into my office?"

Father Coyle patted himself down then exhaled. "I apologise if I have surprised you, but I want to appraise you with the latest development, it simply cannot wait."

Wilson sniggered. "If you've come to tell me of that woman's arrest, you're too late."

The priests' puffed cheeks coloured his face. He delayed his response by marching across the room and settling himself into a leather chair. A frown crumpled his blotchy face. "Yes, she has indeed been arrested. Her child was also taken into care and will be dispatched to an orphanage tomorrow morning." *His lips twitched in sync with his fingers digging into the armrests.*

Wilson simply raised his eyebrows. "Is that it?"

The priest's jaw shuddered. "Well ... I believe with the ringleader removed, her friends will follow – as will her family. They will realise they are unwelcome, that we will not tolerate their practices. We will be rid of them all very soon."

Wilson laid his hands flat on his desk. His head nodded deliberately. "Good, so things will settle and I can continue with my plans?"

The priest's head bobbed. "Yes, of course, there will be no more trouble."

Wilson paused. "You want me to continue funding your school and subsidising the church upgrades?"

The priest's chair creaked. "The community would be most appreciative, and this area will certainly prosper."

Wilson's lips curled inwards, then he blew out a sigh. "You misunderstand me. I have no interest in their appreciation. I simply want assurances that my returns will be commensurate with my investment. The crofters shall pay rentals, there will be no more unrestricted access to produce or feed, and all livestock must be accounted for ... registered to the manor."

The priest shifted in his chair. "Yes, yes, I understand, I am working on it. These people are a little stubborn, used to their ways, but with the troublemakers removed, they are sure to come round."

Wilson leaned forward. "What of the forest? I am still of the view that it is a valuable resource, so now the evil forest dwellers are no longer, I have several options to make it a profitable area."

Father Coyle's sweaty hands twisted his rope belt. "Well, of course there are options, but perhaps in time. For now, it would be advisable to let the dust settle, and implement your strategies slowly."

Wilson stood, and his fists almost burst through his pockets. His eyebrows leaned over slitted eyes. "Their stubbornness is irrelevant, and I have no intention of taking my time. My patience always had a limit, so my advice to you is to get them in line before I do. Unless there is good reason to the contrary, I will flatten the entire area and turn it into something that will create substantial income."

The priest opened his mouth, but a fist flew from Wilson's pocket. "Enough of your whining. I have made myself perfectly clear, you have taken up enough of my time. You may leave."

Breaking the moment of impasse, Father Coyle dropped his belt and gripped the chair arms, but Wilson gestured towards the door. The priest's chest heaved and his chins wobbled. Restrained animosity swirled around the room like bats unsure of where to settle. The priest stood, cocked his head, and turned. When he reached the door, Wilson's voice stung his ears.

"May I also remind you I still have no update regarding my missing men? If you have no explanation, then my trust in your management must be misplaced. You may find yourself no more useful to me than the forest."

The priest swung around but Wilson's attention was already back to the document on his desk. Without looking up, he flicked his fingers into the air and the priest shuffled out the door.

By the time Father Coyle reached Laura's house he was sweating as much as his panting horse. A tornado of anger, fear and humiliation pulsed behind his eyes. His knocking might have shocked the dead, and had Laura not dashed to *open her door, its hinges may not have endured. Laura opened, but gripped the door handle, and before she had time to speak, he barged past, thumping on the wall. "This is not a social visit, and by God you better get in line, or you and your entire clan will find yourselves in a cell so far away no one will ever find you!"*

Wilson slapped the document he'd been working on against the edge of his desk, walked to his window, watched the priest drive away, then marched into the hallway. He barked at the doorman. "Fetch Briggs and Carter."

Two heavy-set men arrived then stood with their hands behind their backs. Dirty brown flat caps hid grimy hair, shielding dull, round eyes fixed on the man before them. Their wide-lipped mouths, missing full sets of teeth, protruded through rough stubble travelling under the collars of flannel shirts, unable to button to the top … a consequence of their trunk-like necks. Bulky boots assaulted the luxurious wool pile, pungent remains of tobacco and ale clinging like invisible shrouds. Neither penetrated Wilson's veneer. He stood two feet away, jaw almost as stiff as his fists now clenched behind his back. As unaffected by their appearance and odour as the soulless eyes of his predecessors staring down at them.

"Do you have what you need? Ready to go?"

Both heads nodded.

"It is time. Start at the far end of the forest next to the crofter's road then work your way around. Be sure to cover the entire perimeter, ending where the forest meets the village. There is no wind, so do not leave any open sections. Do you understand?"

Without averting their eyes or parting their red fleshy lips, they nodded once more. Wilson took a step back, gesturing to the door. "Make certain you remain unseen. Report back to me when the job is done."

After they left, he walked to an open window overlooking the gravelled horseshoe driveway leading out to his vast property. He breathed in the fresh air. Tapping his gold ring on the windowsill scared off a curious magpie. Wilson's desire to solve the mystery of his missing men, and put a stop to the unnerving incidents, was both irritating and inconvenient, but held little of his attention; it formed only part of his aim. Discontent rumbled through the village, and if resistance to his plans worsened, the situation may well become menacing, and costly. His belief in turning this small part of the world into the most lucrative farming and recreation area North of Hadrian's Wall had leveraged the funding he wanted from his family. Now significantly behind in his forecasts, he tired of listening to his father's warning that he was simply attempting to flog a dead horse. His wife had made a hasty retreat to England at the first mention of witchcraft, and would not uproot herself from her London lifestyle to become a permanent farm dweller; unless it became extremely attractive. For that, he needed to show decent profits. She would not risk their two spoiled sons becoming victims of local disobedience or pagan behaviour. He needed to get things under his control.

Outside, immediately below the windowsill, Donald held his breath, praying neither his pounding heart nor the dog sitting three feet away would betray him. Fear ballooned in his lungs, rigid muscles in his back pushed against unforgiving stone. A sudden thud of the window closing dragged the captive air from his throat, and his knees finally regained strength. He sunk into the mud, eyeballing the dog. Reality whacked him like an unexpected gust. He scrambled through resilient rose bushes before bolting upright then sprinting across the now familiar lawns, without a glance at the errant daisies. For a second time, Donald raced to Angus's house breathless and bedraggled, emotions and fears roiling his insides worse than the milk yard churns. This time, his manners gave way to screeching before he even made it to the front door. Fraser ran out, stopping him before he reached the doorstep. Donald's stutter gagged his words until Fraser slapped him.

"Take a breath, sit, calm yerself!" He pushed him to the ground. Donald looked up and his effort spilled out of his eyes. Fraser knelt and grabbed his head between his hands. Donald's body quivered from deep inside, and Fraser's eyes widened. "For God's sake, tell me. Is it Jessie?"

Donald choked, his fingers digging into Fraser's arms. He sucked in as much air as possible, then hissed through tight lips. Each word landed like concrete dropped from a dizzy height. "W-Wilson has sent his men to b-burn down the forest. We have to s-stop them. The women will d-die."

A shadow suddenly loomed over the crouched men, eclipsing the surrounding light. Both looked up.

"What did I hear you say?" Dougal hovered over them, his ashen face and wiry frame almost a spectre of himself, but for the rage in his eyes. Donald shrunk into the damp grass, staring up as though he was a juvenile delinquent preparing for a hiding. Fraser thumped him. His stutter vanished, quelled by the invisible weight of mutual concern and the magnitude of what he needed to say.

"This morning I overheard Wilson giving instructions to his men … the big ugly thugs who hang around the t-tavern bothering the women." He shot a glance at Dougal. "I came to find Angus … then I ran back. Father Coyle was rushing to the m-manor, so I followed him. There was an awful argy-bargy, but when he left, Wilson called in his men … he ordered them to b-burn down the forest." His lips quivered as his fingers twisted into Fraser's sleeve. "The entire forest, everything!"

Dougal stepped forward. Donald's backside buried itself deeper into the grass.

"Get up." Dougal extended a hand and whipped him up off the ground like an overgrown weed. He did the same for Fraser. "Where's Angus?"

"He's gone to get Jessie."

Dougal lifted his arms, anger vibrating each word. "Why? You better tell me, lad, before I set fire to both of you."

At the other end of the village, Angus shoved a heavy-footed Dr MacFarlane through the school gate, prodding his back until they came face to face with an even heavier footed police officer, whose head drooped as the men approached. Angus gave him no place to hide. He stood within inches, squaring his wide shoulders, growling from his belly. "We're here to take Jessie home."

The police officer's wide eyes flashed towards Dr MacFarlane, then back to Angus. His stiff arms relaxed, and suddenly his uniform appeared one size too big. He swiped at his forehead. *"Thank God. I was worried you were coming to hang her."*

Angus lunged at the officer who fell back against the mouldy wall. The width of Angus's shoulders shielded the man from Dr MacFarlane, who retreated into a corner. Angus swung around. *"You stay right there."*

He turned to the officer's colourless face. *"What are you talking about? Who thinks they're going to hang Jessie?"*

His uniform wasn't official enough to hide his discomfort. *"I don't have any idea … I don't know,"* he whined. *"All I heard was she murdered people so they want to hang her. They're coming tomorrow to take her away."*

He kneaded his thighs through dark blue wool trousers hanging over farmer's boots, simultaneously trying to keep his attention on both Angus and Jessie's prison door. Angus stepped back, and the officer gestured towards the door. He shook his head and shuffled. *"I don't want to do this. I want nothing to do with witches. My Mam will kill me just for being here."*

Angus leapt, grabbed his throat, then threw him against the wall. *"My sister is not a witch!"*

Dr MacFarlane remained glued to his corner while the officer scrambled to his feet, scattering mould spores and paint chips. Angus held out a hand, but the officer pushed it away. *"This is not my trouble."* He took a key from his pocket and only just missed hitting Angus with it. *"Take it and get her the hell away from here."*

Angus eyed him. *"You're sure? You're a police officer."*

The young man shrugged. *"I'm only here to make sure she doesn't leave. The priest gave me this uniform. The real police only come tomorrow."*

Dr MacFarlane gasped from his corner. *"Oh, dear God."*

Angus picked up the key then turned to him. *"Seems I don't need you after all."*

When Jessie lifted her head, she beamed as though the messiah himself stood before her. She jumped up, hugging Angus so hard she wasn't sure whose thumping heart was whose. She held his face in her hands. *"Angus, get me out of here. They've taken Lily."*

"Maggie has her." His good news came from behind a deep frown. *"She's taken her to Myna's … that house in the forest."*

Jessie clutched her neck. "Thank God." The damp air still clung to her, and Angus's exasperation with anything relating to the forest added to the chill. She took hold of his hands. "Don't fuss. It's not what you think. Maggie and Myna will look after her, no one can get to her there."

Angus shrugged then glanced over his shoulder to see Dr MacFarlane bolting like a vampire at dawn. "Let's get out of here. This trouble isn't over, Jess. I'm taking Da to his brother first light."

Jessie stepped back. "Well, if it keeps him safe until this all blows over, it's best."

Angus nodded, but Jessie sensed darkness dulling his spirit. "Angus, please don't fret. I will go to Myna. No one will find us. Lily will be safe, I promise."

He shrugged. "I'll sort Coyle ... and Wilson can stick his job."

Jessie reached for him once more. "I'm sorry Angus, I didn't see all this trouble coming to you. I never dreamed it would go this far." She hugged him tight.

Tears filled his eyes. "Aye, it's a right mess you've made this time. Just make sure you stay well-hidden until I can fix it."

"I will, I promise."

They turned their backs on the mouldy room and snuck out the side door, conveniently left unlocked by the temporary police officer. When they reached the street, Fraser and Donald rushed towards them. Their flushed faces and wild eyes froze Jessie's heart, and the momentary flutter of relief in her stomach turned to stone. Donald grabbed Jessie, while Fraser almost knocked Angus off his feet. Donald blabbered incoherently and Fraser gripped Angus's shoulders.

"Wilson is burning down the forest. He's sent his men out, Donald says the spaes live there ... right in the middle of it."

Jessie's skin bristled as she grabbed Donald. "Are you sure? How do you know?"

Fraser pushed Donald out of her way. "It's true, he heard Wilson give the instruction."

Donald clutched his hair. "Myna and the girls are there; we need to get to them. We must get them out of there!"

Angus's face turned ashen. Jessie tried to fight dark images flashing through her mind. Red and black and orange. Their eyes locked, but neither spoke. Fraser looked at Jessie's pursed lips, then at Angus's tight jaw.

"Angus, say something. Jessie, say something."

Jessie's heartbeat thumped in her ears as the ground swirled beneath her feet. She forced her lips to move. "Maggie has taken Lily to Myna."

Chapter 30

GRIPPING DONALD'S HAND TIGHTLY, Jessie dragged him over a log unable to support his muddy boots, so he landed splayed in a heap of damp, moss-topped forest floor. She turned and stood over his lanky, dishevelled body. "Get up! Hurry!"

Donald stood up hastily while a family of twittering nuthatches raced up a tree trunk into the first available crevice. His now Medusa-like curls quivered around his mottled face.

"Stop dragging me. I know the way."

Jessie's hands flew to her waist, her curls tumbling onto her left shoulder. "How do you know the way?"

Donald's stutter resumed, so the only words to escape in one piece were 'Tevia, picnic, home,' none of which she had time or patience to decipher.

"Then keep up with me!"

Donald straightened, then followed her flapping skirts. Jessie's mind churned. Past worries, present crisis and future fears foremost, fighting with her more important navigational process. She'd devised a few routes to Myna's – a necessary requirement to avoid detection by anyone with sinister intentions. Although not the simplest, the fastest route seemed the only option. She flew across slippery rocks, trampled over fallen logs, trudged through boggy patches. Donald's heavy breathing echoed behind. Fleeting questions regarding his familiarity with the forest piqued her curiosity, but she tossed them as she tore through the woods. By the time they reached Myna's door, the burning in her chest had reached her eyes, and she choked back a sob. Her trembling fingers closed around the doorknob. She breathed deep before lunging into the house. Myna and Maggie sat huddled in deep conversation, but froze when the door almost flew off its hinges.

"Jessie, dear God!" Myna shrieked and Maggie clutched her chest.

Jessie rushed in. "We need to get out of here. The forest is burning. Where's Lily?"

Her words tumbled out in an avalanche of urgency, and Myna leapt out of her chair. "Jess, what are you talking about? Sit, you're frazzled."

Jessie stomped so her entire body quivered, dislodging slivers of tree bark and leaves from her wild hair. She punched the air. "Listen to me! We don't have time. If the fire surrounds us, we'll have no chance."

Before Myna or Maggie replied, Donald tumbled in the door then leaned over the back of the couch. Unable to string two words together, he simply pointed to Jessie, nodding so hard he risked losing his head.

Maggie clutched her neck and glared at Myna. "Oh no, I smelled it." Realisation contorted her face. "On my way here. I thought it was your fireplace."

Myna's eyes flew around the room like a startled deer. Jessie stomped once more. "Where are the girls? Where's Lily? We need to move!"

Myna hurried to the back room, returning with the twins – Tevia clutching Lily. For a moment, Jessie ignored the present danger and rushed to her child – happy after her feed and playtime. Tevia's face paled, seeing Jessie so unravelled. She immediately placed Lily into her unsteady arms, but when she looked into Jessie's eyes, her skin tingled, blood rushed to her feet, the ground felt slippery underfoot. Jessie took a moment to squeeze Lily against her heaving chest, sinking her head into her daughter's neck, relishing her familiar, comforting smell. Myna gave instructions while Donald tried his best to appraise Maggie of the situation; without total success, but sufficient for Maggie to pull on her coat and stuff her swollen feet back into her already deformed shoes. Myna called them all to attention then addressed Jessie.

"Are we leaving forever, Jess?"

Tevia gasped, Tavia whimpered. Myna grabbed Tavia's hand, pulling her close. Tevia stood with her gaze fixed on Jessie, her senses on high alert. Jessie glanced at each one, now imprisoned and silenced by fear. She searched for an answer to free them from their terror and calm the panic in their eyes.

"Angus is going to Wilson." She rocked Lily more than necessary. "To make him stop the burning." Her eyes scanned for understanding, finding only blank stares. "We don't know exactly where it started, but if we leave now, we won't get caught by it. We can't take a chance."

Myna closed her eyes for a second then tugged the twins' hands. "Get what you can carry, no more." Myna's eyes searched Jessie's face as the girls rushed to gather their belongings, then her face hardened. "This is my home, Jess. Are you sure Angus can stop this?"

Before Jessie answered, Maggie stepped forward. She placed her hand on Myna's arm. "Myna, let's just be careful … and safe."

Jessie's heart sank, dark colours swirling in her head once more. The girls arrived in the front room, ladened with shawls, blankets, and what little clothing they possessed. Myna called Donald to the kitchen, where he held a sack open while she stuffed it with provisions. Maggie filled a woven satchel with all the tinctures she found carefully arranged on Myna's dresser, as Jessie wrapped Lily in a shawl. While they worked, the walls heaved with unspoken tension and fearful imaginings. Myna looked around her home, and Maggie's bones ached from the weight of her friend's veiled sadness. Tevia and Tavia scurried, flitting like hungry squirrels, nervous tension controlling their movements.

Maggie sidled up to Jessie and stroked her arm. "Don't fret, Jess. Angus can fix this."

Jessie looked up, sighing from deep within her soul. "I hope so, Mags. This is all my fault."

Maggie placed a hand on Jessie's warm cheek. "No matter now. What's for us won't go by us."

Myna broke the onerous atmosphere. "We're ready."

After they had all filed out the front door, Myna turned to look around her home, fighting back tears. "Thank you for everything you've given me." She closed the door, then joined the others on the pathway.

Tevia whimpered. "I can smell it."

Myna took her arm. "Let's go."

Spurred on by a lethal combination of anger and fear, Angus ran faster than he ever thought possible. Similar to Jessie, past worries, present crisis and future fears bombarded his mind, but stronger than the terror they fostered was his desire to make Wilson and Coyle pay for the harm they would cause by burning down the forest. Knowing Jessie and Donald would get to Lily, and evacuate the women safely, provided some solace, but imagining a home destroyed with the occupants still in it was beyond his comprehension – firing his rage. He'd presumed he understood Wilson's thinking, but the tightening vice around his heart confirmed he'd fallen short. Even considering the hardships and troubles in his life till this point, no part of his psyche accepted any person harboured such evil towards others. Similar horror stories from other parts of the country replayed in his mind, one more brutal than the next – hard-working crofters finding themselves without homes or incomes – but still reason evaded him. No amount of consideration on his part would ever justify actions of this magnitude, for what appeared to be on account of nothing more than greed. How he wished he'd trusted his father. His warnings screamed in his head:

"Land as magnificent as this is too valuable for the greedy to ignore."

The moment his boots crunched the gravel leading to the Wilson doorway, his mind emptied, his immediate intention primed. He slowed to a steady walk, should Wilson see him from his window. He breathed into his stomach, wiping sweaty hands on his thighs. Experience reminded him to approach Wilson with deference, to appeal to his sensibilities, even though his gut twitched from the realisation he may not have any. He may have foiled Wilson's attempt to destroy his family, but if the fire got out of control, the entire village would burn, and ultimately Jessie would bear the blame. A quick scan of the windows eased his rattled nerves. He made his way up the familiar stairs to the front door, two at a time, without a sideways glance at the sleeping hounds. He lifted his hand to knock but pulled back before touching the gleaming wood. After a deep breath, and a glance over his shoulder, he rested a stiff hand on the brass handle. Within seconds, his plan to be courteous gave way to the urgency of his mission, so he opened the door, marched his quaking legs to the office, and strode in. Wood pine, tobacco smoke and antique leather assaulted his senses, but it was Wilson's reaction which sent him two steps back when he leapt out of his chair and yelled:

"How dare you! Get out of my house before I have you arrested, along with your sister!"

Angus reeled at the mention of arrest, the rage he'd taken time to subdue before confronting Wilson, smouldering once again. His good intentions succumbed.

"Are you responsible for my sister's arrest?" His forehead creased above wide eyes.

Wilson's lips curled into his moustache. He thrust his hands into his pockets and his shoulders jerked backwards. "I don't think it matters who orchestrated her arrest. If she's guilty of murder, she deserves her punishment. Your risk a similar fate if you don't leave here immediately."

Angus lurched forward, and although the desk formed a physical guard, his temper flew across its smooth leather inlay. "My sister is not guilty of murder, so you have no right to accuse her." He threw his arms in the air. "Father Coyle has twisted your mind, and for reasons beyond my understanding, you seem to believe every word."

Wilson's shoulders moved forward but the rest of his body remained stuck to the carpet. "My dealings with Father Coyle are none of your business! I need not explain myself to you." He removed a hand from his pocket. "Again, I suggest you leave before I have you removed." He pointed to the door.

A sudden crackle from the fireplace jolted Angus from his sparring. "You must stop the fire. You must send water ... and call your men back."

Wilson's moustache twitched. "I do not know what you're talking about."

Wilson's lie stung, and Angus's chest heaved, as though the wall-mounted, peering ancestors had suddenly sucked the oxygen from the air. His fists clenched, and when Wilson's smug expression revealed the depth of his icy disposition, he rushed around the desk, grabbing him by the collar. Wilson's eyes bulged, but Angus leered over him.

"Get your labourers out there with water and get your lackeys back here. You cannot burn the forest, there are people living in it."

Wilson pulled himself free, pushing Angus back against the desk. "This is my land. I will do as I please. You have seconds to get out of here." He pushed Angus aside, heading towards the bell cord hanging next to the fireplace. "If you're still here when my doorman arrives, he will throw you out, and I will make sure you end up in the same cell as your sister."

Angus lunged and grabbed the arm reaching for the cord. "Wait! You need to stop this. You'll kill innocent people."

Wilson teetered then regained his balance. He swung his free arm, which bounced off Angus's shoulder. "Let go of me, you savage! Coyle's right. The less of your kind around here, the better."

Angus straightened from his ankles, smouldering rage exploding from his belly. The air in the room seemed to spin. Wilson's ugly ancestors cackled from the walls while the heavy curtains swept the carpet into waves of advancing fury. Threats and insults bounced around his head in an incomprehensible eddy of noise. The fire, and the smell of burning wood, smothered his remaining iota of belief in swaying Wilson. His fist flew on the end of an arm reinforced with the blood of his ancestors, braced by the love and loyalty of his kin. He almost didn't feel it fly – Wilson didn't see it coming, as he turned to find the bell cord right at the moment of impact. Wilson's reeling sent a surge of satisfaction rushing through Angus's veins like a swig of whisky on a frosty night, but a wave of shock abruptly replaced it when Wilson's head swivelled. The force lifted him off his feet, sending him backwards, and the last thing Angus saw was the underside of Wilson's chin before he crashed to the floor. He closed his eyes for a moment as a ton of regret hit the pit of his stomach. Suddenly, the room stilled as though he were now in the hurricane's eye. The grandfather clock chimed, disrupting his pang of conscience, and he dropped to the floor beside Wilson.

"Get up!" he yelled.

Wilson lay on the carpet in a twisted heap. Angus punched his outstretched leg. No movement, and still the clock clanged. Angus jumped to his feet. Wilson's head sat perched on the edge of the fireplace as though he'd chosen to rest it there. Angus's stomach heaved as his eyes followed a river of red running off the corner of the smooth marble. A ruby waterfall, running gently into a gradually building river formed a shallow pond in the soft pile. Still, no movement. Angus's head thumped. Although he'd only ever seen farm animals die, Wilson's glassy eyes and open mouth defied any other conclusion. Realisation hit and he leapt backwards, staring at the lifeless body, supporting himself on Wilson's desk. Only the sound of his heavy breathing and thumping heart accompanied the unbroken predictability of the grandfather clock.

Angus drew on his survival instincts for guidance. His head refused to lift, and his eyes avoided the stares of Wilson's ancestors firing spears into his back as he staggered out into the empty entrance hall. When one of Wilson's hounds rubbed against his leg, a fleeting moment of panic shocked him. A glance towards the staircase and down the passage bolstered hope. No one – apart from the angry souls interred within the paintings – was any the wiser to what had just transpired.

He eased the large entrance doors shut and stood on the steps of the manor; his soul heavier than the enormous planters flanking him. Irrepressible tears poured, burning his skin as he gazed out towards the forest, his mind numbed by the blackness of his heart. The sun still shone, and tree branches swayed in their normal rhythm. Chickens clucked from the backyard, and two prize stallions swiped flies with happy tails. Angus trembled on the steps, but he recognised the world hadn't stopped to acknowledge the wreckage behind him. The enormity of what he'd done, and the ultimate effects of his action still lay dormant ... as dead as Wilson himself. Until an unsuspecting servant or doorman discovered their master, thereby launching the procedure of hunting him down and destroying his life. Realising the world carried on in oblivion – for now – fired a shock, ungluing his feet, stemming his tears. No one would stop the fire. Wilson's plan would continue. Donald would make sure Jessie and the women escaped in time, but his father's house would be the first of the crofters' houses to burn if the fire crossed the road. Angus's feet skimmed the polished steps, his heart pumped blood into his veins, and he raced down the driveway.

Chapter 31

DOUGAL SAT IN HIS chair, hands planted on his thighs, eyes fixed on the empty fireplace as though it held things visible only to him. He barely looked up when Angus burst through the door. Fraser emerged from the bedroom and grabbed Angus's elbow.

"He's not budging. Says he's not leaving Jessie here – or Mam."

Angus doubled over, sucking air into his heaving lungs. Fraser leaned out of Dougal's earshot. "Angus, what's wrong? Did you make Wilson stop the fire?"

Angus lifted one arm to clutch Fraser's sleeve, gesturing to Dougal. "He doesn't have a choice, none of us do. We need to leave. Right now."

"Ah, no!" Fraser wailed. "What happened? Did that bastard dig his heels in? Is there no end to his badness? Did you not talk sense into him?"

Angus bolted upright and gripped Fraser's shoulders. His glassy eyes and tear-stained face suddenly registered, and Fraser stopped rambling. Angus's lips barely moved. "Wheisht, please." His face crumpled as he squeezed his eyes tight.

Fraser's face paled. "Dear God, Angus, what's happened?"

Angus's head wobbled trying to find its balance, but his knees buckled, and just before he crumbled to the floor, Fraser reached under his arms and guided him to a chair, then knelt and held him. Still, Dougal gazed into the fireplace, engrossed in his own contemplations.

Angus lifted his head, digging his fingers into Fraser's hands until he winced. "We don't have time. It's too late for Wilson to stop the fire. Our time here is done. Get the cart hitched … pack us up. I'll speak to Da."

Fraser's colourless face remained still, words failing him for a moment. Then his head swayed and his hands lost their grip. He only managed a whisper. "Angus, what are we taking?"

"As much as you can." His expression carried more than his words. "We won't be back."

Fraser's body shrunk within his clothes as he walked out the door. Angus willed his tears to wait, breathed in a whiff of white heather from the windowsill, silently begging his mother for strength. He laid his hand on Dougal's shoulder and gazed into the fireplace.

"Da, you need to trust me. It's time to go."

Dull clouds allowed little of the sky to flicker between and above the trees, but Myna needed neither daylight nor starlight to guide her. Her spae instincts came to the fore in complete understanding of the magnitude of their undertaking. If ever she needed strength and wisdom in equal amounts, it was now. She trusted her abilities to deliver them all safely to the tunnel as sure as salmon found their way home, regardless of the uphill struggle. She commanded her troupe with authority.

"Donald, stay behind Maggie; make sure she doesn't fall. Jessie, follow the girls. Tevia, Tavia, stick to my heels." Her voice stirred the surrounding leaves, but no one replied. "Do you all understand?" she barked.

Donald hooked arms with Maggie, yelling from the back. "Aye, we're ready, so let's get moving."

Myna strode into the thickets, shoving any interfering branches or jutting shrubbery sideways; her alternate swipes worthy of David Livingston's approval. Despite their heavily laden shoulders, Tevia and Tavia stepped carefully into the deep muddy impressions left by their mother's boots, keeping pace. Jessie held Lily too tight, so her squeals and demands often stalled progress. She focused on Maggie's laboured breathing, frequently waiting for Donald, who eased her forward with his continuous stream of encouragement. When they reached the well, Jessie insisted they rest for a few minutes, ostensibly to give Lily a break, but a wry look to Myna conveyed her concern for Maggie's wellbeing. A silent Maggie unnerved her more than the faint smell of wood burning she was trying to ignore. The girls sat on the grass surrounding the well. Myna adjusted their bags, making sure everything remained intact. Jessie lay Lily on a soft patch, leaving her to gurgle and wriggle like an upturned beetle. She sidled up to Donald and pulled on his sleeve.

"Maggie's struggling. This next part is tough, so please be careful with her."

Even in the dim light, Jessie watched Donald's worried eyes brighten. "Aye, don't you fret. I've got her. Wherever we're going, she'll be with us."

A sudden waft of smoky air caught Myna's attention. She jumped up, startling the twins. Jessie caught her eye, and both women glanced at the sky as though nudged by an invisible force. Myna looked away. "Come on, time to move."

Within seconds, they regrouped, facing Myna like pupils on a school outing. Donald helped the girls bundle up their bags. He looked around then darted over to the other side of the well. He yanked great clumps of tall grass out of the ground. Returning with bundles of it to cushion the girl's already tired shoulders from their bag straps, he tripped and fell over. Despite the situation, both girls giggled.

"Donald, ye fell oer yer ain feet!" Tevia laughed.

Donald scrambled to his feet, tufts of green flying around him. Colour rushed to his cheeks. "I d-did not!"

His embarrassment irked Myna who chided the girls. "Stop it you two. Get yourselves together."

She marched off to help him, and after brushing grass and dirt from his clothes, she looked down, then understood the cause of his fall. A large dirty boot lay on the grass next to where Donald stood. He pointed to the offending item. "Y-you see. I d-didnae fall oer ma feet."

Myna frowned. "Well, it's big enough to trip over, but how on earth it got here is anyone's guess."

Donald bent, grabbed the boot off the ground, and before Myna said more, he grunted then tossed it into the well. He marched back to Jessie and Maggie, avoiding the girls' sniggering.

Jessie wrapped Maggie's scarves tight. "What was all that about?"

Donald lowered his eyes. "N-nothing. Just the l-lassies being daft."

The boot forgotten, Myna led the group towards the concealed gate leading to the hills and the tunnel. Myna marched on with the twins close behind. Maggie laboured despite Donald's best endeavours. As they approached another rocky uphill pathway, Jessie pushed the girls aside and grabbed Myna's arm. When she turned, Jessie caught her breath. Myna's flushed face and sweaty brow belied her solid stance.

Again, her heart sank and the dark colours filled her mind. "Take the girls. I'll slow down to help Maggie, she's struggling."

Myna shoved her fists into her hips and inhaled. Jessie watched conflict flash across her face before she relented. "Do you remember the way?"

Jessie nodded. "We'll meet you there. Get the girls to safety then wait for us by the rocks. Can you manage Lily?" Myna's eyes widened, and even though Jessie didn't want to split the group, Myna's expression carried a fear she now understood; of being unable to protect your children from harm. She placed a hand on Myna's flushed cheek. "When we get to you, Donald will open the tunnel, then we'll be safe. Now go."

Jessie watched Myna, the twins and her beloved daughter disappear into the overgrown woodland before turning back. Maggie sat with her legs outstretched on a rock large enough to take her weight and shape. Donald cast Jessie a sideways glance, but she ignored him.

"All right, Mags? Take your time, it's not too far now." She prayed her doubt wouldn't betray her. Maggie looked up, kneading her thighs. "I admire your faith, Jess, but I fear it's misplaced."

Jessie gestured to Donald, and they each took an arm. "There's power in you yet, so let's get on with it. Don't want you becoming a bonfire tonight."

Maggie moaned. "Aye, the fire, I'd forgotten about that."

By the time Donald and Jessie reached the mound of rocks concealing their escape route, Maggie's breath rattled inside her chest, as swollen flesh bulged out of boots minus their laces since the latter part of the journey. Myna and the twins rested against a smooth section of wall, and in the dull shade of an overhanging bush, the girls' eyes shone the way curious baby owls search the sky for answers.

Myna handed Lily to Tevia, then jumped up to help Maggie into a comfortable position.

She could not feign her shock. "Oh, my, Mags, you're about expired." She knelt beside her ailing friend. Sweat softened Maggie's wiry hair and her plaid scarf disappeared into her neck folds. Donald eased each foot out of her boots, flinching each time Maggie moaned. Myna grabbed a blanket and rolled it up under Maggie's feet before placing a hand on her forehead. "Och, Mags, this is too much for you."

Maggie reached for her hand. "It is whatever it's supposed to be, Myna. We know that, don't we?"

Myna stood, thumped her thigh then yanked Jessie's arm, pulling her aside. "This is not Maggie's fight, Jess. Look at her."

Jessie stepped back. "It's too late for that now."

Myna's chest lifted. She stepped to within inches of her. "Did you not once – for a second – think about the warnings given to you? About the likely damage to others while you were crusading, hell bent on changing the world overnight? Did you not listen when your mother explained how difficult our world is, and how hard we've worked to keep ourselves safe?"

Jessie reeled from Myna's attack. "If we'd stayed, we might all have burned to death!"

"If you'd only listened to us, it would never have become something to fear. Now it may not just be my home I lose." Myna's voice broke with angry tears. "Even if the forest survives the fire, how will it ever be safe for us to go back?"

Jessie seized her arm. "I did not kill Tom, and you know I didn't kill the smithies!"

Myna pulled away. "None of that matters any more. Now we've helped you, we have become part of whatever they tar you with." She threw her arms in the air before returning to Maggie, leaving Jessie standing alone. A familiar rush of anger bubbled from Jessie's feet up into her chest. Images of Tom's parents, Dr MacFarlane and Father Coyle riled her temper. The chill of the mouldy cell, and the look of resignation on Mrs Ramsay's face when she took Lily away, settled in the pit of her stomach.

She marched across to Maggie, but addressed Myna. "I want you all to carry on until you reach the safe house. Donald will help you. I need you to take Lily with you."

Myna's eyes widened. "What about you?"

"There's something I need to do ... to make sure we are all safe, wherever we are."

Maggie shrieked. "You are not going back there! It's too dangerous."

Jessie knelt and took Maggie's hands. "No one knows this forest the way I do. I'll be back before you've caught your breath."

Maggie's words rattled through pale lips. "You know what's before you, as did your mother, but it doesn't need to be so. You have a daughter now."

Jessie grinned. "Which is why I'll be sure to get back. I would never leave her for you to look after."

Myna grabbed Jessie's arm, but Maggie's voice strengthened. "Myna, leave her be."

Jessie turned to Tevia and lifted Lily. She held her tight then kissed each cheek. Lily gurgled, reached out and clutched a curl of her mother's hair. Jessie looked down into Tevia's wide eyes. "Please look after her. Your mother needs to mind Maggie."

Tevia simply nodded. Jessie freed her hair from Lily's clutches and sat her in Tevia's lap. Lily objected, wailing and reaching for her mother. Jessie bent as Tevia consoled her, and a tear slipped from her eye. "I'm always with you. Till the end of time, and beyond." She kissed the top of her head before cupping her chin and whispering: "Till I get back."

She returned to Maggie and rested her head on her soft shoulder. Fighting back tears, she held her tight. "Wait for me, Mags."

Maggie pressed her cheek against Jessie's head. "I'll be wherever you are."

Jessie stood, then pulled Donald from the mouth of the tunnel, now almost cleared of its protective rocks. She gripped his shoulders. "No matter what happens, you make sure they get to safety. Myna knows the way, so you stay with them. Don't wait for me to get back here. Let them rest a little, but get on your way soonest. I'll find my own way. Do you understand?" Donald straightened and nodded. He parted his lips, but no words formed. Jessie patted his chest. "I trust you, Donald. You have a wonderful soul." She turned and ran down the hill, wood smoke filling her nostrils with each step.

⟳

Father Coyle removed his boots, then filled his wine decanter before Mrs Ramsay knocked on the door and entered. "I'm sorry, father, I didn't know you were here. I just want to put new candles in."

"Yes, yes, get on with it," he grumbled.

As she was leaving, Callan popped his head in. "Father Coyle, I just heard there's a fire in the forest."

The sudden realisation Wilson may have gone through with his plan to destroy the forest, and perhaps him with it, bounced him out of his chair, sending him grappling to get back into his boots. He rummaged around in his desk drawer, then stuffed a velvet drawstring bag into his robe pocket. Callan and Mrs Ramsay watched in shock as he darted around the room. "Finish up then get out," he barked, before thumping down the stairs. His body struggled to keep pace with his mind, forcing him to lean against a wall to catch his breath before sneaking behind a corner. He focused on a door, and didn't wait long before two bulky men appeared. As they turned the corner towards him, the priest stepped out, raising a hand. "I need your services ... urgently."

The men looked at each other, about to laugh, until they spotted the wad of notes in the priest's outstretched palm.

⟳

When Laura heard more knocking on her door her blood froze. She opened it and took two steps back as her chest tightened.

"Seems you've been up to no good with some evil people. Causing trouble for our boss you have. You need to come with us."

Laura's bones appeared to shrivel as she fell against the wall. She turned and looked at her basket of ropes sitting in the corner. "No, no, I'll tell you who you're looking for."

The men glanced at each other before one stepped forward and gripped her arm.

"Take us."

Chapter 32

TRAVELLING ALONE, THE ROUTE back proceeded quicker, and Jessie soon figured out the direction of the fire, and how to avoid it, in relation to where its smell intensified. She didn't fear the fire reaching her, trusting her ability to outrun and outmanoeuvre its course in an area she could navigate blindfolded. She also recognised a hint of damp in the air, praying a storm may arrive to extinguish the entire thing. Frequent whiffs of smoke fuelled her anger as Myna's words rang in her head. They would never be safe, regardless of where they fled. Their enemies determined their course, while their power energised their greed and determination. Unless she could stop them – and she resigned herself to live with the outcome of whatever it took. She trusted Angus to make Wilson see sense, regardless of how hard it may be. The need to repay his sacrifice, redeem herself with her spaes, restore their reputation, pumped through her veins.

With one quick stop at her house, she checked for anything she may have left behind that her detractors might use against her. She closed the door, but stood on her doorstep viewing her beloved garden with fresh eyes. She didn't have time for nostalgia. Her purpose shone brighter than any star. She glanced at the tree where she'd delivered Lily, which only hardened her resolve and raised her ire, so she marched down her pathway, swiping at her spindle berry bushes with each step. She rushed to Father Coyle's office, conscious of the smell of smoke trailing her. The origin and direction of the fire, now as clear as if she'd drawn a map, churned her stomach. After a quick glance up and down the street, she walked up the stairs into the priest's empty office. The dull silence amplified her heartbeat. She looked around, vivid reds, blacks and oranges unnerving her. She made her way to the priest's chair next to his drinks table, sat down then poured a glass of red wine.

The priest soon thumped up the stairs, closing the door behind him, before heading towards his chair. His gasp broke the silence, then he froze. In the seconds their eyes met, Jessie's anxiety dissipated. Angry heat emanating from the priest's face didn't hide the expression in his widening eyes: fear. In the confines of the priest's private space, the shift of power stripped him of both ego and bravado. Until he spotted the glass in Jessie's hand.

"How dare you!" he thundered. "You should be in jail." Jessie stood. The priest stepped back. "Do not come one step closer."

His eyes bulged, but she held his terrified gaze; moving towards him, glass secure between her hands. "We need to talk. You have overstepped, you risk destroying this entire village."

"We will not talk," he blustered, stepping aside then shuffling to the window.

Jessie watched sweat beads fight for space in the furrows between fat rolls on his forehead. His eyes flitted around the room, searching for a safe place, spittle seeping from the corners of his quivering lips. Her heart no longer thumped in her ears, and an unexpected calm softened her words. "Do you intend to have me arrested again? Are you determined to take my child from me?"

"I will have you hung!" he spat. "You will never see your child again." His cheeks throbbed and his robes flapped.

Jessie breathed deep, standing her ground. "Your fears are irrational. We are good people, so there is no need to hate us. We do no one any harm."

The priest swiped a pile of books sitting on a side table. "You are evil! Your forest friends, and your mother before you, evil!"

Jessie reeled from his roar. He marched to the door, yanked it open, and strode into the stairwell.

"Callan, get up here now!"

Jessie walked towards the door. The priest moved away. "I will send the police after you, so don't think you can hide." He looked at the glass still clutched in her hand. "Give me that! How dare you?" He snatched it from her.

She watched the deep red liquid swirl around the wall of the crystal, while her heart thumped. "I'm giving you one more

*chance. We can return to living our lives if you stop this ...
now. You are determining our fates."*

The priest's chest heaved. *"Never! Your days are finished.
You will never set eyes on your child again!"* His
determination thundered in Jessie's ears.

She nodded. *"I'll be on my way then."*

Before reaching the stairs, she turned to see the priest's
temper deforming his face as he placed the glass against his
twisted lips, evil glowing from his eyes. She raised a hand,
then dropped it. He swallowed the entire drink in one gulp,
then tossed the empty glass aside. She walked down the steps
into the street, the sound of smashing glass reverberating in
her ears.

Her stomach spasmed when she spotted smoke swirling
above the treetops on the far side of the forest, too close to her
father's house. It would be the first razed should the fire jump
the road. Descending dark clouds holding a layer of thickening
smoke closed in on each other, leaving only a sliver of light
sandwiched between. Birds raced to make it through the
narrowing gap, flying a gauntlet to safety.

Jessie ran from house to house, bashing on doors, yelling to
startled occupants to get out, and as far away as possible.
Thanks to the humidity of an overcast afternoon with little
wind, news and the acrid smell of smoulder travelled quicker
than the flame's ability to muster strength, providing a
perilous window of opportunity. Farmers and their sons
herded animals down to the river's edge, while daughters
helped their mothers rescue precious belongings, consisting
mostly of food and wool. By the time the fire did rage in the
trees directly across from their homes, most of the crofters
stood huddled by the riverbanks watching the horror of their
beloved forest burning – silently praying it wouldn't turn on
them. An elder clutched her chest, pleading to the heavens:
"What have we done to deserve this?"

Jessie made it to her father's house, rushing through the door
into a cold, empty room. The clean fireplace and empty sink
allayed her fears. She slumped into her father's chair, dropping
her head into her trembling hands as the fluttering in her

stomach calmed. Although Angus may not have been able to prevent the fire, it seemed he did get Fraser and her father out in time. She glanced towards the windowsill where the vase of white heather stood undisturbed by the turmoil. Her chest tightened and her throat ached. She walked over, ran her fingers across the soft white buds, breathing in the sweetness they offered in return. She closed her eyes for a moment, visualising her mother sitting at their favourite place, bare feet dangling into fresh crystal-clear water, surrounded by smooth multicoloured stones.

It took all her strength to clear her mind and run from the house. She recognised from which direction the fire would come, so unless she outran it, the only route back to the tunnel would take her straight into the force of it. She turned off the road, glanced up at the advancing grey clouds, and rushed towards the wall of trees framing the woods. The most familiar of her routes allowed her to run through clearings, jump over old fallen branches, and launch herself off rocks well-used to her feet. Her senses elevated to separate the heady aroma of damp wood and rotting leaves from the lung-stinging stench of wood smoke, prompting her to alter her route where necessary. The occasional crack of a branch snapping away from its trunk, or an unexpected howl from a terrified animal, caught her off-guard, fuelling her flight.

She arrived at the pond breathless, trembling. A deep breath confirmed she'd put distance between herself and the fire, so she stepped to the edge and bent down, leaning over the mossy outcrops and fluttering reeds. The chill of the water tingled her fingers, taking her breath away when she splashed it over her sweaty face. She rested on her haunches, scooping handfuls, instantly cooling her entire body. Her desire to lie down in the thick grass to let the soft blades caress her cheeks – as she'd done her entire life – stood no chance against the pervasive nagging in her brain. The fire would soon cut her off, and she had no intention of taking the only clear route – back to the village – so the quicker she made it to the tunnel, the sooner they would all be safe.

After one last splash of water, she stood gazing into the pond. Ripples settled, and the surface regained its glassy shine, and for a split second she visioned her mothers' face in the watery glow. Her heart swelled. Suddenly, coloured pebbles sparkled in the shallows at her feet, and tadpoles scampered. Rustling from the trees above caught her attention, and she watched an owl scatter leaves as it soared from its resting place out of sight, followed by a blood-curdling screech. When she turned her gaze back to the water, it no longer gleamed. Dark shapes formed, moving across its surface, lengthening, widening into an expanding shadow. Jessie froze as the shadows morphed into shapes – the same ones she'd seen creeping out of the dark walls in her visions: ominous, menacing dark energy her mother had pushed back. The clarity she'd searched for after the visions presented by her stones, jumped to the forefront of her mind. She swung around. Not quick enough to avoid the branch when it crashed against her head, sending her flying into the reeds. The sight of large boots, and the familiar twine of a thick rope crafted by her mother, triggered first relief, then bewilderment, before overwhelming pain consumed her, stealing the light from her world.

✿

Donald sat with Maggie, each of her raspy breaths increasing his anxiety. Even in the dim light, he noticed her colour fade. The more laborious her breathing became, the less her chest moved. Before long, he feared the worst. He released her hand, resting it on her lap, then moved to the other side where Myna sat with her head leaning against the cold tunnel wall. He moved to touch her shoulder, but pulled back. Tevia nodded, so he gently tapped her arm.

Myna's head whipped forward and her eyes shot open. She reached for her chest. "Donald, you near frightened the life out of me."

He leaned forward, concentration stiffening the muscles in his face. "Maggie's really poorly. You need to look at her."

Myna heaved herself off the floor, groaning. It took a few moments for her body to right itself before she moved to kneel beside Maggie. She placed a hand on her forehead and her heart ached. Maggie opened her eyes, greeting her friend with a misshapen smile.

Myna squeezed her hand. "Rest, Mags, Jessie will be back soon, and before you know it, we'll have you in front of a nice warm fire."

Maggie's eyes brightened. "I have a better idea. You take Lily and the girls, go get that fire ready for me. I'll wait for Jessie, she'll bring me."

Myna's reply stuck in her throat, her lips moving silently.

Maggie still held her gaze. "We don't all need to be sitting here. Lily will catch her death, and your bones will ache for weeks if you stay here any longer."

"I'm not leaving you here," Myna panted, "we stay together, we go together."

Maggie's hand tightened around Myna's icy fingers. "I won't have you sitting here, or that bairn getting the consumption on my account. If anyone must wait for Jess, it's me. It's what I want, Myna ... I'll not argue with you." A cough rattled up her throat, echoing in the tunnel. "I don't have the energy to fight you."

Myna clasped both of Maggie's hands, drawing them to her chest. Hot tears filled her eyes. "No, Mags, I can't leave you here. It's not right."

Maggie pulled her hands away then waved to Donald. He bent towards her, feeling her ice-cold cheek brush his. "Get Myna, the girls and that bairn out of here. Look after them, make sure they reach the house safely." Donald's eyes gleamed, his curls shook. Maggie's voice crackled. "Do you hear me, laddie?"

Myna leaned in, wrapping herself around her friend. Uncontrollable tears dropped onto Maggie's shoulders. Her voice broke. "No, Mags, I can't do this."

Maggie lifted Myna's head from her shoulder and looked into her eyes. "You must, it's what Heather would want. Now go, get that fire ready. Jess and I will be right behind you." She pushed Myna back, and Donald dropped to his knees. Maggie took a clump of his hair in her hands.

"Not one word from you. If you do nothing else right in your life, this better be the one thing you do, or Heather and I will haunt you till the day you die."

He stood, closed his eyes, then held his head in his hands. Tevia got up and slapped him. "Help Mam with Lily."

He shuffled to Myna then put the bags over his shoulder. Tevia knelt and Maggie reached out a hand.

"Look after them, Tevia." She stroked her face, wiping a lone tear from her cheek. Tevia hugged her tight, but when she pulled away, Maggie smiled. "You know, child."

Tevia kissed Maggie's hand. "I do."

Before Myna might change her mind, Tevia bundled them up and shepherded them into the darkness of the tunnel. Soon the sounds of their footsteps faded, only the rasping of Maggie's breath, and the occasional trickle of water down the tunnel wall, breaking the hollow silence.

The tunnel seemed to descend into the bowels of a cold damp earth, twisting and turning, testing each step and sense of direction before levelling out. When Myna arrived at a wide area layered with boulders low enough to sit on, she turned to see the sad faces of her motley crew. Her shoulders dropped. "Time to rest."

Donald and the twins each found a spot then lowered their weary bodies to sit. Lily stirred but remained asleep – the comfort of Tevia's embrace shielding her from her dismal surroundings and uncertain safety. The weight of Jessie's and Maggie's absence hung more oppressive than the rough walls, tacit worry more strangling than the gnarly roots of centuries-old trees snaking their way through the damp floor of their underground hell. Donald struggled to get comfortable, so he stepped over the girls to speak to Myna.

"Don't fall oer yer feet." Tevia sniped.

Donald flopped down beside Myna, hissing: "Tell them! It was a boot, not my feet."

Myna turned, and although dark, his eyes shone, his cheeks burned. "Enough, girls, it was a boot."

Donald huffed then settled down beside her. She deliberated for a minute, then her skin twitched. She turned and gripped Donald's shoulders. "The boot, what did you say about the boot?"

"I d-dunno, it was one of those b-boots the worker's wear."

Myna shook him again. "You saw the Englishmen wearing them. Who?" Her voice bounced off the walls, startling the girls. Tevia tried to shush her. "Mam, you'll wake Lily."

Myna snapped. "Be quiet! Think, Donald, where did you see those boots?"

Donald put his head in his hands, pondering. When he looked up, his eyes gleamed in the darkness. "Wilson's smithies, they all wear those boots."

Myna's mind reeled with the memory of Callan, lost in the forest, close to the well. Her heart thumped, her shoulders hunched, she bent over and held her head. The weight of the tunnel air crushed her lungs. Iris, Laura and her injuries, Callan – their faces flashed behind her eyes and her stomach flipped.

Donald leaned towards her. "M-Myna, what's wrong?"

Myna's tears overflowed, running down her cheeks before falling onto her tight fists. She turned to see Donald's wide eyes bearing down on her.

"Jessie!" she cried. "She's in terrible trouble."

Despite the chill, Maggie slipped into a deep sleep. She dreamed she walked hand-in-hand with Heather along a stone path, between the tallest trees she'd ever seen, masses of green foliage dripping from their branches, dancing in the warm breeze. Heather's laugh filled her ears, reaching into her heart. Where the pathway ended, they turned into a field, carpeted with white heather far and beyond their vision. She took a few steps into the field where the sweet aroma swelled her lungs, cocooning her in warmth, and the brightest glow she'd never known. When she turned, Heather was gone ... the pathway disappeared. Maggie opened her eyes, and in the tunnel's darkness, she breathed into the silence. "I'm ready, Heather, take me home."

Heather's face appeared brighter than any sun, as Maggie's gasp fizzled in the air. Within seconds, only the occasional sound of trickling water echoed in the tunnel.

Callan took time to finish his oatcakes, knowing whatever the priest dished out would not make him feel any worse than he already did. His teeth gnawed the inside of his mouth, but still he preferred to think of the smithies down the well rather than preying on his sister, or any young girl. His mind reeled, trying to make sense of the trouble he'd caused simply trying to protect Iris. Father Coyle already branded him a sinner condemned to hell, and his mother was no help in that regard. She may have helped him with the smithies, then covered for him, but why she turned against Jessie, he'd never understand. Those brutal men got what they deserved, but now his life seemed doomed to the mercy of his mother, and Father Coyle.

When he loped up the stairs to Father Coyle's office, he steeled himself for the lashing he would get for taking so long. He couldn't have cared less. His ears hurt constantly from the priest's fat hands, and no sooner would his backside regain its feeling, he'd endure another beating. With each step his legs grew heavier, so by the time he reached the office door, his bones ached.

His spine stiffened quicker than fox ears when he found Father Coyle on the floor, writhing and contorting like a beached porpoise. He scanned the room, unable to find a reason for the priest's condition, until his eyes settled on a shattered, red-stained glass lying next to him. It didn't surprise him to think the priest had again drunk too much, and at last his body was retaliating, but he didn't strike him as being inebriated, or 'buckled' as the other kids would say.

He edged closer, noticing the priest's eyes pop when he jerked his stiff fingers towards where he kept his medicine, but Callan stood frozen, fascinated by the white froth seeping from one side of blue lips. His eyes left the priest's deforming face, sweeping over distorted vestments and one stocking-clad leg kicking the side table as though trying to extricate itself from the remainder of the flab. The spectacle of the priest's condition held his attention, but the seriousness failed to register. Callan's head jolted each time the priest convulsed. His garbled pleading made no sense, but he stepped closer, watching his body shake, then curl into an overgrown foetal position. He watched his lips darkening, the white frothy mess gaining mass, coating his chin. When he leaned forward, bulbous eyes, rivers of blood surrounding large black holes, and what had begun as gurgling, now reminded Callan of pigs squealing when his father tightened the rope around their necks. In a fleeting moment of control, the priest's arm shot out, one finger pointing to his desk. Callan jolted from his stupor, understanding the priest's desperate appeal for his medicine. He glanced at the desk then back to Father Coyle, whose eyes flashed in a spark of acknowledgement – and relief. Callan moved to the desk and opened the top drawer, empty except for a little bottle of pills. He reached for the bottle, but something caught his eye. He paused, spotting a tall, white wax candle, housed in a highly polished silver candlestick. His eyes settled on the dancing flame while the squealing and writhing intensified. He gazed around the familiar room, taking in the weighty brocade curtains he regularly helped his mother remove and clean – the plush carpets with their fringing that took hours to dust, before straightening into the perfect lines the priest demanded. His eyes revisited the silver candle holder, one of so many he'd polished till his fingers blistered. One hand hovered above the bottle as he turned to look at the priest. Every beating, insult and fearful moment at the priest's hands, flashed through his mind, increasing the frenzy of noise.

The priest's squealing, and thumping leg added to his inner torment.

With one hand hovering over the pills, he lifted his other until it reached the level of the candle flame. He held the priest's tormented eyes. Without removing his gaze, his hand turned sideways, knocking over the candle.

Father Coyle's squealing suddenly deteriorated to gurgling from deep within his constricted throat. Both legs jerked, threatening to topple the table. Callan watched flames lick the hem of the curtains before swallowing the offensive carpet fringes. He turned and walked out the door, closing it carefully behind him.

When he reached the street, he looked up at the bright glow lighting up the windows, reflecting its rapid inferno in his glassy eyes. He inspected his trembling hands, unable to see the blood and rope his mind would never forget – the rope he and his mother used to haul the smithies over the wall of the well – and the slap he'd received from his mother after Jessie spotted it.

He curled his fingers into fists and tucked them into his pockets, while the only thought to cross his mind was the priest's demise would sadden no one … and he'd at least done right by Jessie.

The storm Jessie wished for as she'd rushed through the forest now thrashed around her until it developed into a background symphony accompanying her prayers – as the rope tightened around her neck. Thunder and lightning, drums and cymbals, accompanied by various wind instruments finding their climate copy. She welcomed the rain washing over her, confident her magnificent forest would survive. She prayed for Tom, her one and only love, then thanked her guides for the years they shared before his mind rejected reality. He loved his life, and nothing held the power to entice him to leave the peat bogs and lush farmlands, regardless of how harsh or taxing. His determination to stay put, to remain in the place of his ancestors, shone from his eyes; dare anyone question it. Her brave heart and kind soul, for whom no amount of treatment from medicines, concoctions or counsel could stem the demons who tormented him. She would meet him soon ... to continue their journey together.

She prayed for her magnificent Lily, created by pure love; already spreading it like rising sunshine. To have been blessed with such a precious gift, more than she could ever have prayed for, swelled her heart with sorrow and gratefulness.

Lily's journey was about to start; blessed by all her mothers watching over her, guiding her purpose of carrying and fostering the work started by her bloodline. Her mother's warning of the sacrifices she may need to make now broke her heart. Her only consolation was knowing Tevia would nurture Lily's gifts, helping her live as a first daughter – as only a spae can – with their precious stones to guide her, together with the spirits of her ancestors to protect her.

She offered hope for a new life to her father and brothers. She prayed for their forgiveness and understanding, before blessing them with eternal peace in their new homeland.

Amid thunderous noise, wind rattled the trees with such force that their roots clung to each other, gripping the soil the way children grab their mother's skirts when a stranger's leer unnerves them. As Cailleach the weather-witch unleashed her fierce anger at the tragedy unfolding, Jessie's life force waned. Clouds swirled, collided, battling each other for space in a sky now grim and overcrowded. Dark, shapeless rivals crashed, *forcing bulbous raindrops to explode out of the chaos, pounding every bird, branch and blade of grass on their way to the earth – which despite the ensuing damage would recover to continue nature's course, with the help of sunshine and calm days. This mass of black enveloped before snuffing out the remaining light in a frenzy of roaring winds and dense billows. Lightning revealed the tempest in flashes, splintering the sky, piercing the clouds, before obliterating all in a magnetised path to its root source. Birds squawked, farm animals whined, forest wolves howled – forewarning any living creature of a universal anger. Earth wasn't a safe place for now.*

The battering persisted until the fierce energy waned, the wind retreated, the madness subsided. The naturally dense and vividly green forest appeared whipped, stripped of anything not strong enough to hold its ground. Trees stood crumpled, exhausted by the unforgiving attack. Forest flowers lay strewn on the paths like shrapnel, their stalks left bare, lifeless. Remnants of birds' nests lay still, empty, the storm's carnage evident. Forest animals remained hidden ... the fear of fire and storms still holding them prisoner.

The forest stood shocked, paralysed by the onslaught. An ominous squeaking sound of rope against timber broke the ensuing silence while the familiar scent of white heather pervaded the air.

The last thing to comfort Jessie was her mother's magnificent smile, beaming from her radiant face. Her green eyes sparkled as she held out her hand.

THE END

Thank you for reading my book.

This book is the first in a series, so please stay in touch and find out about books 2 – 5 by subscribing to my newsletter:
www.authorallystirling.com

It would be amazing if you would pop over to Goodreads Amazon, Apple, Kobo or wherever you bought your book and leave a review.
It helps other readers get to know about my books and sends virtual encouragement to me!
Facebook.com/authorallystirling
Instagram.com/authorallystirling
Twitter.com/authorAllyS

Acknowledgements

My incredibly talented and supportive writing coach Cathy Eden channelled my inspiration after I barged through her door with a desire to write, immediately! My dedicated writing group girls were the first listeners of this story, without whom I could not have realised this dream. Nikki Malan, Pier Heyn, Tamara Semevsky, Lisa Kane, Melina Lewis, Irene Berman and Joy Watson, your honest input, sturdy ears, and encouragement kept me going. You are all an inspiration to me.

Nicky Malan, your bottomless pit of knowledge, and wine, coupled with your generosity to share both, have made this journey manageable and so much fun! You always said it was a series, and here we are. You are a treasure.

Heartfelt gratitude, love and thanks go to my darling friends Jackie Herriott, Vicki Paynter and Jane Surtees, for the reading hours they spent on early drafts and untidy writing on my behalf. I don't know how you survive me. I owe you lots of wine! You awesome women are my salvation; the family I chose.

Thank you, Collette Kelly. Our Zoom sprints kept me in the writing chair and bolstered my confidence when fatigue set in. Your support and good humour mean the world to me.

I love my cover and design. It was a dream working with Jeanine Henning and Andrea Hoffman. You ladies are the best, your skills are amazing, and I can't wait to see the next ones!

Bernice of BM Admin Services deserves my sincerest appreciation. Her patience, advice and willingness to 'let's try it and see if we can get it right' attitude has been invaluable, and many boxes would not have been ticked without her continued and reliable input.

None of this would be possible without the unwavering support, patience and vast amounts of coffee, chocolate and crisps provided by my long-suffering husband Billy, and ever encouraging, beautiful daughter Robyn – my Bravehearts.

To the great-grandmothers who told the stories, the grandmothers who corrected them, the aunties who spread them, the mothers who passed them on, and the daughters who listened.

To my Dad, my life-time hero, whose laugh I can still hear tinkling around the room when the tales were being told.

It takes a village, and you are all mine.

Follow Ally
Facebook.com/ authorallystirling
Instagram: @authorallystirling
Twitter: @authorAllyS

Visit Ally
www.authorallystirling.com

Chat to Ally
authorallystirling@gmail.com

https://authorallystirling.com/the-sight-of-heather/

Printed in Great Britain
by Amazon